Hackleman
205 Henson Road

The Chosen Ones

THE CHOSEN ONES

Sara Hylton

St. Martin's Press
New York

Library of Congress Cataloging-in-Publication Data

Hylton, Sara.
    The chosen ones / Sara Hylton.
        p.   cm.
    ISBN 0-312-07669-X
    I. Title.
    PR6058.Y63C48   1992
    823'.914—dc20

92-147
CIP

First published in Great Britain by Random Century Group.

First U.S. Edition: June 1992
10 9 8 7 6 5 4 3 2 1

For old friends who have weathered the years and new friends who were strangers yesterday.

The Chosen Ones

1

Greymont is a nice country town set in north rural Lancashire. It has varied industries and is set well away from
that part of Lancashire throbbing under a forest of mill
chimneys. As well as a fine parish church and an
imposing town hall, it also boasts an impressive concert
hall, given to the town by Sir Joshua Garveston – the
father of Sir Gerald, the present baronet. Sir Joshua was
something of a philanthropist, unlike his son who is a
spendthrift and has largely allowed his ancestral home to
run to seed.

Seven miles north of the town stands the stately pile
of Garveston Hall, home of the Garveston family since
the sixteenth century; to the west is Lorivals, once the
home of Brigadier Sir Algernon Lorival and his daughter
Phoebe, but now a well-known school for girls started
by Miss Lorival after the death of her father.

Greymont is surrounded by gently rolling fells and
pretty Pennine villages. The tarn is an anglers' paradise,
stocked with fat trout and perch, and there are several
parks on the outskirts of the town where brass bands
play in the summer on Sunday afternoons. There is a
well-attended repertory theatre and a vast art gallery and
library, also donated by Sir Joshua, whose stone statue
is placed in a prominent position in front of the gallery.

Growing up in Greymont had been a happy experience
for me; it was only later, when sophistication took the
place of innocence, that I came to see the smugness and
snobbery behind the respectable façade of the church-
going citizens of my home town, with their well-scrubbed
children and ordered gardens. With that sophistication it
became easy to be cynical, to find amusement in the
feuds that went on at the tennis club and the golf club,

even when I knew that these were feuds between funda-
mentally decent people who perhaps had climbed the
social ladder a little too quickly, made money too easily.

My father, Arthur Graham, always said there was as
much drama and sin in the smug middle-class community
of Greymont as there was down in London – and he was
in a position to know, because he was employed as chief
reporter on the *Greymont Gazette*. Father was good at
making ridiculous claims: he often did it to start an
argument, particularly with Grandfather Lester, who had
been a doctor in Greymont since his arrival there straight
from medical school at the age of twenty-four. He had
married a local girl and settled down in a large detached
house on the other side of the park, in the élite part of
Greymont. Here lived local councillors and their wives,
professional men, and it was here that the women held
their bridge parties and coffee mornings. Father said he
could learn more from those coffee mornings than he
could pounding the streets and standing at bars in search
of news.

Most people thought father had done remarkably well
for himself when he captured Mary, the younger of Dr
Lester's two daughters, and certainly Mother was sweet
and pliable while Aunt Susan was autocratic, and for
most of my early life I was afraid of her. Mother was
fair and very pretty, with a petite figure and a gentle
smile. She liked pretty clothes with bows at the neck
and slender high heels, while Aunt Susan, who was tall
and angular, dressed well but severely and wore her dark
hair in a bun on the nape of her neck. She had a regal
air when she walked down the street and was treated with
the utmost respect by shopkeepers and acquaintances.

My Aunt sat on church committees and organized
flower shows and dog shows, whereas Mother enjoyed
the gossip over the teacups and evenings out at functions
when she could wear her finery and mingle with local
dignitaries and their wives. Father always maintained
that it was because of Mary being Dr Lester's daughter,

2

rather than his own position at the local newspaper that invariably earned them a place on the top table, and it was true that his dry, caustic wit didn't always go down well with those people in the town who thought they were Somebody.

I could remember Grandfather's long dark surgery at the side of the big house he shared with Aunt Susan, but I had no memory of my grandmother, since she died when I was three. In my mind, there was always just Grandfather, Aunt Susan and Sarah, their housekeeper. My aunt helped with the dispensing and acted as receptionist and secretary, while Sarah cooked and cleaned and generally clucked over both of them like an old hen.

Sometimes I would call there on my way home from school before Grandfather went out on his evening rounds. In summer it wasn't so bad, but in winter the chimney used to smoke, which I thought did nothing for the health of his asthmatic patients who sat dejectedly coughing the time away awaiting their turn. On the big table in the centre of the waiting-room was a pile of magazines and comics for the children, and I enjoyed taking over from Aunt Susan by calling out the patients' names and showing them into the surgery.

When Mother and Father married they bought a corner house at the other side of the park and it was here that I grew up, at number one, Park Road. We faced a pleasant little area of open space with ordered paths and flowerbeds. There was a section set apart for children with slides and swings, and there was a bowling green and two tennis courts. It was through this park that I walked every day on my way to school in the company of my two friends, Barbara Smythe and Maisie Jayson. I liked them both, so it seemed remarkably strange to me that they didn't like each other!

Barbara's father had an engraving works in Greymont and was a local councillor, while her mother was a pillar of St Mary's Church in Ellwood and a prominent member of the Inner Wheel. Father used to say the Smythes were both very conscious that they were on the way up, and were conditioning their only daughter to appreciate that fact.

Maisie's father was a greengrocer and owned the first shop in the parade at the bus-stop beyond the park. The family lived over the shop in what can only be described as cramped conditions. They had a small living room, a medium-sized kitchen and three bedrooms. The bathroom was downstairs behind the shop. Maisie had three older brothers – Bob, Eric and Jimmy. I liked them all, particularly Bob, who was the eldest and treated us to sweets every Saturday before we set out for the village market stalls in winter and the fells in summer.

Barbara never joined us on these excursions, but instead went to the shops with her mother and had afternoon tea in one of the cafés frequented by Mrs Smythe's friends. She couldn't understand my friendship with Maisie, considering the Jaysons beneath her. On one occasion she had the effrontery to say, 'Surely your parents don't like you being so friendly with Maisie Jayson? Her Father's in trade, *and* they live over the shop in that tiny little flat.'

'My father likes Mr Jayson and we get all our vegetables from them,' I retorted.

'Well so do we, but that doesn't mean to say we have to treat them like equals.'

'They are equals. Father says Mr Jayson makes a lot more money than he does, so I reckon that makes them more than equals.'

'Well, of course it doesn't! Your grandfather's a doctor, your father's a journalist, but anybody can be a greengrocer. You have to pass exams to be a doctor and know an awful lot about heaps of things to be a journalist.'

'Well, I like Maisie and I like her family. I'm not going to fall out with her just because you say so.'

'Besides they're Methodists. What sort of religion is that?'

4

'I like going to the Chapel – they sing more hymns than we do and the prayers are different. I get so bored when our prayers are all the same.'

'I don't know how you can say that, Nancy Graham. It's as bad as saying you enjoy going to the Catholic church and listening to all that mumbo jumbo.'

'What do you mean, mumbo jumbo?'

'Well, it's all in Latin isn't it, and nobody but the priest understands a word of it. My father says Latin's a dead language – what good is it to English people?'

'Perhaps I'll go there one day just to see what it's like.'

She turned to face me with the utmost horror on her face. 'Nancy, you can't! What would your parents say?'

'I wouldn't tell them.'

'Because you know they'd be horrified. Anyway, all this has nothing to do with you going to the Methodist Chapel with Maisie. You shouldn't go, it's like being a traitor.'

I related this conversation to Father after the evening meal while I sat in the greenhouse watching him tie up his tomatoes. I was careful to leave out my decision to visit the Roman Catholic church, but I told him everything else. When I had finished I found he was smiling broadly.

'This isn't Barbara Smythe talking, Nancy, it's her mother, and I wouldn't like old Father O'Ryan to hear any of it. He'd be the first to tell you that we're all little better than heathens. Where is your history, my girl?'

'History, Father?'

'Why yes. Weren't we all good Catholics once until old Henry the Eighth elected to divorce his Queen and marry his light of love. The Pope didn't agree with him, so Henry ups and forms his own religion, marries Anne Boleyn and places himself at the head of the Church of England. Haven't you learned any of this at school?'

'I don't remember much about how the Church of England was formed – maybe it's because we haven't yet done a project on Henry the Eighth.'

5

'He was a lecherous old rogue. Woe betide you if you were a pretty girl at the court of Henry, but you'll no doubt be hearing about him and his six wives.'

'Six wives!'

'Why, yes – two of them were sent to the tower and beheaded and two others were divorced because they couldn't produce sons. Next time your friend Barbara starts to give you a lecture on religion, give her as good as you get – tell her about Henry.'

'She's just as nasty about the Methodists.'

He laughed. 'Well, you can tell her they didn't like *our* mumbo jumbo – and see if that doesn't shut her up!'

I loved talking to Father: he was so humorous, and so informative about everything under the sun. When I said as much to Grandfather he chuckled and commented, 'Your father's not always right, Nancy, but I've never doubted his entertainment value.'

At the end of July we would all be leaving our primary school across the park and this became the regular topic of conversation during our weekly visits to Grandfather's house. Usually it started in between the roast and the pudding. It was only just after Easter and the summer seemed a long time away, but invariably Aunt Susan found something to say either about my friendships or my schooling.

'Why weren't you invited to Martin Walton's birthday party?' she demanded one day fixing me with a hard stare. I squirmed miserably in my seat because I *had* been invited there but had lied that I had something else to do. 'I passed the Waltons' house on the way home and the road was filled with cars waiting to collect the children. Mrs Smythe said you weren't there – I thought it strange that you hadn't been asked.'

'I was asked,' I muttered, 'but I didn't want to go.'

'Why ever not?'

'I don't much like Martin Walton and besides, he hadn't asked Maisie.'

Then followed the usual lecture on cultivating the right

6

sort of friendships. In Aunt Susan's eyes, Maisie missed out sadly. Her preference was for Barbara.

I came to dread those Sunday lunches sitting in Grandfather's lofty dining room with its ornate ceiling and dark wallpaper. The furniture was mahogany, lovingly polished by Sarah, and we sat at the big oval table with Grandfather at one end and Father at the other. Grandfather enjoyed his arguments with Father but more and more these days they were interrupted by Aunt Susan, who would question me and lecture me about school and my many misdemeanours.

'I hope you're working hard,' was her usual opening gambit. 'You seem to spend too much time out on the fells with that Jayson girl.'

Father would wink at me and Grandfather would say gently, 'Let the child get on with her lunch, Susan. There's months to go before the summer.'

'She needs to think about it now, Father. Come summer it'll be too late. Mrs Smythe tells me they've got a private tutor in for Barbara.'

I looked up in surprise. Barbara had said nothing to us about all this, but then she could be very secretive.

'Why does she need a tutor?' Father asked curiously.

'He's coaching her in arithmetic, English and history. Mrs Smythe wasn't very forthcoming but it's obvious they think she'll stand a better chance of passing the entrance exam to grammar school if she works hard now.'

'I don't believe in cramming education into a child before she's ready for it,' Father said bluntly. 'I've heard of too many children cracking under parental pressure.'

It was one day during the following week, with the three of us walking home across the park after school when Maisie opened the conversation by saying, 'Mi mother says you're havin' lessons at home now, Barbara. Is that so you'll be sure of getting in at the grammar school?'

Barbara's face blushed bright red before she snapped, 'Why don't you two get somebody to coach you?'

7

'My father doesn't believe in it,' I replied shortly.

'Then you'll end up going to the same school as Maisie.'

'How do ye know which school I'm goin' to?' Maisie retorted angrily.

'I know you're not clever and I know you don't get good marks for your homework,' Barbara said spitefully.

Our sniping was suddenly arrested by the sight of three girls strolling along the path in the direction of the gates. Their school uniform consisted of dark grey skirts and blazers, pink blouses and grey panama hats sporting a pink band. They were junior girls, wearing short grey socks and black patent leather shoes. When they were out of earshot Barbara said reverently, 'That's the sort of uniform *I'd* like to wear. I'd love to go to Lorivals.'

'They only take boarders,' Maisie said tartly, 'an' their parents have an awful lot of money. You can't go there unless you are rich.'

'I could go if I wanted to. In May my father'll be the Mayor of Greymont – they'd be glad to take me.'

'It's silly to board when ye only live a few miles away. Besides, nobody ever goes to Lorivals from round here,' Maisie insisted.

'Well, we'll have to see, won't we?' Barbara replied sweetly, and immediately changed the subject.

The following Saturday I sat with Maisie on the fell above Lorivals, gazing down at the school set in acres of woodland, gardens and playing-fields. Girls were playing tennis on the immaculately kept grass courts while others sauntered across the grounds and the sun shone out of a bright blue sky.

It was windy on the fell and I was glad of my short woollen jacket and the headscarf in my pocket. We had climbed steadily upwards until we reached a small stone tower which the locals called the Pilgrims' Cross. There was a stone plinth at the base so we sat on this, panting a little from our exertions. Below us the small village of Cranbourne went about its business. It was market day and the High Street bustled with morning shoppers while the notes of a brass band came faintly on the breeze. A flag flew bravely from the tower of the church and I suddenly remembered that it was the flag of St George: today was 25 April, St George's Day.

From our vantage point high up on the fell we could see for miles, north and east to the high Pennines, and west to the hills of Cumbria and the distant silver line of the sea. To the south rose the towering pile of Garveston Hall in the midst of its splendid parkland while beneath us rose the majestic turrets and towers of Lorivals. My eyes devoured the scene below: the river wound idly under stone-backed bridges, circling the grounds and playing-fields before it reached the forest and fell sharply over the weir.

A sense of timelessness seemed to pervade the air. It was like a lantern slide, frozen in time, and in the stillness of the air we could hear girls' laughter and suddenly Maisie blurted out, 'Would you like to go to Lorivals, Nancy?'

'Dad's not rich enough – he could never afford the fees.'

'But what if he could? I wouldn't go there, it's a snob school. They'd turn their noses up at a greengrocer's daughter, and a reporter's daughter, come to that. Barbara might be all right though as *her* father's 'bout to become Mayor.'

I laughed. 'Oh Maisie, you are funny. Why are we talking about Lorivals when none of us are going there?'

For a few minutes my friend was silent, sitting with her arms round her knees, her face strangely pensive. Then she surprised me by asking, 'Why didn't you go to Martin Walton's birthday party? Was it because he didn't invite me?'

'I didn't want to go. I don't like him very much.'

'But was it because he didn't ask me?'

'That came into it. I thought it was mean of him to ask Barbara and me and leave you out.'

9

'I didn't mind, I don't like him either. I reckon Barbara's stuck on him, don't you?'

'I reckon she is.'

We dissolved into laughter and jumping to our feet, started to run down the hillside, not pausing once until we reached the stone steps against the wall.

It was Monday morning when the three of us met again on our way to school. Barbara was taller than both Maisie and myself. She had dark brown hair, worn tied back from her face in a tartan silk bow. Her legs were long and slender, and her eyes were as green as a cat's in a cool pretty face. Maisie on the other hand had a head of flaming red curls, a pretty gamine face dusted with freckles, and lips that smiled constantly over small gleaming teeth. She was small and wiry, and there were times when her hazel eyes grew dark and stormy with the sulks. As for myself, I was fair with dark blue eyes and in those days considered myself quite unremarkable. Maisie wished constantly that she didn't have red hair and freckles, I wished I was dark and mysterious but Barbara seemed complacently happy to be Barbara.

She enthused about Martin's party, the presents and the food, the guests and the entertainment, but when Maisie and I asked no questions she said airily, 'Martin isn't going to the grammar school in September. He's going to Ramilees Hall, so I don't suppose any of us will be seeing much of him after that.'

'Not even you?' I couldn't resist saying, and was rewarded by the warm pink colour flooding her cheeks.

Maisie giggled. 'Everybody can see you're sweet on him. I can't think why.'

'He's clever, that's why, and the Waltons have the loveliest house – it's the sort of house I want for myself one day.'

'He's stuck up an' snobby,' Maisie went on relentlessly. 'I couldn't live in a field with Martin Walton.'

'It's just as well then,' Barbara retorted, 'because you're not likely to be given the chance.' With a toss of her head, she strode away from us, her dark hair blowing in the wind, her school satchel flung angrily over her shoulder.

We hadn't gone far when Martin Walton himself passed us with a curt nod and seeing Barbara ahead lengthened his stride to catch up with her. We giggled together, particularly when Barbara turned back and gave us a self-satisfied smirk.

Martin was the only son of a solicitor with a thriving practice in the town; his mother sat on the Bench and on several charity committees. A tall boy with a thin clever face under straight dark hair, he was something of a loner and not too popular with other boys of his own age since he was undeniably clever and inclined to flaunt it.

'They'll be two of a kind if she marries him,' Maisie grumbled.

'Gracious me, Maisie – that's years away! I don't want to marry any of the boys I know now.'

'You don't?'

'Well, of course not. I want to meet somebody when I'm older, somebody new, don't you?' I smiled at the blush staining her freckled face. I knew very well that Maisie was just as besotted with Tom Standing as Barbara was with Martin but the two boys were very different. Tom's father was a farmer and the Standings lived high up on the fell overlooking the river. He was a cheerful boy with a shock of straw-coloured hair, and he was always well to the fore on the school sports field but lamentably behind in the classroom. Anybody more different than Martin it would have been hard to imagine.

2

'If she's good enough she'll go to the grammar school, if not she'll go to the other one. She's doing her homework, and we've encouraging reports from her teacher. I've told you before, Susan, I won't pressurize her!'

Once again my father was defending me against one of Aunt Susan's regular tirades. For the time being she had to be content with that, but a lot was to change before I left primary school at the end of July.

Greymont Council had always given generously to the Governors of the local grammar school, to equip it with new classrooms, a larger gymnasium and land for the extension of the playing-fields, but when the Governors asked for money to build a swimming pool the Council dug in its toes and said enough was enough. It had always been a tradition that the Mayor of Greymont was invited to serve on the Board of Governors during his term of office, but after the affair of the swimming pool Barbara's father, who had become Mayor after the local elections in May, was not approached. Such a snub to the town's first citizen and his lady was unheard of and Father, in his usual way, was vastly amused.

'That'll put the cat among the pigeons,' he said. 'I doubt if young Barbara'll be going to the grammar school now.'

'Where will she go, then?' Mother said. 'Where else is there?'

'There's the Convent School in Ellwood – that has a good reputation, but I know where Mrs Smythe would like to send her.'

'Where's that?'

'To Lorivals.'

'I doubt if Lorivals would take her,' my mother

objected. 'I've seen the prospectus and it states plainly enough that the school is for the daughters of the nobility, the gentry and officers in the service of the Crown.'

'My dear girl, that's archaic. Miss Phoebe Lorival has been dead for over fifty years now. All that probably worked well enough in her day, but times have changed and a school that size can't exist on fresh air. Girls like Barbara Smythe will be made very welcome there.'

'But they don't take day girls, Arthur, and it's ridiculous that Barbara should go as a boarder when she lives only a few miles away.'

'Well, whatever happens I can't see Joe Smythe letting this snub pass without some form of retaliation.'

The grammar school triumphed: they got their new swimming baths, thanks to generous donations from the parents and a hefty bank loan. A war of words took place in the *Gazette* between the Council and the school and unhappily, the headmaster, Mr Haverfield wrote a scathing attack on my father's write-up of the events which annoyed him considerably. The headmaster was known to be something of a despot, unused to criticism of any kind and his next action was to inform Grandfather that he intended to change his doctor.

Grandfather said he wasn't unduly concerned. He had never liked the man, who was self-opinionated, arrogant and petty-minded. Mother was tearful, Aunt Susan was furious, Father was noncommittal. Quite suddenly my future took a different path.

Sunday lunch in Grandfather's dining room was the battleground and as always Aunt Susan was the first one to enter the fray. 'What's to be done now?' she demanded. 'Obviously Nancy can't go to the grammar school, not after what they've done to Arthur and Father.'

'The school's done nothing to *me*,' Grandfather said mildly. 'If Mr Haverfield wishes to change his doctor it has nothing to do with the school.'

'But everybody's talking about the school,' Aunt Susan protested. 'They've even sent out invitations to attend the opening of the pool although it's months off, and they've deliberately snubbed people who have been more than good to them in the past. Oh, I know that man's at the bottom of it. Children are being taken away from the school because of Haverfield's attitude and I for one don't want my niece to go there.'

'But where else is there?' Mother cried.

'There's Lorivals – she can go there.'

We all stared at her in amazement then Father said sharply, 'Are you mad, woman? Where do you think I can find that sort of money?'

'You're angry my dear,' Grandfather put in mildly, 'Perhaps we should discuss this later when you've had a chance to simmer down.'

'I am angry,' Aunt Susan agreed, 'Quite apart from their snub to you, Father, I've been told that Mrs Haverfield has had a lot to say about my invitation to sit on the Bench. According to two of my friends who are already Magistrates, she said in their presence that she didn't think it a good idea.'

Two days later Aunt Susan arrived at our house as we were finishing our evening meal and I knew immediately that she had something important to discuss. There was a determined look on her face as she sat opposite Father, clutching her handbag. Her voice was adamant as she announced, 'I've spoken to Father about sending Nancy to Lorivals and he's come round to my way of thinking. Nancy's his only granddaughter and your only child – we all owe it to her to do the best we can for her. We don't want her to go to the grammar school – and I was outraged when I saw her climbing up a lamp-post the other afternoon. She sees too much of the Jayson girl and those brothers of hers. I don't mean any disrespect but my only niece is not to mix with a greengrocer's brats. Now Father has said he will pay her school fees. Don't say anything yet, Arthur – it will come out of the

14

money he expects to leave to Mary and me, but that's beside the point.'

'And does Dr Lester know how astronomical the fees at Lorivals are?' Father enquired dryly.

'They're not nearly as high as you might think: I've spoken to Barbara Smythe's mother. They're sending Barbara there, so if they can afford it we can too.'

'That is nothing to go by. A few years ago Joe Smythe was a very long way from being affluent, but since he got on the Council and started that engraving business in Greymont he seems to have prospered. We all know what that means, don't we? You scratch my back and I'll scratch yours.'

I could stand no more of it, and before anybody could say another word I cried out, 'Why doesn't somebody ask *me*? I don't want to go to Lorivals, I don't want to live away from home. They'll all be stuck-up and horrible and I hate their uniform. Please, Father, don't listen to Aunt Susan. I promise I'll never climb lamp-posts again.'

'Be quiet, Nancy!' Aunt Susan said sharply. 'You're far too young to appreciate what's being done for you. You're being offered opportunities far in excess of anything your mother and I had. We had to be content with Pritchard's Secretarial College, and travelling into the town night and morning.'

'Why can't I go there, then? I'd rather go there than Lorivals.'

'Pritchard's no longer exists, Nancy,' Father said evenly. 'They closed their doors during the war and they've not been opened since.'

'I took the liberty of telephoning the headmistress of Lorivals this morning and she's agreed to see us next Wednesday afternoon. In the meantime, she's sending brochures so that we can look at them beforehand.'

'I can't go with you,' Father said sharply. 'I'm due in court next Wednesday afternoon; that case on the arson down at the wharves is coming up.'

'It doesn't matter. We can look at all the brochures

15

together and talk them over on Sunday afternoon after lunch. If Father's paying the fees he should know what is going on.'

'You haven't said anything, love,' my father said to my mother, who sat gazing helplessly from one to the other.

Aunt Susan fixed her with a stern gaze, and after a few seconds she said quietly, 'It would be nice for Nancy to go to Lorivals, Arthur, and it is good of Father to offer to pay the fees.'

'But Mother, I don't want to go,' I cried helplessly.

Father looked at me a little sadly then said, 'Don't worry, Nancy. Perhaps we'll find the fees are too much after all, and if not, you could love it there.'

I sat in sulky silence after lunch on the following Sunday while the grown ups discussed my future at Lorivals. The fees were accepted by Grandfather regardless of the amount and they all talked enthusiastically about the school which had once been a stately home.

'I can't think why they don't take day girls,' Father said wistfully, 'Nancy'll be living just a few miles away and yet we'll only see her during the holidays.'

'And a good thing too,' Aunt Susan snapped. 'She'd be at Lorivals during the day, and nights and weekends she'd be off with that Jayson girl.'

'There's nothing wrong with young Maisie,' Grandfather said gently. 'She's bright, she's pretty and she's a good girl at home. It's talking to Joe Smythe's wife that's turning you into a snob, Susan.'

'I remember Nellie Smythe when she was a little freckle-faced kid not unlike Maisie Jayson. Her father was a cobbler over at Cranbourne and her mother did a bit of cleaning for old Mrs Ewing. She seems to have forgotten all that in her newfound prosperity,' Father said provocatively.

'Why shouldn't she forget!' Aunt Susan retorted. 'Her husband's the Mayor of Greymont and he's got a good business – she's entitled to be proud of how things have

16

turned out for them. It's nice for Barbara to be going to Lorivals, Nancy. You'll have one friend there at the very outset.'

'I don't like the uniform,' I muttered as a last stand.

'Of course you like the uniform,' she said dismissively. 'It's charming and original and besides, it will suit your colouring beautifully. After we've had the interview with Miss Clarkson and you've looked inside the school you'll change your mind about everything. Mrs Smythe tells me Barbara's delighted to be going there.'

I felt angry and defeated. My future had been arranged without my being allowed a single opinion. I had thought Father would be more supportive and I was hurt and bewildered that I would have to leave home to become a boarder at Lorivals.

On the way home Father sensed my anger and misery, and taking hold of my hand he said gently, 'You'll have long holidays Nancy, longer than you would have had at any of the schools in Greymont, and we'll see you whenever it's possible. When you've settled down you'll probably love the place. It has a very good reputation. I'm allowing your grandfather to pay because I think in the end it will be good for you. You'll be having a chance denied to a great many other girls.'

'It's a chance I don't want, Father,' I cut in sharply.

'I didn't want a lot of things when I was your age, pet. I didn't know what was good for me. One day you're going to realise what we're doing is for your future and you'll thank us for it.'

'How ever am I going to tell Maisie that I'm going to Lorivals?'

'Why not cut across there and tell her this afternoon? It's better than waiting until Barbara is with you.'

It was true. I couldn't tell Maisie in Barbara's company. All the same I couldn't think it was going to be easy.

By the time I reached the Jaysons' shop it was after four in the afternoon. The boxes and baskets filled with vegetables and fruit had been taken in because it was Sunday and the front of the shop had been swept clean. I rang the bell at the side door, and after a few seconds I heard footsteps running down the stairs.

Maisie's brother Bob opened the door, and he looked down at me with a friendly smile. 'Maisie's upstairs helpin' Mother to get the tea ready. Ye can go up, Nancy – ye know where the kitchen is.'

There was a smell of frying bacon and new bread, and when I entered the kitchen Mrs Jayson glanced round from the stove and Maisie looked up from the table where she was busy buttering muffins. Her face broke into a wide smile. 'We didn't expect you, Nancy. Are ye stoppin' for yer tea?'

'Oh no, Maisie, I've just come back from Grandfather's. If you're busy it can wait until tomorrow.'

'Nay, lass, she's not that busy. Take Nancy into the livin' room, Maisie. One of the boys can finish butterin' the muffins.'

The tiny room was crowded. Mr Jayson sat in his big armchair in front of the fire with his account books spread out in front of him, while Bob sat beside him with a sheaf of papers on his knees and the two younger boys were at the table poring over their usual jigsaw puzzle.

Seeing my hesitation Maisie said quickly, 'We can go into my bedroom if ye like Nancy. It's quiet in there.'

Maisie's bedroom was small as well. There was a single bed in the corner, a slim wardrobe and a plain chest of drawers. There was no space for a chair so we plumped down on the bed.

She looked at me expectantly and some of my anxiety must have shown in my face because she said sharply, 'What's wrong, Nancy? Ye look all upset.'

'I am upset, but I don't quite know how to tell you why.'

'Tell me? Tell me what?'

18

'I'm going to Lorivals in September. It was decided today at Grandfather's.'

She stared at me aghast, then her face became sharp and pinched with anger.

'So you're goin' wi' 'er instead o' wi' me.'

'We don't even know if we'd be at the same school anyway, Maisie. After the summer we might not even be together any more.'

'Oh yes, so you're clever and I'm not – is that what you're sayin'?'

'We're good at different things, that's all.' She didn't speak but sat looking down at the floor, her hands clenched in her lap, and I thought tears were not very far from the surface. 'I'll have long holidays and we'll be together then. I'll have those to look forward to.'

'In time you'll not even think about me. You'll make other friends – we'll drift apart.'

'Well, of course we won't! You'll always be my best friend. I don't even want to go to Lorivals – it's all been decided for me.'

'Your Aunt Susan, I suppose.'

'How did you guess?'

'Well, I'd best get back to the kitchen. We allus have bacon an' egg, an' muffins for Sunday tea – it's easy and mi Mam's worked hard enough in the shop all week. You're welcome to stay if you want to.'

'Thanks, but I'd better get home. I ate too much at lunchtime.'

The smell of cooking bacon was delicious but I knew if I stayed it would stick in my throat. We got off the bed and went back into the living room. Bob looked up with a smile saying, 'Well, you'd best take off your coat if you're staying, Nancy.'

'I'm not. I have to get home. I can let myself out, Bob. I'll just say goodbye to your mother.'

Mrs Jayson was busy laying the kitchen table assisted by the two younger boys. We've set a place for you, love,' she said warmly. 'Ye like bacon and egg, don't you?'

'Yes, but I have to go Mrs Jayson, thanks all the same.'

She looked from one to the other of us and taking in Maisie's dour face she said sharply, 'I 'ope you two 'aven't been quarrelling.'

'No, of course not,' I reassured her.

'Well, our Maisie's face looks sour enough to turn the milk. What is it, lass?'

'It's nothing, Mam. Leave me alone,' and then with a sob in her throat Maisie spun round and rushed back to her bedroom.

I looked at Mrs Jayson helplessly. 'Maisie will tell you all about it later, Mrs Jayson. We haven't quarrelled, honestly.'

'Well, ye can let yourself out, love. Eric – go an' tell our Maisie her tea's ready. I don't want her sulking in her bedroom.'

I was glad to let myself out into the fresh air. My thoughts were filled with Maisie's bitterness but my own unhappiness was if anything greater than hers. I didn't want to go to Lorivals, I didn't want to leave my home and I viewed my immediate future with depressing uncertainty.

3

On Wednesday morning I toyed with my breakfast and Father said gently, 'You and Maisie still friends, love?'

'She's very upset. Nothing's the same any more – she thinks I'd rather go with Barbara than her.'

'She'll get over it, love. You'll both make new friends.'

I didn't answer him. Instead I applied myself to my breakfast which tasted of nothing at all.

'I'd like to be able to take you over to the school,' he was saying to Mother, 'but I can't manage it. I have a busy day in front of me.'

'That's all right, dear. Susan is coming round in a taxi about eleven.'

'I can't think why she doesn't have some driving lessons, she must spend a small fortune on taxis.'

'Father won't teach her to drive, and I don't suppose you would either.'

'Not likely! Before I knew it, she'd be teaching *me*!'

'I wish you two got along better. Susan's really very kind and generous. I know she's got a sharp tongue in her head, but she means well.'

'I'm not sure her interfering with Nancy is the right thing. She could go up there to Lorivals and hate every minute of it. We're nobody special, Mary. I'm just a reporter working on the local rag. Nancy will be mixing with girls from a completely different background.'

'Times are changing, Arthur. Many of the old families are now short of money and people who never had any are suddenly quite affluent. You only have to look at Garveston Hall. Susan went up there to a flower show last summer and she said the place is terribly shabby. The paintwork is disgraceful and even the stonework is crumbling in places.'

'I'd like to bet the old man's cellar is well stocked, though.'

'Maybe, but he's halved his workforce on the parkland and the younger boy's been sent to Ramilees. The older boy went to Harrow.'

'Perhaps it's not so important for the younger son to go to Harrow; Phillip will inherit the title and the Hall.'

'No, Arthur, it's usual to send all the sons to Harrow, and if something happens to Phillip, Mark is the next in line.'

'Is all this supposed to make me feel better about sending Nancy to Lorivals, Mary?'

'Well, of course not. I'm only pointing out that times are changing.'

As he left the breakfast table Father bent down and ruffled my hair. 'Go up there and show 'em, love, I know you can do it!'

It was a warm, late spring morning. The hawthorns were bursting into fresh green leaf and there were primroses under the hedgerows. On any other morning I would have revelled in the drive along the country road with the fells misted above us but as we finally entered the great iron gates of Lorivals I was wishing I was miles away.

The building stood on three terraces and the morning sun glinted on mullion windows and Pennine stone. Multi-coloured pansies bloomed in giant stone urns set along the terraces and as our taxi came to a halt on the lower terrace I could see that the great oak door was studded with brass and that a cleaner was busily polishing a huge brass knocker.

It was Aunt Susan who swept up the steps before us, and Aunt Susan who addressed the cleaner who had turned round to eye us with a tentative smile. 'We have an appointment to see Miss Clarkson the Headmistress. Is it all right for us to go in?'

'If ye'll ring the bell on the hall table, ma'am, somebody will look after you.'

I had expected Lorivals to be unusual, but on first impression it didn't resemble a school at all. The large hall was panelled in dark oak and there were old-fashioned portraits on the walls. A shallow carved stair-case swept up from the entrance and divided on the first floor. On the landing hung a very large oil-painting of a man wearing a splendid uniform in bright scarlet and gold. One long slender hand curved round the hilt of his sword and his steely blue eyes seemed to be watching us as we waited down below.

Seeing me staring at the portrait Aunt Susan said sharply, 'That is a painting of Sir Algernon Lorival, Nancy. Apparently there is one of his daughter Phoebe in the hall used by the students at the back of the house.'

At that moment a small silver-haired woman appeared. She was wearing a tweed skirt and beige silk blouse, and she smiled in the friendliest fashion, which succeeded in dispelling much of my awe.

'Miss Clarkson is expecting you in her study,' she said. 'Now, which one of you is Mrs Graham?'

'I am,' said Mother shyly. 'This is my sister, Miss Lester and this is my daughter, Nancy.'

The newcomer smiled. 'I'm Miss Harris, Miss Clarkson's private secretary. Will you come with me?'

We followed her through a door at the back of the hall and now I could hear voices and laughter, interspersed by music and the sound of girls' voices singing. Miss Harris explained that the music room was directly above us and if we liked she would show us round the School after our interview with Miss Clarkson.

We were ushered into a large sunny room at the end of a long corridor overlooking the playing-fields, and a tall slender woman dressed in navy stood up from behind her desk to receive us. I was aware of white walls on which hung several water colours and the delicate hues of chintz covering the chairs and hanging at the windows. Our feet sank into a soft green carpet and the air was fragrant from a vase filled with carnations standing on her desk.

'Will you bring coffee, Miss Harris – unless you would prefer something else?' she said, addressing us with a friendly smile on her lips.

'Thank you, coffee would be very nice,' Aunt Susan replied.

The Headmistress indicated that we should sit opposite her, then fixing me with a direct gaze she said, 'Do you wish to come here to Lorivals, Nancy? I must explain that we have never before taken girls who live so close to the school, but this year we have decided to change things. The Mayor of Greymont's daughter will be a pupil, and you also I hope.'

She sat waiting for my answer and I was dismally aware of Mother staring down at her gloves and Aunt Susan boring into me, willing me to say the right thing. I was no more capable of lying to Rachel Clarkson on that morning when I was ten years old than I was when I left Lorivals eight years later. Looking her straight in the eye I said firmly, 'I don't know whether I want to come here or not. I'm happy going to school in Greymont.'

'But you would soon be changing to a secondary school after the summer holidays anyway, my dear. That too would be strange to you, Nancy.'

'I know, but I would be able to carry on living at home – that is really what I would like to do.'

'I see.' She turned to look at my mother and aunt sitting in uncomfortable silence. 'It would seem we have a reluctant pupil here, Mrs Graham,' she said dryly.

'My niece is ten years old, Miss Clarkson,' Aunt Susan interrupted stiffly. 'I doubt very much if she's really aware of the chance she's being offered.'

'Most of my pupils are reluctant when they come here, Miss Lester. Many of them are from abroad, others from the south of England. They arrive, see the dark hills and the lonely fells and they yearn for the sunshine and the softer scenery they have left behind. Later, they grow to love Lorivals *and* the scenery that had once seemed so unfriendly. You have an advantage over them, Nancy, as you already love the hills and our sometimes stark countryside. Only the school is left for you to love and I can assure you that you *will* love Lorivals. I have yet to hear a single student say she is not happy here, and wants to leave.'

At that moment the coffee arrived, brought in by a girl wearing a spotless white apron over a short black skirt. Miss Clarkson busied herself serving it, indicating that I should hand it round. There was a large plate filled with shortbread and when Aunt Susan reached out for a second helping Miss Clarkson said, 'The shortbread is home-made, indeed everything we eat is either made on the premises or grown in the grounds. We have an extensive vegetable garden and orchard, and the sheep and cattle you can see through the window in the library are ours. Highmoor Farm has always been part of the estate.'

'How many girls do you put in a bedroom?' My mother asked tentatively.

'Sometimes four, sometimes five. In most cases the girls are instant friends.'

'Will I be with Barbara Smythe, Miss Clarkson?' I asked her.

'I think that would be a very good idea, Nancy. A familiar face on your first morning here would be nice.' A knock at the door interrupted her and Miss Harris entered to say that a Mr Fray was waiting to see the headmistress. 'I must ask you to excuse me, ladies. Mr Fray is the father of one of the girls who is leaving us in the summer, so naturally he wishes to discuss her future with me. Miss Harris will take you round the school so that you can see for yourself what lies in front of you. Goodbye, Nancy – I am looking forward to your joining us in September.'

We each shook hands with Miss Clarkson before following Miss Harris' slim figure down the corridor. Despite my misgivings I was impressed with Lorivals. The art room was a great studio on the first floor with huge plate-glass windows overlooking the fells, and the music room was equipped with a grand piano and long cupboards containing other instruments. The gymnasium was every girl's dream and it was only when we reached the bedrooms that I was less enchanted. After my room at home they appeared unduly spartan. Narrow single beds stood beside a single locker and wardrobe, and in some cases the windows were small and the carpets worn.

Aunt Susan stood in the centre of one of the bedrooms, her expression disapproving. 'The fees are so high one would have thought they'd spend a little more money making the bedrooms comfortable,' she remarked acidly.

'We don't want to alter the character of the place, Miss Lester,' Miss Harris said mildly. 'Half the charm of Lorivals is the fact that much of the school is exactly as it was when Miss Phoebe first envisaged the place as a girls' college. The facilities for learning and leisure are marvellous, while the bedrooms have a certain faded charm, I think.'

'They're faded, all right,' Aunt Susan said with Northern bluntness. 'Why, the girls will hardly have sufficient room to get dressed. Where are the bathrooms?'

'There are two on every corridor, and adjacent to the gymnasium there is an extensive shower block.'

By the time we reached the entrance hall, girls were running down the stairs from their classrooms to the dining hall, but they showed little interest in us. For the first time I began to admire their grey pleated skirts and pale pink blouses and my heart lifted a little from the doldrums it had been in since last Sunday luncheon.

That evening, Father asked a great many questions about our visit to Lorivals and Mother enthused about the beauty of the school and its setting. It was only when she came to the bedrooms that her story became less than enthusiastic. 'They were so cramped, Arthur,' she

26

complained, 'just a locker and tiny wardrobe. In some rooms the carpets were practically threadbare, and it felt chilly. What are the rooms going to be like in winter?'

'Good schools have never been noted for their luxury, love. I believe that sort of environment is supposed to make men of them, or rather Spartan women.'

'All the same, I shall worry about Nancy in the winter. Even Susan grumbled about the bedrooms.'

'Then they must be spartan. You'll have a lot to talk over with your friend Barbara in the morning, Nancy.'

The next morning Barbara was waiting for me at the park gates but there was no sign of Maisie. She avoided me during the break and when lunchtime came she hurried off in front of us. Barbara sneered, 'She's annoyed because we're going to Lorivals and she isn't. As if *we* care!'

I cared very much. In the late afternoon I hurried after Maisie across the park but she would not turn round when I called her but merely ran as fast as her legs would carry her through the gates. This state of affairs lasted all week and one evening I complained bitterly to my father about it.

'Don't worry, Nancy. It's natural for her to be upset. She's going to miss you and you're going to miss her, but life's like that. People come and go – you'll find that out the older you get.'

'Do you think I should go to her home and ask to see her?'

'No, I don't. Let things take their course, love. By the end of the summer you'll probably be the best of friends again but if you're not, try not to worry. You win some and you lose some.'

A few days later I set out to walk across the park alone. Barbara walked well ahead with Martin Walton and Maisie as usual had hurried on already. I was feeling sorry for myself and angry with all the adults who had conspired to send me to Lorivals when a voice beside me suddenly said, 'Hallo, Nancy. I was hopin' I'd see you on your way home. Now what's wrong between you and our Maisie?' The voice belonged to Bob Jayson. He fell into step beside me but I was reluctant to talk until he added, 'She's drivin' our Mam mad with her tears and she's off her food. We've all asked 'er to tell us what ails 'er but she just sits there tight-lipped and sayin' nothin'. I told our Mam that if I saw you in the park I'd ask you straight out.'

'Why do you think I know anything about it?'

'Because she mooned about the house all over the weekend, and you 'aven't been round for some time. What's wrong love?'

In halting tones I told Bob about Aunt Susan's conviction that I should go to Lorivals, and Grandfather's offer to pay for me. I told him about our interview with the headmistress and I also said that I wasn't keen to go but wasn't old enough to please myself.

'So that's it,' he mused. 'Well, it's a great school Nancy, or so they say. You'll be mixin' with the upper crust there and no mistake.'

'I don't particularly want to mix with the upper crust.'

'I don't suppose you do, but it'll please your Aunt Susan. My, but she likes her own way. I hate servin' her in the shop; she was right uppity with mi father t'other day over his best bananas and the shop filled with customers. I don't think he'd be sorry if she took her custom elsewhere.'

'She doesn't get on too well with my father, either. He says she's bossy, she interferes too much.'

'Well, now that I know what ails our Maisie I'll see what I can do. I suppose you still want to be friends with her?'

'Oh yes, Bob I do, I really do – I've missed her terribly. I'd give anything for Maisie to be coming to Lorivals with me.'

He grinned. 'I can't quite see our Maisie at Lorivals, but you never know. My Great-Aunt Maud's just died and left our dad all her savings. It's a tidy little sum, but I shouldn't think he'll be spending it all on our Maisie.'

We parted at the gates. Bob was sixteen and due to leave Greymont Comprehensive in the summer. His future would be in his father's shop, which he didn't seem to mind since he already helped there in all his spare moments. Father said all three Jayson boys would eventually go into business: he'd heard that Mr Jayson intended to put in a bid for the ironmonger's next door when old Mr Mosely retired.

It was several nights after my meeting with Bob that Father came into the kitchen while Mother was getting the evening meal and I sat at the kitchen table doing my homework. He placed a large basket of fruit on the table in front of me. 'I got Jaysons to make up the basket for me when I saw your friend Maisie was helping in the shop, Nancy. I've been having a long talk with her father. This morning she was interviewed for a place at Lorivals, and what's more – they've accepted her!'

'Are you sure?' I gasped excitedly, with shining eyes.

'Absolutely sure. I got it from Mr Jayson himself. He says nothing's too good for his little girl and he can afford it. He's come into money from old Mrs Marshmont, his Aunt Maud. Walked about like a tramp she did for as long as I can remember, and left thousands. Anyway, that shop's a goldmine on its own account. He can well afford to send young Maisie to Lorivals.'

'Don't the boys mind?' I couldn't help asking.

'Nay, Maisie's always been a bit spoilt, being the one girl with three brothers. Besides, the lads are happy where they are – it's a good business with room for the lot of them.'

'Should I go down there, do you think?'

'No, you sit back love and wait to see if she tells you herself. She knew her father was talking to me, so she'll know I'd pass on the news.'

Contrary to recent events Maisie waited for me the following day and so as not to miss anything, Barbara too caught up with us. Her face was a picture when Maisie announced, 'Did your father tell you I'm to go to Lorivals, Nancy?'

I heard Barbara's quick intake of breath, and before I could reply she snapped, 'You're lying, Maisie! Lorivals would never look at you.'

'Well I've been accepted, so there. Mi dad and me went to see the headmistress yesterday, and she told me I'd be welcome at the school. She told mi dad it was high time Lorivals was becomin' more democratic like.'

'She'll not be putting you with us, though, Barbara said quickly. 'Did she say who you'd be sharing with?'

'She said it would be nice for the local girls to arrive there on the same day in the autumn. We'd all know one another and be instant companions. Most of the girls have to start making friends, so we're luckier than most. I didn't tell her you and I had never been friends.' At the park gates Maisie treated us both to a bright smile before she hoisted her satchel across her shoulder and started out across the road.

Thoroughly put out Barbara said angrily, 'I'm not going to Lorivals to be with Maisie Jayson. That was one of the reasons I had for wanting to go there, to get away from her and girls like her.'

'If Miss Clarkson thinks Maisie is good enough to attend Lorivals it's not for you to say she isn't. I'm glad she's going and if you've any sense you'll start being nice to her. You'll be the one out of step if you don't.'

With a toss of her head she marched away, leaving me with the feeling that the immediate future would be anything but plain sailing.

Maisie and I discovered our old camaraderie in the long summer months. In late July we said our farewells to the little primary school across the park and Barbara departed with her mother to a cottage her father had taken just outside Whitby for the whole of August.

My parents both loved the Lake District and we invariably spent some part of August near Ullswater or

Derwentwater, but this year Father had hired a cottage in Wastdale, a more remote part of Cumbria where he told me I would find the deepest lake and the highest mountains.

When I asked Maisie what she was doing about holidays she said somewhat plaintively, 'I reckon we'll be going to stay with Aunt Edith and Uncle George in Derbyshire. It's not really a holiday, because we all help on their farm and in the house, but she's mi mother's only sister and Mam looks forward to the visit.'

When I told Father he said immediately, 'Why not ask Maisie to come with us? It might broaden her horizons a little.'

I was surprised when she seemed doubtful about the invitation. Her first reaction had been one of delight, but now I could tell she was having second thoughts.

'You would like to come, wouldn't you, Maisie?' I persisted.

'I'd love to come but it'd be expensive, more expensive anyway than goin' to Aunt Edith's. Mi Dad's already spendin' a lot more money on me than the boys are gettin'.'

'I can't think any of your brothers would mind.'

'That's just it, they wouldn't. It's my conscience that's troubling me.'

When I told my parents about Maisie's misgivings Father said, 'She's a thoughtful girl, your Maisie, but tell her all she'd need is spending money, and there won't be many shops to spend it in.'

Maisie was still doubtful, but Bob became my ally. I told him about his sister's reluctance to come with us, and her reasons for declining. He grinned down at me. 'She's been listening to our Mam nagging our Dad about the money he's spending on her. Mi mother's not adventurous – she likes her money in the bank where she can keep her eye on it. She thinks holidays are an unnecessary expense ye see, and believes it's ridiculous our Maisie going to Lorivals. You know mi father's taking over the ironmonger's, I suppose?'

'Yes.'

'She thinks that's ridiculous, too. Mam hasn't got a business head on her shoulders: she's telling mi father that one shop's quite enough for the area, that having two is foolish and wasteful like.'

'So you don't think your mother'd agree to Maisie coming with us to the Lake District?'

'No, she'd say she was havin' too much money spent on her and it's time she learned it doesn't grow on trees.'

'I see. Well, I won't mention it again, Bob. I don't want to cause trouble in the family.'

'Leave it with me Nancy, I'll talk to mi mother. You'll see, she'll let Maisie go with you.'

Two days later I met my friend flying down the street with her red curls blowing in the breeze, her feet hardly touching the ground, and a broad bright smile on her face. Long before I reached her she was shouting, 'I *can* come, Nancy! I *can* come!'

Father always said it wasn't just the scenery or the weather that made that holiday so much joy, it was Maisie's enthusiasm, her gasps of delight at the deep dark beauty of the lake and the towering hills that surrounded it. The weather too was kind to us. In the entire fortnight we only had one day when the rain fell incessantly and the lake loomed in front of us sombre and eerie, majestic in its circle of rugged screes and lonely mountains.

It was chilly and we spent the morning collecting kindling and logs so that Father could build a fire. The tiny cottage felt cosy as the firelight fell on shining brass and copper and Maisie said appreciatively, 'This is the day I'll remember best, Nancy. I've loved every minute of it all, but this is the best – the firelight and the warmth inside, while outside there's that long dark lake and those mountains.'

'It's not the prettiest lake.'

'I know, but it's the grandest, isn't it? I reckon it's the wildness that makes it so different.'

'Are you looking forward to going to Lorivals now, Maisie?'

'I'm resigned to it. I just hope we're together, as Miss Clarkson promised. She said she hoped we'd make other friends, a great many of them, but I know they'll all be stuck-up like Barbara Smythe. They'll not want to be friends with me.'

'Well, of course they will! Perhaps Barbara'll change when she's no longer living at home.'

'She'll be worse, not better.'

'I don't think so. Her father's rather a nice man, it's just her mother who's snobbish, like my Aunt Susan.'

Maisie grinned. 'Your Aunt Susan says she doesn't want to be served by our Bob anymore, because she doesn't get all her own way with him. Dad panders to her likes and dislikes.'

'She's always been Mother's big sister and she rules Grandfather with a rod of iron. I think Father's the only person she's not entirely sure of – they argue all the time.'

'I've had such a lovely holiday, Nancy. I'll never forget these last two weeks, never.'

'There'll be lots more, Maisie.'

Oh, the optimism of youth, the conviction that life will go on in the same way without changes or deviation. We had an awful lot to learn.

4

It was a misty September morning when Father deposited me on the steps of Lorivals carrying a new suitcase and wearing the pink and grey school uniform which I had once professed to dislike.

Cars were coming and going while Father stood with his arms around me on the lower terrace. 'Try not to be homesick love,' he encouraged. 'It'll soon be half-term, then there's Christmas and all of three weeks to spend at home. Besides, you'll have Maisie and Barbara, they'll be just as homesick as you.'

I clenched my fists to stop the treacherous tears from falling down my cheeks, relieved when I saw Mr Jayson's shabby old Austin depositing Maisie at the end of the terrace. Nobody seemed remotely interested in us. Girls were greeting one another enthusiastically and only a few seemed nervous and less than happy. There was a stir among the girls standing on the terraces when Greymont's black Mayoral Rolls Royce swept along the drive, and the new Mayor and Mayoress descended from it with their daughter Barbara. They were both wearing their mayoral chains.

Mrs Smythe's eyes swept the crowd with every expectation that they would rush forward to greet her. When they merely resumed their conversations which the arrival of the car had interrupted she seemed rather less sure of herself, and after a brief farewell to her daughter immediately returned to the car and sat in the back seat staring straight ahead of her. Alderman Smythe behaved rather more affectionately, and then the car was returning down the drive and Barbara was standing next to us, pale and tearful.

Maisie showed the vindictive side of her character by

saying acidly, 'I hope they don't think you were showin' off.'

'What do you mean, showing off?' Barbara demanded.

'Arrivin' in the Mayoral car, that's what I mean.'

'I didn't want to come in that, it was Mother's idea.'

I was pleased when a plump girl standing nearby turned to ask, 'Is this your first day too?'

'Yes,' I answered for all three of us. 'I'm Nancy Graham and this is Maisie Jayson and Barbara Smythe.'

She shook hands with each one of us in turn, then taking a crumpled bag of boiled sweets out of her pocket handed them round. 'I'm Norah Peabody. Perhaps I'll be put with you – they say there's either four or five to a dormitory.'

By this time we were moving into the building, and a porter was shouting for order and asking us to leave our luggage in the hall to be sorted out later. A long low table was set out in the hall and four mistresses were sitting at it. The girls formed queues and I allowed Norah to line up before me.

When it was her turn the young teacher who I learned from the card set before her was Miss Meachem said, 'You are in room three on the second floor, Norah. You will be in there with three other girls and your luggage will be taken up. Please put your things in the locker and wardrobe, then leave your suitcase outside the room so that the porter can collect it and put it in the basement store.' Norah moved away and it was my turn.

After hearing my name Miss Meachem looked down the list in front of her then with a bright smile said, 'You three are the local girls. You'll be pleased to know that Miss Clarkson has placed you together in the same dormitory. It is Room Five on the second floor and you will be sharing with two other girls, Amelia Urquart and Lois Brampton.'

Maisie was openly relieved that we were to be together, and even Barbara didn't think it was a bad idea. Needless to say we very quickly became known as the village girls although Barbara was quick to protest that Greymont was not a village but a fair-sized town. It made little difference.

'I wonder who's coming in with us,' she mused anxiously while we were putting our things away upstairs. 'I hope it's somebody we can get along with.'

'I hope so too,' Maisie said feelingly, 'then you needn't spend so much time with us.'

'Nancy happens to be my friend too,' Barbara said haughtily.

We were saved from further argument by the arrival of the school porter carrying two suitcases which he placed at the side of the two empty beds.

As soon as he'd gone Barbara swooped on the nearest suitcase which was somewhat battered and bearing a great many labels. 'Look at these,' she exclaimed. 'Hong Kong and Singapore, Brisbane and New York. "Miss Lois Brampton" – who do you suppose she is?'

Maisie was busy examining the other suitcase. 'This is a "Lady Amelia Urquart". Gosh, shall we have to call her Your Ladyship?'

'Don't be silly, Maisie, of course we shan't. She's just a pupil like the rest of us.'

Barbara was however very impressed and I quickly surmised that she intended to make one of the newcomers a special friend. Maisie said as much as we made our way down the stairs to the hall where we were to congregate later that afternoon. 'She'll have no time for us with those two in the dormitory,' she said darkly.

'We don't know yet what they'll be like.'

'I don't suppose she'll care – it's enough that one of them is a Lady and the other's much-travelled.'

Neither Lois nor Amelia arrived that afternoon, and an older girl who came into our room later and introduced herself as a prefect informed us that they would be arriving the following morning. Miss Clarkson would be speaking to all the new girls tomorrow promptly at two o'clock in the music room.

'When do we start lessons?' Barbara asked.

'Keep your eyes on the notice board in the corridor downstairs, and it'll tell you all you need to know. Lessons start the day after tomorrow. Do any of you play any sport?'

We all admitted to indifferent tennis and hockey, and somewhat disdainfully she said, 'Well, we'll see what you're worth during the next few days. We play hockey, netball and tennis here. We also have riding lessons if you're interested and ballroom dancing. Perhaps you'll tell the other two when they arrive.' She walked over to the two cases and scanned the luggage labels casually, then turning away remarked, 'We don't have any kowtowing at Lorivals, remember. Miss Clarkson frowns on it, and there are a good number of titled girls here already.'

She left the room without another word and after she'd gone Barbara said indignantly, 'What did she mean about kowtowing?'

'She means Lady Amelia is no different from us,' Maisie said sharply.

'I don't believe in kowtowing,' Barbara replied hotly.

'Then why did you arrive in the Mayoral car?' Maisie asked.

'Why don't you stop it the pair of you!' I said angrily. 'You're like two cats spitting at each other. We're here in the same bedroom whether we like it or not, and I don't think it's a good thing for the two new girls to see you arguing all the time.'

Neither of them spoke. Barbara carried on unpacking her suitcase, thrusting things hastily into her locker then slamming the drawer shut while Maisie sat on her bed idly swinging her legs with a sulky expression on her face.

Our evening meal was eaten at long tables in the dining room, and because we were the new girls our places were at the very end near the doors, through which a draught blew unremittingly. There were only two empty places

37

at the table and we assumed these were for the two girls arriving the next morning. Miss Clarkson and her staff occupied the top table and they were served first after Grace was said.

A girl sitting opposite cried into her soup and Maisie had little appetite for the plain fare set before her. The meal was unimaginative but wholesome, and although I had little appetite I made a show of eating when I caught one of the older girls watching us pointedly.

After supper Miss Clarkson said we should spend our first evening writing letters home, then we were dismissed into the common room or to our dormitories to comply with her request.

Barbara and I wrote long pages in which we gave a detailed account of our first day at Lorivals while Maisie confined herself to a page and a half of erratically written script which I felt sure would tell her family little.

Promptly at nine o'clock we went back to the dining hall for cocoa and biscuits, then we scrambled for the bathrooms and hurried to reach our respective dormitories before the lights went out at ten o'clock.

We lay in our narrow beds silent and miserable until a prefect came, but after a quick glance to reassure herself that we were in our beds she left, closing the door quietly behind her. I heard Maisie sobbing until Barbara tearfully told her to stop, that it was the same for all of us. So passed our first day at Lorivals and I asked myself plaintively how I was going to bear the years ahead.

The next morning we familiarised ourselves with the layout of the school and the playing-fields, and as the morning progressed I began to feel happier about the future. It is true we were still feeling strange amongst girls who had been at Lorivals for some time, but as we met and talked with other newcomers we quickly realised that our fears were their fears also, and that at one time all the girls who now went about with smiling faces and cheerful greetings had been in our position.

The fresh air gave us an appetite for lunch, which proved to be far more palatable than dinner the night before; momentarily Maisie forgot about her mother's steak and kidney puddings and deep apple pies. We were advised not to forget Miss Clarkson's address at two o'clock and I suggested that we go back to the dormitory in case the two missing girls had arrived.

We found the room in something of a mess. A small dark-haired girl was busy unpacking. Her suitcase rested on Maisie's bed and on the other beds were piled underwear and clothing, as well as a long sports bag holding a tennis racket. The newcomer was pretty, with short brown hair and huge hazel eyes. I noticed at once that she was not in school uniform but wearing a beige tweed skirt and matching silk blouse. Barbara was the first to introduce herself.

'I say, I'm most awfully sorry, I've spilled out on to all your beds, but these things'll be put away in no time,' the girl said quickly.

There was nowhere for us to sit, and I asked if we could help since she appeared so completely disorganised while Barbara insisted, 'I suppose you are Lady Amelia?'

She smiled. 'Actually no, I'm Lois Brampton. Did you think only a Ladyship could be so much in need of a lady's maid? I'm always like this when I'm unpacking and I've had to do so much of it.'

'You'd best hurry up,' Maisie advised. 'We're to have a talk from the headmistress at two o'clock.'

Lois turned to look at Maisie with a half-smile on her face, obviously unused to her abruptness and the north country accent which was much more obvious in Maisie than in either Barbara or myself.

'Have you had lunch?' I asked, to soften Maisie's terseness.

'I had something on the train and I got a taxi from the station at Greymont.'

'Didn't your parents bring you?' Barbara asked in some surprise.

'My father lives in Brussels, he wasn't able to get leave.'

'How about your mother, then?' Maisie asked.

'My parents are divorced. Mother lives in the States – I don't suppose she even knows where I am.'

I tried to give her a warning look but Maisie went on oblivious 'Your mother doesn't know where you are! Doesn't she care?' Lois Brampton merely permitted herself a small smile before returning to her unpacking while I took hold of Maisie's arm and shook my head as a warning to say no more.

At that moment the door opened and another girl stood in the doorway. There was something about Amelia Urquart that instantly set her apart, but it was not her nobility, rather an inner calmness, a serenity which made her seem older than her years. In a soft, low-pitched voice she announced, 'I'm Amelia Urquart. This is my dormitory, I believe?'

Barbara was again the first to introduce herself while Lois scooped her things off Amelia's bed and apologised saying, 'I'm sorry, you'll want to unpack. I've spilled over a bit.'

We waited for Lois to change into her school uniform then just before two we left the dormitory on our way to hear Miss Clarkson's address. It was at the top of the stairs that we realised Maisie was missing and Barbara said impatiently, 'Oh never mind her, we'll all be late if we wait for Maisie.'

It was Amelia who said, 'You go ahead and save places for us. I'll wait for Maisie.'

Barbara had the grace to blush and that was the moment when I discovered a deep and abiding admiration for Amelia Urquart, which was to stay with me through all the years we remained together at Lorivals. Perhaps it never really left me – not even in those days when the difference in our stations became desperately plain.

During her short speech, Miss Clarkson said we must all regard ourselves as Lorivals girls and be proud to be such. It was at Lorivals that we would learn values of comradeship and stability that would sustain us all our lives – values which Miss Phoebe Lorival had so clearly envisaged when she started her school.

I looked at Miss Phoebe's portrait taking pride of place above the dais in the music room: such a small sparrow of a woman, with her pretty gentle face framed by soft brown hair. Poor Miss Phoebe who had been prevented from marrying, forced to stay close to a domineering parent who had ruled his house and his servants like a despot. Had she really found true satisfaction in turning this lovely old house into a school, shattering its peace with the sound of girls' voices, the quiet footfalls of discreet servants replaced by the rushing tread of innumerable pupils . . . I wondered if her pale little ghost wandered about the rooms and passages, searching for a peace that had gone forever.

5

Seven years of eating, sleeping, playing sport and studying together made us five girls closer than sisters. We grew from gauche and awkward childhood into the sort of young women Lorivals invariably produced – poised and graceful. When I first met Amelia I couldn't see that Lorivals could teach her anything, for even in those early days she seemed to be perfect. To me she was so incredibly beautiful and capable that I couldn't believe it when they chose *me* to be Head Girl instead of her.

As usual, the omission raised not a ripple in the incredible composure, not even when Barbara passed several snide remarks, and Maisie was loud in her congratulations.

Gently Amelia said, 'Nancy deserves to be Head Girl, Barbara. She's worked so hard and she's popular with everybody. We should all be delighted for her.' Barbara had the grace to look embarrassed and the moment passed without further words.

In the summer of 1972 Amelia invited me to spend two weeks at her parents' place just outside Hereford. To avoid any feelings of excluding the other three she added, 'I've asked my parents if I can invite all of you before we leave Lorivals, so perhaps Nancy can come for two weeks in August and Lois for two weeks after that. I'd like you to come for Christmas, Barbara, and Maisie in the New Year.'

Maisie was quick to demur, saying that she liked to be at home for the whole of the Christmas holiday as it was the busiest time at her father's shop. Later she admitted privately to me, 'I like Amelia, Nancy, but I honestly don't want to go to her home. I'd just feel out of place.'

'Maisie, why should you?' I said stoutly.

'I couldn't ask her back, not with Eric and Jim there. You know what they're like, always squabbling and neither of them speaking the Queen's English.'

'Amelia wouldn't mind, she'd probably enjoy it.'

'Besides we've not the room, not even with the flat over both shops. There's still boxes of oranges and apples, and stock piling up in the passages. I don't mind if I don't go to Amelia's. You and the others must, but I honestly don't want to.'

Amelia accepted her refusal and did not try to persuade her. 'I don't think Maisie would be happy at my home,' she confided. 'We never do anything exciting – Father's engrossed with his stamp collection and Mother's so vague about everything except her roses and the local agricultural show. She's always called upon to help judge the dogs and she's a founder member of the pony club.'

It was the first year I had spent apart from my parents in the summer holidays and Father said somewhat wistfully, 'We'll miss you love, but I suppose it's what we can expect, now you're a young woman.'

'Don't you want me to go, Father?'

'Well, of course we want you to go. Your Aunt Susan would be mortified if you didn't – when Nellie Smythe starts telling all her cronies that her daughter Barbara is spending Christmas with her schoolfriend, Lady Amelia Urquart at Lord Urquart's country seat, she'll be able to say that her niece was there in the summer. You can't deny her that pleasure, my dear.'

'Aunt Susan doesn't change, Father.'

'If anything she's worse than you remember. Susan's dined out for months on your elevation to Head Girl. Between her and Nellie it's an ongoing battle.'

'Oh dear, I do hope I'm never like Aunt Susan, it all sounds so terribly childish.'

I was impressed with Drummond, the home of the Earls of Urquart. It was a vast stone-built house in acres of parkland on the banks of the River Wye just a few miles from Hereford and Amelia's parents received me gracefully if somewhat absently.

I was introduced to her father in the rose garden where he was busy tying up several of the rose trees that a gale in the night had flattened. At first I thought he was one of the gardeners in his battered felt hat and flannel trousers that had once been white. He was wearing an old Harris tweed jacket and there were carpet slippers on his feet, but even so he greeted me with an olde worlde courtesy that I found completely charming.

In no time at all we were helping him to tie up his rose trees and with an absent-minded smile he said gently, 'I'd forgotten you were coming home today dear, your mother's at some committee or other. How did you get here?'

'By taxi from the station, Daddy. I didn't bother to tell you I was arriving today, I knew you'd forget.'

'So you think your old father's pretty hopeless, do you?'

She smiled at him across the rose beds. 'I think you're a darling Daddy but I warned Nancy you'd have your head in the clouds. How's Mummy's new litter?'

'Thriving and puddling all over the hall. It's time they went – their mother would agree with me if she could talk.'

Seeing my look of surprise Amelia said, 'One of Mummy's dogs – her Yorkshire Terrier, Nancy, she spoils her terribly. There – that's the last one, Daddy. Are you going back to the house now?'

'No, I'm going to the greenhouses. Have you shown your friend round the place?'

'Not yet, Daddy, we've only just arrived. Besides it's too nice to stay indoors. I thought we'd take a walk across the park.'

'Show her the deer and the swans, they're what most people come to see.'

As the days passed I began to realise why Amelia seemed to float through life like some graceful swan herself, with hardly a ripple to trouble her on the even waters of her life. Firstly there was the unending peace of the countryside, the placid river and quiet, picturesque villages. Then there were her parents, incurious about our life at Lorivals, assuming that Amelia was happy there but untroubled if she were not. They accepted me graciously as one of her friends but showed no further curiosity. I had expected them to smile when I related some of my father's stranger experiences, but they were no more interested in my family than they were in me.

We spent our time driving about the lanes of Herefordshire in a trap pulled by Jenny, a sleek and beautiful pony. We rode across the fields and we went with Lady Urquart to flower shows and dog shows. The puppies were adorable and she had found homes for all of them. At the local dog show she presided over the proceedings, but it was her own black labrador that won first prize, and similarly, it was Lord Urquart's rose that took the cup at the flower show – more, I thought, out of a sense of tradition than because it was the most beautiful rose on show.

Lord Urquart escorted me round Drummond proudly showing me portraits of his ancestors and of himself in the uniform of a Brigadier. I also saw oil paintings of Amelia's two brothers, Charles and Cedric, the first in the uniform of a Colonel in the Guards and the second in Naval Officer's uniform. I felt I was obliged to ask questions so I asked cautiously, 'Do both your sons live in England, sir?'

'Charles lives over at Meriton but of course one day they'll live here. Cedric lives near Dartmouth and my other daughter is based in Falmouth.'

Later when I mentioned her brothers and sister to Amelia, she said, 'I was an afterthought in my parents' lives. My brothers and sister were adult when I was born. Cedric was at sea and I never saw much of Charles. Of course, he and his wife visit quite often but they're

45

in Canada just now so you won't meet them. My sister Celia lives in Cornwall, she's not due for a visit.'

How impersonal it all was and yet I could understand Lord Urquart's love for that great stone house set in the midst of a beechwood with ivy climbing up to the clustered chimneys. Amelia told me the gardens had been trampled down by Cromwell's army and at night when I lay in my huge bedroom overlooking the orchard I could hear the rustling of the leaves in the wind and if I closed my eyes I could imagine some long-dead Lady Urquart passing my door, her silken skirts swishing against the skirting boards.

By the time I left Drummond I was homesick for my father's quick humour and the normal everyday sounds of the Greymont milkman clanking his bottles along the path and the cheerful whistling of our newspaper boy. Amelia had to remind her parents that I was leaving that morning and they came to the front of the house to see me off. I thanked them for their hospitality and Lady Urquart said graciously, 'You must come again, Nancy. We are always glad to meet Amelia's friends.'

I had the distinct impression that five minutes after I left she would find it difficult to remember my face and I wondered what Lois would make of Amelia's parents when she arrived later in the day. It could be that Lois would relish the sense of permanency surrounding Drummond since there was precious little of it in her own life. She received long rambling letters from her mother in America as well as expensive presents, and she made excuses constantly not to visit her father in Europe. We had learned early on not to ask questions and when holidays came round Lois was invariably asked to spend them in our respective homes. Barbara's mother and Aunt Susan didn't entirely approve of Lois. They frowned over her parents' divorce and said the girl's brittle and independent attitude to life was plainly a result of her upbringing.

On my return from Herefordshire Father met me at

the station. 'I'm so glad to have you back, love,' he beamed. 'Now you'll have to get accustomed to living with the peasants again. Did you enjoy yourself?'

I chatted to him in the car on the way home and he listened with a smile when I told him about the flower show and the dog show, the old beautiful house and the miles of parkland, then when I had finished he said dryly, 'Your Aunt Susan's waiting all agog to hear about the holiday – it'll be Sunday lunch as usual, Nancy.'

'How is Grandfather?'

'He doesn't complain but he's looking much older these days. He'll love having you at home. Another twelve months and you'll be leaving Lorivals. When is the next holiday?'

'We have three days in October when I thought it would be nice to ask Lois here, and then Christmas.'

Lois did come to stay at Greymont in October but she said her father had arranged to come to England for Christmas and they would spend it together in a London hotel. Maisie confided in me that her mother had said she could invite Tom Standing and his parents for Christmas day and looking at her bright red cheeks and obvious embarrassment I asked, 'Do you like Tom Standing as much as ever, Maisie?'

'I suppose so, in spite of the last seven years at Lorivals.'

'What are you going to do when you leave in the summer – marry Tom or get a job?'

'Miss Chandler says I could do well as a Domestic Science teacher but I'll need good A-levels in other subjects before I can teach and I'm not too happy about those.' When I remained silent she added somewhat anxiously, 'You're thinkin' it's been a waste sendin' me to Lorivals, and you're right. My brothers laugh at my posh accent and I've no real ambition. I just want to leave school and help out at home until I get married. You think that's awful, don't you Nancy?'

'Not if it's what you want. Do you know for sure that Tom wants it too?'

'No, but I'll have a good idea after Christmas.'

Lois was unenthusiastic about meeting her father. While she dragged her suitcase on to the floor prior to packing she surprised me by saying, 'I'd give anything to be coming home with you, Nancy. I don't want to spend Christmas in London.'

'But it'll be wonderful, Lois! Think of all those interesting places to see, and the theatres.'

'I don't suppose he'll be on his own, he never is.'

'What do you mean?'

'He'll have some girl with him, probably somebody I've never met.'

'How can you expect to meet your father's friends when you never go to see him,' I said logically.

'You don't understand,' she muttered miserably, and it was true that I didn't. Her mother had remarried, so surely she couldn't hate her father because of her mother? It had to be something else, something deeper, but as usual I asked no questions.

My father came to collect Barbara, Maisie and me on the morning we left school for the Christmas holidays. It was mild and some of the leaves of autumn still lingered on the beech trees that lined the drive. We chatted cheerfully on the way into the town but I thought Father seemed unusually silent and it was only after we had dropped Maisie off that he turned to say, 'I'm taking you on to your father's office, Barbara. Your Mother's got a meeting this afternoon so there'll be nobody at home.'

After he had helped her out with her luggage he returned to the car but before driving off he said quietly, 'I have some bad news for you, love. Your Grandfather died yesterday – it was a heart attack.'

I could feel the sudden tightening in my throat and

the pain of tears stinging my eyes. 'Why didn't you tell me he was so ill?' I cried plaintively.

'He's not been quite himself for months, love, you saw that in October. He died very quietly in his chair in the surgery waiting for his next patient. There was nothing anybody could do.'

'When is the funeral?'

'Christmas Eve. We shall be going to his house on Christmas Day as usual. Your Aunt Susan has said nothing must change, but both your mother and I would have preferred her to come to us.'

'I shall hate going to Grandfather's when he isn't there any more,' I sobbed.

How could Aunt Susan expect us to believe nothing had changed? Grandfather's favourite chair stood empty and lonely before the fire and it was the same at the dining table. I felt that she had quite deliberately left his presence all around the house. His favourite pipe lay on the mantelpiece and his best-loved cardigan was draped across the back of his chair. His slippers were on the hearthrug and a book he had been reading lay open on the table beside his chair.

Father said it was morbid to leave things lying about, but Aunt Susan said sharply, 'I like to think he's here enjoying Christmas with us as usual. I'll put his things away when I'm good and ready.'

'Are you going to go on living here, Aunt Susan?' I asked.

'No. A new man, Dr Jarvis, will be taking over this practice and I've decided to look for something out of the town. I had thought of Ellwood – the village is quite nice.'

'You'll have more travelling when you want to come into the town,' Father said reasonably.

'I can cope with that. There's old Mrs Crossley's house going just on the outskirts of the village – I've always rather liked that house.'

'Don't you think it's too large for you, Susan? Mrs

Crossley had half the rooms shut up,' Mother said quickly.

'I can't do with a small house. I have the furniture for a larger house and I'm certainly not getting rid of any of it. It's all good stuff. I'll get nothing for it secondhand and I'm not disposed to give it away.'

My parents made no further comment and Sarah came in to collect the plates before bringing in the Christmas pudding. Christmas had always been one of my favourite festivities but not this time. The pudding stuck in my throat and where once we had made much of handing the presents around today they were simply placed on the window seat in the living room and we opened them in silence, saying polite thank-yous, afraid to be enthusiastic.

We left promptly at nine and at the door Aunt Susan said briskly, 'We'll need to see the solicitor early in the New Year, Mary. Perhaps Nancy should come with us, she's mentioned in Father's will.'

'Are you going to make an appointment, then?' Mother asked.

'I already have. It's for January the second at ten o'clock. I'll meet you outside their office in the Square.'

Even the weather was wrong for Christmas. As we trudged across the park our feet scattered the leaves of autumn which still clung to the paths and lawns, and it was damp and misty. When we reached the park gates we stood for a few moments listening to the Salvation Army band playing Christmas carols, and I thought miserably that it was the only bit of Christmas cheer we had had all day.

Once inside the house Father stoked up the fire and brought out the sherry, then went to a corner cupboard and lifted out several parcels wrapped in brightly coloured paper which he handed to Mother and me.

'Why, Arthur!' Mother exclaimed. '*More* presents?'

'I knew what it would be like at your father's house.

Susan should have come to us, it was like having dinner with a ghost.'

'I know dear, but she's bound to miss him, they were very close.'

'You're forgetting how they quarrelled, how she got on his nerves and how she bossed him about. I wasn't sure whether it was grief or remorse that was making her hang on to his things.'

'Do you really think she'll buy that house in Ellwood?'

'If she fancies it she will. Now, enough of Susan – open your parcels and let's see what you think of them!'

One of my parcels contained a narrow gold chain and single pearl pendant, the other a beaded evening bag, while Mother's contained a new black leather handbag and a quilted dressing gown. We both showed our delighted appreciation of Father's gifts, then he poured out the sherry, chocolates were produced and we settled down in front of the television for the rest of the evening. For the first time that day it seemed like Christmas.

6

Once term had started again, we spent all of our free periods at Lorivals revising and worrying about the exams ahead. The days passed in a blur of essays, the nights in memorising our notes. I began to feel drained and badly in need of a complete change of scene, however brief, before the A-levels were inescapably upon us. Lois, who was much more relaxed about the whole thing, had a practical suggestion.

'Why not come with me to Austria at Easter for a quick break, Nancy? It's my father's suggestion. He is going to work in Vienna in the spring and he has the loan of a house near the lakeside in Igls for a week at Easter. I said I'd go if I could get a friend to come with me.'

'I'll have to ask my parents but I'm sure it will be all right. Will it be terribly expensive?'

'Not at all. Dad says he'll foot the bill, all you'll need is spends.'

When I asked Amelia what she intended to do with her life after quitting Lorivals she merely smiled that sweet ethereal smile of hers, saying she wasn't sure. It was something she'd have to think about. Barbara thought she'd be working for a time in her father's office, but she also informed us that at Easter she was going with her parents and the Waltons, including Martin, to Scotland. The men would play golf and Martin would give her lessons. I began to believe that Maisie and Barbara had the same aspiration – to marry the boy they had loved since childhood. When I said as much to Lois she replied acidly, 'It wouldn't be enough for me – marriage is *very* overrated.'

Lois was a seasoned traveller so it was I who was excited about my first flight into Innsbruck airport while she remained unconcerned. Her father was there to meet us and my first thought was that he looked far too young to be her father.

Mr Brampton was tall and slim with a boyish smiling face and fair hair, and he was immaculately dressed in a dark grey suit. He came forward with outstretched arms and a bright smile on his face, and Lois was swept into a warm embrace before he greeted me.

'So this is Nancy,' he said, smiling down at me. 'I'm David Brampton – how do you do. We're going to have the most marvellous time in Igls, girls. Ever been to Austria before Nancy?'

'No, this is my first time abroad.'

'Even better, then. Now come along – I've left Gloria hanging on to the trolley. I daren't leave it for a moment otherwise it would be taken.'

'Who is Gloria?' Lois asked somewhat sullenly.

'My new secretary. She's a great girl, you'll like her.'

We followed Mr Brampton out of the lounge, trying to keep up with his long strides and I could see that Lois' face was faintly mutinous. Catching my eye she muttered savagely, 'I knew there'd be a woman somewhere, there always is.'

I wondered why it mattered so much. I didn't have long to think about it however, because after a wave of his hand a girl was walking towards us across the foyer, pushing a trolley before her.

Gloria was beautiful, tall and slender with long auburn hair and a red fox coat slung over her shoulders. Her smile was warm and friendly.

It was dark when we drove up to the chalet on the plâteau above Innsbruck. The city was spread before us like a jewel and I could smell the pine forest and hear the lake gently lapping against the shore. I gasped with delight as we entered a room lit by lamps and with a huge log fire burning in the grate. I was aware of a pine floor scattered with rosy red rugs, and huge brass containers filled with grasses and branches of bright red berries. Gloria said, 'We knew you'd love it. Tomorrow we can discover the lake and the walks through the forest.'

'We'll build a fire on the shore and eat from the barbecue. This is a private beach but when the weather's fine most people do it. Now then, I expect you two girls are ravenous,' Mr Brampton said jovially.

'We ate on the plane, Dad. I'd really like to get unpacked and I'm not in the least hungry. Nancy may like something.'

'Well, of course,' Gloria said amicably. 'I left a chicken cooking in the oven and there's fruit and cheese. The cheese is local Nancy, and very good.'

Lois and I unpacked in an uncomfortable silence and when I had put everything away in the huge drawers under the massive wardrobe I said, 'You are coming to eat, Lois, aren't you? Gloria's taken the trouble to prepare something – I think you should.'

'Don't lecture me, Nancy. I'm not hungry but I am very tired. *You* go ahead by all means.'

The chicken and young vegetables were delicious. They were followed by fresh woodland strawberries and cream, ending with the local cheeses which, as Gloria had promised, were excellent. Mr Brampton produced a bottle of light German wine and after we had eaten he said with a fond smile, 'I have an excellent secretary, Nancy. Not only does Gloria breathe efficiency at the office, but she also cooks an excellent meal.'

I was embarrassingly aware of the look that passed between them. Gloria was obviously in love with him, but how much her employer returned that love was not disclosed in his handsome amused face.

Lois was fast asleep when I went into our bedroom, and I was very quiet so as not to disturb her. I hoped the start of our holiday was not going to set the pattern for the rest of it but I was not optimistic.

For me that short week was an enchanted time. We

were taken into the city to dine in a popular Tyrol restaurant where there was a great deal of yodelling and thigh-slapping, and we sailed and fished in the lake and walked in the forest. At first Gloria and David accompanied us everywhere, but I was glad when they decided we were capable of getting around on our own.

Gloria was trying too hard. She desperately wanted Lois to like her, and I cringed at those moments when Mr Brampton caressed her arm or ran his fingers through her long silken hair. I saw the look of disdain on his daughter's face, and I turned away in embarrassment. On our walks I never referred to the subject until the day Lois surprised me by saying, 'You like her, don't you?'

We were sitting high up on the hillside overlooking Igls. The sun shone in a clear blue sky and it was so still we could almost hear the silence. When I didn't answer her immediately Lois said, 'She wants you to like her, she's falling over backwards to please him and us.'

'I think she's nice,' I said cautiously, 'and she's also very beautiful.'

'But of course, all my father's women friends have been beautiful.'

'Is that why you don't like her, because she's your father's mistress?'

'I like her well enough. I just don't care to see her being silly about my father when I know what he's like.'

'She's not hurting you by being in love with him, and she can't help it. If you should be angry with anybody it should be your father, not Gloria.'

'Now you're beginning to understand, Nancy,' she said with a grin. 'If you stay here long enough you might even put two and two together and make four instead of five.'

'What do you mean by that?'

'It's not Gloria I dislike, it's my father, and I dislike myself for feeling that way. I want to love David, I want to like being with him, but I can't – and it's women like Gloria who have taught me to dislike him. Come on, I'll race you to the chalet.'

She streaked ahead of me but I made no effort to catch up with her. I was glad that the holiday was coming to an end. I was glad to be going back to Lorivals . . .

The exams were over, the results were out and I was not displeased with mine. Father said I'd done well to get three good grades in maths, English, and French, and Barbara, Lois and Amelia had also obtained respectable results. Maisie hadn't been so lucky but didn't seem to mind her grade Es in history and scripture.

Now all the talk was of the senior dance which took place in the main hall of Lorivals for the girls who would be leaving at the end of the summer term. Over the years we had heard about this dance, and as juniors had sat silent and intrigued peering through the balustrade from the regions above while the older girls we envied danced in the arms of young men and boys until midnight. Miss Clarkson informed us that we would be permitted to invite a boy to the dance, maybe a brother or friend of the family, and that in addition several of the boys from Ramilees School would be invited.

For weeks the dance was the sole topic of conversation: in the dining hall and the gym, in the dormitories and on the playing-fields. Maisie was quick to inform us that she was bringing Tom.

'Who will you bring, Barbara?' I asked, even though I already knew the answer. I asked Martin. I asked him at Easter and he said he'd be delighted to come,' she answered proudly.

Lois said she would take her chance with the boys from Ramilees. There was nobody in particular whom she wanted to invite. 'Have you decided who you're bringing to the dance, Nancy?'

'There's nobody I want to ask, either. I'll stick with you and hope one or two of the Ramilees boys asks us wallflowers to dance.'

'They'll be as diffident as we are,' Amelia said with a

smile. 'They've spent most of their lives in the company of other boys, so they'll be shy with girls. I'm bringing Phillip Garveston – our families have been friends for years.'

I stared at her curiously. In all the years I had known Amelia she had never once mentioned the Garveston family, now suddenly out of the blue Phillip Garveston was being invited to be her dancing partner.

'I'll invite Mark Garveston too if you want Nancy. He's nice, you'd like him,' she carried on and suddenly I had a vision of Garveston Hall and felt strangely out of my depth and unsure of myself.

'Perhaps he'd like to come alone and find a girl for himself,' I said sharply, but Amelia only laughed.

'I think he'd rather I found someone for him: the last time I saw Mark he was very shy.'

We didn't discuss it again and Amelia must have taken it for granted that I had agreed, for a few days later she said, 'I had a letter from Phillip this morning. He says Mark will be very happy to come to the dance and make up a four – I knew he would.'

It was exciting getting ready for the dance. As usual, Lois had received a generous cheque from her father and on the Saturday before the event she went into Lancaster and came back with a wonderful confection in kingfisher-blue shot taffeta. The dress had a low-cut neckline and a wide bouffant skirt made in three tiers lined with sparkling net. Personally I thought it far too old for her, but she went on to produce silver dance shoes with three-inch heels and silver earrings that dangled almost to her shoulders.

The vision of Lois in her expensive attire put my own pretty pale pink crêpe-de-chine dress right in the shade. Faced with this competition, Barbara adamantly refused to wear the cornflower blue dress her parents had bought for her in Greymont and insisted that she too, should have something a little more exciting. After that she went into Kendal with her mother the following Saturday and returned with a jade green taffeta dress that went some way to stealing Lois' thunder.

Maisie decided she would wear white, which earned the approval of every mistress at the school, since they considered white to be young and virginal, but Amelia was the greatest surprise of all.

She showed us a dreary dress in an indeterminate shade of beige and I wasn't even sure it suited her colouring. I reserved my opinion until the night of the dance when I quickly changed my mind. The dress, which swathed Amelia's slender figure like a second skin, stopped short just below her knees, where it fluted gracefully. She made Lois and Barbara appear overdressed and Maisie and I look pretty-pretty and unfashionable. Her only jewellery was a long single row of pearls which Barbara confided were real, and small pearl studs in her ears.

A buffet table had been set out in the small hall and the larger hall where the dance was being held had been decorated with huge urns of flowers from the garden. As it was a warm summer's night, the windows were open letting in the scent of flowers.

The boys from Ramilees arrived in a coach; wearing their school uniform, well-scrubbed and polite, they sat along one wall eyeing the girls nervously until one by one they drifted across as they had been instructed to do.

A four-piece band occupied the dais at the end of the room, and couples slowly plucked up courage and took to the floor, some of them more expert than others. I saw Maisie shepherd Tom into the hall, where they took their seats just within the door, watching the dancers and occasionally smiling into each other's eyes. I thought Tom looked rather out of place in his casual trousers and tweed sportscoat. It was hot in the hall and after a time he removed his coat and placed it at the back of his chair revealing a cream shirt and green tie.

When they took to the floor I couldn't help noticing Tom's brown laced shoes, but as they passed us by I smiled at him and he grinned back at me. I liked him.

He was decent and honest and he had cared unwaveringly for Maisie since childhood.

Barbara was dancing in the arms of Martin Walton, a strangely mature and elegant young man in his dark dinner jacket, dancing efficiently and decorously, and sporting a dark moustache which made him look older than his years.

Lois was in the arms of a small sixth-former from Ramilees. He marched her up and down in a style that would have done credit to the drill ground, and when his steps faltered as they constantly did, he apologised with a scarlet blush on his face.

I was feeling agitated. The Garveston brothers had not arrived and girls were looking at us curiously because we sat aloof from the others and had already refused dance invitations on the grounds that we were waiting for our partners.

Unconcerned Amelia said softly, 'Phillip's always terribly unpunctual. Daddy says he'll probably be late for his own funeral.'

'Have you seen a lot of him?' I couldn't resist asking.

'Quite a lot. Our families have been friends for years. Lady Garveston is more or less an invalid but his father's quite a dear even if he has let the Hall go to seed.'

'That's a terrible shame. It's a beautiful building.'

'Yes, it is. Of course, with money it could be restored. I expect Phillip will see to that one day – ah, here they are at last.'

There was a stir amongst the dancers and the staff when Phillip Garveston and his brother Mark entered the hall. For one thing they were both tall and handsome, but they were the only two men in the room wearing tails. With a bright smile in our direction they crossed the floor to our side. Introductions were performed, and I found myself looking up into a pair of clear blue eyes and a face that smiled charmingly as Mark Garveston asked me to dance with him.

7

Young and in love – how magical the phrase, how magical the fact. I had not known how easy it would be to dance with somebody and fall in love, so that years later, the strains of a particular waltz would make me feel immeasurably disturbed.

I only know that I had never been so alive before: it seemed that on that evening the curtain rose and the stage was set for everything that followed – the love and the joy, the pathos and the tragedy.

It was illogical, really, to throw my heart away after one rare breathless meeting which came to an end when Mark politely took my hand and thanked me for a delightful evening, but his eyes had said so much more . . . or so I believed.

Three days later we stood in the main hall listening to Miss Clarkson deliver her farewell speech. She wished us well and told us we must never forget that the stamp of Lorivals was on all of us and would remain with us throughout our lives. We must do it honour in our chosen paths and never forget that there would always be a welcome beneath its roof for us, 'the chosen ones'.

How impersonal the dormitory seemed now with the white bedspreads immaculately covering the narrow beds and our huddle of suitcases packed and waiting to be taken down the stairs.

We stood in an uneasy group searching for words, but are there any words that dear friends can say, when they knew it will end in goodbye? Maisie shuffled her feet in embarrassment, something she had always done when she was confused and unhappy. Lois, more matter-of-fact than any of us said briskly, 'I hope my taxi isn't late. I don't want to miss my train.'

'Father could have dropped you at the station,' Barbara said, 'there'll only be the two of us.'

The porter came in for our luggage, and after him the housekeeper, who glanced around the room quickly, saying, 'I hope you haven't been sitting on the beds. Everything must be fresh and waiting for the new girls. I expect the place will soon be busy with parents wanting to look around and I'll have my hands full.' None of us spoke, and after another quick inspection she went out, leaving us to follow in her wake.

A shiny black car stood below us in the car park and Maisie waved down at it. 'It's Dad,' she told us. 'He said he'd be bringing his new car. Eh, what a beauty – we've never had one as big as that before!'

Somehow her words broke the ice, and we were laughing and kissing one another when Amelia said suddenly, 'We must keep in touch. We've all got each other's addresses, but shall we make a vow here and now that in ten years' time, wherever we are, whatever we're doing, we will meet. It'll be such fun, and we'll have so much to talk about.'

Maisie replied slowly, 'Ten years is an awful long time, Amelia. We'll probably all be married with children we're unable to leave.'

Amelia would have none of it. 'We must all make the effort to meet ten years from today on the twentieth of July at my house – wherever that is. We'll have a nice long weekend together when we can all talk about ourselves. I'll be reminding you of it as the time grows near but I want you all to promise you'll come. There's no getting out of it!'

We fell in with her mood, promising and believing in it, with laughter on our lips and anticipation in our hearts, then Mr Jayson was putting his daughter's case in the car and she was tripping down the steps to join him.

Lois' taxi was the next to arrive and we all urged her to let us know as soon as she had got settled somewhere. She had told us she aimed to find a job in London; her father would help her so it would probably be a post in one of the Ministries, then as we were waving her off a long open tourer was being driven into the car park and the man at the wheel gave a wave. Amelia said with a bright smile, 'Phillip is punctual for once. I'm glad, we have a long drive in front of us.'

I stared after her. Phillip Garveston had got out of his car and was loading the boot with her luggage, then after a swift embrace she was sitting in the car with him, waving her hand as they drove away along the drive.

'I wonder if she'll marry him,' Barbara was saying. 'I must say she was pretty cagey about him all these years. I didn't even know she knew the Garvestons until the day of the dance. I notice his brother didn't come for *you*, Nancy.'

'There's no reason why he should – my father is coming for me.'

'But you were at the dance with him.'

'I know, Amelia asked him.'

'Oh well, we might have the stamp of Lorivals all over us, but you're not an Amelia Urquart and that's the sort of girl he'll be looking for.'

I didn't speak, but I was aware of a sickening resentment which was in danger of bringing an angry retort to my lips. I was quick to repress it, glad that at that moment my father's car arrived followed almost immediately by Mr Smythe's.

For the last time I looked up at Lorivals, with the sun gilding its mellow stone, the shafts of light falling on far towers and hills and dark old trees, and beyond the gentle river and banks of verdant green. I felt the tears prickling my eyes and Father held out his handkerchief with a tender smile. I was weeping for Lorivals and a youth that seemed to be ending on that warm summer's day.

There was no pressure on me in those first few weeks to find work. It was summer, and much hotter than usual.

When the sun shines on England it atones for all those low-hung leaden skies and rain and dim moist fogs. Even that dampest of English places, the Lake District, took on a golden warmth. Father was the first to broach the subject as we sat on the banks of Ullswater in August, waiting for the fish to bite.

'Have you thought what you want to do, love?' he asked gently. 'I thought you'd leave Lorivals with all sorts of high-flung ideas.'

'I'd like to come on to the *Gazette* for a time if the editor agrees. I have my shorthand and typing, but I'm not sure if I'd be any good at journalism.'

'Your examination results were excellent – and you know what the job involves. What are your friends doing?'

'Lois is getting a job in London – she said she'd write when she's fixed up. Maisie's learning to be a farmer's wife and Barbara doesn't seem to be worrying about a job as yet. I expect she'll help run her father's business.'

'I would think Barbara's more interested in becoming Mrs Martin Walton,' he said dryly.

When I looked at him sharply he grinned at me. 'It's your Aunt Susan, Nancy. She's seen Mrs Smythe in the shops looking at clothes suitable for the bride's mother.'

'Surely she doesn't want to get married yet? She's only eighteen!' I couldn't resist saying.

'She's always been years older than her age, love. Have you heard from your friend Amelia?'

'No.'

I had written to Amelia twice but had received no reply, and I felt faintly hurt about it. In my foolishness I had nourished a hope that she would keep in touch, that the happy foursome of the dance at Lorivals would continue, but apart from asking me if I had enjoyed the occasion she had never referred to it again. Angrily I asked myself how she could ignore my shining eyes and blushing cheeks whenever the other girls had teased me about the occasion, but then when had I ever known

Amelia to step out of the sublime serenity which seemed to cushion her against the normal everyday happenings of life.

'When do you want to start with the paper, love?' Father asked now without taking his eyes from the lake.

'As soon as we get back. You've spent all that money on my education, so I should think about paying you back.'

'Nay lass, your education didn't cost me anything, and there's to be no talk of paying us back. If you're happy and doing what you want to do that's all any of us will ask.'

'Including Aunt Susan?'

'You can leave your Aunt Susan to me.'

So at the end of August I went to work on the *Greymont Gazette* in a very junior position. I accompanied one of the photographers to weddings and funerals, and dutifully went to plays and concerts where I earnestly took notes in uncertain shorthand and then laboriously deciphered and typed them up. It was a very different world from Lorivals.

One Monday evening late in September when I arrived home wet and miserable after spending several hours shivering on the edge of a local football pitch, Father met me in the hall saying, 'I have to go into Lancaster on Thursday, love, and I'll be away all day. Think you can handle a big funeral for me?'

'I am so sick of funerals. Who is it this time?'

'I've heard this afternoon that Lady Garveston died this morning – the funeral is to be on Thursday at two pm at the village church in Cranbourne. All the Garvestons are buried there. It'll be a big occasion and good experience for you, Nancy.'

With the selfishness of youth I spared not a tear for dead Lady Garveston: my one thought was that Mark would be there. He would be surrounded by people, but across that crowded churchyard our eyes might meet and

64

I would see in his that special look I had seen on the night of the dance. I did not think of his grief at losing his mother.

It seemed to me that all of Greymont, Cranbourne and every surrounding village had turned out for the funeral. The church was packed to suffocation so that we were unable to set foot in it, and people lined the paths and clustered about the gravestones. The photographer said angrily, 'What a waste of time! We'll get nothing in all this, Nancy – the national press is here.'

'But we *must*, Joe! Ask them to make room for you.'

'I'll do my best. If I were you I'd get over to the grave, show them your press card.'

I left him jostling and pushing for a place with the others, while I scrambled over the gravestones to get nearer the great granite cross which was set above the Garveston vault. There was a cold wind blowing right off the fells and I pulled the collar of my coat high about my ears and buried my hands deep in the pockets. My feet were freezing on the muddy path.

We could hear the intoning of prayers and the singing in the church, and then at last they came out, walking slowly, the longest funeral procession I had ever seen. I spotted Mark at once. He was walking with his father and elder brother behind his mother's coffin. Dark-suited and bare-headed, the autumn sunlight gilded his blond hair and in those first few moments I had eyes for nobody else. The family were surrounded by friends and relatives dressed in mourning, and then I saw Amelia, walking between her parents. She looked neither to left nor right, but as they passed us her mother turned her head and her eyes stared straight into mine. They displayed not a sign of recognition but I was not surprised. I had known on the day I left Drummond that she would not remember me, not even if we'd met accidentally the next day.

The immediate family had descended the steps into the vault and the rest stood around the doorway with their heads bowed, unmoving until the doors opened again and the family came out into the churchyard.

The mourners paused only a little while to read some of the inscriptions on the wreaths then they turned away and made for the gates. As Amelia and her parents passed I held out my hand and gently touched her arm. She turned to stare at me, and for a moment I thought that she too did not know me, then suddenly she smiled, that vague, beautifully serene smile and murmured, 'Why, Nancy. How nice of you to come,' then she had moved on with her parents and I was left gazing after them.

With my eyes swimming with tears I turned away and made for the small iron gate at the back of the church-yard while everybody else followed the funeral party to the front gates. I reached the road and started to look for the photographer, then I felt somebody take hold of my arm and looked round into Mark's blue eyes.

He smiled soberly. 'I thought it was you, Nancy. I hadn't thought you'd be interested in my mother's funeral – it's a bit of a peepshow, isn't it?'

'It's part of my job, Mark – I'm a reporter on the *Gazette*. I don't enjoy going to funerals!' Realising how rude and tactless I had been, I said more gently, 'I'm so sorry about your mother.'

His face relaxed and he said ruefully, 'Thanks. I'm sorry that I haven't been in touch but the summer seemed to go so quickly and then Mother's health deteriorated pretty rapidly. You've left Lorivals?'

'Yes, in July.'

'Amelia and her parents are here, have you seen them?'

'Yes.'

'We can't talk now Nancy – can I telephone you one evening?'

'Yes, of course.'

He hunted in his pocket and brought out a small notebook and pencil and automatically I gave him my telephone number. 'It won't be this week as we've a lot

66

to see to and have people staying at the Hall until after the weekend. I'll telephone you next week, I promise.'

I smiled while he briefly squeezed my hand, then made his way through the crowd towards one of the cars.

I waited by the roadside until all the cars had passed. I didn't see Mark again, but I saw Amelia sitting stiffly with her parents in their chauffeur-driven Daimler. One of the women standing nearby said to her companions, 'That's young Lady Amelia Urquart and her parents. She's going to be the next Lady Garveston.'

'How do you know?' someone asked.

'I work at the Hall, don't I? Them that works there have known for years that one day she'll marry the Honourable Phillip – and the sooner the better.'

'What do you mean by that?'

'She'll bring some money into the family, won't she? If she leaves it too late there'll be nothing to come to the sons. The house'll have fallen down round our ears.'

'Bad as that, is it?'

'Well, the master's spent no money on it for years. The roof leaks in most of the bedrooms and there's hardly any glass in the conservatory. The plumbin' makes a noise like the Cranbourne brass band and there's chinks ye can post a parcel through in most of the window panes.'

'Poor Lady Amelia, she'll not be getting much out of it.'

'Oh, she'll be all right. They say her father's got plenty o'brass and she's the youngest of his children and most likely the apple of his eye.'

Over our evening meal at home we talked about the funeral and Father approved of the report I had written although he made a few alterations.

'You're coming on, love,' he said with a smile. 'We'll make a journalist of you yet.'

When I told my parents that Amelia had been at the church, Mother said, 'She'd have been pleased to see you there Nancy. Did you two get a chance to talk?'

'No, there were too many people and she was with her parents.'

'Well, you know her parents, don't you?'

'Yes, but like I said there was a crowd. I heard one of the women standing near me saying Amelia was going to be the next Lady Garveston. Have you heard anything, Father?'

'No, but then that's not my kind of reporting. That's womens' gossip.'

I decided not to mention Mark to either of my parents. For one thing, he might not keep his promise to telephone and for another there was Aunt Susan to consider. Any indications that I was friendly with Mark Garveston would end with the entire town busy speculating. Mrs Smythe was the first one she would crow to – and it was a risk I couldn't take.

I waited all the following week for the promised telephone call and when it didn't come, felt angry with myself that I had allowed Mark to see I was interested. On the Friday morning I went into Greymont to write up a local art exhibition and was walking thoughtfully round the gallery when a voice said in my ear, 'What do you think of them, Nancy?' I turned sharply to find Mark looking at me with a smile on his face. Before I could reply he went on, 'I telephoned you this morning. Would it be your mother who answered?'

'Yes'

'She told me you were here so I decided to come along and hunt you out. What on earth are you going to say about this lot?'

'Some of them are better than others. For instance, I rather like this one.'

'You do?'

'Well, yes.'

It was a picture of a Pennine homestead, the rolling moors and clouds filled with rain and a shaft of golden slanting sunshine breaking through. I thought it captured perfectly the dark dismal hills and the sudden changing rain clouds.

Mark was standing looking at it critically with a small frown on his face and I couldn't understand why. This was the sort of scenery he had grown up with, the wild countryside visible from any window at Garveston Hall – so surely he had to see how authentic it was? Instead, he turned away with a wry smile.

'You don't like it?' I said in some surprise.

'When one has grown up surrounded by decent paintings it isn't really surprising, Nancy. Anyway, I'm not artistic so don't let me influence you – I'm a bit of a moron when it comes to painting. Can we go somewhere to talk?'

'This is my job, Mark. I have to go back to the office and type up a few paragraphs about it.'

'But you eat lunch, surely?'

'Yes, I have an hour for lunch.'

'Well then, let's go and eat somewhere. The Blue Bell does a good meal.'

That was the start of it: the drives into the country and the Saturday race meetings accompanied by the gay brittle crowd of young people who were his friends, and the flowers that came almost daily so that there was no chance of keeping our association from my parents.

I needed time to consider. I thought I loved Mark desperately, but I was unsure about the way our friendship was progressing. It wasn't really what I wanted. For one thing, his friends were not my sort of people. The girls came from nouveau-riche families; they were spoiled and none of them went out to work. The boys too seemed to talk of nothing beyond the next race meeting. I was accepted as Mark's girl, but when they all chattered about expensive holidays and hobbies I had nothing to contribute.

On one occasion they were giggling about seeing Amelia with Mark's brother at one of the race meetings and Joanna, who always had the most to say, said sarcastically, 'Amelia's the most awful prig. I suppose that's what Lorivals does for you.'

Stung to retort I said quickly, 'I was at Lorivals with Amelia, and I don't think she's a prig at all. Neither am I, come to that.'

There was a long uncomfortable pause before Joanna gave a short laugh and commented, 'I thought one had to be a member of the landed gentry to get to Lorivals – not that I'd ever want to go there, the school is far too restrictive.'

After that they treated me coolly but Mark seemed not to notice.

When I learned that Amelia was staying at the Hall I told Mark I would dearly like to see her again but he said hastily, 'You wouldn't have anything in common with her these days, darling, and I've never got along with Phillip. They're two awful bores.'

Inevitably my parents wanted to know more about the boy who sent me flowers and reluctantly I told them. 'But please, Mother, I don't want Aunt Susan to know,' I begged. 'You know what she's like.'

'Really Nancy, she's always been very good to you. It's thanks to her that you went to Lorivals in the first place – a fact that no doubt is standing you in good stead now,' she said firmly, but Father was more understanding.

'She'll also entertain her cronies with the fact that her niece is keeping company with the Honourable Mark Garveston, and Nancy isn't ready for that yet, are you love?'

'No Father, I'm not.'

'He's obviously very fond of you, darling,' Mother stated. 'These flowers must cost a fortune.'

'Flowers don't commit him to anything Mary, and if Nancy doesn't want your sister to know we should respect her wishes,' Father said warningly.

Inevitably, my secret soon became public knowledge. Greymont was a small town and we were seen at the theatre and snatching an intimate lunch in some country inn. I knew the day was rapidly approaching when Aunt Susan would demand to know what was going on.

Matters came to a head one Sunday after lunch when she slammed down the coffee pot then turned to face the three of us with a determined look on her face. 'Well! Do I have to ask what is going on, or are you going to tell me?'

'Tell you what?' Father asked calmly.

'You know what I'm talking about, Arthur. How long has Nancy been friendly with the Garveston boy?'

'We would have told you eventually,' Mother was quick to say, 'but they are simply good friends. Nancy met Mark at a school dance and they've kept up the friendship, that's all.'

'Well, I don't like it when I hear people gossiping and don't know the facts. They're talking about it at church, in court, and they're even talking about it in the hairdresser's. Has this Mark been to the house yet?'

'Why no,' Mother replied. 'Like I said, Susan, they're only friends.'

'Well, from what I hear it's been going on since the summer and I think it's high time you invited the boy to meet you. That way, you'll know if he intends the friendship to be permanent.'

I sat at the dining table angry and mortified and after looking at my set face Father said dryly, 'Oh, so you think I should be asking if his intentions are entirely honourable Susan, and be discussing the sort of dowry Nancy will get.'

'Well, of course not – I just think you should make him welcome in your home. Let him see that Nancy comes from a respectable background even if it *isn't* Garveston Hall.'

Ignoring Father she fixed her sister with a stern look, and after a few minutes Mother said weakly, 'Perhaps we *should* invite him to tea one day, Arthur. How about at Christmas?'

71

Immediately lunch was over I escaped from Aunt Susan's with the excuse that I had promised to walk over to see Maisie in the afternoon.

'What has she to say about your friendship with the Garveston boy?' Aunt Susan asked sharply.

'I haven't discussed Mark with Maisie. I don't see an awful lot of her now as she's often up at the farm.'

'Did you know that her brother got engaged to George Gibson's girl last Saturday?' she informed us. 'I reckon Bob's the nicest of the Jayson boys and Mary Gibson'll make him a good wife. She's used to serving customers, she helps out in her aunt's confectioners at the weekends.'

On my walk through the park I found myself thinking of those childhood days when I used to meet up with Maisie and Barbara at the gates, but there were other children now playing near the dovecotes, racing after their balls along the leaf-covered paths.

Mr Jayson himself opened the door for me, his face wreathed in a welcoming smile. 'Well, hello lass,' he said. 'We don't often see you around here these days. Maisie's in the parlour with her mother and the rest of the family's in the dining room waiting to be fed. Have you eaten?'

'We had lunch at Aunt Susan's, and I told them I'd be home for tea.'

'We can't tempt you, then?'

'I'm very easily tempted when it comes to meals in your house, but I did promise to be home.'

'Say hello to the others first then,' he said, opening the dining room door for me to pass in front of him. The two younger boys, now sturdy teenagers were sitting at the table looking through a pile of magazines with the crockery pushed aside. Mary Gibson sat with them, but when I entered the room she rose and went to sit on Bob's knee with a proprietary arm round his neck. I think she resented my friendship with the family. I smiled a greeting at them all, and the two younger boys grinned back.

Following me into the room Mr Jayson said, 'The new doctor's all right love, but the town's still missing your grandfather. You always knew where you were with him, and he'd come out to see you no matter what time o'day it was. Now – can we offer you a sherry, at least?'

'No, I'd better not. Thanks all the same, though.'

'Well, then, you run along into the parlour, and you might remind them that we're all waiting to have our dinner.'

I knew immediately I entered the parlour that something was wrong. Mrs Jayson sat in her favourite chair with a look of extreme sorrow on her face, and I could see that she had been crying. Maisie's expression was defiant. Her face was flushed and angry and she stared at me sullenly without speaking.

I stood uncertainly in the doorway until Mr Jayson's voice came from behind me saying, 'Come on then, Mother. Isn't it time you started to do something about our meal? Let the two girls talk by themselves.'

She jumped to her feet and with head averted passed in front of me, closing the door behind her. I took her vacant seat then, unable to stand the silence any longer I said gently, 'I can see I've come at a bad time, Maisie. Shall I go away?'

Suiting my actions to my words I rose to my feet but Maisie said sharply, 'There's no need for you to go, Nancy. I'd rather you heard it from me direct, since everybody else'll know soon enough. I'm pregnant. Mam and I have been rowing all morning, ever since I told her about the baby.'

I sank back into my seat, utterly shocked and querulously she went on, 'I suppose you think it's terrible. I know the sort of things the neighbours and everybody else'll be sayin': look at all the money mi dad spent to send me to Lorivals and here I am pregnant and only been out of school a few months.'

73

'What are you going to do?' I asked sympathetically.

'What I've always wanted to do, marry Tom.'

'But you're so young, Maisie. You have all your life before you.'

She looked at me then, and in her look I sensed genuine pity. 'Don't be feeling sorry for me, Nancy. We're glad about the baby – we *want* to get married. The only thing I regret is the money I've cost Dad – he'd 'ave done better to spend it on the boys. Sendin' me to that posh school was the silliest thing when all I ever wanted to be was a farmer's wife, Tom's wife. I learned nothin' there that'll make me an asset on the farm. I spend every hour I can now, trying to catch up on how to feed the chicks, cook for the farmhands and see to the cattle.'

'You'll be living with Tom's parents, then?'

'Yes, we've talked it all out.'

'What do his parents think about the baby?'

'They think we should have waited, but they're still pleased for us. We'll live with them for the time being until we find our feet, but it was always going to be Tom's farm one day. When they think we're ready his parents will retire and we'll 'ave the place to ourselves.'

'Your life's like an open book, Maisie – you know already exactly how it's going to be.'

'Yes, and that's a lot more than you do, Nancy.'

'What do you mean?'

'Can you honestly say you're as sure of Mark Garveston as I am of Tom? Is he going to marry you – have you met his folks, been welcomed into his home? Oh, I know you go around with that snobby crowd but I couldn't be botherin' with any one of 'em miself. They ride their horses across the farmland and Tom's father's forever complainin' because they leave the gates open. They're just plain selfish. And they give him a mouthful of abuse – he says the girls are worse than the men.'

'I don't suppose Mark is with them when they ride there. He knows better than to leave farm gates open.'

74

'I've never heard that he was with them, but they are his crowd, I've seen him in their company.'

Deciding to change the subject I asked, 'Have you decided when you are getting married?'

'In about three weeks. It'll be a very quiet wedding, with just Tom's folks and mine. Mam's upset because I'm not wearing white and a floating veil but I've told her I don't want that. A big wedding would cost a mint o' money and we can put it to better use. I'll be choosing a dress I can wear again and again, and I've asked my Cousin Alice to be my bridesmaid. I hoped you wouldn't mind, Nancy.'

I did mind. Hadn't we always said we'd stand by each other? Seeing my disappointment she went on gently, 'If things had been different mi mother'd have insisted on a big wedding and you'd have been my chief bridesmaid I promise, Nancy. Alice and her sister would have been bridesmaids as well. As it is, there'll be so much talk. Oh, do try to understand for my sake.'

'I do understand. I'm just so very sorry it has to be this way.' I was close to tears.

'You'll be able to be Barbara Smythe's bridesmaid. I expect she'll ask you, Amelia and Lois as well.'

'Barbara's getting married?'

'You mean your Aunt Susan's not mentioned it?'

'Not as an actual fact.'

'Well, I heard Mrs Smythe talkin' in the shop on Saturday mornin'. Her Barbara's gettin' engaged to Martin Walton on her nineteenth birthday and they're being married at Easter. He's going into a solicitors' partnership somewhere in the Midlands and they're lookin' for a house there.' That's one weddin' that'll set Greymont alight!'

As I walked home along the dark streets in a chill drizzle my mind was filled with talk of weddings. When I turned the corner I saw a large car outside our gate and recognised Mr Smythe's Rover.

When I entered the sitting room four pairs of eyes

looked up expectantly. Mr Smythe sat with a large whisky in his hand and the sherry bottle stood open on a small table between my mother and Mrs Smythe. I went to sit on the arm of Father's chair and immediately Mrs Smythe said meaningfully, 'And how do you like the food at the Golden Lion, Nancy? We thought it had become a bit expensive after the last people left.'

'I thought it was quite good, but I've only been there once.'

'We saw you there with Mr Garveston. You two are getting to be quite friendly.' I didn't speak, and Father squeezed my hand gently. 'We've called to tell you that our Barbara is getting married at Easter,' Mrs Smythe went on self-importantly. 'They're down in Cheltenham this weekend house-hunting. Martin's going into partnership there – he's done very well to get into such a good firm of solicitors. I just hope they find somewhere suitable to live, as houses there are scandalously high in price.'

'They'll be getting married at St Mary's, I suppose?' Mother put in.

'Oh, of course, and it'll be a big wedding. The Waltons have a lot of friends and so have we. Then there are the councillors – some of them will have to be invited. I rather think Barbara'll be asking you to be her bridesmaid, Nancy. She's no cousins she wants to ask, but I know she was thinking about the girls she was at school with.'

'All four of us?' I couldn't resist asking.

'Well you, Lois and Amelia at any rate,' she replied tartly.

'I thought Maisie Jayson was part of the Lorival crowd,' Father said dryly, and immediately Mrs Smythe bristled with a quick reply.

'From what I see of Maisie Jayson she'll be standing in front of the altar well before our Barbara. She's monopolised that boy Standing since they were children.'

I kept what I had heard that afternoon to myself, intending to confide in my parents as soon as the Smythes had left. Now, Mother very deftly turned the subject away from Maisie and they started to talk about something else.

8

Barbara informed me that she and Martin had found a darling old house in a village quite close to Cheltenham. She enthused rapturously about the beauties of the town and the countryside and produced samples of material and colours she had decided upon for her wedding at Easter.

'Of course you'll be my bridesmaid along with Amelia and Lois. I can't very well invite Maisie – I suppose you've heard about her?'

'Yes, she told me herself.'

'Don't tell me she was proud of it!'

'She's never wanted anybody but Tom.'

'I've only ever wanted Martin, but I'm not in the sort of mess that Maisie's in.'

'Have you heard from Lois and Amelia?'

'I've heard from Lois. She's quite happy to be my bridesmaid and I was wondering if you could put her up for the weekend.'

'I'm sure we can, we'll all be glad to see her.'

'I haven't heard from Amelia, but I expect she's here, there and everywhere. Anyway I'll expect to see her at the Civic Ball in a couple of weeks' time.'

'Why would Amelia be there?'

'Hasn't Mark told you? The Civic Ball is being held at Garveston Hall this year. Sir Gerald has decided to throw the place open for public functions – I expect they could do with the money.'

'I don't suppose Mark intends to be present.'

'Oh yes, I'm quite sure he will be. The family have asked for several tickets to be sent over, about a dozen I think.'

'I see.'

I waited for Mark to mention the event, but one evening when one of our crowd started to discuss it, he changed the conversation rapidly. Nevertheless, I was so sure he would invite me that I spent a great deal of money on a new evening gown which I managed to smuggle into my wardrobe without either of my parents seeing it. At night before I went to bed I repeatedly tried it on and paraded in front of my mirror. It was quite plain, the beauty being in the deep turquoise silk taffeta which rustled enchantingly when I moved and it caught the light. My next purchase was a pair of silver kid evening shoes with ridiculously high heels, and these too I kept hidden.

Pride forbade me from asking Mark about the Ball directly; instead I anguished alone and in secret so that every time he dropped me outside the house my heart was filled with resentment.

It was only three days before the Ball when Father asked idly over the breakfast table, 'Will you be going to the Civic do over at Garveston Hall next Friday, love?'

'What "do" is that, Father?'

'You mean that young man of yours hasn't mentioned the Civic Ball?'

'I don't suppose he'll be there or he would have done. Are you and Mother going?'

'Not this year. We have another function on the same evening.'

'But you always go to the Civic Ball.'

'So you *do* know about it, Nancy.'

'Yes, well . . . I remember Barbara going on about it when she was here.'

He said nothing more, but I was aware of his eyes watching me from time to time across the table, and the sympathy I surprised in them renewed the resentment that had plagued me for days.

Friday came and went. I saw my parents setting out for the dinner they were attending and Father said gently as he waited for Mother in the hall, 'Don't be upsetting

79

yourself about the Ball, Nancy. He's probably not even there, and even if he is he'll be regarding it as a family duty. Mark will have a good explanation, never fear.'

How endless the evening seemed. I was tempted to catch the bus and go to the cinema in Greymont, but lethargy overcame me. I was eaten up with self-pity, and at eleven o'clock when I knew the dance would be in full swing I went upstairs to my room. I took the gown out of the wardrobe and laid it on my bed, then the tears came and I threw myself down on top of it and sobbed into my pillow. Much later a strange sort of calmness came over me, generated by anger and shattered pride. Resolutely I folded the gown and together with the slippers placed them in the largest suitcase I could find and with the help of a stepladder and a torch placed them out of sight in the loft.

Two days later Barbara came over to the house with the pretence of discussing her wedding plans. As she chattered on about material and colours I tried to respond intelligently, willing her to talk about the Ball, yet resenting the fact that I knew this was the real reason for her visit. At last in her usual devious way she got around to it.

'Martin only went back this morning or I'd have come round sooner,' she said without looking at me. 'Amelia was at the Ball with Phillip Garveston. They announced their engagement the day before.'

'I see.'

'She was wearing sapphire blue. I must say, it did much more for her than those awful beiges she used to wear.'

'Did you manage to speak to her?'

'Well, of course. I asked her why she hadn't answered my letter, but you know Amelia – she was all sweetness and light, full of apologies that she'd been so busy with her engagement, and her mother hadn't been well, and she'd been in London when it arrived. She can't be my bridesmaid, unfortunately. She'll be down in London on family matters. I think she's to be married in Hereford Cathedral next year some time.'

I was burning with the desire to shout at her, 'Was Mark at the Ball? Who was he with?' but restrained myself. I willed my face to appear nonchalant while she chattered on about Amelia, and when I felt I couldn't stand it a moment longer she said almost as an after-thought, 'By the way, Mark Garveston was at the Ball. He came with the rest of the family and danced most of the evening with a girl somebody said was in their house-party. I must say he looked terribly bored for most of the evening and she wasn't a bit pretty. Do you know who she was?'

'I have no idea.'

'I'll ask Mother. She'll know because she was intro-duced to most of the Garveston party.'

I didn't need Mrs Smythe to tell me the name of the girl in question, as Mark himself told me when he met me coming out of the office several days later. He took my arm as though nothing had happened, squeezing it gently against him and smiling down at me with all the old admiration in his eyes. I warmed to him, then angrily moved away. It was not going to be that easy for him. He suggested a country inn for lunch. I accepted, but kept the conversation so light that he looked at me ner-vously from time to time. Afterwards, he tried to make a future date but when I kept prevaricating by saying it might not be possible, out of sheer exasperation he cried, 'What's wrong, Nancy? Something's eating you – I sup-pose it's that wretched Ball.'

When I didn't answer he took my arm and forced me to look up at him. 'I never wanted to go to the damn thing in the first place,' he said. 'I tried to get out of it but somebody had to look after Jane Leadbetter. She was a house-guest – it was my duty.'

Again I remained silent, and his face bore a sulky little boy's expression as he tried to explain. 'Don't tell me you wanted to attend, Nancy. Why on earth didn't you say something? In any case, I was bored stiff.'

'Who is Jane Leadbetter?'

'Lord Leadbetter's daughter, they're old family friends. If you knew Jane you wouldn't be jealous. She's a nice enough girl but she's as plain as a church mouse.'

'I'm not in the least bit jealous of her. How could I be? I don't even know her.'

He became ingratiating, holding my hand and stroking my fingers. 'I'm sorry Nancy, I didn't think you'd mind so much. I'm an idiot, that's my trouble. All night I was thinking about you, wishing it was you dancing in my arms . . . It won't happen again, I promise. The gang are going to the Rugger Ball in Greymont in a few weeks' time and we'll go to that one together.'

I was almost placated. I could wear my new gown and dance all night in Mark's arms, but it wouldn't be the same: I wouldn't be Mark's girl in Mark's home, I would again be just one of the crowd.

For weeks Aunt Susan had not pursued the subject of Mark Garveston, but now she was renewing her insistence that my parents invite him into the house.

'No wonder he didn't ask Nancy to the Civic Ball up at the Hall – the poor boy isn't sure whether you're going to accept him or not,' she maintained.

After she had left, my parents talked over the idea. Father was unenthusiastic. 'Nancy's too young to be serious about this boy and besides, he's too fly. What are his prospects? He's no job that I know of and I do not like the way he behaved about the Ball, whatever his excuses.'

I was quick to defend him and after a while Father shrugged his shoulders philosophically, saying, 'All right, then. You must arrange it with your mother, Nancy, but don't be surprised if he tries to get out of it.'

Mother decided that we should ask him to tea on Boxing Day. 'I think tea's a better idea than lunch, since he might think he would be expected to stay for the rest of the day, and if we invite him to an evening meal he might have something planned. I think tea at four would be very nice, and if you both wanted to go out later we wouldn't mind.'

When I mentioned it to Mark I was sure he read the anxiety in my eyes because he said instantly, 'I'd love to come, Nancy. Please thank your mother. What time do I arrive?'

'About four o'clock. We can go out later, if you like.'

'Well, we'll see. I'm not sure what's happening at home. Amelia and her parents are coming for Christmas and there'll be others dropping in all the time.'

Mother was visibly nervous on Boxing Day morning as she polished the silver and brought out the best china, and Father said acidly, 'I thought you'd polished the silver just a couple of days ago. Why can't this boy accept us as we are?'

'Please, Arthur, don't spend all day in your woolly jacket and your carpet slippers,' Mother retorted. 'If I can make an effort so must you.'

A small banquet was laid out on the kitchen table ready to be taken into the dining room because Mother said it was impossible to serve tea in the lounge and expect Mark to balance plates and cups and saucers on his knee. There was a trifle and all sorts of fancy cakes, thinly-cut sandwiches and sausage rolls, and I was despatched upstairs to put on my best afternoon dress while Father was inspected from head to toe before Mother was satisfied he looked respectable.

Mark was early by five minutes; he arrived in a flurry of flowers, chocolates and cigars wearing a casual hacking jacket which made my father seem stiff and conventional in his best lounge suit. He was charming and smiling and Mother soon warmed to him. It all went remarkably well until we moved into the dining room, where Mark eyed the table and the repast spread out on it.

'How very nice,' he said graciously. 'I do hope I can

do justice to it. We had an enormous lunch at home – there's always so much food around at Christmas time.'

Before we took our places at the table he stood looking up at the Lowry painting which was my father's pride and joy. He gazed at it for several minutes but when he came to the table he made no comment and somewhat anxiously I asked, 'Do you like it Mark? Father's very proud of it – it's genuine.'

He smiled. 'I'm afraid I don't really understand Lowry's work. I get confused by all those matchstick figures. Was Lancashire ever *really* like that, do you think?'

My heart sank. This was going to be the sort of argument my father excelled in.

'Well of course you wouldn't remember, you're far too young. I'm too young myself,' he said easily. 'However, I remember the mill chimneys, the corner shops and the pubs. I enjoyed listening to my grandfather talking about the Whit Walks and the sound of clogs on cobblestones. Your own grandfather was a cotton man – surely he told you stories of old Lancashire, the sort of Lancashire Lowry painted.'

Good-humouredly Mark responded, 'I expect he did, but like me he wanted to forget it, which wasn't very difficult from the windows of Garveston Hall.'

'It's part of our history, lad.'

'But must we constantly be reminded of it? I get very tired of my friends in the south looking on the north as a dingy dismal place nobody would ever wish to visit.'

'There are a great many beautiful places in the north, and southerners are missing a lot if they don't recognise the fact.'

'I'm not talking about the scenery, Mr Graham, I'm talking about the poverty – the grimness of the streets, the greyness of towns dominated by mill chimneys. I'm not surprised that young people hanker after London and the glamour of the south when so much of this primitive gloomy stuff is rammed down our throats.'

It was all going wrong. Father sat with a frozen face because for once in his life he was losing the argument while Mark gave my mother his gracious undivided attention, but he ate only sparingly of the food spread before us.

All father's radical leanings came uppermost as he started out on several attempts at conversation, and always Mark treated his utterances with respect but barely concealed irony, and then to my horror Father said, 'Have you thought what you want to do with your life, Mark? Nancy tells me you haven't yet decided on a career.'

Mortification filled my soul as I recognised Mark's haughty stare which said quite plainly that it was none of my father's business. Heedless to the antagonism, my father pressed on. He was not a journalist for nothing; he had met opposition in many forms over the years but it had been his job to sift and pry, to drag information from reluctant participants and today was no exception. Mercilessly he continued his interrogation while I squirmed in anguish and if Mother tried valiantly to change the subject he was having none of it.

'Don't schools bother these days?' he asked in apparent innocence. 'When I was a lad our last year at school was one big attempt to slot us into some career or other.'

'I have several things lined up,' Mark said tersely, 'but it has nothing to do with the school. I shall please myself about my future.'

'What lines are you thinking on, then?'

'Well, nothing's been decided. My father isn't hurrying me.'

'I've come across a fair number of you young chaps in my work, and mostly their leanings are towards the race tracks, either horses or cars. I wondered if you were any different.'

'I could go into horse training with Patrick Arden. He's having some success this season and I've put out one or two feelers, but since you mention it my first love *is* cars. I'd like very much to join the Lotus team, particularly as I drive one of their cars.'

His tone was insolent, his words barely hiding the condescension he was feeling and I knew he was angry. He objected to these questions about his future and my father sat back in his chair with a look of grim satisfaction on his face. He didn't like Mark: his interrogation had been designed to show him up as a wastrel, a good-time boy, and Mark new it. Desperately I wanted the afternoon to be over and at last Mark looked at his watch and with an apologetic smile at my mother said, 'I am sorry to break up the party Mrs Graham but I must be going. It's been delightful.'

He shook hands with my parents then I walked with him to the door.

I sensed his relief at leaving my father's antagonistic presence. I wanted to cover the moment with excuses but none would come and then he bent his head and brushed my lips gently with his own before I watched him striding away from me into the night. I couldn't think that he would ever want to see me again and at that moment I hated my father and hated myself for the angry disloyal thoughts that were making me tremble with suppressed rage.

I heard the sound of voices in the kitchen and the clatter of plates but I was not yet ready to face them, instead I ran upstairs and spent the next half hour in my room sitting on the edge of my bed with my thoughts in turmoil. At last I heard Mother calling to me and reluctantly I sauntered downstairs. She was standing in the hall, her face anxious and then Father was there looking so contrite that I knew he was well aware of what he had done.

He was over-hearty, placating as he put a careless arm round my shoulders as we walked into the lounge together. 'Well, I think that went off all right don't you love?' he said gently, before I spun round on him with accusation on my lips and tears in my eyes.

'Oh Father, how could you? All those questions about a job, all that radical talk Grandfather used to love and Mark obviously hated.'

'I told you she'd be upset,' Mother put in but Father merely stood back from me, his face sterner than I had ever seen it.

'I thought they were questions that needed to be asked,' he said firmly.

'But not tonight, Father, not the first time you'd met him.'

He went to sit in his armchair and picked up a book he'd been reading as if to say the topic was closed, but I wouldn't let it go. I stood in front of him full of misery until he wearily laid the book aside. 'You wanted me to like him didn't you, Nancy, and I wanted to like him – but I couldn't. He's not the man for you, love.'

'Why isn't he – what's wrong with him? Doesn't it make any difference that I want him? I love him, don't you care about that?'

'I don't want you falling in love with the first man who flatters and flirts with you and I still maintain that he's aimless. He has no job, and those silly leanings towards this and that glamorous, unrealistic line of business didn't endear him to me either. Besides, I can't forget the way he treated you about that Ball up at Garveston.'

'He explained about that. He didn't want to go – but they had house-guests and he was expected to escort one of them. He's taking me to the Rugger Ball to compensate.'

'That's just it, love. He'll take you to the Rugger Ball with all his noisy friends, but he won't take you to a function at his father's place where you could meet his family and see Amelia. You were friends at Lorivals but that doesn't seem to count for anything now she's engaged to his brother. Can't you see love, underneath all that soft soap he's a bit of a snob. He admires you, he might even think he loves you, but when the chips are down I doubt if you're the girl he'll want to marry.'

'You don't want me to have anybody, do you? You're jealous because Mark's not like you, you don't understand him and never will.'

'Don't speak to your father like that,' Mother admonished me. 'Of course he isn't jealous of Mark! Both of us only want what's best for you – all the same, Arthur, I did think you laid it on a bit thick. The poor boy didn't come here for the Third Degree.'

'He could mature I suppose,' Father mumbled, 'but I'd have to see some signs of it before I could like him.'

'He was right about some of the things he said,' Mother said thoughtfully. 'He didn't like your Lowry and I can understand that. Times are changing – why must we be constantly reminded of Lancashire as it used to be?'

'Mark Garveston wasn't looking at the painting as a work of art. He wasn't even beginning to see the colours and genius of it. He was simply looking at a Lancashire that has gone forever, and he was glad it had gone. It's not the Lancashire he would have wanted to be associated with.'

'I don't see anything wrong in that, Arthur,' Mother persisted. 'We should be glad that times have changed. Nobody really wants to go back to forests of mill chimneys and those dark dismal streets.'

'You're not seeing my argument, love. I don't want a return to those times either. I just want someone to look at my picture and recognise the brilliance of the artist.' After that he gave up, and I felt a rare satisfaction in thinking he had lost the argument.

For nearly two weeks I didn't see Mark and Father remarked acidly one evening over supper, 'Isn't it the Rugger Ball next Friday?'

'I don't know. It's your fault if Mark doesn't get in touch.'

'If he doesn't he'll only prove how right I was about him.'

Two days before the Ball Mark telephoned me at the office and in those few moments we spoke as if we'd met only the day before. My spirits rose and once more I was happy and hopeful. At the Ball his admiration was there for all to see: he loved my dress, my hair, my beauty and for that night at least I believed we were in love, hopelessly ecstatically in love. For days I existed in a haze of joy that even Father's cynicism failed to diminish.

My euphoria lasted until Barbara's wedding. She arrived one evening with her mother and father, bringing her wedding list, and my parents crossed off the gift they intended to buy while I chose something else which had her mother's approval.

Mrs Smythe talked incessantly about the wedding reception, the photographers and the display of presents in a room set aside for them by the hotel.

'I thought you might be having the civic hall,' Father said dryly.

'Well no, the catering isn't all it might be and the hotel is putting some of the guests up so we decided on that. We thought at one time we might ask if we could have it at Garveston Hall but they've turned one or two people down recently and we didn't want to risk that.'

'Who have they turned down?' Mother asked curiously.

'Well, they didn't even want the Hunt, and one of the Golf Clubs was refused. We couldn't find out why but everybody seems to think it's Lady Amelia who is putting her foot down. Apparently her father's pumping money into the place: they've taken on a shoal of gardeners and decorators are working night and day. Barbara's had a present from her ladyship, mind.'

'Really, what did she send?'

'A picture. Personally I don't care for it, but I've no doubt it's the real thing. Martin said he'd have it valued.'

I did not miss Father's cynical smile and Mr Smythe said slyly, 'If it's valuable they'll have it in their living room. If it's not, they can always put it away in one of the bedrooms.' The two men chuckled together, while Mrs Smythe gave her husband an angry look before changing the subject.

Barbara had chosen rose pink for the bridesmaids' dresses, saying she thought the colour would suit both Lois and myself, while she was having her dress made in Lancaster by the most expensive fashion house in the county. She told me she had chosen cream parchment satin but disclosed nothing else.

'Martin's cousin is to be best man,' she informed us, 'and I'd like my cousin Ernest and Mark Garveston to be the groomsmen. Would you like to ask Mark for me Nancy, or do you think the invitation should come from me?'

'I think you should ask him yourself.'

'Oh very well, he's bound to come since you'll be there. Surely he'd like to be a groomsman.'

'I expect so.' Across the room I looked into my father's eyes and once again I was aware of the doubt in them whenever Mark's name was mentioned.

On the following Saturday Mark and I drove out into the country for lunch and right from the outset he seemed so preoccupied that I hesitated to mention Barbara's wedding. The meal was eaten largely in silence and it was only later when we drove through a hailstorm that he said sharply, 'Hang this wretched weather. I was hoping we might have driven to the coast but it looks as though we'll have to content ourselves with a cinema or something.'

'What's wrong, Mark?'

'Wrong! Why should something be wrong?'

'You've been very quiet all through lunch.'

'I'm sorry Nancy, I didn't think you'd notice. I'm not very happy about this wedding at Easter.'

I stared at him in surprise. 'Have you had your invitation, then?'

'Yes, I've been asked to be a groomsman. I don't know either of your friends – why should they ask me?'

'I wish they hadn't but I suppose it's because I'm one of the bridesmaids. Don't you want to do it?'

'Look – I don't think I can attend the wedding. Lord Urquart is expecting us to spend Easter at his place and it's something I can't really get out of.'

'Couldn't you drive there immediately the wedding is over?'

'It isn't convenient, Nancy. It would mean driving up from Hereford and then back again, surely you can see that.'

'Yes Mark, I see it very well.'

'I'll send them a nice present with my apologies, and perhaps you'd back me up. I don't want to appear too ungracious.'

The doubts were now certainties: I knew that our love affair really was on the way out. I was not the sort of girl Mark Garveston would ever marry. He would look higher than the daughter of a small-town reporter. Oh, the affair would drag its feet a little; there might be the odd strained meeting and weary telephone calls that meant nothing, and in the end there would be half-hearted expressions of regret. We were too young. He had his way to make – I would find somebody more worthy . . . platitudes contrived to let me down gently, but I had no doubt that they would come.

As we drove back across the fells the mist came down and driving claimed all Mark's attention so that out of necessity we remained silent. It was only when we approached the town in steadily driving rain that I realised I wanted to go home. There seemed no point in prolonging the agony of being with Mark when I was so certain that our time together was coming to an end anyway.

He turned to ask, 'Have you thought what you'd like to see? I'm not even sure what's on.'

'I think I'd rather go home if you don't mind Mark. It's a wretched night.'

He didn't answer me immediately, then as we drove towards the park he said softly, 'You're sure, Nancy?'

'Yes.'

He offered no resistance, and in a few minutes we were drawing up outside the front gate. 'Shall I telephone during the week?'

'I shall be out quite a lot this week. Goodbye, Mark.'

I was glad it had been brief. There had been no regrets, no protestations of missing me, no promises neither of us could keep. I felt frozen inside and my teeth were chattering as if with cold. For what seemed like hours I sat in front of the fire without bothering to switch on the lights, and then when it started to splutter and die down I realised that it was after eleven. I made myself go into the kitchen to make coffee which I took up to my room. For hours I lay tossing and turning, long after I heard my parents' footsteps pass my door, but it was my dream that brought the treacherous tears into my eyes so that when I awoke in the morning I could feel them wet on my cheeks.

I dreamed about our last day at Lorivals when we had stood bright-eyed and hopeful listening to words that had sent us out of the hall believing that we were the chosen ones, girls on whom Fortune had smiled, whose futures shone bright and cloudless before them. On that cold grey morning I awoke with a sense of betrayal, that it had all been a lie.

Lorivals had not made me the sort of girl Mark Garveston could marry and I felt his rejection so keenly I choked with the pain of tears in my throat. I never cried for him again.

9

All Greymont turned out for Barbara's wedding at the parish church of St. Mary. The guests were a mixture of civic dignitaries and fashionable upper-crust residents, with the women vying with each other as to who would be considered the smartest; even Mrs Smythe had difficulty in keeping her end up. It was all a very far cry from Maisie's modest wedding some months before at the Methodist Chapel, which had been attended by only the immediate families.

Lois arrived the evening before and I went with Father to meet her train. She seemed to have grown taller, and be altogether more sophisticated than the girl I had known at school. Her camel-hair coat was elegant, and she had let her hair grow so that it swung round her shoulders as the walked; I felt countryfied trotting beside her. She kept up a steady chatter as we walked to the car, and it was only when we were unpacking her suitcase in her bedroom that the old Lois emerged and throwing her arms round me she sighed, 'I've been so looking forward to this weekend, Nancy. We've such a lot to talk about.'

We talked long into the night, sitting on the edge of her bed drinking hot chocolate and eventually Mother said if we didn't get some sleep we'd hardly be awake for the wedding next morning.

Lois betrayed little surprise when I told her we'd lost touch with Amelia, and little more when I explained about Maisie. She was sympathetic about Mark, but reassuring. 'You're too young to be serious yet. You'll meet lots of men in the future and anyway, who'd want to marry a man and be related to Amelia when she's been so keen to keep away from us!

'I can't think she can have changed all that much.'

'Maybe she was always like this, and simply adapted at Lorivals so that we'd get along with her.'

'Perhaps.'

'Now tell me about the wedding: will there be any nice men waiting to make a fuss of us?'

'I'm sure there won't. The best man is Martin's cousin and very much engaged to a girl in Greymont. One groomsman is only sixteen and I'm not sure who they've asked to be the others. One thing, the hotel's good so I can promise you a decent meal.'

'Oh well, I suppose that's something to be thankful for!'

'Tell me what's been happening to you, Lois. Do you like your job? Have you somewhere nice to live? Oh, there's so much I need to know.'

'And I've so much to tell you. I'll start with the job. I've a lot to thank my father for with that, since I'm working at the Foreign Office as a secretary, very much a junior, of course. I do get to meet people, civil servants and MPs and we do have a pretty good social life.'

'How is your father, Lois?'

'Oh, he's all right, still the proverbial Peter Pan. Gloria's married to some country cleric and they're living in Somerset, but as you can imagine there have been a string of females since then. The current one is a girl I'm setting up house with.'

I stared at her in surprise. 'You mean you actually like this one?'

'I like her well enough, but I've grown up a lot since Gloria. I know that Marcia's no more important to Father than any of the others, but what's more important, Marcia knows it too.'

'You say you're setting up house together?'

'Yes. She also works at the Foreign Office as a secretary, that's how we met, and how my father came to know her. Let me tell you about the house, Nancy. It's in Hammersmith: after you've picked your way through the market stalls and crisp packets littering the High Street, you suddenly turn down this little alleyway and there's a large, old-fashioned iron gate with a smashing garden beyond. It's so unexpected after the sordid streets of Hammersmith and the house is as picturesque as the garden. It has a quaint terrace and stone stairs leading up to a glass door, and there's a big bay window. The rooms are lofty and spacious.'

'How can you possibly afford such a treasure?'

'Wait 'till I tell you. A very old lady lived there and for years she didn't spend a bean on it. The decoration was Victorian, there was damp everywhere and the kitchen and bathroom are a disaster but the possibilities are endless. The Council have taken the old lady into care and she won't sell. The house will be sold eventually when something happens to her, but for now we're renting it, and at the weekend and whenever any one of us has a spare moment we're working on it. There are three of us – Marcia, me and Joyce. Joyce is a friend of Marcia's; she works for one of the airlines so she's away quite a lot. We've roped in as many men as we know to help get the place shipshape but of course it wasn't possible to do much in the winter. You'd love it, Nancy – and I'd like you to come down for a holiday once we feel it's up to scrutiny.'

'It sounds wonderful! Oh, you've done much more with your life than I have, Lois.'

'Not really. My father helped with my job and one has to live somewhere.'

'Do you have a man friend?'

I saw the warm delicate colour flood her cheeks and rather self-consciously she said, 'Nobody special.'

'Why are you blushing then?'

Lois laughed. 'Oh well, there is one man, you're quite right, but we've never been out together. I've only even met him once or twice, so you could say I've a crush on him, nothing more.'

'But perhaps there will be more?'

'And perhaps he doesn't know I'm alive.'

'Oh Lois, not you too.'

'No – I could never love somebody like Mark. The man I'm crazy about is much older and more sophisticated. He's terribly ambitious and everybody says he'll go far – he has that sort of dedication. I don't ask questions because I don't want anybody to know I'm interested in him, but I do listen to the gossip. There's always so much of it and every little thing I hear about him is very precious.'

'Is he married?'

She turned away abruptly and went to stand at the window. After a few minutes she said in a small voice, 'He lives alone and like I said, I don't ask questions. I don't want to know about other women, even a wife. Why don't you come to work in London, Nancy? Surely you don't intend to stay on the local paper forever – where is your ambition?'

'I'm not sure yet what I want. At first I thought it was Mark, but now I realise he wasn't an ambition, merely a desire.'

'You'd soon find a job. The ministries are always looking for girls with your acumen. You have Lorivals behind you, remember, and my father would help.'

'I'm not sure how my parents would react if I said I wanted to work in London.'

'Try them, but wait until I've gone. I don't want them thinking I've given you wanderlust.'

Barbara made a beautiful bride, and there were gasps of admiration from all sides of the crowd as they watched her glide along the path towards the church on her father's arm. Dark and slender, the heavy folds of her cream satin gown fell away into a long train while a headdress of pearls and orange blossom kept her long delicate veil in place. Lois and I walked behind her, both more or less the same height; our rose chiffon gowns shimmering in the morning sunlight. After the ceremony when we left the church I seemed to tower over Cousin Ernest and Lois grinned at me sympathetically.

Later she said, 'It reminds me of that evening at Lorivals when I had to dance with all those serious young boys from Ramilees. They were all so tongue-tied and most of them had six feet. Why couldn't one of us at least have had Martin's cousin.' There was no time to answer her, for the organ music swelled and ahead of us we could see the crowds of people thronging the churchyard.

Lois' visit unsettled me. I became increasingly disenchanted at the *Gazette*, despite my good fortune at being taken on there. It all seemed so banal, the interviewing of couples celebrating Golden and Silver weddings, the social clubs and charity garden parties, the minutiae of provincial life. Father sensed my restlessness.

I found him one evening sitting in his study with the daily newspaper in his hands, but he was not reading it. He was looking at the article on the front page and a photograph of the journalist who had been wounded in a confrontation in the Middle East.

I took the paper out of his hands to look at it and he said with a little smile, 'That's what I really wanted to do, love – travel the world, visit all the trouble spots and write columns everyone would want to read – and look where I ended up . . . I knew this young man's father. We worked on the same paper once but he went on to better things while I stayed on in Greymont with the local rag. He must be very proud of that boy of his – I reckon he's the best journalist in the country today.'

I stared down at the picture of a tall, smiling young man with his right arm in a sling. He had a devil-may-care look about him in his khaki shirt and shorts and there was a charm in his smile – charm, and a certain ruthlessness.

'Why didn't you do what you wanted to do? Was it meeting Mother?'

'No, I wasn't married then but my father died suddenly and circumstances kept me at home, then I married your mother and somehow I just drifted. Don't think I've been unhappy, love, it's only when I read things like this report that I become restless and feel I've wasted a lot of time.'

I was thoughtful. It seemed that I too was wasting time, and if I said as much Father might see things my way but Mother was a different proposition. She constantly said how nice it was to have me at home, to go shopping with and share woman talk with.

At the beginning of July Maisie gave birth to a little boy. I was invited to the christening and to the farmhouse afterwards for refreshments. The baby behaved beautifully, Tom looked every inch the proud father and Maisie sat holding her son in plump contentment. Later, when he had been put down for a nap, she came to chat and already it seemed to me that she had a matronly air.

'I'll write and thank your folks for the lovely present they've sent for the baby,' she said happily. 'Everybody's been so kind and we've hardly had anything duplicated.'

'How have you settled down at the farm?'

'Really well. Tom's mother says I might have been a farmer's wife all my life. I was sorry not to have seen Lois at Easter. We'd gone away for a break all that week, still, it was a good excuse not to have to go to Barbara's wedding!'

'Now, Maisie, she made a lovely bride and as for Lois, she's changed. Nowadays she's very sophisticated and fashionable.'

'Well, she always was fashionable – too fashionable for Miss Clarkson's liking, but I expect she's got it right now.'

I laughed. 'Yes, I rather think Miss Clarkson would approve of Lois now.'

'I was sorry about you and Mark Garveston you know, but I never thought it'd come to anything.' I smiled briefly. Only Maisie could have put it quite like that.

Unabashed she went on, 'I don't suppose any of us'll ever hear from Amelia again. She's made it quite plain that we're not her sort.'

'I expect she's busy with her wedding plans.'

She shook her head. 'No, it's not that, Nancy. It was all right to mix with us at school because she didn't have any choice but now she has, and we're expendable.'

I raised my eyes a little and Maisie laughed. 'That's a big word for me, isn't it – it's what our Bob said about her. Bob should have gone on to do somethin' better than servin' in the shop, he always was the clever one.'

'Has Bob fixed a date for his wedding to Mary Gibson?'

'Just before Christmas. They're buyin' a house up the road so they'll be handy for the shop, and when Mam and Dad retire they may come and live up here.'

'I hope Bob and Mary will be very happy.'

'She's all right but she's a bit jealous of you, Nancy. She thinks our Bob fancied you at one time and that's why she doesn't have much to say to you.'

Later that night, when I went into father's study to see if he had left any notes for the morning, the newspaper was still open on his desk. I picked it up and looked again at the photograph: Noel Templeton, our man in Tel Aviv. Restlessness surged within me. It was time to move on.

Towards the end of the summer I had one long rambling letter from Barbara. It was filled with enthusiasm about her new home and life in Cheltenham, from which I gathered that the Waltons were already part of the Gloucestershire social whirl. Over the next few months, Lois wrote often – about the house, her job, nights out at the theatre and dinner parties with her father and his friends. In every letter she urged me to visit and to think about finding work in London. This did nothing to still my restless impulses.

It was a raw blustery day at the beginning of December

and I had been detailed to report on a hockey match between the girls of the local grammar school and St Mary's Social Club. I was chilled to the bone as I stood disconsolately at the edge of the pitch with my feet frozen in the thick mud, desperately trying to breathe some life into my stricken hands.

As I clomped my way back across the playing-fields towards the icy pavements, I was hailed by a cheerful voice. 'It's Nancy Graham, isn't it? What are you doing here?'

I turned to see Miss Edge, our former games mistress at Lorivals, striding along behind me and I reflected how she had never seemed to feel the cold. Her homely face was red and shining, and she was wearing the same familiar thick slacks and sweater.

I smiled, waiting for her to catch up with me, then I replied, 'I work on the local paper, so I have to write about the match.'

'And I was seeing what the opposition had in the way of talent. We're playing the grammar school next week: will you be writing about that one?'

'I'm not sure, but it's possible.'

'I thought you'd have been into something more exciting than working for the local newspaper. Your father's a reporter, isn't he?'

'Yes.'

'Oh well, that explains it. Do you keep in touch with the others?'

'With Lois Brampton and Maisie Jayson, or Maisie Standing as she now is. Barbara Smythe is married, too, and living away in Cheltenham.'

'And Lady Amelia?'

'Preparing for her wedding, too, I expect. I no longer see anything of Amelia.'

Miss Edge made no comment, and after a little while remarked, 'I wonder why the flags are at half-mast on all the public buildings around here. I noticed it as I came along this afternoon.'

'I don't know. Perhaps Alderman Biggins has died; he's been an invalid for such a long time that whenever we see a flag at half-mast we assume it's on his account.'

'Oh well, we'll soon know. I've left my car along the road there. Can I give you a lift?'

'No thank you, Miss Edge. I have to get back to the office. I can walk there in a few minutes.'

I watched her drive away in a burst of exhaust fumes then started to hurry down the hill in the direction of the town. I had not gone far when I met my father climbing up. He said quickly, 'You needn't go back, Nancy. Everybody's out so you might as well write your report in comfort at home. Was it a good match?'

'I'm too numb to remember, I'm still half frozen.'

He smiled. 'Oh well, you'll soon warm up.' He seemed strangely preoccupied as we started our climb back and unwilling to talk. We left our outdoor clothing in the hall and went straight into the kitchen where we heard Mother getting the evening meal.

'I'm glad you're both home together,' she said, turning round with a smile. 'You're early. Susan's just been on the phone: she tells me all the flags are at half-mast. Is it Alderman Biggins at last?'

'No, it's Phillip Garveston,' my father said heavily. Into the silence he added, 'He was flying home from France with another chap when their plane crashed into a hillside in the Midlands. They both died. I expect there'll be a full report on the six o'clock news.'

We stared at him, stunned, and he went on, 'I can't give you any more details that that. I went along to the Town Hall but they didn't know very much. The national press will have picked it up by now. We'll be reporting it secondhand.'

'But that's terrible!' I cried finally. 'Poor Amelia, and her wedding was to take place so soon.'

Pictures were shown on the six o'clock news of the shattered plane lying against a bleak hillside. Phillip Garveston's friend John Reynolds had been piloting his own plane: the pair were returning from a brief visit to France.

'That's another Garveston funeral we shall be covering,' Father said softly.

So once again I stood in the churchyard surrounded by a multitude of people waiting for the funeral cortege to arrive. All around me I was aware of speculation from people who were obviously employed up at the Hall.

'I wonder what'll happen now,' one woman was saying. 'Lord Urquart's poured thousands into the Hall so that his daughter'll have something worthy of her, and I doubt if them Garvestons have the brass to pay him back.'

'How's she taking it, do you think?'

'They don't show their feelings, the aristocracy, not like us they don't. Polly says she's like a piece of ice, that composed and serene, it's almost as if she doesn't know what's happened, or doesn't much care.'

'Oh, she'll care all right. Like you say, she'll not be showing her true feelings, not in front of the servants at any rate.'

And so they went on until I felt I would scream. After a while Father took hold of my arm saying, 'We'll stand over here, love. I can't endure much more of this gossip. You'd think they'd lay off this morning at least.'

Silence at last descended over the churchyard as the funeral procession made its solemn way along the path. Amelia walked between Sir Gerald and Mark and I thought she had never looked more beautiful. There was no expression on her pale composed face while beside her Sir Gerald seemed to have suddenly aged. He leaned heavily on his stick and his face was grey and lined in the freezing wind that swept across the churchyard. Mark too was different. This was not the boy who had so charmed me with his laughter and gay, airy demeanour that promised much and meant nothing. Now he was the heir to an old and honourable name, and to estates that had belonged in his family for hundreds of years.

I made no effort to attract Amelia's attention, although I intended to write to her. Once, for a quick moment, my eyes met Mark's across the crowd. He nodded briefly, then the funeral party was walking away from us to the waiting cars.

That night I told my parents that I wanted to quit the *Gazette* and Greymont itself. There was a room for me in Lois' house in Hammersmith and I hoped to find work in London.

Mother was tearful while Father merely said, 'What sort of work do you want to do, love? Lois was in the happy position of having her father at the Foreign Office, but all I know is newspaper work.'

'You told me when I went to Lorivals that the world would be my oyster,' I reminded him, 'and I did well at school, although I've never wanted to go to University. I've been thinking a lot, and I could take a proper course at a Secretarial College, to really bring my shorthand and typing up to scratch. I can always come home, can't I, if I'm making a mistake?'

'Well, of course you can love, but you'll need some money in London, enough to start you off and pay for that secretarial course at any rate.'

'I'll pay you back Father, as soon as I get a job.'

'There's no need,' Mother put in quickly. 'Father didn't leave you anything, Nancy, he divided his money between Susan and me, but I always intended to open a high-interest account for you with some of it.' I embraced her and she continued anxiously, 'I don't know what your Aunt Susan's going to say, mind. She'll not be in agreement with your gallivanting off to live in London and leaving your training at the *Gazette*.

'She was responsible for Nancy going to Lorivals,' Father said sharply, 'so surely she must see that her niece is worthy of something better than working alongside me on the local rag.'

10

Lois had prepared me for the peace of the garden after the bustle of the streets of Hammersmith. Giant horse chestnuts shed their branches across the grass and brittle golden leaves crunched under our feet as we walked up to the front door. Both the door and the large window on the right of it had been painted recently, but not very expertly. Lois smiled when she saw me looking at them.

'They need another coat yet Nancy, but the paint doesn't dry well in this weather. They'll have to wait now until the spring.'

'The garden's lovely.'

'Well, I told you about that, didn't I? Please don't be too critical about the house – try to visualise it when it's to our liking.'

In the kitchen a big iron stove and a gas boiler of ancient lineage took up one corner. A huge Welsh dresser stood against one wall, its shelves filled with Willow Pattern crockery which Lois informed me had all been bought cheaply at one of the local markets and chosen because it was easily replaceable.

There was a large table in whitewood in the dining room and several unmatching chairs set around it. There was also an old sideboard against the wall and a small walnut table bearing a silver tea service which Lois said had been a present from her father. This room had the bay window.

In the lounge were four or five assorted armchairs and an elderly television set near the window. The carpets on the floor were badly worn, and Lois told me they had come with the house but would be replaced when funds were more plentiful.

Lois, Marcia and I would have the three rooms at the

front of the house because we were at home much more than Joyce.

'By the way, you owe me ten pounds for your bed, Nancy,' Lois said smiling. 'Mrs Mellor at the secondhand shop got it for me, but you'll have to supply the bedding yourself.' Indeed, apart from the bed and one cane-bottomed chair my new bedroom was empty, but Father had given me a hundred pounds at the station when he took me to catch the train, with the instruction that I shouldn't be afraid to spend it on things I needed at Hammersmith.

When I told Lois about the money she said, 'We'll go to the shops this afternoon and buy what you need immediately. We can do the salerooms later in case you want to buy a secondhand wardrobe and dressing table. In the meantime, feel free to use anything of mine.'

The bath was badly stained but Lois assured me it was quite clean.

'We've promised ourselves another, one of these days,' she grinned, 'but I've turned down my father's offer to pay for things. Marcia was a bit peeved about that because she felt if I didn't accept things from him she couldn't, but I want to be independent. Anyway, I think her affair with Dad is on the way out. She's gone into the country with some friends this weekend and he didn't seem very concerned.'

'Does it always end like that?'

'Oh, mostly,' she answered cheerfully. 'They all get the message eventually and Marcia's no fool – she knew almost at once that there was no future in it for her.'

'You don't seem to mind as much as you once did.'

'I don't mind at all. If Dad wants to play at being Peter Pan there's nothing I can do about it. Sometimes he's a delayed adolescent, at others he's an aging Casanova. I find both roles equally nauseating, but I've learned to live with it. Come and see my room.'

I followed her down the passage to a door at the far

end which she flung open, then stood back so that I could enter the room before her.

Lois' bedroom was the same size as mine, but there the similarity ended. The paintwork was new and although the wallpaper was faded and needed replacing, the curtains and bed coverings were in a pretty chintz and on the floor beside the bed lay a lovely Chinese rug. Her wardrobe was a huge oak affair while the dressing table was walnut; both were sadly in need of restoration. I walked over to the window and looked out into the garden and Lois came and stood beside me.

'I told you the house was a mess, Nancy. I suppose it's much worse than you expected.'

'No, of course it isn't. If I can get my room to look like this I'll be delighted. We'll never manage to decorate the rooms ourselves though, they're far too lofty.'

'Yes, but Joyce knows somebody, a friend of her brother's who's in the trade. He said he'd come and take a look at the house and give us an estimate.'

'I hope I can get a job quickly, but I need to brush up my office skills before I can even think of applying.'

'A part-time job at the weekends would help.'

'Are they easy to come by?'

'There's one going at the local library on Saturdays. The money's not much but it's something.'

'I'll go along later and make some enquiries.'

I was amazed at how quickly things began to fit into place. Marcia returned from the country on Sunday evening and as I looked into her clear hazel eyes I was reminded of Gloria. They were all of a pattern, Lois assured me – girls who were sophisticated and knew how to dress; girls a man would be flattered to be seen with, girls who would accept what they couldn't change. Marcia was in her early thirties. She was a secretary to somebody of importance at the Foreign Office and she had not made the mistake of making David Brampton the centre of her universe. Marcia had cut her teeth on men like David and she knew the score only too well.

106

I soon enrolled on a crash course at a good secretarial college recommended by Marcia, and in the evenings I studied German and Chinese.

Both Marcia and Lois were amused at my desire to learn Chinese, and Marcia said with some irony, 'Why Chinese, for heaven's sake? What sort of job are you looking for?'

'I don't know – I just thought it might come in useful.'

'It would if you were thinking of emigrating to Hong Kong.' They both giggled.

Joyce Carruthers was considerably more supportive. She was a pretty blonde girl who whisked in and out of our lives. She applauded my ambition to learn Chinese, saying, 'The airlines would be interested, I'm sure. If I hear anything I'll let you know, Nancy.'

Three months at the secretarial college saw me with a first-class diploma and I was progressing well with the languages. Lois hinted strongly that I should have no difficulty in finding work within one of the ministries but strangely enough, it wasn't what I wanted. Listening to Lois and Marcia going on at great length about MPs and ambassadors, influential civil servants and an army of Secretaries who themselves had secretaries of their own convinced me that this was not for me.

There was a new man in Marcia's life and I guessed he was somebody rather important since he arrived to fetch her in a large dark limousine and she was spending almost every weekend in the country. I asked no questions but one Sunday morning when Lois and I walked in the park Lois said, 'I don't want to be like Marcia. She reminds me too much of all those other girls father collected for a time and then discarded.'

'Do you know who Marcia's latest boyfriend is?'

'I've a good idea, and if it's who I think it is he'll certainly never marry her, he's married already.'

'Happily married?'

'He and his wife are still living together. If they were apart I could understand it, but as thing are I can't.'

For a while we walked in silence then my friend said in a small voice, 'That's why I'll never talk to anybody about the man I'm in love with, not even you.'

'I can't understand why you're so secretive, Lois. He never comes to the house for you, he never telephones that I know of . . . is he married, too?'

'I don't talk about him because there's nothing to talk about. I love him but he doesn't love me. He knows me well enough but we only meet when I'm with my father. He mixes with the same crowd in government circles.'

'So how can you be in love with him? You might not even *like* him if you knew him better.'

'I know I only have to look at him to feel weak at the knees. He makes me behave like a stupid child, Nancy. All of a sudden tonguetied and gauche. The only thing that keeps me sane is knowing I'll see him again. In the meantime, I try to find out as much as I can about him.'

'How do you do that?'

'I listen when others talk about him. I know all about his work, his flat in London and his Club. I know about his family, I even know the sort of things his manservant shops for.'

'What possible satisfaction can you get from that?'

'I walk round the block where his flat is and look up at the windows. I know everybody who goes into those flats. I know where he eats out, which theatres he goes to, when his mother comes to town, what sort of Christmas presents he buys and who he gives them to. I could write a book about him – Mr Nobody's life story by an unknown woman.' She stopped by a tree and rested her forehead against the trunk in an attitude of despair.

I stared at her in shocked surprise. 'Lois, I can't believe you're involved with something so terribly unhealthy.' I took her gently by the arm and we strolled on. 'I loved Mark but it was a young wholesome sort of love, and at one time I like to think it was mutual. This man gives you nothing but pain! You're besotted with a dream.'

'I know, but that's my fault, not his.'

'But it's crazy! You could be meeting somebody meanwhile. You're so pretty, any man would be thrilled to have you as his girlfriend. As it is, you're wasting your youth on some chap who doesn't even know you're alive.'

As if she hadn't heard me she went on, 'I was miserable all last week. I told you and everybody else I had a bad head, that I was sickening for something, but it wasn't true. I saw him coming out of his flat with a girl, quite a young girl, and she was very pretty and well-dressed. They were laughing together as though they knew each other very well. He called a taxi, then he got hold of her arm and they waited at the kerb. He kissed her cheek and helped her into the taxi, then he stood there until it moved away and she sat waving to him through the back window.'

Lois gulped and then continued in the same monotone. 'I couldn't sleep that night; I couldn't get the pair of them out of my mind. I was so sure that he was in love with her, that she had been staying at his flat but I was determined to find out about her. I had to, or I'd make myself ill worrying about it.'

We walked on for a few minutes in silence. I couldn't believe it was Lois behaving like a lovesick schoolgirl. The conversation was distasteful to me, but oblivious now to my feelings she said, 'I made myself be very nice to his secretary. I invited her out to lunch and she's so full of herself and her job that it didn't take much to get her talking. I learned that the girl was his niece, his sister's daughter. She's getting married in August. You've no idea how relieved I felt. That night I went to the theatre and ate a huge box of chocolates. It was my present to myself for doubting him and finding I'd made a mistake.'

'Lois, you have no right to doubt him. He isn't answerable to you.'

She turned her head and grinned at me. There was

nothing remotely mischievous and lighthearted in her grin. It was conspiratorial and quite unnerving.

I was worried about Lois' fixation with this unknown man. On some occasions when she had accompanied her father to a dinner or other function she'd return in the early hours with shining eyes, excited and wanting to talk throughout the night. *He* had been there. Sometimes I had to insist she left my room so that I could get to sleep. I heard her sobbing in her room and she refused all offers of help. Her misery was not caused by any ill-treatment on his part, but merely because he either hadn't been there, or had been with a group of other people. The whole thing was unhealthy and soul-destroying, and I believed that if she didn't get to grips with this obsession, Lois would have a nervous breakdown.

With this in mind I spoke to Marcia, and was surprised when she merely shrugged her shoulders philosophically, saying, 'Oh, she'll get over it. The trouble is, Lois always minds too much about everything – her father, his women friends and this fellow.'

'Do you know who he is?'

'No. She doesn't talk about him to me, and in any case, Nancy, I'd rather not know.'

I had applied for several jobs in central London. One was with the Bank of England, one at the Home Office and another with a pair of Oriental importers. The last one appealed to me the greatest. The firm had branches in Singapore, Hong Kong, Bangkok, China and Japan, and I hoped my progress in Chinese would recommend me to them. While I waited for replies, I decided to go home for the weekend. I had nothing planned – Lois was spending the weekend with her father and some of his friends in Brighton.

It was so good to be back in Greymont, a part once more of the bustling market scene, and to see the mist hanging low across the Cumbrian mountains and smell the salt-laden breezes swept inland across the marshes. I was needing the calm normality of my parents' home without in any way wishing to return there permanently. I told myself that Lois' emotional problems would pass: perhaps I should have discussed them with my parents. From early childhood I had been taught to be open about things which troubled me. We were a family, and a family was there to help and bring anxieties out into the open, but Lois' problems were largely of her own making and my parents would deplore the fact that I felt involved.

We had a lot to talk about. Father thought I should have stuck to journalism and the fact that I was learning Chinese both amused and dismayed them. It was over coffee when I saw the doubtful look that passed between them and in the next moment Mother said anxiously, 'Are you going to tell her, Arthur?'

I looked at him quickly, seeing his hesitancy, and I asked sharply, 'What is it? Is something wrong?'

'Haven't you seen the papers this morning, love?' Father said calmly.

'No, there wasn't time to buy one. I knew you'd have one here.'

He got up from his chair and went to the magazine rack, then I watched him open the paper to find the page he was looking for. With a little smile he reached out and handed it to me.

There was a picture of Amelia standing on the terrace of her father's house Drummond, with her arm linked in Mark's; the heading leapt out at me: HAPPINESS AFTER TRAGEDY. The paragraph below the photograph informed me that Lady Amelia Urquart, who had lost her fiancé, the Hon. Phillip Garveston in a flying accident at the end of last year, was now engaged to his younger brother Mark. The wedding would take place quietly later in the year. After the honeymoon they would take up residence at Garveston Hall. Mark was smiling down at Amelia but she was not looking at him; her face stared out of the page, serenely beautiful, and in that moment I asked myself if there was anything, love or great joy, pain or devouring tragedy, any emotion that could remove that composure from her beautiful face.

'It doesn't matter, does it love?' Father said gently. 'You're over him now, aren't you.'

'Yes, it all seems a long time ago.'

'Well, thank goodness for that. Your mother thought we shouldn't tell you.'

'I'd have heard about it sooner or later and it's better coming from you. How's Aunt Susan?'

'Expecting us for lunch tomorrow. Susan doesn't change.'

'And the Jaysons?'

'Bob's married and his wife's helping in the shop. Maisie's heavily pregnant again and it's rumoured the Jaysons intend to retire at the end of the year so they'll be handing over the business to the boys.'

'I'd really like to see Maisie while I'm here, but if we have to go to Aunt Susan's tomorrow there may not be enough time.'

'I'll run you up to the farm in the morning and collect you in time for Susan's. Maisie'll be so glad to see you, Nancy. Whenever she sees your mother she always asks about you.'

We found Maisie in the chicken run, her cheeks rosy red from the chill wind and her exertions. She was wearing several thicknesses of outdoor clothing which made her look like an apple dumpling topped off with a bright red woollen cap. She was obviously pleased to see me and taking my arm like she used to when we were children she said, 'Come along into the parlour, Nancy. I'll make coffee and you can tell me all your news.'

'Are you alone?' I asked her curiously, because the house seemed so quiet.

'They've gone over to Carnforth and taken Peter with them. They do so dote on him. I tell them not everybody wants a toddler runnin' about the place but they took no notice. I just 'ope he behaves himself!'

Her eyes sparkled, her face shone with happiness and

when she told me about their joy at the advent of a new baby I couldn't help thinking that, of the five of us Lorivals girls, at least Maisie had found what she was looking for. Some deep sense of loyalty prevented me from confiding in Maisie about Lois. I merely said I was happy in London, and contented myself by telling her about the house we lived in, my secretarial college training, job applications and all the small incidents I could remember from the last few months.

By the time Father picked me up just before lunch, Maisie and I had done equal amounts of talking. I had dutifully admired the new baby's layette and the nursery which Tom was re-decorating.

'When will you be up here again?' she asked me wistfully at the front door, giving me a loving hug.

'I'm not sure, but at Christmas, definitely.'

Aunt Susan thought the Chinese lessons were a waste of time. She said I should jump at the Home Office job if it was offered me – after all, I couldn't afford to be blasé about regular employment and a pension at the end of it. What is more I was well rid of that Mark Garveston. How could he even think of marrying his dead brother's fiancée in such indecent haste?

She talked and we listened, just as we'd always done, and it was only later when Father was driving me to catch my train back to London that he said dryly, 'A few months ago she was saying you must have done something quite dreadful to turn young Garveston off. Now, it seems, you're well rid of him!'

It was almost midnight when my taxi pulled up near the house in Hammersmith, and only a single light was burning in an upstairs room: Lois' room. After dumping my weekend case in my room I knocked on her door. She was sitting in her dressing gown writing letters and her welcoming smile was entirely normal. She told me she was writing to her mother, and she was interested in my

113

weekend, how my family were and the news of Maisie's baby.

'How have things been with you?' I asked her.

'Come and look at my dress,' she invited.

She left her chair and went to the wardrobe, bringing out a confection wreathed in layer after layer of tissue paper which she laid on the bed.

'It was frightfully expensive but Dad contributed. Here, help me to unwrap it.'

The gown was lovely, of jade wild silk with a tiny waist and a long full skirt. Completely plain, it stood out on its own without any attempt to decorate it with diamanté trimming or pearls, and I could only hazard a guess at what Lois had paid for it.

'Is it for something very special?' I asked curiously.

'*Very* special. Two old friends of Dad's have just returned from Brazil after four years. They have a house in Gloucestershire and we've been invited for the weekend. There will be quite a large house party and Dad says we'll have to dress for dinner on Saturday evening. They've always been most formal.'

'And will He be there?'

'I made sure of that before I told Dad I'd go. Think of it, Nancy! A whole weekend, Friday to Sunday, and I'll probably be the youngest there. He's just got to notice me.'

'Oh Lois, I do hope so. You worry me.'

11

During the following week I saw little of either Lois or Marcia for my time was taken up with interviews for jobs. I was one of several girls interviewed at the Home Office by a middle-aged woman and an elderly gentleman who both seemed unimpressed by my secretarial diploma and my public school education. I left the building feeling rather pessimistic and went for coffee with one of the other applicants. She said with a rueful smile, 'One wonders exactly what they're looking for. I expect they've already found someone but the jobs have to be advertised. Got anywhere else in mind?'

'I have an interview at the Bank of England and with a firm of importers, but after this morning I'm not very hopeful.'

'There are plenty of jobs around, but the Civil Service seems to be the most difficult to enter. I wanted to make it on my own but I do have an uncle at the Ministry of Transport, so perhaps it's time I asked him to pull some strings.'

I thought my interview at the Bank went quite well, but again I was told I would be informed later by post after all the applicants had been interviewed. Feeling very discouraged now, I made my way to the importers, expecting similar treatment there. However, nothing could have been more different. I was shown into a tasteful room where my feet sank into a thick oriental carpet; tall vases stood on intricately-carved ebony stands, and objects of jade and ivory were displayed about the room. I was served faintly scented China tea in a delicate cup I could almost see through, and as far as I could ascertain there were no other girls waiting to be interviewed. I began to feel more composed.

A charming oriental girl came to retrieve the tea tray. She bowed and in a slightly sing-song voice announced 'Mr Papadraos has been detained, but he will be here presently.'

I wondered if Mr Papadraos was Greek, but I did not have long to conjecture. After a few minutes the door opened again and two men entered the room. One was tall and portly, the other small and slender. Both of them bowed over my hand then went to the other side of the desk and sat facing me.

The tall man had iron grey hair and a severe, lined face, but when he smiled the severity suddenly disappeared and a warm friendliness took its place. The smaller man was oriental. He leaned towards me and said politely 'You are learning Chinese, Miss Graham. That is good.'

He beamed at me through his thick horn-rimmed spectacles and for the first time in days I felt somebody was interested in my accomplishments as a person. They invited me to talk about my life, and I told them freely about Lorivals and my short training as a journalist. When I had finished more tea was served and Mr Papadraos said finally, 'We would like you to come to work for us, Miss Graham. Your work will not be merely secretarial, for you will handle articles of great value during the course of your work, and will come to appreciate their worth, the materials from which they are made, and their place of origin. Perhaps you will have the opportunity to travel in the Far East yourself – it will depend very much on how well you cope with the opportunities that are presented to you.'

I stared at him in some surprise, and with a little smile he said, 'You are surprised about the opportunity to travel? You may not know it, my dear, but we are a world-wide company with branches in all the large cities in the Far East. We were impressed by your application, since Lorivals is known to us, and by the fact that you have troubled to begin the ardous task of learning Chinese. You will continue with your studies?'

'Yes, of course – if that is what you want.'

My feet hardly touched the ground as I left the office. The salary was much more than I had hoped for, so I bought an expensive navy blue skirt and white silk blouse and a pair of plain navy court shoes to celebrate. They seemed entirely business like and quite in keeping with my new status. I hurried home, wishing there was somebody there to hear my good news.

Mrs Merrill our daily cleaner was in the kitchen putting on her coat when I arrived home and she said with some relief, 'I'm glad you're back, Miss Graham. I'm just off, as I go to Miss Holland on Wednesday afternoons as you know but I'm a bit worried about Miss Brampton. I think she's sickening for flu, or bronchitis. I've made her a cup of tea but I think she needs the doctor. I have to get off or I'll be late.'

'When did she get home?'

'About half eleven – somebody brought her home from the office. I've seen her tucked up in bed, but she looks really queer.'

I only had to glance at Lois' flushed face and glassy eyes to know she was really ill. She was shivering and all her limbs ached, but when I suggested calling the doctor she immediately cried, 'I don't want the doctor, Nancy. He'll just keep me in bed and stop me going to Gloucestershire. Even if it kills me I'm going there!'

'It's obvious that you're not fit.'

'I will be. I'll fill myself with hot drinks and aspirins. If I see the doctor that's all he'll prescribe. You're not to tell my father, Nancy. I'll be better for Gloucester – after all, it's a whole week and two days away.'

I warmed soup up for Lois and fed her pain killers. I could hear her dry choking coughs, and she said her chest was hurting and she couldn't breathe properly. On Sunday evening I spoke to Marcia.

'We should send for the doctor and tell her father,'

Marcia said practically, and I agreed with her, but when we said as much to Lois she became tearful and excited, extracting promises from us that we were both reluctant to keep.

'It's ridiculous,' Marcia grumbled. 'She can't possibly go to Gloucestershire next weekend – her father'll never take her in that state.'

'What can we do?'

'Nothing yet. Hope she comes to her senses, I suppose.'

'Do you know why she's so desperate to go?'

'I've a good idea.'

'Who is he?'

'I'm not prepared to say – oh, not because of any promise I've made to Lois but because it's all on her side. If it's who I think it is he'll not do anything about Lois. For one thing, he won't create a scandal within the department – there's never been any surrounding him that I know of – and for another, he's a friend of her father's. She's a fool to think it's going to change, because it won't. Now if she's no better in the morning we're going to tell David and get the doctor in.'

'She'll never forgive us.'

'We're saving her life – she might thank us for that one day.'

If anything Lois was decidedly worse the next morning. Gasping for breath her face was grey against the pillow and I agreed we should not waste any more time. The doctor arrived and diagnosed pneumonia. David Brampton insisted that his daughter be removed to a nursing home in Kensington where she could be properly looked after.

By this time Lois was too ill to care either one way or the other about Gloucester.

It was a week of coping. I was now one of those thousands of girls who stream out of the tube stations every morning armed with copious handbags containing make-up, paperbacks and homemade sandwiches. I had never felt so alive! At lunchtime I pored over heavily-illustrated books of oriental art, and read about the various Chinese dynasties that had produced these works. Mr Ho Ying complimented me warmly on my dedication.

In the evenings I went to see Lois, who was now recovering slowly from her bout of pneumonia and insisting that she would be well enough to travel on Friday evening.

Her father was equally adamant that she would not be going anywhere, and here he was backed up strongly by the nurses and doctor in charge of her.

'What's so important about this weekend?' he queried in puzzlement. 'There'll be plenty of those, my love. I won't hear of it so you'd better get the whole idea out of your head.'

By Wednesday evening Lois knew it was hopeless. I found her tight-lipped and lethargic, but when her father arrived at the nursing home her first question was, 'Who will you be taking in my place?'

'Do I have to take somebody? I'll probably go alone.'

'You never go anywhere alone,' she replied wearily. 'I want you to take Nancy, please, Father. She never goes anywhere as she doesn't know many people yet. Please, Dad – it's what I want.'

He looked at me doubtfully, and I was quick to say, 'I couldn't possibly go, Lois. I won't know anybody there and besides, I've nothing to wear for an occasion like that.'

'You can wear my dress, we're the same size.'

'I couldn't wear it. If you don't go to this one there'll be others.'

'I want you to go and I want you to wear my dress.'

Across her bed my eyes looked into her father's and then he smiled. 'Of course I'll take Nancy, I'll be glad to. How soon can you leave your office?'

'I believe it's four-thirty on a Friday, but I'm not sure if I should go.'

I couldn't argue with them both. Lois was persistent and her father obviously wanted to avoid a scene, so in the end I capitulated. Soon afterwards David Brampton kissed her briefly and left after assuring me that he would pick me up at my office at half-past four on the Friday afternoon.

After he had gone I looked at Lois sternly but she merely grinned at the ease with which she had got her own way.

'How could you, Lois? It's obvious David doesn't want to take me. There's probably somebody else he'd much rather take.'

'Probably,' she said dryly, 'but you're the one who can tell me all about it when you get back. I'm not going to tell you who He is, but you might be able to guess. I don't propose to say whether you're right or not.'

'He's a fixation, Lois. How I wish you'd get him out of your mind.'

'Borrow anything of mine you want. In the daytime they wear tweeds and in the evenings they dress up. Wear the jade gown on the Saturday, since that's sure to be the most formal occasion. They won't bother on the day you arrive, so you'll just need a simple afternoon dress, and on the Sunday you'll be driving back after lunch.'

'What do they do all weekend?'

'Sometimes they ride, sometimes they walk, but most of them simply sit around swapping stories and reading newspapers. Sometimes there's a game of bridge – do you play?'

'Not very well, I'm afraid.'

'Oh well, you can opt out of that one. There'll be enough guests who do play.'

'You're going to lie here feeling sorry for yourself, thinking about me enjoying myself.'

'I'm not very sure you're going to actually enjoy yourself – most of the time you'll find it deadly dull. By the time you get there Dad'll be quite proud of escorting a girl young enough to be his daughter. Incidentally, take care – he can be quite a charmer.'

'Do you have any other instructions for me?'

'If you fall for the man I'm in love with I'll kill you. If he falls for you I'll kill myself.'

She appeared to be joking but with Lois I couldn't be sure these days. I snapped irritably, 'There'd be a better chance of my avoiding him if I knew who he was.'

'I'm not asking you to avoid him, Nancy. Let the devil do his worst.'

It was the first time I had driven through the Cotswold countryside and I was enchanted by it. David Brampton was a charming and easy companion and I had not missed his look of approval when he took my weekend case out of my hand outside my office door. I was wearing my new skirt and blouse, and a short, navy-blue jacket loaned to me by Marcia which I hoped he had not already seen.

He professed not to know the names of the other guests but added that when we arrived he would probably find he knew most of them. I felt he would have been very surprised to learn that his daughter knew the name of at least one of the guests . . . David was a good conversationalist, and as he recounted some episode from his years spent in the Bahamas, I thought of my father, who had so wanted to be a traveller on the world scene – and I felt the sharp pain of his disappointment.

'By the way, won't the others think it strange that you are bringing me?' I asked tentatively.

'Well, of course not. I phoned them first to explain the situation. You'll find them very charming.'

Indeed they received me most graciously, and my spirits lifted when I looked through my bedroom window at the large garden and rolling countryside which surrounded it. I was told to go down to the drawing room as soon as I'd unpacked; dinner would be at eight-thirty because there were one or two people who hadn't arrived and it would be quite informal.

I wore a black silk skirt covered with a design of

scarlet poppies and with it, a soft black woollen sweater; my only jewellery was a pair of long silver earrings.

That I had chosen correctly was evident when Mr Brampton whispered, 'You look lovely, Nancy. Some women should never wear black, but with you it's perfect.'

I was introduced as, 'Nancy Graham, my daughter Lois' schoolfriend who has taken pity on me because Lois is ill.'

I doubt if many people in the room believed that explanation, nor did I miss the polite but faintly dismissive smiles which my escort accepted with easy savoir-faire, more flattered than disconcerted.

As the evening progressed I found myself inspecting my fellow guests and speculating on who amongst them could have so enthralled Lois that he had become the centre of her universe. By the time dinner was over I had decided on his possible identity.

He came late, apologising for his tardiness and blaming the evening traffic and an accident on the road. He was tall and arresting with a sort of arrogance in his bearing, and as he leaned forward to hear the conversation of the woman sitting beside him, the lamplight found red-gold lights in his blond hair. Once across the dinner table his eyes met mine and he smiled, inclining his head the merest fraction of an inch.

Later in the evening I asked David his name and with a little chuckle he said, 'He's the youngest man in the room, but don't let that fool you. He's not the youngest in experience.'

'What do you mean?'

'Oh, some scandal a year or two ago concerning some young woman at the Bulgarian Embassy. It was all sorted out, but it put him back a bit in the promotion stakes. I think Ian Owen's now recovered from that setback.'

'He's attractive and I rather think he knows it. Has Lois met him?'

'Come to think of it, she has. He made quite a play

for her at the last house-party we went to together. You have been warned, my dear.'

At that moment we were joined by an elderly gentleman who was introduced to me as Brigadier General Sir Robert Foster. He said heartily, 'Trust young David here to have purloined the prettiest girl in the room. Let an old soldier have a look in, dear Boy.'

So Dear Boy left us to chat while Sir Robert went on to discuss his latest hunter and the charger he had never forgotten from World War One. Across the room I met the eyes of a man chatting to our hostess and he smiled sympathetically. I had noticed him earlier when he came to sit at the dining table. He was attractive, with a thin clever face and grey eyes. His smile was charming and yet he had a little boy lost look, although he moved easily from one group to the next, equally at home both with the men and the women.

By the end of the evening we had still not been introduced, and people were now settling down to play bridge, he amongst them. I wandered into the library and entertained myself by looking at pictures and old prints. I found a book on the shelves relating to ancient Chinese porcelain and another showing the treasures of Central Asia, so I settled down in a large chair in front of the fire to enjoy them.

It was much later, and the fire had died down considerably, when the door opened and the man I had noticed earlier came into the room. He stared at me, then quickly said, 'I'm so sorry. I came in to browse – I didn't realise there was anybody in here.'

'That's perfectly all right. I play a very inferior game of bridge, so I found it more interesting to come in here.'

He walked across the room to look down at me. 'What are you reading, then?'

I handed over the book on Central Asia and he raised his eyebrows a little. 'I'm impressed. I wouldn't have thought this subject was a young girl's forte.'

'I know very little and need to know a lot more. I

123

started work in a firm of oriental importers last week and I'm only just beginning to realise how much I have to learn.'

'Which firm is that?'

' "Treasures of the Orient". A Mr Papadraos is one of the partners.'

'I happen to know him very well. Over the years I have bought several articles from him, of jade, and porcelain. What sort of work will you be doing?'

'At first I thought it would be purely secretarial, but now I realise it's likely to involve much more than that.' I felt faintly piqued by his attitude. The stranger had made no effort to introduce himself, nor to ask me my name, and after a few moments when I watched him settle himself into a chair with a magazine in his hands I replaced the books I had borrowed and wished him a quiet goodnight.

I had the distinct impression that he believed I was one of David Brampton's run of girlfriends and that the story about his daughter's illness had merely been a cover-up. I felt unreasonably angry. These men had known Lois' father for a great many years and were no doubt conversant with his foibles. Why should I care what they thought – I would probably never see any of them again! At the same time I *did* care and I resented this one man's assumption more than the rest.

I didn't sleep well. At first light I was standing by my window watching the mist flit eerily across the lawns, absorbed by the antics of a vixen who minced daintily across the grass to stand poised and ready for flight at the sudden clatter from the bushes, but it was only a pair of magpies who emerged to skim effortlessly into the trees.

I bathed leisurely and dressed in a tweed skirt and thick sweater – an outfit that Lois had assured me would be quite in keeping with anything the other women would be wearing. It was quiet as I ran down the stairs, for not even the staff appeared to be up and about. I left the house through the conservatory door, which I had no difficulty in opening.

There was no wind and no frost. I marched briskly towards the perimeter wall and tall iron gates, then walked down the lane and explored the village. Then for a while I walked along the banks of the river until the church clock chimed eight o'clock, when I retraced my steps.

The village was coming alive now. Newspaper boys were on the streets, there was a delicious smell of new bread and farmers were delivering produce to the ring of market stalls. I wanted to linger but thought by this time, the other guests might be coming down for breakfast and I didn't want to appear tardy.

I was almost back at the gates when I encountered a man coming from the opposite direction. It was my visitor in the library from the night before. He smiled, holding the gate open so that I could pass in before him, then he fell into step beside me.

'You're early,' he remarked in a friendly tone. 'I hope you slept well.'

'Oh, yes. I walked right into the village, as nobody was awake up at the house when I left.'

'It must have been very early!'

'Yes, it was.'

'I sleep very badly in the country. I'm not accustomed to the silence – one gets so used to the sounds of London.'

'Yes – not that I've been in London very long.'

'Where do you live?'

'In Hammersmith. I share a house with Mr Brampton's daughter Lois and two other girls.' He had the grace to look disconcerted, and then I felt my mouth twitching with laughter and seeing it, he too laughed and I giggled, 'I knew you didn't believe his story about my being Lois' friend but in this instance it's true. My name is Nancy Graham, and I was at school with Lois.'

'I see. Please forgive me for thinking otherwise. It was

none of my business, anyway, but I have known David for many years. He's a charming fellow, and who am I to blame him for the company he keeps? My name is Desmond Atherton, by the way.'

I had already heard of Desmond Atherton, from Lois' father and Marcia. Apparently, he was a man who was going places, a diplomat of some stature – not a man given to meaningless chatter or idle speculation. As we continued our walk back to the house I stole a look at his attractive clever face and thought that had I been in Lois Brampton's shoes it would not be Ian Owen I was finding so attractive, but Desmond Atherton.

The rest of the morning passed uneventfully. Some of the guests elected to drive to a nearby point-to-point meeting while others, myself included, preferred to explore the Cotswold countryside. I watched a party of them drive off in high spirits and wrapping up warmly I set off once more towards the gates. This time, I took the opposite direction to the village and walked quickly, revelling in the freshening breeze. The road climbed until from the summit I could look down at the cluster of redroofed villages and warm Cotswold stone. My attention was captured by a tiny stone church with a squat tower and I made my way towards it.

I loved old churches and this one was surrounded by ancient yew-trees and a beautifully constructed lychgate. The gravestones were very old and some of them belonged to children. I was busy deciphering one of them when a voice beside me said, 'Most of them died of outbreaks of cholera, I believe. One can only begin to imagine the sadness which descended upon these old villages at such a time.'

I turned to see Desmond Atherton approaching, and caught my breath at the charm of his smile; it was like the sun coming out after a period of shadows.

'You didn't want to go racing,' he stated.

'Not today.'

'You don't care for it?'

'Oh, but I do. I spent many weekends going to race meetings when I lived in the north, but this afternoon I just wanted to discover the countryside by myself.'

'And I have intruded.'

'Oh no! Do you often spend weekends in the country?'

'I do try to, but I wish it could be more. Are you happy being away from home in London?'

'I think so. I haven't had a lot of time to feel homesick, and besides, now that I have a job and more money I hope to start going to theatres and concerts. There's so much to do and so much to see! I'm hoping I can persuade Lois to join me.' My excitement seemed to amuse him.

'You say you were at school together – whereabouts?'

'We were at a place called Lorivals. I don't suppose you've heard of it.'

'Oh, but I have. My sister Edith was at Lorivals – one had to be rather special to get into that school, I seem to remember. A lot of fuss was made.'

'But not any more. I'm afraid they've had to lower their standards somewhat.'

Desmond Atherton didn't attempt to disagree with me but merely smiled, then said, 'Have you had enough of old churches yet? There's a delightful inn at the edge of the village where we could have lunch, if you like.'

'I was beginning to feel peckish.'

'Well, there'll be a sort of buffet laid on at the house for those who have been too indolent to go out. Some of them like to read the newspapers and talk shop, but I'd much rather eat out. Will you join me?'

In many ways Desmond reminded me of my father, but without his caustic humour. Over lunch I told him about the *Greymont Gazette*, and a little about my family and the years at Lorivals. However, I made no mention of Mark Garveston or Amelia Urquart. It was not because I felt any sense of hurt because a love affair and a school-girl friendship had gone awry, the reason was more subtle than that. It was only when we were letting ourselves

127

back into the house that I realised Desmond Atherton now knew an awful lot about me – while I had learned comparatively little about him.

The race-goers returned in high spirits just after five and David confided that he'd had a good day. I noticed that Ian Owen was in the party and as we left after tea to go upstairs to our rooms he walked beside me up the staircase.

'Don't you like racing?' he enquired, smiling down at me.

'Yes, but I went walking instead. We had lunch at one of the old inns in the area.'

'We?'

'Mr Atherton and I.'

He offered no comment, but just smiled briefly. I thought to myself, so this is the man with whom Lois is infatuated – aloof but possessing a charm that would make him attractive to women. Poor convalescent Lois, how she would have loved to go to the race meeting! All the time I was dressing I was planning what I would tell her about the weekend.

Surveying myself in the mirror before going downstairs I was more than reassured: the heavy folds of my borrowed dress emphasized my height and slender figure, and the colour suited my honey-blonde hair and fair complexion. When I bumped into David leaving his room, his eyes lit up and he whispered, 'You'll be the prettiest girl in the room tonight, Nancy! That dress is really lovely.'

'It was kind of Lois to lend it to me.'

'Don't worry about that, my dear. I'm the one who paid for it and no doubt she'll wangle another one out of me for the next occasion.'

At the dinner table I was seated between David and Ian Owen and this gave me an opportunity to chat with him. Our conversation was desultory, however. His eyes admired me but he was more interested in the talk at the table. I was no competition for scandal in high places, or more seriously, current unrest in various trouble spots and the political situation at home.

Once I looked up and found Desmond Atherton watching me. He smiled sympathetically and seeing the smile Ian Owen turned towards me saying, 'You must be very bored by all this shop-talk, Miss Graham. Didn't your friend warn you what it would be like?'

'I'm not bored, Mr Owen, I'm just feeling a little inadequate.'

'There's absolutely no need for you to feel inadequate. Think instead of the glamour you are lending to this table. We do rather selfishly tend to talk shop, with the idea that everybody is equally interested.'

After that he made an attempt to chat with me. We talked about London, the plays he had seen recently and the art exhibitions he had attended, the others joined in and I was content to listen. There was a lot of discussion on a forthcoming concert starring a famous tenor and the rush to obtain tickets. Desmond Atherton asked across the table, 'Will you be going to that concert, Nancy?'

'I'm not sure. The tickets will be very expensive.'

'Yes, I'm afraid they will. Perhaps another year.' He smiled, and I warmed to him anew. He was remembering our conversation earlier in the day when I had told him I had only just started to earn money in London. When the others looked at me curiously he adroitly changed the subject.

Ian Owen continued to chat politely, but I knew he was only half-listening to my words. His head inclined towards me, his lips smiled but I felt they would have continued to smile even if I had started to talk in Chinese.

12

We said our goodbyes amid much genial good humour. Desmond Atherton had left after breakfast, my last memory of him being a smile across the breakfast table, and when the Brigadier remarked that he was leaving early he answered that he had a call to make on his way into London.

We joined the others in a light buffet lunch, then we too made our way to the car and I noticed that Ian Owen was still there, chatting easily to a couple standing with drinks in their hands. He waved his hand to us and David said with a light laugh, 'The talk goes on and on, Nancy. He's young and ambitious – every word, every contact might be important. I was like that once, but not any more. Perhaps I never had the right sort of dedication.'

I wondered how he would have reacted if I'd said I thought his daughter was in love with Ian Owen, but I wasn't sure, and even if I had been I couldn't have told her father. She would never have forgiven me.

Several days later David Brampton telephoned me to say that he had taken Lois home to his London flat until she was well enough to return to Hammersmith. He asked if I could go round that night to see her.

'I'm quite worried about her, Nancy,' he confided. 'She doesn't seem interested in anything, she didn't even mention the weekend – and when I started to talk about it, she said she didn't want to know.'

'Perhaps she's upset that she couldn't go,' I said anxiously.

'Well, just have a chat to her please, she'll talk to you. Lois and I haven't always been on the right wave-length.'

I found my friend curled up in a chair with a book

on her knee. She looked more like herself, but there was a wary look in her eyes and when I said brightly, 'Don't you want to know about the weekend, who was there and what we talked about?'

'Not particularly.'

'But Lois, there's so much to tell you! Don't you even want to know what they said about your dress?'

'It's your dress now, Nancy.'

'Then at least let me pay you for it out of my salary.'

'There's no need. How's the new job?' So we talked about my job and after about half an hour she said wearily, 'Do you mind if I ask you to leave now, Nancy? I still tire easily.'

Feeling acutely despondent and helpless, I left, and several days later she returned to Hammersmith.

That Monday morning, I was surprised to receive a telephone call at the office from Desmond Atherton. I recognised his low clipped voice instantly, and my mouth went suddenly dry as I struggled to regain my composure.

'I remember that you said you would dearly like to go to that concert, and I happen to have two spare tickets. Something very urgent has cropped up on that evening and rather than waste them, I'd like to pass them on to you.'

'Thank you very much, Desmond, but please let me pay for them.'

'Certainly not. You do have a friend who would go with you?'

'I'm sure Lois would love to go – I'll ask her this evening.'

'I'll put the tickets in the post for you. Let me have your address.'

The tickets arrived two days later and I waved them across the breakfast table saying happily, 'Tickets for that concert, Lois! It's next Tuesday evening – will you come?'

Marcia looked up in surprise. 'How on earth did you

manage to get those, Nancy? They're like gold-dust, they must have cost the earth.'

'Somebody I met in Gloucestershire last weekend who can't go because he's got a more pressing engagement remembered that I'd said how much I would love to go. You will come won't you, Lois?'

'Yes, of course.' She brightened up. 'I'll meet you in town for a meal beforehand.' It was only when Marcia had left the room that she added quickly, 'Who is giving us the tickets?'

'Desmond Atherton, I expect you know him.'

'Yes.' The reply was terse but I had come to expect this sort of curt rejoinder to most of my attempts at conversation.

I saw little of Lois in the days leading up to the concert but I had her promise to be on time. All day I looked forward happily to the evening ahead, so much so that Mr Ho Ying commented with a toothy smile, 'You are very jolly today, Miss Graham. Perhaps you go to meet a nice young man?'

I laughed and he went on, 'You are a very pretty young lady, maybe you meet a young man when you go with Mr Brampton.'

'I'm only happy because I'm going to hear some wonderful music this evening.'

'Ah. You like Italian tenors?'

'Yes.'

'And you enjoy your work with us?'

'Very much. I am learning something new every day.'

He nodded, well pleased, and it was true. Most of all, I loved those times when I went into the galleries and could observe our rich customers examine and discuss the articles which they were wealthy enough to buy. My favourite client was an old man who never bought anything. With their usual courtesy, my employers allowed him to browse among the treasures. By the way he stroked the objects I could tell he was a connoisseur, and I loved the gentle, absent-minded smile with which he accepted the cup of tea I sometimes made for him. On the afternoon of the concert he was the last to leave the gallery and as I hurried down the road I saw him waiting at the bus stop, probably still immersed in the past and finding it more rewarding than the present.

I was early at the Greek restaurant where I had arranged to meet Lois but when she hadn't arrived after half an hour I decided to go ahead and order my meal. I couldn't believe that she would let me down, but by the time I had finished eating she had still not turned up and I began to feel anxious. It was getting late so I had to hurry to the concert hall. I left her ticket at the box office, in the hope that she would pick it up there if something had happened to detain her.

The seats were excellent and I looked around me with interest. I had not been there many minutes before I saw Ian Owen enter the hall in the company of an elegant woman in her late thirties. He seemed in high good humour as they laughed with their heads together.

There was rapturous applause for the orchestra and the majestic figure of the tenor himself, and then I gave myself up to the magic of his voice, which effortlessly filled the enormous auditorium. I had looked forward to the evening for days, but now, although the music was a joy I was very conscious of the empty seat beside me. By the time the interval arrived I knew Lois was not coming.

As I hurried home after the concert I was torn between anger and anxiety, and when I heard laughter and conversation coming from the sitting room I threw open the door furiously. Marcia and Joyce were sitting on the settee in front of the fire and they turned, startled at my explosive entrance.

'I thought Lois was in here,' I gasped.

'I thought she was with you,' Marcia said.

'No, I waited at the restaurant and she didn't come, and she didn't turn up for the concert, either.'

'Oh well,' Marcia shrugged philosophically, 'I've stopped trying to understand Lois these days. I haven't seen her since breakfast.'

I made an excuse that I was tired and wished them goodnight – somehow I wasn't in the mood for careless chatter. My dreams were troublesome and I awoke with a start, seeing from my bedside clock that it was almost three o'clock. All desire for sleep left me; I got out of bed and struggled into my dressing gown. I was plagued by all the anxieties of the previous night, and wanted to see if Lois was ready to give me an explanation.

My slippers made no noise as I walked along the corridor, and without knocking on her door I opened it and went inside. The curtains were not drawn and the room was lit up by the street lamps which cast eerie shadows on the walls and ceiling. I looked towards the bed but it was empty. I snapped on the light in disbelief, but the bedclothes were not disturbed and I sank down on to the edge of it desperately afraid. After a few minutes however, commonsense got the better of me and I went to her wardrobe to see if I could discover what she might be wearing.

Her best camel coat had gone, and hesitantly I went to stand at the window. For a second I thought of rousing Marcia, then deciding against it hurried to my room and started to dress, throwing on jeans and a thick sweater. Grabbing my coat and a warm scarf, I ran silently down the stairs and let myself out of the front door.

The damp night air felt cold, and shivering a little I hurried to the gate and opened it. The empty street stretched before me but I made myself hurry towards the lights of the main thoroughfare ahead. Two vagrants occupied a bench outside the little park, snoring heavily. I paused. It was foolish to go on – I had no idea where to look. Instead, I should be telephoning her father, or if the worst came to the worst, the police. Disconsolately I made my way back to the house and then I saw her, coming from the opposite direction and walking slowly like a sleepwalker. I took to my heels and ran towards her.

She stared at me dully and I stared back. Lois' hair hung damp and dark round her face and for a moment there was no recognition in her gaze. Then she smiled, the saddest smile I had ever seen and I felt the rush of tears into my eyes. Practically I said, 'Lois – what are you doing here? You should have been in bed hours ago. You're absolutely soaking – do you want another bout of pneumonia? Come back to the house and I'll make you some coffee.'

She allowed me to take her arm and lead her through the gate, then waited like a child while I unlocked the door and drew her inside. I heated milk and made two mugs of coffee, shivering and clenching my teeth to stop them from chattering. Lois accepted the coffee without a word and I sat beside her at the table, relieved when the hot drink brought some semblance of warmth into my limbs. After a few minutes I asked gently, 'When did you last have something to eat?'

She looked at me absently. I might have been asking when had she last visited Mars, then after a few moments her face cleared a little and she said faintly, 'I'm not hungry, thank you.'

'It's very late, where have you been?'

'Walking.'

'Alone?'

'Yes, of course.'

'Lois – it's well after three in the morning. You can't have been walking all night. Please tell me where you've been and what you've been doing.'

Her eyes grew wild and solemn like a hurt child, and like a child she said, 'Please don't scold me, I can walk if I want to. I like walking.'

'If you've finished your coffee we should go to bed. I can't think that you'll be fit for work in the morning.'

At the mention of work some degree of awareness crept into her expression and for the first time my anxiety seemed to reach her. 'I'm sorry you were worried, Nancy. I'm perfectly all right, honestly. What time did you say it was?'

'After three.'

'Oh dear. I've finished my coffee now, I think I'll go to bed.'

With a murmured goodnight she left me staring after her, with the realisation that I would learn nothing more that night.

Several days later she said to me 'When is that concert, Nancy? I've forgotten where we decided to meet.'

'The concert was last week. I waited but you didn't come so I went to it alone.'

She stared at me in disbelief, then to my horror put her head in her hands and sobbed uncontrollably. After a while she said in a shaky voice, 'Was that the night you came to look for me?'

'Yes.'

'Nancy, I'm sorry. Do you hate me very much?'

'I don't hate you at all. I'm just feeling so very helpless that you're obviously, very unhappy and I don't know what I can do about it.'

'There's nothing you can do, there's nothing anybody can do.'

'If it's so hopeless, don't you think you should try to forget about him? Because of him you're losing your identity, you're letting your friends and your father down. Is a man who doesn't love you worth all that?'

It was almost as if she hadn't heard me. Instead she said as if suddenly remembering, 'I thought I could go there first and still be in time to meet you, yes, that's what I thought – and then the time just went on and on and because I'd waited so long I had to go on waiting until he went out.'

'He went out?' I prompted gently.

'Well, yes. I knew he was in, I saw the light in his flat. There's a little teashop almost opposite so I waited in there.' She giggled. 'The waitress kept on serving me tea and gawping at me, then she brought the bill and said they were closing. She wasn't very nice – she could see I was waiting for somebody and it had started to rain.'

'Who were you waiting for?' I asked, but she ignored my question.

'I had to stand in a doorway and people kept on staring at me so I pretended to look up the road as though I was waiting for somebody. I saw him come out but I don't know what time it was. He was wearing a dinner jacket and he hailed a taxi instead of driving himself. He was alone but I knew he must be meeting somebody so you see I had to wait for him to come back to see if she was with him.'

'How long did you wait?'

'I knew he wouldn't come back until much later so I went into an Italian Restaurant and had a meal. I've been there many times before – I like going there, it's so near his flat. I can go there and feel close to him. I know the names of all the men who visit him, I know some of the women, too. I learn about those from his secretary.'

Every word she uttered left me horrified. This was a cruel and agonising obsession and while I wanted to tell her that Ian Owen had been at the concert in the company of a woman obviously well known to him, I couldn't; instead I had to listen to her gentle plaintive voice saying, 'I waited and waited but he didn't come back. Then a policeman asked me who I was waiting for and he was kind, he told me I was getting wet and it was time I went home. I wandered about a bit after that, but I didn't dare go back to his flat in case the policeman was still there. I don't remember much after that until you met me in the street.'

'Lois, you promised when I came to London that we'd do things together, but we never have. Why don't you come home with me for Christmas? My parents would love to see you again – and then in the New Year we could make a real effort to do all the things we promised ourselves.'

She stared at me for a few minutes, then started to hunt in her handbag. 'I'd forgotten about Christmas. I've got a letter from my mother somewhere, I think it's Christmas when she's coming.'

After a few minutes she found what she was looking for and opening out the letter she started to read through it.

'Yes, here it is. *"We'll be arriving on the 21st of December and will be staying at the Grosvenor House Hotel. We hope to see a great deal of you, darling."* She doesn't say if the brat is coming with them.'

This was more like the Lois I knew and I laughed. 'He's probably changed a lot since you last saw him. You might even like him now.'

'So you see why I can't go to Lancashire with you, Nancy. I'll have to see Mother, and Dad I suppose, although the last I heard he was hoping to join some friends in France for Christmas.'

'Will he see your mother, do you think?'

'I'm not sure. Oh, it's all very civilised – they do speak when they meet, they even manage to appear quite solicitous about each other's welfare but I'm never very sure how much sincerity is behind it all.'

In the days leading up to Christmas I saw little of Lois. One Saturday afternoon she arrived home carrying brightly wrapped presents but I was on my way out to the Barbican Centre, where there was an exhibition of Lowry's paintings. I was staring at one canvas in rapt attention when a voice behind me said, 'One either likes Lowry or one doesn't. Personally I do like his works, without ever wanting to own one.'

I turned to find Desmond Atherton smiling down at me. 'Tell me how you enjoyed the concert?' he said smoothly.

'It was wonderful. Thank you so much for letting me have the tickets.' He didn't ask about Lois and I was glad – I didn't want to tell him that one of the tickets had been wasted.

We loitered together around the exhibition and by the time we left it was dark and a fine drizzle of snow was falling.

'I wonder if we shall have a white Christmas,' I mused. 'I can't ever remember one.'

'You are going north for Christmas?'

'Yes.'

'Then you might just manage it. If it is snowing in London it's probably snowing twice as much in the north.'

I held out my hand, saying, 'It was nice meeting you again. I hope you have a good Christmas.'

'Thank you, Nancy. Shall we start it tonight by your having dinner with me – that is, unless you've nothing better to do.'

I wanted to accept his invitation but underneath my coat I was only wearing a plain black woollen skirt and matching sweater, with a double row of imitation jade beads. 'I'm not sure that I'm dressed for dining out,' I said uncertainly.

'I'm taking you somewhere where the food is excellent and one doesn't have to dress up. People go there to eat well rather than to be seen.'

The restaurant was a charming place lit by discreet wall-lights and candlelight, and we sat at a corner table where we could see everybody who entered. While Desmond scanned the wine list I was very aware of his profile, the sheen of his fair hair and when he looked up and smiled my heart lurched painfully.

He was a man who could converse easily on many topics, and be a good listener as well. I found our dinner together an exhilarating experience.

We had reached the coffee stage when a couple entered the restaurant and I found myself staring at the man curiously. I felt I should know him, and yet I was equally sure that we had never met. As they passed our table

Desmond looked up and said quickly, 'Well, this is a surprise! We don't often see you in London, Noel. Has the shoulder healed well?' Desmond had risen from the table and the two men were shaking hands while the girl looked on with a smile. Then Desmond was introducing me to Noel Templeton and his companion, whose name was Libby.

After they had moved on to their table and Desmond was sitting down again he said, 'I should have told Noel that you were once in journalism. He would have been interested.'

I remembered him now, the man in the picture on Father's desk, the man he admired so much, and in a small voice I said, 'I can't think Mr Templeton would be very interested in my sort of journalism. It was very provincial and small-time.'

'We all have to start somewhere, my dear.'

'I know, but he's made the big time, hasn't he? Do you suppose the girl is in journalism too?'

'Perhaps.'

'She's very attractive.'

He smiled. 'Templeton isn't married. I see very little of him but whenever I do he invariably has a pretty girl with him. He leads an exciting life. Next week he could be in the Gulf or South America – wherever there's trouble, in fact.'

'Being married to a man like that could be a fairly harrowing experience.'

'Yes, indeed. Maybe that's the reason he's in no hurry to settle down.'

I looked across the room to where Noel Templeton and his companion were chatting amicably and to my consternation he looked up, inclining his head with a half-smile. They were still dining when we left the restaurant at just after ten, but as Desmond helped me on with my coat I felt their eyes on us and we turned to call goodnight.

Desmond laughed as we made our way out into the

street. 'Noel is curious,' he said easily. 'I don't often entertain young women to dinner.'

I believed that his words were designed to tell me something – but I wasn't sure what. I knew nothing of his private life, not even whether he was married, separated or single. All I *did* know was that Desmond Atherton attracted me so strongly I hadn't wanted the evening to end, and a vague feeling of loss washed over me when he hailed a taxi to take me home.

'I live within walking distance, Nancy. Have a very happy Christmas,' were his parting words.

13

Suddenly I was a child again, sitting in Aunt Susan's dining room with its heavy mahogany furniture and view of snow-capped lakeland hills. Her tongue had lost none of its sharpness as she argued with Father about the new young doctor in Grandfather's surgery and the discrepancies of the Council and its workforce . . . Mother as usual took no part in all this, busy no doubt with her own thoughts. I diplomatically kept my head down, savouring the wonderful home-cooked food.

Father grinned at me mischievously across the table. 'Are you going to see Maisie, love? I told her mother you were coming home for Christmas.'

'Oh yes, definitely. Do you happen to know if Barbara's with her parents this Christmas?'

'She doesn't seem to come home very much, if at all,' my mother said. 'Her parents have been down there to visit her and Martin several times, but I don't think her father's too happy about things.'

Maisie was rather more forthright when I saw her on Boxing Day. The new baby slept in her pram while Peter played quietly with his new toys in front of the fire. The living room was littered with Lego, wrapping paper and animals: two enormous tabbies sat on the windowsill and a dog gnawed at a rubber bone on the hearthrug near the child. In one corner of the room a budgerigar chattered in its cage and seeing me looking round the room Maisie said apologetically, 'It's that cluttered, Nancy. If I'd known you were coming today I'd have made an effort at tidying it up. You know what Christmas is like.'

'You've a lot to do Maisie, you can't have much time to yourself.'

'Well, I'm not too houseproud when the children are

around. After all, I want it to look like home: I'm not one for pushing them in a room and closing the door behind them. When Tom gets home tonight everything'll be straight and in its place. This has been our busiest time, what with the fowl to be plucked and dressed, and all the delivering.'

'But you're happy?'

'Heavens yes, didn't I always say I would be? I love being a farmer's wife. True, I never have a minute to myself, but I enjoy it anyway. Now I want to hear about you, Nancy. You live a far more exciting life than me.'

I told her about my job, I even told her about Desmond but I didn't confide in her about Lois. Maisie with her happy ordered life would never in a thousand years understand the disorders of Lois' tormented mind.

'Do you ever hear from Barbara?' she queried.

'Well, no. She sent my Christmas card to Greymont, so perhaps she hasn't got my London address. I never expected her to write to me, though. She always did say she was a rotten correspondent.'

'She doesn't seem to come up here much these days. Leastways, I've never seen her and my mother says according to Mrs Smythe they're far too busy. They've joined the tennis club and they both play golf. Barbara's on all sorts of charitable committees and her husband's making money hand over fist. It wouldn't matter to me how much Tom was making, I'd never stay away from my folks. You wouldn't, either.'

'No, I suppose not.'

Maisie produced tea and Christmas cake, then went to rummage in a drawer of the sideboard, returning with a newspaper cutting which she thrust into my hands. 'Did your Dad show you this, Nancy? I kept it specially to show you.'

It was a photograph of Amelia and Mark standing in one of the rooms of her father's house. She was wearing her wedding dress and looked as she always looked – serene and ethereal. Her long gown was simple but exquisitely cut, and she was wearing a large hat trimmed with flowers. Standing beside her Mark looked elegant in his grey morning dress but it was Maisie who put my thoughts into words. 'They look to have about as much life in them as that statue in the background! It's a marriage of convenience, that's all, like the ones you read about in one o' them romantic novels.'

'Except that it doesn't appear to be so romantic.'

'She's living here at Garveston Hall now. Apparently she shops in the village and is always nice to the shop-keepers and the villagers. I can believe that easily enough. Amelia always was nice to everybody.'

'Yes, she was. I wonder if she's really happy?'

'Well, one thing's for sure – we'll never know! Just like we'll never have that reunion she was so keen on. She won't be bothering with us now.'

I thought a lot about Amelia as I tramped down the farm-track towards the village, and that night when I got home I said to Father, 'Maisie showed me a photograph of Amelia's wedding. Did you get to print one in the local paper?'

'We didn't bother. The national papers all reported it, so by the time we could have got hold of something it would have been old news.' My father had aged: there was more grey in his hair and he looked tired. When I asked him if he was well he merely grinned and said 'I'm getting too old to stand on frozen football pitches love, and I've had a bad cough I can't seem to get rid of. Don't say anything to your mother, mind. You know what a worrier she can be.'

On my return to London, the house in Hammersmith felt unwelcoming and cold. I hurried to light the gas fire in the living room before going upstairs to unpack. On my bedside table I was surprised to find a note propped up against the lamp. I recognised Lois' handwriting: the note was to tell me that she was dining out with her mother and stepfather and I was invited to meet them at their hotel on New Year's Eve.

Lois' mother was an older version of her daughter, while her stepfather was jovial and anxious to entertain us. They showed us photographs of their lovely big house and their son Brett, who was back in the States with his American grandma, recovering from a tonsillectomy. I felt embarrassed when Lois merely looked through the snapshots in a perfunctory manner. To cover her moroseness I chattered on endlessly, and when the couple invited me to visit them again with Lois in the near future, I accepted their invitation, although I felt pretty sure we would not be taking advantage of it.

'You young things should be at a fun party seeing the New Year in, instead of dining with us. What happened to your boyfriends?' the stepfather said heartily.

'I hope you'll tell us when there is someone,' her mother said plaintively, but Lois changed the subject abruptly, then surprised me by saying it was time we left, as we were in fact due at some friends' to see the New Year in.

There were no friends, but I think Lois' parents were relieved to put us in a taxi at half-past eleven and kiss us both goodbye. The streets were filled with revellers but Lois sat sulkily in her corner of the taxi and I said, 'Why did you have to lie to them? They were trying to be so kind and it is New Year's Eve, after all.'

'They embarrass me,' she answered shortly. 'They try *too* hard.'

She sat at the kitchen table while I made coffee, then we took it into the living room. For an eternity we sat in silence, then something of Lois' old humour surfaced; she said smiling, 'I've got a bottle of wine in the fridge, let me go and fetch it. Like you said, Nancy, it *is* New Year's Eve.'

As we sipped our wine, I chatted on about Maisie and her family, and then introduced the subject of Amelia's wedding, but I thought Lois was only half-listening. Curled up in an old-fashioned velvet chair, glass in hand, her eyes were watching me and yet I suspected her

145

thoughts were miles away. After a while she made an effort at conversation saying, 'Dad's joined a skiing party in France for this holiday. He said he wasn't asking me to go too because I ought to spend some time with my mother, but that wasn't the real reason, of course. More likely he's got a new girl with him.'

'Oh Lois, you can't be sure.'

'I know David better than you do. We all dined together on Christmas Eve, and it was gruesome. My stepfather was hearty, Mother was subdued and Father over-friendly. The tension was awful. You don't know how lucky you are to have a normal family.'

I made myself ask her. 'Have you seen Him over Christmas?'

'He's gone away. At least, he isn't at his flat.'

'Why don't you make a New Year's resolution to get over this man? After all, there's nothing to remember, nothing you've done together.'

'When I know there's somebody serious in his life then I'll make the effort. Until then, there's always hope.'

We finished the bottle of wine and Lois began to unwind. We found ourselves laughing at our early days at Lorivals, and then she stood on the hearthrug and did a remarkably accurate performance of Miss Clarkson's farewell speech. 'You are the chosen ones,' she chirruped. 'Never forget that the stamp of Lorivals will be on you always.'

'Do you feel like a chosen one?' I asked her tipsily.

'But of course. Here we are on New Year's Eve all alone drinking a bottle of plonk. There's Maisie with her brood, probably the happiest of the lot of us, and Amelia with a make-do marriage.'

'What about Barbara? At least she's living like a chosen one.'

'She's a Mrs Newly Rich – hardly the sort of existence Miss Clarkson meant.'

'Why don't we go out on to the street and join in the revelry?'

'Yes, come on! We shouldn't be sitting here like two old maids getting quietly sloshed.'

We grabbed our coats and ran towards the gate, about to fling it open when we looked at each other in sudden doubt. Catching hold of Lois' arm I cried, 'Do we really want to go out there and have some drunken youths embrace us as though there's no tomorrow?'

Quietly we closed the gates and returned to the house.

The galleries of Treasures of the Orient were busy in the New Year period and I stayed close to Mr Papadraos in the hope of absorbing some of his words of wisdom about the articles on display.

Once I saw Desmond Atherton come into one of the rooms and despite his apparent interest in a selection of 15th-century ink-blocks, I felt sure he had come to see me, and I wished my heart would stop thumping so painfully. It was much later when he joined me to chat knowledgeably about Chinese art while Mr Ho Ying smiled approvingly before wandering away diplomatically.

'When did you get back to London?' he asked softly.

'Last Wednesday.'

'And what did you do on New Year's Eve? I almost called you.'

'I dined with Lois' mother and stepfather who are here from America.'

'Then it's just as well I didn't. I have a god-daughter who has a birthday next week – I know she collects miniature boxes, so will you look at them with me?'

We had a good selection, but I felt he had asked me to help him so that we could stand together – he was quite capable of choosing one without any assistance from me. He picked them up one by one, asking me which one I liked, and we both agreed on his final choice of one the colour of a butterfly's wing its lid of delicate gold filigree. I wrapped his gift in a sheet of elegant paper finished off with a tiny gold rosette, so absorbed in my task I wasn't aware that a plump woman in a flimsy peach outfit had joined us until she said overbearingly, 'I would love to be able to wrap a parcel like that but I'm afraid mine go sadly awry. Which one did you finally choose, Desmond?'

'What a pity you didn't see it before it was wrapped,' Desmond replied easily. 'I chose the pale blue box, as my god-daughter is particularly fond of blue. Thank you,' he said formally, holding out his hand for the small parcel.

I turned away and joined Mr Ho Ying who smiled and whispered, 'That was Mrs Etherington-Grant – she will not buy anything. She knows she can purchase similar items more cheaply in Hong Kong.'

'She lives in Hong Kong?'

'Yes. Her husband is a British Trade Commissioner there. She will know Mr Atherton well from his time in the colony.'

She was walking between Desmond and her husband into one of the other galleries now and my attention was claimed by an elderly gentleman who also wished to look at the tiny boxes. I did not expect to see Desmond again so I was very surprised when he returned to the gallery just before closing time. He came straight to me, smiling at my surprise.

'I intended to ask you before, Nancy, but not in front of Mrs Etherington-Grant. The woman's a born gossip. If you haven't another engagement, will you have dinner with me tonight?'

'I'm not sure if I'm suitably dressed.'

'Please don't worry – you look charming. Let's go – I have my car in the car park at the back of the gallery.'

As we emerged into the stream of evening traffic I looked across the road to see the Etherington-Grants hailing a passing taxi. Desmond smiled cynically, but made no comment. I felt momentarily uncomfortable until he covered my hand with his and with a brief smile said, 'I knew the Etherington-Grants in Hong Kong. He was tolerated, but she was an inveterate gossip – nobody was spared. I have the distinct feeling that she's kept tabs on me all afternoon.'

'Do you mind?'

'I mind that she knows anything at all about my whereabouts or my friends, but while in Hong Kong she was formidable, here in London she is relatively unimportant. Don't let her worry you, my dear. As far as you're concerned, she doesn't matter.'

I had no idea at that moment just how much she would matter at a future stage in my life.

Lorivals had not prepared me for loving Desmond Atherton. It had conditioned me for boys like Mark, quick to laughter and too sure of themselves. Young men who drove fast sports cars and fancied themselves on the tennis courts, boys who were not ashamed to boast about their conquests but who were basically immature.

When I thought about loving Mark I knew now that that too had been immature, my first excursion into womanhood. Our relationship had never been destined to last, but I had no certainty that this new love was destined to last, either. I was in love with a man who was as elusive as the Scarlet Pimpernel. To be with him was ecstasy but I never knew, when he said goodnight, when the next meeting would be, only that there would be another time.

Spring turned into summer, and summer into autumn and if there were days and weekends when I didn't see Desmond our next meeting would feel the same as if we had met only yesterday. He opened my eyes to the beauties of gently flowing rivers and long country twilights, to ancient castles and rolling downs, and in the evenings to music and great orchestras, but I came no nearer to learning his true feelings about me.

Deliberately I asked no questions, and hence knew no

more about the real Desmond than I had known during that first weekend in Gloucestershire. By tacit agreement he never came to the house in Hammersmith for me, but invariably met me at work or in some favourite restaurant, and although I knew now where he lived, he never invited me to his flat.

I desperately wanted to ask Marcia if she knew anything about his background, but pride prevented me and I did not want to ask Lois. She had not wanted to confide in me about the man she loved, so why should I talk to her about Desmond? Besides, Lois was seldom in the house these days. She avoided me at breakfast and whenever I suggested we go to a cinema together she invariably had something better to do.

One morning I saw her walking in St James' Park with a middle-aged woman I had not seen before. They sat on a bench to eat their sandwiches and it was the older woman who did most of the talking while Lois seemed to hang on to her every word.

I believed this woman to be the secretary of the man Lois was in love with, for how else could they have had anything in common? The woman was plainly dressed and I allowed my imagination full rein. I thought she would be efficient and loyal, dedicated to a government job with a decent pension at the end of it, and probably with one or two aging parents to support. She would be flattered to be made much of by a younger woman with an obvious crush on her boss, flattered that she was able to reveal something of his private life yet able to remain discreet about his public one.

I felt faintly sickened as I watched Lois' gentle probings, wishing I could walk over to their bench and join them but knowing I would not be made welcome, not by Lois at any rate. I waited until they had finished their sandwiches and began their walk back to the Foreign Office, still chatting, unaware that they had been under observation.

It was the end of November and I was glad that we

were quiet at Treasures of the Orient so that I could get away early. Desmond had bought tickets for a new play which was getting rave reviews and we were to dine early. Halfway through the afternoon I was told that there was a telephone call for me and thinking it was Desmond ringing to say he might be detained, I was surprised to hear Aunt Susan's voice at the other end of the line.

'I'm glad I could get you without much trouble,' she began in a strangely shaky voice. 'It's your father, Nancy. We'd like you to come home, today if that's possible. It's urgent, my dear.'

'But what is it, Aunt Susan? Is Father ill?' For a few seconds there was silence, and in a trembling voice I urged, 'Aunt Susan, what's wrong?'

'Your father's dead, Nancy. He had a massive heart attack at the *Gazette*. Your mother needs you at home.'

I sank down on the nearest chair feeling suddenly faint and utterly disbelieving. People were kind, cups of tea appeared and a taxi was summoned to take me home so that I could pack what was needed for the journey and my stay in the north. I was doubly touched when on offering to pay for the taxi I was told that Mr Papadraos had already settled up with the driver.

It was while I was packing that I suddenly remembered Desmond. Somehow I had to let him know, but how? He had told me he would not be in his office during the afternoon and the restaurant did not open until five-thirty. There was no alternative but to leave a message at his flat. Hurriedly I scribbled a brief note, informing him what had happened.

Asking the taxi driver to wait, I ran quickly up the steps leading to the opulent block of flats where Desmond lived. An elderly man stood at the desk in the main hall sorting out mail and I interrupted him quickly to ask if he would hand my note to Mr Desmond Atherton immediately he came in, hoping against hope that Desmond would return home before leaving for our rendezvous. The porter laid my letter on one side after assuring me that he would see Mr Atherton received it and then I hurried out of the building.

I was at the top of the steps when I saw Desmond and another man walking up towards me. Our eyes met, and if there was relief in mine, in his I read first of all surprise, and then for a split second only, annoyance. It went so quickly I could have imagined it, but in my misery I knew I hadn't. For that one brief moment I was a nuisance, I was bothering him by encroaching into that world he had been so determined to keep private, and my vulnerable young pride and shock at my beloved father's death brought the sharp tears into my eyes. I would have run past him if he hadn't caught hold of my arm.

'Nancy,' he said. 'Is something wrong?'

'I'm sorry I came to your flat, Desmond,' I sobbed. 'I couldn't think how else to let you know. I'm going home – my father is dead.' I put a hand over my eyes.

'Oh, you poor child! When did this happen?'

'I can't talk now, I have a taxi waiting, I must go.'

'Then I'll go with you to the station, you mustn't be left alone.'

'Please, I'd rather go alone. I'm all right. I've left a note for you at the desk.'

'Will you let me know when you're coming back? I'll meet your train.'

'Very well, I'll let you know.'

I tore my arm away from his grasp and rushed headlong down the steps. In the taxi I looked up to find him staring after me, then I sobbed bitterly into my handkerchief. My father was dead and I had no faith in a future with Desmond. I had not imagined it: I could see it still, that cold haughty stare that had been there for only a second before the shutters had come down.

14

I missed my train by ten minutes and there was over an hour to wait for the next one. I was shivering with cold and misery as I took my cup of coffee to an empty table in the refreshment lounge.

Around me was conversation and laughter. People were waiting to meet friends, others preparing to travel, but I felt completely isolated from them as memories brought hot stinging tears uncontrollably into my eyes. It had always been my father who had brought enchantment into my life. Mother was the sweet elusive one, too ready to be dominated by an older, more intrepid sister, while Father had opened my eyes and ears to life with its joy and mystery, its adventure and its tragedy. Now he was dead and I would never listen to him again.

I groped in my handbag for a handkerchief but looked up sharply when I saw a man's hand already holding out a large clean white one for me. Peering through a blur of tears I took the handkerchief and dabbed at my eyes, then when they cleared a little I looked again at the face and recognised it.

Noel Templeton was looking at me gravely, his dark eyes sombre in his lean tanned face. I stumbled over an apology.

He smiled. 'I was sitting over there when you came in,' he said gently. 'I thought you looked upset and I wondered what had happened. You don't have to tell me if you'd rather not, although sometimes it helps to talk about it, even to a stranger.'

'You're not a complete stranger,' I said in a trembling voice.

'Well, no, not if you can count the times we've dined in the same restaurant.'

'Before that, I'd heard about you from my father.'

'From the newspapers, I suppose?'

'Yes, he was a newspaper man, a local reporter up north.'

'Was?'

'Yes. He died yesterday – I'm going home to his funeral.'

The eyes darkened and his face showed concern. 'I am sorry, what a rotten journey you're embarked on. I know we've been introduced but I can't for the moment remember your name.'

'Nancy Graham.'

He nodded. 'I am sorry, Nancy. Do you have a mother, brothers and sisters?'

'Only my mother.'

'You say your father was a reporter on a local paper, which is how most of us start out. Which paper was it?'

'The *Greymont Gazette*.'

'That's strange, my father started his career with the *Gazette*.'

'I know. My father knew him. He showed me a picture of you one day and said that you were the kind of journalist he'd wanted to be, but somehow or other it had eluded him. I worked with him on the paper for a while after I left school, but I got awfully tired of reviewing local weddings and sporting events.'

'I know, that's when I decided I had to move on. But you're not in journalism now?'

'No, I work for a firm of oriental importers.'

'You don't regret it?'

'No, I'm very happy there but I scribble in my spare time.'

'Oh well, if you ever get fed up with your job if writing is in you it will surface.' He smiled before consulting his watch, and I felt he had been talking about journalism to keep my mind occupied with other things than my father's death. 'I'm catching the next train for Manchester – is that your train, too?' he said, rising to his feet.

'No. I'm going to Lancaster – my train isn't due for another half hour.'

'Then I must go. Keep the handkerchief, I have another one.' He held out his hand and took mine in a firm grip. His hand felt like an anchor and I had the urge to hold on to it, to drown in the concern I read in his eyes, the sweetness of his smile, then I was watching him shoulder his way through the crowd that hung around the station hall.

If only my father had been alive, he would have delighted in hearing that I had actually been speaking with Noel Templeton. Once more a wave of misery passed over me and I wept a little into Noel's handkerchief.

Rain was dancing on the pavements when I emerged from Lancaster station but the daunting rush of evening traffic was over and I had no difficulty in making my way to the bus stop where I was relieved to find a bus waiting to start its journey to Greymont. There were few travellers, and I sat looking through the window at the grey city drenched in rain, the street lights shining eerily through the gloom.

The streets of Greymont were practically deserted and I put up my collar to trudge the distance to my home. My case was not heavy, but coping with luggage and an umbrella was not an easy task and I was glad when I arrived at the front gate. Through the glass in the front door I could see that a light burned in the hall and I hunted in my bag for my key.

As I closed the front door behind me I could hear voices at the back of the house and then the door opened and light streamed out of the dining room into the hall. For a moment my mother and I stared at each other without speaking then I went forward and put my arms around her. She was crying quietly.

For several minutes we talked about the rain, my

155

saturated coat, my dripping suitcase, then when I had taken them into the kitchen to dry I went into the dining room. A tall, well-built man stood on the rug in front of the fireplace and when I entered he smiled and held out his hand.

'You probably don't remember me,' he said pleasantly. 'I'm Roger Fellows. I lived next door until I emigrated to Canada some years ago, but you were only a youngster then.'

I only vaguely remembered that we had had neighbours who had gone to live in Canada, but without waiting to hear if I remembered him or not he continued, 'I hope I've been of some assistance to your mother. It was providential that I should be visiting the old country when your father died.'

Mother turned quickly to say, 'Roger's been very kind, Nancy. He's helped with all the funeral arrangements and Arthur was so careless about things. Some of his papers were here, some were at his office, but everything's going to be taken care of now.'

'Thank you, Mr Fellows,' I said quietly.

'Please call me Roger,' he said easily. 'I'm glad to have been of service.'

'Aunt Susan said Father died very suddenly,' I prompted my mother.

'Yes, but he hadn't really been well all summer. He'd been out all afternoon standing in the cold at old Alderman Biggins' funeral, and instead of coming straight home to write his report he went back to the office. It was there that he had the heart attack. They took him to the hospital, but he was already dead. They couldn't do anything.' Her voice broke and she struggled for control. 'Now, have you eaten, Nancy? We had something at around five – I wasn't hungry but Roger's been out all afternoon seeing to things, so I did bacon and egg. Will you have that?'

'I had something in London, Mother, so I'm not hungry. Shall I make some tea?'

156

'You go into the other room and chat,' Roger said quickly. 'I'll make the tea and bring it in to you.'

The fire in the lounge had burned low so while Mother added coal I looked round the familiar room. Nothing had changed – it was still a charming room, with a pale green carpet on the floor and chintz covers on the suite. When Mother turned to face me again she indicated a small desk standing open near the wall on which already stood a pile of letters.

'Your father was very well thought of, Nancy. All those have already arrived – it's nice to know Arthur was well-respected. I'll be glad when the funeral's over, though. It will be a large one.'

She was right about the funeral. Employees of the *Gazette* stood together under the dripping trees, headed by Mr McKay the owner of the newspaper, and there were representatives from the police and the fire services, social clubs and dramatic societies and so many others my father had written about.

After the service Mr McKay came to speak with me, his face kind. Taking my hand in his firm grip, he began, 'Well, love, we'll certainly be missing your father. He was the best reporter we ever had, irreplaceable. You could have been like him if you'd stayed. Why didn't you?'

'Itchy feet, a need to spread my wings.'

'And you haven't regretted leaving journalism? Your father was a bit upset about that.'

'I'm happy in my job, it's interesting and different.'

'Well love, if you ever feel like coming back to Greymont we'll find a place for you on the *Gazette*. You won't forget, will you lass?'

I walked to the church gates with Barbara's father while her mother stayed to look at the wreaths which covered the ground round the church.

'How is Barbara?' I asked, sad that she had been unable to attend.

'Well, we don't see much of her these days, Nancy.

Her mother likes to visit down there, and then she goes on and on about their house, their friends and their money until I feel like telling her to pipe down but they don't come up here much. Look at Maisie there, happy as a sandboy with those bonnie children of hers. Now that's how I wanted to see our Barbara – I was hoping for a few grandchildren.'

'It's not too late, Mr Smythe.'

'Oh, but it is. They don't want children – they'd interfere too much with the good life they think they're having. Me and Martin don't exactly see eye to eye, which means me and Barbara are not as close as we used to be. Aye well. Is there a young man in your life, love?'

'Nobody special.'

'But there's plenty of time – getting married from the schoolroom wasn't a good idea where our girl was concerned but I must say it's worked for young Maisie Standing.'

We ate our funeral tea at Aunt Susan's: the talk was all about the service and the flowers, and I was glad to see that Mother was bearing up well. It was Roger Fellows who brought up the question of Christmas and Aunt Susan was quick to say, 'We always spend Christmas Day together. When are you due to return to Canada, Mr Fellows?'

'At the beginning of December, Miss Lester. I promised myself a month in England and I'd like to be home for Christmas.'

'Do you have a family?' I asked him.

'My wife died five years ago and we never had any children. I have a sister who lives close by and I've a very nice house in a small town called Hamilton. Life's been good to us out there.'

'You've been so kind, Roger. I don't know what I'd have done without you,' Mother said gratefully.

'You'd have had to manage,' Aunt Susan said tartly, 'like a lot of other people. And anyway, you had me to help you. You'll be here for Christmas I hope,' she ended, eyeing me sternly.

Before I could answer Roger said quietly, 'I've been trying to persuade Mary to come to Canada for a few weeks. The change would do her good, help her get over this sad time more quickly. I believe I've almost convinced her.'

'What will people say?' Aunt Susan snapped. 'The first Christmas after Arthur's death and you gallivanting off to Canada. Besides, you should be at home for your daughter.'

'But why should she?' I cried. 'I don't have to come home for Christmas, I can stay in London and spend it with Lois. Do you want to go to Canada, Mother?'

She stared at me nonplussed for several seconds, then hesitantly she said, 'Well, Roger has been trying to persuade me but I wasn't able to think straight. Now I think it might not be a bad idea. I'll be all alone when you've gone back and frankly, I was dreading the next few months.'

'When are you all alone?' Aunt Susan cried, outraged. 'I'm here, aren't I!'

'Well yes, I know you are dear, but you have your committees, magistrate's duties and friends I haven't even met. I couldn't expect you to be with me all the time and neglect your other commitments.'

'Then you'll come,' Roger urged eagerly.

She looked at me, and I nodded my acceptance so that she turned to say, 'Yes, I will Roger. Just for a week or so. Thank you for your kind invitation.'

'For a month or so Mary,' he said firmly. 'It will be winter with a vengeance in Canada, there'll be snow everywhere but that doesn't say you won't love it. Stay until the spring, stay as long as you want.'

He was looking at my mother with affection, like a big shaggy dog and I knew he was in love with her. For my mother it was too soon – all she wanted was a shoulder to cry on, a time to lick her wounds, a time to heal, but I was sure that in the months to come some-thing warmer than friendship awaited her in Canada. I had never been surer of anything in my entire life, but the certainty only made me sad and I found myself remembering the cold withdrawn expression in Desmond's eyes.

That night I wrote to him to say I would be travelling home on Sunday evening and expected to arrive in London around nine-thirty. The ball was back in his court.

15

My train back to London was late by half an hour and it was a chill misty evening when I finally stepped down on to the platform at Euston Station. I had no certainty that Desmond would be there to meet me but my heart lifted when I saw him walking swiftly along the platform. He smiled and suddenly my heart raced when he put his arms around me and held me against him.

'Here, give me your case,' he said, 'you look frozen.' He took my case in one hand and held my hand in the other, walking quickly towards the bright lights of the foyer. Only once he looked down at me and in a gentle voice said, 'Was it all very terrible, Nancy?'

I nodded. Later I would talk about it, but not now when I knew my voice would tremble with emotion.

'I've asked my man to leave supper out for us – just a few sandwiches and coffee. I didn't think you'd want to eat out tonight.' I stared at him in the utmost surprise. I couldn't believe that I was being invited to his flat when I remembered his look of annoyance before. He smiled down at me. 'I don't suppose you had anything on the train, I know what Sunday travel is like.'

'No, I thought you would be taking me straight home.'

'We can't talk in the car and I'd rather take you to my flat where it's warm and comfortable. Your friends will probably be out anyway, so you could be going home to an empty house.'

I said nothing more, and then we were getting into his car and driving into the misty drizzle of the night.

I had known his flat would be tasteful. Firelight fell on old prints and leather-bound books. A long low table stood on the hearthrug and this was set with delicate china and silver. I allowed Desmond to take my coat while he indicated that I should sit near the fire and I looked round at the warm lovely room with its deep leather chairs and beautiful Chinese rugs.

There were photographs on a table near the long velvet drapes and others on the mantelpiece but before I could look at them, Desmond was coming back to me followed by a servant carrying a tray. I saw at once that he was an Oriental, but without looking at me he occupied himself by pouring coffee for us and when this was done he left, walking noiselessly out of the room.

Desmond invited me to take cream and sugar saying casually, 'I can recommend Chang Lee's sandwiches, he is an admirable servant in every respect.'

'He's Chinese?'

'Yes. I was with the diplomatic service in Peking for several years, and he has been with me since then.'

I realised I was very hungry and Chang Lee's sandwiches were excellent, as Desmond had said. We ate in silence and slowly I began to feel warm and alive, extending my hands to the blazing fire, luxuriating in its glow. Then Desmond said gently, 'Now you can tell me about your father and your visit home.'

I talked without tears, about Father's death and the old friends surrounding his grave. I told him about Mother's proposed visit to Canada and that I couldn't possibly go home to spend Christmas with Aunt Susan. When the tale was told he got up from his chair and pulled me up into his arms.

'I want to comfort you Nancy, but only time can do that. I don't think you should go home for Christmas, it will be miserable for you with your mother away.'

'She'll be away until the spring – she didn't exactly say so but I know she will. I think she might marry Roger Fellows when she's had time to think about it.'

'Would you mind about that?'

'Yes I'd mind, but I wouldn't blame her. She has her own life to live.'

'And you have yours, which is why you shouldn't go

162

home for Christmas. It's several weeks away, something will turn up.' They were not the words I had wanted to hear, and gently I drew away from him and moved towards the fire. He would have followed me but at that moment we heard the telephone ringing shrilly in the hall and then Chang Lee was there to inform Desmond of the call.

I could hear his voice, pleasant and conversational outside the room and I looked up at the photographs on the mantelpiece. They were of groups of people at various functions – dinners and shooting parties, and some of the faces I recognised from the house-party in Gloucestershire.

I moved over to the table and saw at once that here the photographs were different, more personal. One was of a boy with thick blond hair, wielding a cricket bat and laughing delightedly on a sunny afternoon in a garden, then there was one of the same boy in a group of others, all wearing blazers and school scarves, and yet another of him sitting on the grass with a little girl leaning against him while a woman sat in a garden chair smiling down at them both.

I felt my heart give a sudden sickening lurch as I picked up a photograph of a group standing before the unmistakeable frontage of Drummond, the family home of the Urquart family. I stared down at it with searching eyes that threatened to imprint it into my heart forever.

It was a picture of Lord and Lady Urquart standing with Desmond, Amelia and the unknown woman and the two children; the boy and little girl were looking up plaintively, and the girl grimly held on to the hand of the woman smiling down at her. Standing next to Desmond was Amelia, wearing a pretty silk afternoon dress in soft blues and greys, with her dark cloudy hair hanging loosely round her shoulders; her arm was linked into Desmond's, and both of them were smiling into the camera.

I did not hear Desmond return to the room, then he

163

was taking the photograph out of my hands, looking down at it as though seeing it for the first time, and the room was silent save for the coals crackling in the grate. When he looked up at last our eyes met and I sensed in his a strange misery.

He replaced the photograph on the table and went to stand on the hearthrug looking down into the flames, his face inscrutable. After a few seconds I went to stand beside him, neither of us speaking, until he reached out and drew me into his arms.

'Why did I see you looking so surprised when I came back into the room?' he asked softly.

'I recognised the house. You see, I was at school with Amelia Urquart.'

He held me away from him and looked down at me curiously. 'That was the only reason you were surprised?'

'Yes, of course. I stayed at Drummond once – it is very beautiful.'

'You felt no curiosity about the others?'

'Not then, no. I was too surprised at seeing Amelia and the house. Why, who are the others?'

'My wife and children.'

It came again, the sudden sickening lurch in my heart and the old pain of rejection which left me breathless with anger and resentment. Gently he held me against him while his voice started to talk about the years of his life of which I could have no concept, and the people in those years and I listened with my head against his breast, his chin resting on my hair.

'I met Celia Urquart in my last year at Oxford. She came to a ball at the invitation of a friend of mine and I fell instantly in love with her. I had been told I had a brilliant future in front of me and she was a suitable partner for me, beautiful and rich, and the daughter of a peer. By the end of that summer we were embarked on a future supposedly rosy with promise. We were the beautiful people, the golden people on whom Fortune

164

smiled, and it's true, Fortune did smile for a great many years.

'Our son Edward was born in South Africa. He was beautiful, healthy and bright. We adored him and although we spent many periods away from him abroad during his early childhood, he was very happy at Drummond. Amelia had been something of an afterthought in her parents' lives and she was only ten when Edward was born. They were great friends.'

He left me and went back to the table, returning with the photograph of the group. He looked down on it with a strangely sad expression, then held it out to me. 'Nancy – did anything strange strike you about this photograph?'

I took it and stared down at it again. At first it seemed like any family group – smiling faces against the façade of a beautiful house on a warm summer's afternoon. Amelia and her sister were very alike with their patrician beauty and calm smiling serenity, then for the first time I began to see something not quite right about the little girl.

She leaned against her mother in a somewhat ungainly pose, and although she smiled her eyes had a vacant stare. Hesitantly I whispered, 'The little girl . . .' then I paused, staring into his eyes which had suddenly grown dark and sad.

'My daughter Dorinda. Perhaps it was a mistake to have another child, for Edward was nearly eleven . . . but she was beautiful and adorable, then when she was three she had meningitis which left her with brain damage. She will never be able to walk, she can't speak – in other words she's like a pretty rag doll. She knows her mother, but she doesn't even remember me.'

'Oh, Desmond, I am so terribly sorry. How sad that is.'

'Yes. I have to spend most of my time in London for obvious reasons but Celia prefers to live in Cornwall. It is very ironic that this child who was supposed to heal our tottering marriage is responsible for keeping us apart.

165

We now live very separate lives but that is how things are.'

'You stay together for the sake of the child.'

'And appearances. I'm ambitious, Nancy. The only thing I have left is my career – Celia knows that, and now I'm being brutally frank in allowing you to know it also.'

He was spelling it out for me plainly and without subterfuge: I could love him but we had no future together. Celia was his wife and would remain so, and yet I was not proof against his arms drawing me into his embrace, his voice against my hair saying, 'I can't divorce her Nancy, not even when she won't live here in London with me, but the child is mine. I must share the responsibility even if more often than not it is at a distance. The doctors have told us Dorinda will not live to maturity – and after she's gone, who knows what will happen between Celia and me? I can only tell you that in the immediate future I can't promise you anything. I can't hold up your life – you're young and beautiful, and you're worth much more than I can offer you.'

'What are you offering me, Desmond?'

'A life of stolen meetings, all without participation in my public life. Uncertainty, loneliness, no light at the end of the tunnel, the wondering and waiting for some intangible dream . . . A woman has to be strong to stand all that.'

'She also has to be desperately in love, Desmond,' I murmured, staring into his face.

'And you think you are desperately in love, my dear?'

'I know I am. I don't want anybody else. I only want you – if you love me nothing else matters.'

I believed it. When he took me in his arms and kissed me there was nothing more certain in the world. I listened happily while he talked about those times when we would be together, and then in the distance we heard the quiet closing of a door and Desmond said, 'That is Chang Lee going home. He doesn't live in.'

In amazement I looked at the clock on the mantelpiece and saw that it was almost midnight. 'It's so late,' I exclaimed. 'I should go home.'

'There's no need, you can go to work from here.'

'Isn't this the one place where I shouldn't be?'

'We shall have gone before Chang Lee comes in the morning. Besides, he's the perfect servant – discretion itself.' For a moment Desmond stared thoughtfully into the dying fire, then rose to his feet and pulled me after him. 'You're right, Nancy. There's no romance for you here, nor for me. Next weekend we'll go down to a lovely little inn I know just outside Winchester. My parents used to stay in it when they came to see me while I was at school there. Now I'd like to go back there with you, will you come?'

'You know I will.'

'Come along then, I'll take you home. There won't be much traffic at this time of night.'

It was only when we were driving back to Hammersmith that a certain sanity began to encroach into the euphoria of the past few hours and the future began to face me stark and unadorned. I knew I loved Desmond, but for the first time I asked myself whether I was strong enough to face what he was offering, and what I would do if my strength failed . . .

16

I had had two years of Desmond and another Christmas Eve had arrived. I found myself nostalgically remembering other Christmases, with my family around me. I was all alone in the house in Hammersmith. Lois was with her father in Amsterdam, a sulky miserable Lois who hadn't wanted to go but considered his invitation to be better than nothing, and Marcia was in Essex with several cousins. Joyce was in Miami.

Every tick of the clock was like another hour of my life passing. A caustic telephone call from Aunt Susan in the early morning hadn't helped. I explained to her that I had been too busy at the shop to get away before and Sunday, especially Christmas Eve, was impossible for travelling. In any case I couldn't bear to be spending Christmas with Aunt Susan. The last time I had visited her the questions and recriminations had gone on all weekend, and I vowed she wouldn't see me again for some considerable time.

My mother had married Roger Fellows in the summer and was now living in Canada with no mention of visiting England in the foreseeable future. Desmond had gone to see his wife and children in Cornwall, where supposedly they would be one happy family on Christmas Day at least.

Strangely enough I never felt like the other woman in Desmond's life. He seldom spoke about Celia so that she remained a vague shadowy person who was there but unimportant. I was the sacrificial lamb on the altar of his ambition. His career was more important than his wife, his children or me, and there had been many times over the last two years when I had wanted to run, to distance myself from his charm, and his wise, gentle smile . . . but then he was back in my life bringing with him companionship and ecstasy, and my pain and doubt melted away and were forgotten until the next time.

It was never Celia who kept him from me, it was always his work. I couldn't talk to anybody about him, certainly not Lois who was still wallowing in her own misery after all these long months or Marcia, who I often found looking at me with those world-weary eyes and who I was sure already sensed my frustration without knowing who was responsible for it.

Desmond seemed to know instinctively where it would be safe to dine, which theatre we could go to. When we were out he was invariably attentive, but in the way one is with a visiting relative, which was the role I automatically adopted whenever we came into contact with anybody he knew. Lorivals had not conditioned me to be just a part of the background to someone's life: he sensed my anger and was quick to reassure me that it wouldn't always be this way. One day something would happen and the whole sorry mess would be sorted out. He never actually said what the sorting out would entail – death or divorce – he only asked for my understanding. He already had my love.

I ate my solitary Christmas Eve snack sitting forlornly in front of the television. I had decorated a small tree bought at one of the street markets and on the table at my side was a box of chocolates and a bottle of sherry. The electric fire stared back at me impersonally, making me long for pine logs and leaping flames. I was in no mood for television party games and forced jollity, instead I switched channels to a macabre play concerned with ghostly happenings and vague misted shapes appearing suddenly along clifftops accompanied by the cries of gulls.

There followed a programme of nostalgic music of other years and Hutch's rendering of *These Foolish Things* sent me into the kitchen with tears streaming down my face and deep resentment in my heart. I was sitting at the kitchen table drinking my coffee when I heard the telephone shrilling in the hall. Hopefully I went to answer it, rewarded at hearing Desmond's voice saying anxiously, 'Nancy darling, are you all right? I rang before but there was no answer.'

'I had the television on and the door was closed, so I didn't hear the phone. Merry Christmas, darling.'

'Nancy, I hate you being alone there. Wasn't there somebody you could spend Christmas Eve with?'

'I didn't look for anybody, I preferred to be alone.'

'Why didn't you go north to stay with your aunt?' I didn't think that remark merited an answer and after a few moments he said, 'I'm leaving here on the twenty-ninth because I have to be at the Ministry for something rather important. I'll telephone you when I get back.'

'What is the weather like in Cornwall?'

A moment's silence, then, 'We're not in Cornwall, Nancy, we're at Drummond. Celia wanted to be with her parents, as her father hasn't been well.'

'I see. How is Dorinda?'

'Much the same, unfortunately, but the poor love enjoys the company of Edward. Your friend Amelia and her husband and children are here, too.'

'Amelia has children?'

'Yes, twin girls, toddlers.'

'Christmas at Drummond must be very nice.'

'Nancy – I'd much rather be spending Christmas with you. Although I love being with Edward, I'm not particularly enjoying the rest of the holiday. It's not to be compared with that week we spent in the Ardennes.'

'Goodbye Desmond, I'll see you when you return to London.'

'Goodnight darling, sleep well.'

Sleep well! When it got to 3 a.m. I hadn't slept at all. Earlier I had heard the carol-singers from the local church pass by, and then the chiming of several clocks and the intermittent laughter of partygoers on their way home. I was obsessed with thoughts of Desmond in the bosom of his wife's family: in my imagination I could see Amelia, with her lovely, serene face, fussing over her children, and Mark playing the proud father for the benefit of her parents. I couldn't think straight, I could only wallow in cynicism, telling myself that Celia was living in a fool's paradise because Desmond loved *me*. Then I cried into my pillow wondering why, when he loved me so much, he wasn't with me instead of them. Christmas Eve had turned into Christmas Day, and it stretched in front of me like a desolate wilderness . . .

I asked no questions about Desmond's stay at Drummond, and he was wise enough not to speak of it. The stealthy pattern of our meetings continued, and my resentment grew. In the moments when I thought about my life logically, I knew that Desmond had never lied to me. Scrupulously honest, he had warned me that this was how it was going to be. I couldn't accuse him of dishonesty and yet now I was despising his honesty, wanting the unattainable.

It was one Sunday afternoon in spring. We had driven down to a favourite restaurant situated in the leafy lanes of Surrey. The sun shone out of a clear blue sky and I was wearing a new dress and jacket of which Desmond had warmly approved. The weather was so mild that people were sitting outside at tables under the trees to eat their lunch, and as we made our way through the gardens I suddenly heard Desmond mutter, 'Damn!'

He was looking at a small group of people seated at one of the tables – a man with two women and three young children. One of the women had greeted us, and in the next moment Desmond was at their table, smiling down at her. I paused uncertainly; her eyes were on me, curious and somehow familiar. I was sure I had seen her somewhere before.

Desmond held out his arm to draw me forward saying, 'Nancy, this is Miss Wilton, a toiler at the Foreign Office like myself. May I be allowed to buy you all a drink?'

In the hustle of ordering and paying for drinks he omitted to introduce me by name and I wondered if this had been done deliberately. I stood smiling stiffly, and then Desmond was saying, 'Please excuse us – we have lunch ordered in the restaurant and I think we should tell them we've arrived, don't you, my dear?'

We murmured our farewells, and then Desmond and I were walking along the drive towards the restaurant and he was saying through gritted teeth, 'I didn't expect to meet her here! She's always efficient and discreet but we're all aware of the tittle tattle that goes on in high places.'

'You can always get away with it by telling her I'm your little cousin up from the country,' I snapped sharply.

'I don't intend to tell her anything at all. I brought you here hoping for a bit of peace when I could conveniently forget the Foreign Office and all those who work there.'

We ate an excellent lunch, mostly in silence, but later over coffee I noticed Miss Wilton at the window smiling and waving her hand. Desmond responded gallantly and then she was gone.

I was trying desperately to remember where I had seen the woman before, but couldn't think. It was when we were driving back in the late afternoon that I suddenly remembered – she was the woman I had seen talking to Lois all that time ago in the park! Outwardly calm I asked, 'Doesn't that woman we met this afternoon work as a secretary to Ian Owen?'

For a brief moment Desmond's eyes left the wheel to stare at me solemnly, then he sighed. 'Must we talk about her, Nancy? She really isn't important.'

'If she's unimportant why won't you talk about her?'

I knew he was annoyed with me for being insistent, with himself for minding so much, and with the circumstances which made life so complicated. The day was spoilt, like so many others recently.

In the early evening Desmond dropped me a few streets away from the house in Hammersmith saying he had letters to write and a long document to read. He promised to telephone me during the week.

Joyce was letting herself in at the front door and with a bright smile she turned to say, 'I've got four whole days before I need to fly out again. Does your fella have a pal?'

I laughed. 'I'm afraid not, and I'm sure you don't need me to find you a manfriend.'

'It's awfully early to be parking you for the evening.'

'I know, he has work to do.'

'I hope you know him well, because that's usually a good excuse for a man to get home to his wife and kids.'

'I do know him well.'

'Right – in that case I shall remain silent. I suppose there's nobody else at home?'

'Marcia's away for the weekend and Lois has gone somewhere with her father.'

'Well, I'm going to have a bath and slip into something more comfortable than this uniform. Join me in the lounge for a drink in an hour?'

'Of course.'

We were drinking sherry and chatting in the lounge when we heard Lois come in and go straight to her room. Joyce raised her eyebrows ruefully, saying, 'Is she still carrying a torch for the same man?'

'She must be. Perhaps I should ask her about her weekend? Sometimes she wants to talk, and sometimes she's not inclined to say a thing.'

I found Lois with her weekend case on the floor, flinging the contents on the bed before putting them away. She looked up when I entered the room and I realised at once that I would have to tread warily. I sat on the edge of her bed and for what seemed an eternity she went on putting things in drawers, ignoring my existence, then unable to stand it any longer I said, 'Did you have a nice weekend, Lois?'

'It was all right.'

'How is David?'

'Well enough.'

'Look, it's ages since we spent a day or a weekend together – can we do that soon?'

She turned to stare at me. 'I thought you had better fish to fry these days, Nancy. I don't want to know who he is, only if it's serious.'

'As serious as it can be at the moment. I love him, but he isn't free to marry me.'

'I see. I'm so sorry, Nancy – is there a chance it might be different one day?'

'I don't know, I'd like to think so. Dare I ask about you?'

Her eyes clouded and she sank down beside me on the bed. 'I only said I'd go with my father this weekend because I was so sure He'd be there. He should have been but he didn't arrive.'

'Why are you so certain about his movements?'

'I have my contacts.'

'Lois, it isn't enough. Do you still never meet or actually speak to him?'

Her eyes grew bright with cynical humour. 'Oh, we pass the time of day if we accidentally meet in the corridors of power. He bids me a charming good morning, and sometimes asks if my father is well and when I propose to join David in Holland or elsewhere.' She giggled. 'He doesn't know that I watch his flat and talk to his secretary. He probably thinks that I'm a nice little thing who blushes when he speaks to me and is probably shy.'

'I wish you could meet somebody else,' I said slowly.

'I meet a lot of men, I work with men and sometimes I eat lunch and dinner with them! I'm just not interested in any of them that's all.'

'He's an obsession. It's been going on for over two years now. Lois, I'm frightened for you.'

174

'Did you say we should spend a day together,' she interrupted. 'How about next weekend?'

'I'm not sure about next weekend – can I let you know?'

'You're waiting to see if your man is available. Nancy, if you ask me, you're as obsessed as I am.'

I bit my lip in annoyance, then said quickly, 'Shall we spend the entire weekend in the country? We'll go to some nice little inn somewhere where the food is good and we can spend our time walking and exploring. Somewhere in Oxfordshire might suit.'

'Suppose your man telephones to say he's free?'

'Then I'll say I have another engagement. He'll understand, it's the sort of relationship we have.'

So we spent the weekend in the Vale of Aylesbury at a small country inn, and we did go for walks, but the visit wasn't a complete success. Lois was no longer the Lois of Lorivals, with her sense of humour and bubbling laughter. Too often she was silent and morose and I knew her thoughts were far away.

It was fairly late when we arrived back in Hammersmith and walking up the stairs together Lois said, 'It's been like old times, Nancy. Can we do it again soon?'

'Yes, of course.' I was delighted to hear her say this.

'He won't mind?'

'He's often away and anyway, you're my friend. You're important, too. I'll let you know in good time when he's out of London next.'

'Perhaps we can have lunch one day in the meantime. I'd like that.'

'Oh yes, so would I. Let's make it Tuesday.' I went to bed cheerfully, thinking that at least in the immediate future, something of our old camaraderie was back in my life.

17

After we had eaten lunch the following Tuesday, Lois and I walked in St James' Park then we sat on the grass watching the ducks splashing merrily on the lake. It was a warm sunny day and the crowds around us were dressed in light summer clothing. I looked at Lois sitting with her back against a tree, hugging her knees. She had had her hair cut short and with the sun on her brown arms she looked more like the schoolgirl I remembered than she had done for months.

A warm smile suddenly illuminated her face and she raised her arm to wave. To my dismay, I saw the woman Desmond and I had met in Surrey walking across the grass towards us and I scrambled quickly to my feet.

Lois indicated that she should join us, making room for her to sit down while I remained standing. 'Marion, I'd like you to meet my friend Nancy Graham. I told you we were having lunch together. Nancy, this is Marion Wilton – Marion works as a secretary at the Foreign Office so you can say we're colleagues.'

For the second time in weeks I found myself taking the woman's hand and murmuring a greeting. If she recognised me, she was discreet. Our talk was about the excellence of our lunch, the warm sunny weather and the antics of two small boys playing leapfrog on the grass.

'Just like my two nephews,' she laughed. 'What a handful they're turning out to be.'

I smiled politely, remembering the children I had seen with her in Surrey. After a few minutes I looked at my watch saying, 'I don't know about you people at the Foreign Office, but it's time I went back to work. I do have a little walk.'

'Where do you work, Miss Graham?' she enquired.

'I work for a firm of importers, "Treasures of the Orient" they call themselves.'

'Do you really? Oh, I love looking through the windows of their premises. All those lovely vases and the jade, and gorgeous Chinese carpets – things I'll never in a thousand years be able to afford.'

'I know, I look at them with some degree of longing too, but at least I enjoy handling them and working with them.'

'Yes, indeed. It's been nice meeting you again, Miss Graham.' She blushed. It had been a slip of the tongue and for a moment Lois looked at me sharply but then Miss Wilton was chattering quickly to cover her words. 'I think we should be getting back too, Lois. My, what a morning I've had, and the afternoon likely to be similar.'

I left them, walking quickly in the opposite direction, thinking that by this time Lois would be asking the other woman where she had met me before. I wondered if that obviously discreet secretary would tell her what she wanted to know.

However, I forgot about Miss Wilton in the weeks that followed. Desmond monopolised me and it would seem my weekend with Lois had made him feel I was not entirely at his beck and call. In any case I saw little of Lois, and even Marcia remarked that she was out more than usual, arriving home very late and seemingly not wanting to meet us at breakfast.

'Perhaps she's found someone at last,' I said hopefully, but she only shook her head.

'I don't think so. She's always alone when I see her, unless she's lunching with Marion Wilton, and I can't think they have much in common, at least on the surface.'

'What do you mean by that?'

'Well, they are in a different age group to begin with, and Marion's hardly the sort of woman who could contribute much towards Lois' well-being. She lives with her widowed mother at Barnet, and her only conversation is her brother and his wife and children. She never gets away on holiday unless it's a long weekend with them about twice a year and her mother's very demanding. Lois must have some other reason for taking up with Marion, or vice versa – it would be interesting to know what it is.' I said nothing more, but from the look on Marcia's face I knew she was well aware of why Lois was so friendly with Marion Wilton.

Desmond gave me good warning that he expected to be visiting the Soviet Union in the autumn and would be out of the country for several weeks. I never asked questions but for some reason he was more informative about this trip than usual. He seemed excited, even gratified by it and through it all I saw for myself the burning ambition that meant more to him than his wife and children – and me.

Our meetings were spasmodic now. They consisted of snatched meals when I listened to his excuses about why we couldn't meet more often, and rare nights at his flat, when I tried to tell myself that he loved me as desperately as I loved him.

Two days before he was due to leave for Russia he telephoned to invite me to his flat. 'I'd like to take you out for a meal, darling,' he said gently, 'but I simply haven't the time. Will you bear with me, eat a few of Chang Lee's sandwiches and supervise my packing?'

I took a taxi from the gallery and arrived around six o'clock. Chang Lee opened the door with imperturbable blandness and the briefest of Oriental smiles, then Desmond stood with his arms around me saying eagerly, 'Darling, I'm so glad you could come, I'm in an awful mess. There's coffee and sandwiches on the table there, help yourself.'

Two suitcases stood open on the floor and he was moving quickly from the bedroom to the living room carrying sheaves of papers while Chang Lee quietly placed piles of immaculate shirts into one of the cases. They had not bothered to draw the curtains so that was the first thing I did after looking down at the stream of traffic passing the flats, and the long lines of people waiting across the way for their buses.

'You did well to get here so early,' Desmond said, not bothering to look up from where he stood near the bureau busily writing notes in a small notebook. 'If I don't make notes I shall forget what I'm doing,' he explained with a brief smile.

It did not take me long to realise that I should never have gone there. Chang Lee left before ten, after reassuring himself that the cases were safely packed, labelled and placed ready in the hallway. I sat watching Desmond leafing through innumerable papers, sometimes with a frown of impatience, at others with satisfaction. Then there were the telephone calls taken in his study where I couldn't hear the conversation.

He was kind and he was apologetic. At eleven o'clock he pushed his papers away with a wry smile saying he would need to work long into the night and suggested taking me home. I believe he was relieved when I insisted on getting a taxi and after saying he was sorry I had had to spend such a boring evening, he kissed me tenderly, promising to write while he was in Russia and that he would contact me immediately he arrived home.

All the way home I was angry with myself, with Desmond and with life in general. I had been a fool to believe that a few brief moments of ecstasy could ever compensate for a lifetime of loving, tenderness and belonging . . . As I had told myself so often in the past two years, it was time I finished with Desmond Atherton. If only it was as simple as that. During an evening as fraught as this one, I had not had the nerve to tell him I was pregnant.

As I climbed out of the taxi and paid the driver, I looked up at our house in amazement. An ambulance stood outside the front door and lights streamed into the night from the open door. I could see people moving about in the hall, then two ambulance men appeared carrying a stretcher on which rested a small slim form.

I threw a handful of money at the cabbie and raced towards the ambulance. I had almost reached it when Marcia caught hold of my arm and I turned to stare in her pained, horror-filled eyes. 'You can't do anything, Nancy. It's Lois – she's dead.'

'Dead!' I echoed stupidly.

'You'd better come inside where we can talk.'

I followed her into the house where Joyce stood in the hall, trembling and tearful. With her was a tall man whom Marcia introduced as the doctor. After a few moments two police officers came running downstairs and one of them said to Marcia, 'Did the Inspector get your statement, miss?' She nodded briefly. 'In that case we'll be going. I'm sorry it was too late for anything to be done.'

'We've cleaned up the bathroom,' said the other. 'We're used to this sort of thing so you needn't be afraid to go in there. Somebody will call round in the morning to see if we can do anything else.'

After that they left and the doctor said to Joyce, 'You'd better get off to bed, young lady, you've had a nasty shock. Have a warm milky drink and take one of these tablets – it'll help you to sleep.' He held out a small bottle containing a few white tablets which Joyce accepted with a shaking hand, then he too departed leaving us staring at each other in the hallway.

Practical as always Marcia said, 'I'll make some cocoa. We can talk in the kitchen.'

Like docile children we followed her into the kitchen. Mechanically, I set out cups and saucers and Marcia made the milky drink, while Joyce sat with her head in her arms sobbing quietly. When at last we were sitting round the table with our cocoa in front of us, I stared at Marcia helplessly, my eyes filled with questions I couldn't put into words.

180

'Joyce found her,' Marcia explained quietly. 'By the time I got home the police and ambulance were already here. Joyce can tell you what happened.'

Joyce raised her ravaged face to stare at us, but the tears started afresh – more sharply than I intended I said, 'Joyce, please! I need to know – please tell me what happened.'

She dabbed at her eyes, and pulling herself together with what I can only describe as a supreme effort she said tearfully, 'I got in around seven and Lois was in the bathroom. I was going out later so I knocked on the door and asked her how long she was going to be. She didn't answer so I went into my bedroom and got into my dressing gown, then I went back to the bathroom and knocked again. She still didn't answer, and I was cross with her so I pounded on the door.'

The tears started afresh and she sobbed, 'I wish I hadn't been so cross, I wish . . . Oh, I don't know what I wish. I should have known something was wrong.'

'How could you know?' Marcia said reasonably. 'Go on with your story.'

After a few moments she said, 'I came downstairs and made myself a cup of tea, then about twenty minutes later I went back to the bathroom. The door was still locked so I called out to Lois again. I thought she might have fallen asleep in the bath but there was no answer and I couldn't hear a sound. Again I waited. I was still angry but I had begun to be frightened. I went into her bedroom. Her raincoat and scarf were thrown across the bed and her clothes lay in a heap on the floor. It looked as if she'd just come in, taken all her clothes off and gone straight to the bathroom so I went back there and knocked on the door again. It was so silent, Nancy!

'I was so terrified when I ran out into the street that I was prepared to invite anybody into the house to help me, but luckily there was a policeman walking down the road and I ran after him, calling out for him to wait. He stared at me as though I was demented, running down the road in a dressing gown in the pouring rain, but he came back to the house with me and helped me pound on the door then he said, 'Something's definitely wrong, I'll get this door open, while you go downstairs and get hold of an ambulance. She might have fainted in the bath.

'I'd hardly got back upstairs when an ambulance arrived – it must have been in the area. By this time he'd broken the lock on the door and was in the bathroom . . .' She paused, her eyes wide with horror at the scene which had confronted her. 'Lois was lying in the bath and the water was blood-red and dripping onto the floor. She looked just like a big red rag doll and when the constable tried to pull her out of the bath his feet were sliding all over the place. He called for me to help him but I couldn't touch her and then the ambulance men were there. They stretched her out on the floor and tried everything they knew to bring her round but they said she was already dead. She'd slashed both her wrists, you see. Do you think if I'd sent for them sooner they'd have been in time? It's my fault, I know it is.' She shuddered.

'Well, of course it isn't your fault,' Marcia said staunchly. 'You did everything you could – how were you to know she'd do anything so dreadful? Look, drink up and take one of those pills. I'll come upstairs and see you into bed.'

Marcia left the room with Joyce while I set about washing up the cups. I acted like a zombie. All this was just a nightmare and soon I must wake up to a new normal day, but then Marcia was back in the room and we sat at the kitchen table facing each other. She said, 'Lois' father is being contacted by the police. He'll be here tomorrow and he'll have to know everything.'

'Of course – poor David! He'll be devastated. Look, must he really be told everything?'

'Well, of course. That foolish obsession she's had for years, almost since the first day she went to work at the

Foreign Office, although why she suddenly realised today that it was hopeless I can't imagine. I saw her earlier on this afternoon having tea with Marion Wilton. I'd have joined them but they had their heads together and were talking very confidentially – I smiled, but they didn't invite me to join them.'

'I've met her, she's Ian Owen's secretary, isn't she?'

Marcia stared at me. 'No, she's Desmond Atherton's secretary.'

I stared at her incredulously, and for a few moments felt the room slipping away. Then hoarsely I cried, 'Oh no, it can't be Desmond! I don't believe it.'

'So he's the man you've been around with these past few years. I must say, I'm surprised.'

'Surprised!'

'Well, yes. There's never been any scandal around Desmond, no other woman, no string of dollies. He's always been the blue-eyed boy, the one who was destined for high office, and people pitied him his invalid daughter, applauded his devotion to his lady wife and his brilliant son. Well, well, I must say our Desmond's covered his tracks remarkably well.'

'How sordid you make it sound,' I said bitterly.

'I'm sorry, Nancy, I didn't mean to make it sound sordid, only human. I thought Desmond was different from all the others, with their nice tidy little affairs tucked underneath their belts. Most of the affairs are light-hearted, and only in one or two instances has there been a rare old scandal. I must say, you probably mean a great deal to him, Nancy. Desmond Atherton isn't noted for behaving like a Casanova.'

'Why didn't Lois ask me about him? Why did she never talk about him? If I'd known Desmond was the man she was in love with, on that weekend in the Cotswolds I'd never have become involved with him. I assumed it was Ian Owen – a fatal error. 'She just never told me.'

'She never told anyone, but I'm still not sure what

183

brought it to a head tonight. What could Marion Wilton have to do with it? She's Desmond's secretary, not the keeper of his conscience. He wasn't likely to discuss his private affairs with her.'

I told her quickly about the brief meeting we had had with her that Sunday in Surrey and Marcia said, 'Yes, but surely that wasn't enough to make Lois want to take her own life? She would have come to you for an explanation. And anyway, Marion Wilton wouldn't have told her about you.'

Quite suddenly I was remembering that row of people standing dejectedly in the rain at the bus stop opposite Desmond's flat. Any one of those huddled figures could have been Lois. She had told me often enough how she watched his flat for hours . . . The burden of believing her death was my fault was almost more than I could bear.

The tears rolled uncontrollably down my face and Marcia said briskly, 'Look Nancy, none of this is your fault. Most girls in a similar position to Lois would have either tried to make a relationship with Desmond Atherton, or consigned him to the devil and looked around for somebody else. The fact that she made him into an obsession was unwholesome and just a little mad. We know the way her personality deteriorated. You simply must not think that any of this is your fault, or Desmond's either, for that matter. He never knew, and even if he had what could he have done about it?'

'I know that, but she's dead, isn't she? Lois was my friend and I loved her. Desmond will just be horrified that she died the way she died, sorry for her father David and sorry for me because Lois was my friend, but he'll be oblivious about his part in it. I feel that I hate him now.'

'The Foreign Office will be alive with the drama in the morning, so he'll probably get to learn of it before he leaves for the Soviet Union. No doubt he'll telephone you.'

184

'I doubt it, he'll be far too busy. He'll probably even get his secretary, the wonderful Miss Wilton, to write a letter of condolence to David Brampton.'

The suicide of a diplomat's daughter made headlines in the morning paper and at work there was unspoken sympathy on the faces of my colleagues. When I arrived home in the evening Marcia was there before me, saying that she had spoken to David Brampton and he intended to come to the house later to see us. We therefore ate a hasty meal in the kitchen, cleared away the dishes and were sitting in the lounge watching television and waiting for him to arrive.

We sat with frozen faces watching the evening news that showed our house, followed by an interview in Lancashire with Miss Clarkson, who calmly stated that Lois had been a clever and popular girl showing great promise.

'They've certainly made the most of today,' Marcia commented dryly, then suddenly the scene changed and we were looking at a picture of Heathrow Airport and an Aeroflot jet waiting to take off for an important diplomatic mission. There was the usual procession of conservatively-clad diplomats and then Desmond appeared, smiling and urbane. Beside him, poised and chic, her arm through his, was Celia, his wife.

For a few moments I felt faint and had to clutch at the arms of my chair for support. I looked at the screen through a blur of tears. Celia resembled Amelia so much. She had that same elusive charm, that cool assurance, and how elegant she was in a fur hat and full-length dark mink coat.

Suddenly Marcia sprang up from her chair and went to switch off the set. Confronting me, she said sharply, 'He didn't tell you his wife was going with him, of course?'

I shook my head. I was trembling with anger and hurt. The months and years of loving Desmond suddenly seemed worthless, and with the hurt was a deep punishing hatred. If he had walked through the door at that moment I could willingly have killed him. I hated him for me, for my child and I hated him for Lois.

Seeing my fury Marcia said gently, 'Hate him by all means, Nancy, but you must never blame him for Lois' death. He had absolutely nothing to do with that. Our nerves are still raw from last night, and having David here later is not going to help. You must get a grip on yourself.'

I accepted the brandy she brought me, drinking it in one quick gulp so that stinging tears came into my eyes. I coughed and spluttered at its sharpness in my throat.

In one blinding moment I knew I would not be waiting in London for Desmond to return.

The brandy must have helped, because an unnatural calm seemed to take hold of me and allowed me to face David Brampton dry-eyed and coolly logical.

He told the three of us that there would have to be an inquest, and he would send for his ex-wife. His voice trembled now and again when he spoke, and looking at his lined grey face David Brampton seemed a hundred years older than the man who had escorted me to Gloucestershire on that eventful weekend. Gone was the bright smiling charm against which Lois had always railed; suddenly that confident man had been replaced by someone who was finding great difficulty in coming to terms with his loss.

'I can't understand it,' he said in a low, hesitant voice. 'She was such a game little kid, always full of fun, ready for anything. She was fearless on a horse, and on skis. Oh my God, why did she do it? She had enough money, she had a good job and friends. She always told me she was happy in London. When the police told me, I immediately thought some bastard had let her down and she was pregnant, but they say it's nothing like that. If it wasn't a man, then, what was it?'

He looked at us desperately, but Marcia and I remained silent.

Appealingly he said, 'You'd known her for years, Nancy. Surely you knew Lois was never the sort of girl to do this. Oh, I know she could be difficult, more so after her mother and I split up, and she always hated my mistresses. I thought it was just girlish jealousy, but now I suspect it was something else – some flaw in her personality, something none of us could see. How did she get on at the Foreign Office, Marcia?'

'She made friends quite normally. Everybody is horrified at what has happened.'

'And you're sure there was no man, nobody she was remotely interested in?'

'If there was we never knew his name.'

He stayed late, covering the same ground again and again, then he left after asking us to attend her funeral.

In five days it was all over: the inquest brought in a verdict of suicide while the balance of Lois' mind was disturbed. As I stood with Marcia and Joyce at her funeral, I caught sight of Marion Wilton with a group from the Foreign Office, but she never looked up. Marcia muttered, 'I wonder if she's feeling the least bit responsible for what happened.'

Again I found myself remembering that line of huddled figures opposite Desmond's flat. Fate had been so cruel: why on that night had it been left to me to draw the curtains, thus revealing myself starkly against the light? And Fate hadn't done with me yet, for I had a momentous decision to make.

I had to talk to somebody and Marcia was the obvious choice. For days I debated with myself as to how I should tell her, but in the end I told her unemotionally, neither asking for pity or censure, and she responded in a like manner for which I was grateful.

'Do you intend to tell him when he returns?' she asked calmly.

'I don't intend to be here when he returns.'

'You're leaving the Gallery?'

'I'm not sure. They've given me a few days' holiday, supposedly to get over Lois' death and its trauma, which will be long enough I think to have an abortion, then I've got to start thinking seriously about the future. I can't be here when Desmond comes back, Marcia. I have no confidence in my strength if I see him again.'

'Can I help?'

'You can tell me I'm doing the right thing. You can tell me Desmond and I have no future together, you can tell me I have the right to destroy an unborn child, one he wouldn't want to know or rear.'

'You're sure about that?'

'Oh yes, I'm sure. Much as I love Desmond, I know that his ambition overrides all. Celia at least adds some sort of lustre to him, even from her place in the background, but I'm just a sideline and I don't ever want to become a nuisance or an encumbrance. After I've had the abortion my life must change, but as yet I have no idea which path it should take.'

She made no effort to dissuade me nor did she come out with any well-meaning clichés. I was grateful for her coolness, knowing it was a façade designed to cover a real sympathy for my plight. Even after the termination she asked no questions but showed by her friendly desire to cosset me that she understood and approved of my actions.

18

On the night before I was due to return to the Gallery I slept fitfully, obsessed with the changes I must make to my life. Daylight brought no answers to the many problems I faced, but it was the arrival of the morning paper and a photograph of Noel Templeton on the front page that made me suddenly think of the paper. Mr McKay had told me there would always be a job for me on the *Gazette*. I immediately decided to telephone him during the morning.

However, I wasn't thinking straight. I was so set on getting away from London that I had forgotten our old home had been sold months before – I would have nowhere to live except with Aunt Susan.

It was mid-morning before I got the opportunity to speak to Mr Papadraos, and then I stated baldly that I had decided I wanted to go back to journalism and living in the north.

'You say there is work for you there, Miss Graham?' he asked evenly.

'Yes, I'm sure there is. I wanted to speak to you first, but Mr McKay did offer me work on the paper if ever I decided to go back.'

'It was sad about your friend, very sad but I have thought for several months you have not been happy, Nancy. There was some other reason for the shadows I saw in your eyes, some man perhaps.'

Strangely, I didn't find my employer's words offensive or presumptuous. His face was kind, his voice gentle, and I looked down at my hands lying in my lap without answering him.

'Will it help to run away? You are happy here, we value you. You cannot have your friend back if you leave us – and why let some man change your life? If and when you leave here, you should have a better excuse.' I looked up at him sharply and he smiled. 'If he cares enough he would follow you, if he doesn't he will let you go without lifting a finger to stop you. Either way it is unsatisfactory. I have a better solution.'

I waited, surprised, and he went on, 'When you first came here we told you there was a strong possibility that you would be able to work overseas. That opportunity has now arisen but it will mean that you will be living in the Far East for three to four years. We do not allow our people to go for a period of less than that.'

'The Far East,' I echoed, feeling dazed.

'Hong Kong to be precise. You are an ideal choice, since you have taken the trouble to learn some Chinese, and you have worked well and learned well. In Hong Kong you will meet a great many people, and travel broadens the mind like nothing else you can think of. You will work at our galleries there and if you think what you have seen here is wonderful, you will be doubly enchanted there.'

'But where would I live? When would you expect me to go?'

'As for the first you will share a flat with a young lady who works in one of the Government Offices. I have it on good authority that it is a charming flat in a popular area where many British people live, and for the second, I would require you to go out there as soon as possible. You have a passport, of course?'

'No, not at the moment.'

'Then you will need to get a passport photograph taken. Let me have it and we will do the rest. I would like you to leave no later than a week on Saturday.'

It was happening too quickly. I could only sit in my chair staring at him and Mr Papadraos said gently, 'Perhaps you would like to think about it, talk it over with a friend, but not for too long or I must send someone else.'

Unsteadily I rose to my feet, and he came to open the door for me. His final words were, 'I hope you will not disappoint me, Nancy. Believe me, this is what you should do. I am a man and I know men, so do not waste your youth and beauty a moment longer on the unattainable.'

I thought about it all morning. The other staff envied me my chance and gave me every encouragement. I telephoned Marcia and arranged to meet her for lunch and when I told her my news, her eyes opened wide. She said sharply, 'You'd be mad not to go! I'd give the earth to have an opportunity like that. Why on earth are you hesitating?'

'There's so much to think about. What about my room at the house? You and Joyce can't possibly manage the rent on your own.'

'You'll be well-paid, Nancy. You could contribute a retainer to keep your room. Joyce has already said she'll have no difficulty in letting Lois' room and probably one of the others. Really, if you don't grasp this opportunity with both hands, what will you do? It's my bet you'll stay on in London hoping against hope that one day in the distant future Desmond Atherton will ask you to marry him.'

'No, I was going to ask if I could have my job back on the *Greymont Gazette*.'

'Then you'd hope he'd follow you, beg you to go back to him, and if he didn't you'd be even more desolate. Put yourself completely out of reach Nancy, salvage your pride. Believe me, I know what I'm talking about. I only wish I'd taken the advice I'm handing out to you, then my own life would have been very different.'

'I shall have to write to Mother and then go home to see Aunt Susan – I couldn't just go out to Hong Kong without saying goodbye.'

'Well, why don't you? You have about ten days – go out and get your picture taken then ask Mr Papadraos for a few days' leave. He won't begrudge you that, I'm sure.'

I could tell my employer was delighted with my decision and he readily gave me permission to go home. Home was Greymont, but the house where I had been born looked very different when I passed it on the way to Aunt Susan's. The row of conifers lining the short drive had gone, and in their place stood some plastic urns, in which I had no doubt flowers bloomed in the springtime, but now they stood dirty and empty at regular intervals along the drive.

I wished now I had taken a taxi or a bus to my aunt's village, but I was carrying only a light bag and had been so anxious to see old landmarks. Now I was nearing the Jayson shops, and hoping I could pick up a bus there without being seen. Three of the shops in the parade now belonged to the Jayson family. They had taken over the ironmonger's and the butcher's in addition to their greengrocer's shop, so that only the newsagent's remained at the other end of the row. As always the vegetables, fruit and flowers were spread out across the pavement and I had almost reached the bus stop when I was hailed by a loud voice. 'Hey, Nancy Graham! Don't tell me you're passin' wi'out callin' to see us.'

It was Maisie's younger brother Jimmy. He was standing on the corner, his face wreathed in smiles, staring across the road at me, and there was nothing else for it but to cross the road to join him. He was wearing a clean white coat and seeing me looking at it he said with a grin, 'I'm the grocer – my father always said it were a good trade so when he bought the third shop that's where I fitted in.'

'How about the others?'

'Eric's in the ironmonger's and the fruit and veg belong to Bob. Dad is the business manager – keeps an eye on us all. I'll tell our Bob you're here – he'll be that glad to see you, Nancy.'

'Don't get him out of the shop specially, Jimmy. I'll call again, I'm here for several days.'

'No problem. Come into the shop, it's cold standin' on the pavement.' I would have preferred to walk on but by this time he was holding my arm and propelling me into the shop.

Bob's wife was at the counter serving a woman customer with fruit, her face unsmiling and without welcome. Not so Bob, however, who came out of the living room at his brother's request. His face lit up when he saw me, and then he had his arms around me and he was kissing my cheek and smiling down into my eyes.

'We read about your friend, Nancy,' he said quietly, 'It must have been a terrible shock for you. Our Maisie was really upset. I remember Lois, she was a nice jolly little thing, hardly the type to do anything so awful, but it just shows, you never really know anybody.'

'Everybody who comes into the shop's been talkin' about it,' his wife Mary said spitefully. 'Some of them remember her stayin' with you. All that money spent on her education, and for what? Wasted. Look at Maisie – she didn't need to go to that posh school to end up as a farmer's wife. The money would have been better spent on Bob or one of the other boys.'

'Nay Mary, I always knew I was coming into the shop. What would I have wanted with a college education?'

'Greymont'll be unexciting after London,' she said sharply to me. I didn't answer and she went on, 'I tek it you'll be goin' up to see Maisie?'

'I'd like to, it's been ages since we've met.'

'I'd go in the afternoon if I were you, she's more time to be bothered then. And what about your friend Lady Amelia? I suppose you'll be visiting her. She gets most of her greengrocery from us – sends one of the staff with her order and we deliver it to the Hall.'

'Are you likely to be staying in London for good now?' Bob enquired politely, rescuing me from his wife's sharp tongue.

193

'I'm going out to the Far East at the end of next week. I've simply come up here to say goodbye to Aunt Susan and collect a few things I might need.' As Mary Jayson's eyes grew round and her mouth opened to speak I added hastily 'I really must be going, or she'll think I've got lost. I'll probably see you both again before I leave.'

After I left the shop I decided I had had enough of nostalgia for one day, and went to wait in the queue for the bus to Ellwood.

The following afternoon I climbed the fell to Maisie's farm. I was glad I had put on a pair of Wellingtons as the field and farmyard were inches deep in mud. I was also glad of the old raincoat I had borrowed when a pair of sheepdog puppies leapt up at me ecstatically.

Tom came out of the barn to see what all the fuss was about, and when he saw it was me a broad smile illuminated his face. He cried, 'Go straight in, Nancy, you'll find her in the kitchen as usual. Eh, she'll be that glad to see you. Have you been slimming? You've lost weight.' I laughed and shook my head.

Maisie stood at the kitchen table rolling pastry, but it didn't deter her from putting her arms round my neck and kissing me, then we were laughing together as we brushed the flour from my coat.

'Why didn't you write and let me know you were coming?' she scolded. 'You're not running off early this time, I hope. You must stay and eat tea with us.'

'I'd like that, Maisie.'

'Tom'll run you back in the pick-up. It's dark about half-four at this time of year and the fields are that muddy. Let me get these pies in the oven and then we'll have a cup of tea and talk.'

She chatted as she worked, about Tom and the children, the harvest and the house, and while she talked I looked round the big farm kitchen at the comfortable fireside chair with its worn cushions, the huge oven and old Welsh dresser and seeing me looking round Maisie said, 'Nothing's changed, Nancy. I'd like some new cushions for the chair and a new rug on the floor, but there's allus something else to spend our money on. We've two children to think about now and heaven knows, they take everything we've got. They're growing so fast!'

'Where are the children?'

'Well, our Peter goes to play-school in the village, and Alice the youngest'll go next year, thank goodness, then I might have a bit of time to myself. I've got help – one of the farm labourer's daughters comes every day to see what she can do. Today she's taken Alice to her grandma's. She only lives in those cottages you can see through the window, and the old lady likes to see her. Mind, she'll stuff her with sweets so that she won't want her tea, but I don't say anything, because she's ever so kind. And Nancy, I see your aunt at church most Sundays, and guess what? She's nicer to me now than she ever was when we were youngsters.'

'She's mellowed a little, but not much.'

She laughed, popping the last pie into the oven, then after washing her hands she smoothed them over her red curly hair saying, 'I should get it done properly, but there's never the time. I'll make a cup of tea and we'll go into the parlour to drink it.'

When I told her about Hong Kong in some anxiety she said, 'What on earth is making you go all the way out there? I thought you were happy in London.'

'It's an adventure, and the people at the gallery have asked me to go.' I couldn't tell Maisie about Desmond. She was now a nice, respectable young woman far removed from my sort of life. She would be sorry for me but she would think it just retribution that I was suffering. I deserved to suffer for even thinking I could take a man away from his wife and children and in the next few moments I knew I was right not to tell her.

'It was terrible about Lois. I cried all night about her,

and everybody around was asking me why she'd done it, as if I'd know when I haven't clapped eyes on her for years. They all said the same thing, that it was probably some man she was involved with. Was it Nancy?'

'We don't know why she did it – she could be very intense about things, as you probably remember.'

'But you were living in the same house! Surely you must have known something was wrong?'

'Lois didn't confide in me. It was just one of those terrible things that happen.'

'Oh well, it was a real tragedy. By the way, I spoke to Amelia at the Agricultural Show the other day. She's a patron and she was there with her little girls. They're lovely, and she's so proud of them. I wasn't going to bother to speak to her – after all, she's never bothered about any of us, but when she smiled I just had to go to her and meet the children. Then last week I saw her again. She was riding through Ellwood on her horse and she smiled and said hello, just like she always did. I thought she might have mentioned Lois, but she didn't, so I didn't either. She told me she was looking after her sister's daughter while her mother was abroad. Our Bob's wife said she's heard in the shop that the girl was poorly, not quite all there if you know what I mean.'

'I called at the shop yesterday and saw Bob and his wife. The two younger boys have their own shops now, I see.'

'Yes, Dad saw to that when the shops went up for sale. He said they should all have something of their own.'

'You and Tom look very well, Maisie.'

'Yes, it's a healthy life out there in the fields, even at this time of year. And I'm happy enough. I've got one decent coat which I wear for church on Sunday and most of the time I'm in a jumper and skirt covered with an apron. Sometimes I'd like to go down to the shops in Greymont and buy something really extravagant for myself, but then I think about new shoes for the children and I stay where I am. Were you a bit upset about your mother getting married again, Nancy?'

'A little. I thought it was too soon.'

'So it was. Your aunt sold the house for her – was some of the money left for you?'

'My father left me six thousand pounds – the rest went to Mother. I hadn't expected anything, so I just put it in a high-interest account for a rainy day.'

'Well, I can tell you that I'll get nothing from *my* father: it'll all go to the boys. I had mine when he paid for me to go to Lorivals, and much good it did me. I'd have been better helping out in the shops and sharing in the will one day.'

Suddenly she grinned across the table at me. 'Do you ever think about that last talk Miss Clarkson gave us before we left Lorivals? She called us the chosen ones, but I reckon there's only me and perhaps you who's really happy.'

'Why do you say that?'

'Well, you never see Amelia with her husband. He's always off to race meetings, where he's been seen with different women, and when they are together it's her children she bothers with, never her husband. Then there's Barbara in her posh house, chairing a lot of lah di dah committees and never wanting a family. Her mother might think she's in clover but her father doesn't. We don't see either of them up here. Then there's Lois, that's the most terrible thing of all.'

'Then there's me and you,' I prompted gently.

'Well, I'm happy enough, although you've not given much away. For all I know, you might be very happy to be leaving England and living halfway across the world.'

All the time I was packing my small bag a few days later, I was thinking about my walk on the fell the afternoon before. Deliberately I had taken the path where

I could look down on Lorivals and because it was a Saturday I had met many of the girls out on the fell.

Wearing the distinctive grey and pink I had once worn they passed me with brief smiles or totally ignored me, and where I had thought to stand looking down on the school I found a group of older girls there before me. Young, confident, conditioned to believe that the world was their oyster, now they were just girls giggling over something that amused them, but how would the years ahead shape them? Probably not as Lorivals intended.

Lorivals was a world of women, but what would the world of men do to them? In ten years' time would they still be as sure, would they still be able to look at the world with wide honest eyes and know that all the dreams they had nurtured had now come true – or would they be disenchanted with life as the chosen ones?

'Nancy, your taxi's here,' Aunt Susan's voice called up to me, and zipping up my holdall I collected my handbag and ran down the stairs.

'One of these days,' she said calmly, 'I'll get a car of my own and take some driving lessons. The price of taxis is ridiculous – wouldn't you just think this driver would charge me a little less for using him so often?'

I put my arms round her and kissed her, and she looked at me doubtfully. 'I do wish you weren't going to Hong Kong, child, it's too far away. It's not somewhere you can just catch a train and come home for weekends. Oh dear, suppose you're not happy there?'

'I will be, Aunt Susan, and I'll write as soon as I'm settled.'

'Will you write to your mother too and tell her what you're up to? She said she hoped you and I would visit Canada next year.'

'You go Aunt Susan, she'll be glad to have you.'

'I'm not going all that way on my own.'

'Well, I'm going to Hong Kong on my own.'

'You're a lot younger than I am, and a lot more foolhardy. Run along now, the clock's ticking away.'

Greymont was sleepy on this chill afternoon. The people we saw on the streets walked with their heads down against the wind which swept down from the fells and the dark clouds looked heavy with rain. Lights were already lit along the platforms and it would seem I was the only one waiting for the train into Lancaster where I had to change for the London Inter-City express.

This time there would be no Desmond waiting for me on the Euston platform, and such a strong feeling of desolation swept over me that my eyes filled with tears. How much would he mind when he returned to London from Russia and found me gone? Would he feel anger, resentment, or would there be relief that his blessed career was safe as well as his strange and separate marriage? I had no idea, but for myself I only felt a forlorn and desperate abandonment. It was worse than a bereavement – that I could have accepted, but to know that somewhere the man I loved lived and breathed but didn't love me enough, was misery.

19

How can I describe Hong Kong with its splendour and its squalor? Even after twelve months it never ceased to amaze me. At night in the velvet dark it sparkled like a gigantic diamond when every light in its myriad sky-scrapers shone into the darkness and reflected in the dark waters of Victoria Harbour. The harbour too was alive with all manner of craft. Chinese junks sailed side by side with opulent yachts, bustling ferries nosed their way between giant ocean liners and planes dropped out of the night sky and glided along the runways which seemed to reach out like long ghostly fingers into the South China Sea.

How different was daytime Hong Kong, with its noisy streets and Eastern clamour, the buildings strung with banners and mysterious dirty alleyways disappearing behind hotels which were among the most luxurious in the world. Powerful limousines moved through the heavy traffic, while on the hillsides, refugees from Communist China lived in shacks which the rains and mud regularly washed away.

I had lived in Hong Kong for a year and was still entranced by the place. I loved the crocodiles of children walking to school in the morning, beautifully dressed in snowy-white dresses and wearing soft panama straw hats on their ebony hair. I had never seen such well-behaved clean children, but I knew many of them came from overcrowded apartment blocks, or worse still, those derelict shacks. There were times when I felt ashamed of our comfortable flat with its sun terrace, its exquisitely tiled bathroom and modern kitchen, but when I voiced my anxieties to Sally Merton, my flatmate, she only said, 'It's better not to think about it, Nancy. We can't be held responsible for all the refugees pouring into Hong Kong. They're not our people, they don't hold British passports, we simply give them sanctuary. They are told before they come that they must stay in Hong Kong ten years before they can have any hope of getting an apartment, but still they come. Look at the size of Hong Kong! It's tiny – it's bursting at the seams and the seams are not elastic.'

In my work at our sister gallery I was faced with objects of incredible beauty, and it seemed incongruous to me that all this could co-exist with so much that was ugly and unclean. I had been welcomed warmly by the one Englishman and his Chinese staff at the Hong Kong branch of Treasures of the Orient, and I was happy in my work. Sally was engaged to a Sergeant called Guy in the Hong Kong police force, but when she did have free time we explored the colony together. We took the tram to the top of Victoria Peak where we could stare down on one of the most glorious harbours in the world, and we ate in excellent Chinese restaurants and occasionally on the jumbo floating restaurant in Aberdeen Harbour.

Several times I went with Sally and Guy to the Happy Valley racecourse, and Guy invariably brought along an escort for me – some fresh-faced young Englishman who was glad to spend an afternoon in the company of a girl from home. These encounters fizzled out when my dates realised I wasn't interested in romance: it was too soon, and none of them were capable of erasing Desmond's memory.

I thought about him often and as time passed my anger against Desmond mellowed. I had so many things to be grateful to him for. He had shaped the jolly, North Country girl I had been when I first arrived in London into the sort of woman who could converse easily with men and women of every level. It was not Lorivals which had done this, and certainly not Mark with his young brash humour, it was Desmond. I remembered now the low timbre of his voice, answering my questions

201

patiently, opening my eyes to people, music, paintings and ideas, a smile always present on his clever, attractive face.

I liked Sally Merton. She was one of those happy-go-lucky girls who asked no questions but offered a shoulder to cry on if I needed it. I had told her a little of my history but she sensed my need to put it all behind me and I was grateful to her for this.

'I've been asked to invite you to a party my boss' wife is giving next Saturday,' she said one day. 'She's a great one for inviting people not long out from home, and she was quite insistent that I bring you.'

'That's very kind of her.'

'I'm not so sure. I've been out here four years and I've never known her do anything without a hidden motive.'

'Well, there can't be a hidden motive about me – I don't even know your boss' wife. Is the party in the evening?'

'Around six o'clock. They have a lovely old house halfway up Victoria Peak, an Old Colonial sort of house with a large garden. From the terrace you can see as far as Macau and China too on a clear day. You could enjoy it, for the drinks will be plentiful and the food's always good. She knows everybody in Hong Kong, even the interesting people who've just arrived so you could find it very enjoyable.'

'What does one wear for a function like this?'

'Oh, something reasonably sophisticated – a cocktail dress. That black dress you wore the other evening would be perfect and black does suit you. Was it very expensive?'

I nodded. I had bought the dress in London for my birthday, to wear during the evening Desmond had planned for us to celebrate it. The dress was simple but exquisitely cut, and I knew the moment he saw it that Desmond approved.

As I emerged from my bedroom into the living room

on the night of the party, Sally eyed me critically saying with a smile, 'You look lovely, Nancy!'

'So do you. Did you buy your dress here?'

'Would you believe at Stanley Market? I can't possibly afford the prices in the shops here. It's not bad – everybody will have seen it before, but then there's nobody there I'm likely to be interested in, anyway.'

'Wasn't Guy invited?'

'Gracious no. Fiancés are never included.'

'Why is that, do you suppose?'

'I'm not sure. I suppose if they invited everyone's partner, their house would be crowded. I'll not tell you anything about my boss' wife – you'll form your own opinion before the end of the evening.'

We took a taxi to the house on Victoria Peak and already a stream of cars seemed to be arriving. Lights from the house lit up the garden dramatically. A Chinese servant took our wraps and indicated that guests were mingling in the drawing room and outside on the terrace. As soon as we entered the room a tall portly man came over to greet us smiling profusely. I knew him instantly: he was the man I had seen in London walking round the Gallery with his plump wife in pale peach.

My heart sank. I hadn't bargained for this, and although Mr Etherington-Grant showed no sign of recognition I was wishing already that I had made an excuse not to come. He advised us to circulate freely, and immediately summoned a wine waiter and another carrying a tray of canapés.

Sally was busy telling me the names of some of the government officials standing about the room, most of them accompanied by their wives, and then I saw the hostess herself descending upon us. She was gowned in white, heavily encrusted with shimmering bugle beads, her blonde hair immaculately dressed, her face made up to pink perfection. She came with extended hands, greeting Sally first as, 'My dear Miss Merton, I'm so glad you could come. A night without that handsome fiancé of yours will do no harm, and this is your friend Miss Graham?'

I took her jewelled hand in mine, aware of her bright blue eyes and thick dark blue mascara, her soft, pink-lipped mouth smiling its welcome, and aware too that her eyes did not smile, they remained speculative. Turning to Sally she said archly, 'There's an old friend of yours over there, Miss Merton. It's Timothy Greaves, back in Hong Kong after six years. Do have a word with him dear, he's such a shy young man.'

Obediently Sally left and Miss Etherington-Grant's attention reverted to me. 'Now let me see, I'm sure we have met before, but for the moment I can't remember where. We have met before, haven't we, Miss Graham?'

'I saw you in the premises of Treasures of the Orient in London, Mrs Etherington-Grant. You were looking at miniature boxes.'

Her face cleared. 'Of course, and you were assisting Mr Atherton. Such a charming man, and flying so high after his successful trip to the Soviet Union. Of course, everybody knew he was destined for great things. For one thing he has all the right connections.'

I didn't speak, allowing my eyes to slide away from hers to survey the room in general.

'How are you enjoying it here in Hong Kong?' she continued with a smile.

'I like my work, and I'm finding everything very different, but interesting.'

'Will you allow a seasoned veteran to give you a little advice, my dear? I do it for all the British girls fresh out from home. Be very circumspect here; it is a small community and scandal never loses anything. You're a very pretty girl, and men being what they are will always be intrigued by a lovely face. And yet the man never suffers, the girl always does.' Her expression was gentle, benign even, and if it hadn't been for her eyes, as cold and hard as chipped amethysts, I might have thought she really cared about my reputation. However, she was really warning me off every man present because she knew about Desmond, and when I remained silent she pressed home her advantage.

'Of course I knew Desmond and dear Celia very well when they were out here many years ago. It's unfortunate that Celia doesn't wish to live in London; it means that Desmond is often lonely, poor man. It's easy to understand why he needed the company of somebody else, and you're such a nice pretty little thing. There's no question of divorce, however. They will stay together, if not for themselves, for the children.'

'What Mr Atherton does is not my concern, Mrs Etherington-Grant and if you'll forgive me saying so, what I do is no concern of yours.'

Her face coloured briefly and grew hard. 'Well, of course, if you are not prepared to take good advice when it is well-intentioned then that is your affair. Do enjoy my party, Miss Graham.'

She walked off stiffly, bristling with annoyance, and across the room Sally looked at me doubtfully. I was seething with resentment, but after a few minutes, humour took its place. I had made an enemy of a very influential woman. I should have bitten my tongue, pretended to be grateful for her advice, instead I had been impulsive, but it was done now and I had too much pride to ask her to excuse my rudeness.

I sauntered out on to the terrace and stood looking across the harbour where a huge liner, lit from stem to stern, gleamed like a dowager duchess in the centre of a stream of passing junks. For a brief moment I felt the sting of tears upon my face. I would have given anything to be leaving Hong Kong on that ocean liner. I had come halfway across the world to escape but here was this wretched women forcing me to remember.

I sipped my champagne, aware that people were dancing on the terrace and all around me was laughter and conversation. I was about to turn away, wondering how soon I could decently leave when I found my arm taken in a friendly gesture and a voice said evenly, 'Come and dance with me, you divine creature.'

I looked up into the smiling eyes of Noel Templeton, and then we were dancing and from the doorway, Mrs Etherington-Grant was watching us with an expression of anger on her pretty vapid face.

'I do meet you in the most unlikely places,' he said easily. 'How long have you been in Hong Kong?'

'Twelve months. I have a job here.'

'And Mrs Etherington-Grant felt she should take you under her wing?'

'Something like that.'

'Why you, I wonder?'

'The girl I share an apartment with, Sally Merton, works for the government.'

'Well, I don't know her but I *do* know Mrs Etherington-Grant – indeed, all Hong Kong knows our hostess. Are you having a good time?'

'Not particularly. I was just wishing I hadn't come.'

'That goes for me, too. She insisted and I hadn't anything else on, but I do think that after a decent interval you and I could make our excuses and leave.'

'Would that be very rude?'

'Not at all. I have work to do and you have a headache. I'm being very chivalrous in taking you home.'

'And in her eyes I'm running true to type.'

'What do you mean by that, I wonder?'

'I've been advised to be very circumspect, and there I go, leaving her house with the first man who asked me.'

He laughed. 'Then we'll be two people of whom she doesn't approve. I can't begin to tell you the number of dinners I've sat through in the company of some woman she's found for me. She disapproves of bachelors and single girls as pretty as you. She thinks we're all pred-ators, as dangerous as marauding polecats.'

The dance came to an end and smiling at me engag-ingly he said, 'I know a small restaurant not far from Deep Water Bay where I can promise you the best food in Hong Kong. Perhaps we should tell your friend we're leaving.'

I looked around the terrace but couldn't see Sally, only Mrs Etherington-Grant bearing down on us. I found my friend sitting on a sofa in the drawing room, listening to a very earnest young man in a somewhat bemused fashion. When I told her I was leaving she merely said, 'Don't worry about me, Nancy, Tim'll see me home. Is he nice?'

'Someone I knew in London.'

'I'll see you later then.'

I collected my wrap before going towards the Etherington-Grants, who were chatting with Noel at the door. Our host was genial, his wife considerably less so, and we left like two naughty children earning her disapproval.

For a while we drove in silence while Noel gave all his attention to the thronged streets of Hong Kong Island, then we were on the coast road heading for Aberdeen. It was dark with only the car headlights illuminating the road ahead, then after a momentary brightness that was Aberdeen Harbour we were in the dark again heading for Deep Water Bay.

'Did you ever see the film *Love is a Many Splendoured Thing*,' Noel enquired. 'There's been a rerun of it many times. Most of the action in it takes place at Deep Water – the scenery around there is quite beautiful. You'll not see much of it tonight, but we can maybe see it another time.'

The restaurant Noel took me to was little more than a bamboo shack, but there was a primitive charm about it and the food was wonderful. When we had reached the coffee stage, he fixed me with a keen stare and said 'Now you can tell me what that woman said to cause you so much pain. I watched you cross the terrace with stricken eyes and I thought at one stage you were crying.'

It did me good to talk about it all to Noel. He had seen Desmond and me together in London and he knew Desmond – I didn't know how well – but certainly enough to converse with on a friendly footing. I spared myself nothing, neither the hating nor the loving. When the tale was told we sat in silence for some time before I looked up to find him watching me closely. Then he grinned and for the first time that night I relaxed.

'So,' he said finally, 'it's all over, and you've run away. Did you run away because you were afraid when you saw him again you'd go back, no matter what he'd done, or did you run away and mean it, that you don't ever want to go back to him?'

'I don't want to go back. I want to learn to live without him – I want to be calm whenever I hear his name or see his face in a newspaper. I *won't* be the other woman in his life! I know that one day I shall have to return to London and I want to be strong enough to resist him.'

'But you're not strong enough yet?'

'Apparently not, if that woman can upset me so much.'

I was surprised when he changed the subject abruptly by saying, 'I spoke to my father about you and he remembered Arthur Graham straight away. He said he could have been a great journalist if he hadn't stayed too long on a small paper. It's a pity you didn't follow in his footsteps.'

'Mr McKay said he'd take me back any time I wanted to return. Actually I didn't know many people when I arrived here, and I didn't have nearly enough to do so I wrote an article about Hong Kong and sent it to the *Gazette* in Greymont to see if it was any good. You know, a "Local Girl in Hong Kong" type of feature. They printed it *and* paid me for it! I was so thrilled.'

'Good for you. Do you have a copy?'

'Well yes, but you'd think it very mediocre. I couldn't possibly let you see it.'

'How do you know what I'd think? I'd *like* to see it – may I?'

'All right, I'll steel myself for your pulling it to pieces.'

'I wouldn't do that in any case. I'm off to Peking for

a few days tomorrow but I'll telephone you when I get back. Perhaps we could have dinner together again.'

'Thank you, I'd like that.'

He looked up at the windows of the flat when he dropped me at the front door. There was a light burning and he said briskly, 'It looks as if your friend's returned home from the party. You'll have a lot to talk over.' He took my hand in a firm grip, then I watched him drive away into the night.

Sally was sitting in her dressing gown playing Patience on a small tile-topped table when I opened the door and she looked up with a smile.

'How long have you been in?' I asked her.

'Oh, about an hour. Tim's not a social animal, he was getting very bored with the party and I suggested he brought me home. I think I was only invited so that I would take you.'

'Why do you say that?'

'Mrs Etherington-Grant asked a lot of questions about you – whether we got on, did you get many telephone calls from England, who your parents were, what sort of background you came from. Don't worry, Nancy, she's well-known on the island, and totally detested by a good many people. She made life hell for a girl in one of the Government offices a few years ago because she thought her husband was getting a little too friendly with her. It was nonsense, of course – nobody in their right mind would risk annexing Mr Etherington-Grant.'

'I'm rather glad I don't work in one of the Government offices.'

'The only authority she has is through her husband and everybody knows he's under her thumb, but she can make life difficult with those hints at scandal she trots out. The fact that you went off with Noel Templeton really set her back on her heels. Any day now she'll be warning you that he's a confirmed bachelor, too free with women and that you're wasting your time.'

'How does she know what I'm doing? I should have

thought she'd have been pleased that I'd transferred my affections from a married man to a bachelor, not that my affections are involved.

Sally threw back her head and laughed. 'Things are going to be very interesting! Noel Templeton doesn't give a hoot what she thinks, and she can't do you any harm regarding your career. I'd be wary though, this is a very small island and we are a small community within it. She could make trouble for you Nancy, although, I never understand why people listen to her when we all know what she's like.'

Sure enough, several days later, Mrs Etherington-Grant came into the gallery on the pretext of looking at a new delivery of jade items. I was busy at the time with another client but she dawdled deliberately then when my customer left, she approached me, and smiled in the friendliest fashion.

'Good morning, Miss Graham. I came in to look at the jade but it really is too expensive for what I want. It's a wedding present actually, but for a couple I don't know all that well. I rather like the look of those pictures – may I see one or two of them?'

They were exquisite paintings of flowers and birds on deep cream satin set in narrow bamboo frames; she had me holding them at a distance against a wall, changing from one to the other until with a shrug of her shoulders she said, 'They're *both* very beautiful, but I'm not sure. Perhaps I'll wait until Mr Etherington-Grant can come with me – he's so much more positive than I. Did you enjoy the other evening, Miss Graham?'

'Yes, thank you very much. It was so kind of you to invite me.'

Slightly disconcerted she said quickly, 'I wasn't meaning the party, dear, I meant your evening in the company of Mr Templeton. Noel's such a dear boy, such very good company. All the girls are a little in love with him.'

I remained silent, occupying myself with replacing the pictures while she warmed to her theme. 'Of course, one can't really blame him for never having a serious relationship. He lives such a bohemian life, and also a very dangerous one. A wife would be a serious encumbrance.' Then, in a voice a little above a whisper, 'Forgive me my dear, but I don't want you to be hurt a second time. That would be too awful.'

'You are kind to concern yourself about me, Mrs Etherington-Grant but there's really no need. I knew Mr Templeton in London – his father knew my father, so you can say we're old friends.'

'Really?' she said with raised eyebrows. 'You know he's in China at the moment.'

'Yes.'

'After that he's likely to go off to some other trouble-spot. It's an exciting life for a man, but a totally dreadful one for any woman connected with him. I would hate it myself. Well, I'll think about the pictures, Miss Graham – I'm always spoiled for choice when I come here.' She smiled again graciously and made her way self-importantly through the gallery and out of the door.

I wanted to laugh. She was ludicrous – a silly bored woman with not enough to do except create scandal and interfere in what didn't concern her. Nothing she said would ever affect any feelings I might have, now or in the future, for Noel Templeton.

20

It was several days later, after his return from Peking, that Noel and I swam in the warm limpid sea they called Deep Water Bay. I was the first out of the water, rubbing myself dry before lying out in the sun listening to the cries of the gulls above me. Presently Noel dropped down by my side saying, 'Did you bring that article of yours with you, Nancy?'

'Yes, it's in my bag, but I warn you it's awfully trite.'

'I'll be the judge of that.'

'How was Peking?'

'Restless. One senses it – the whole world's restless. Maybe global peace is just a pipe dream, since there's always war in some part of the world. Maybe we are indulging in a fool's paradise.'

I saw he was sitting up looking pensively out to sea, his eyes half-closed against the sunlight and I discovered the first faint stirrings of attraction for this man with his hard lean body, tanned by the sun, his keen good-looking face and dark sculptured hair blowing gently in the wind.

Noel was considerably younger than Desmond, and he didn't have Desmond's world-weary expression, the expression of a man without illusions, a man versed in cynicism, a man fashioned by diplomacy to be all things to all men. Noel was in a different mould, like a young eagle, keen and eager and forever searching, a man who didn't have the time to become jaded with the adventures life had to offer.

I was conscious of a feeling of excitement. If I could suddenly think like this wasn't it sure proof that Desmond's image was receding in my mind? I didn't want it to be replaced by a new torment, however. I didn't want to fall in love with Noel Templeton, to replace one disaster with another.

At that moment he turned his head and looked down at me, then with a little smile bent down and kissed me. For a few seconds I lay quietly on the sand, then I raised my arms and placed them round his neck allowing his arms to creep round me and the embrace went on and on until we separated to lie quietly side by side upon the sand.

He made no effort to kiss me again, and after a while I produced the article I had sent to Mr McKay and he read through it. He made no comment while I waited anxiously for him to reach the end, then with a smile he said, 'This is good, Nancy, it's very good. How much did he pay you?'

'Fifty pounds.'

'It should have been three times as much.'

'It's only a small local paper,' I protested. 'They don't have that kind of money.'

'I'll bet he sold many more copies when he published this, with all those friends and neighbours agog to hear what one of their local girls was up to. You're not going to stop here – you'll write others, of course.'

'I hadn't thought of it. I wouldn't know where to place them.'

'All those people who read the first feature will be waiting for the next. They'll want to know how you're making out, where you eat and who with, who you're in love with and anything else you can dream up.'

'If I was in love with anybody I certainly wouldn't put it into print.'

'Very discreet of you Nancy but seriously, you mustn't stop here. You have your father's gift – he'd be so pleased to know you hadn't entirely given up on journalism.'

'I know. Father would have been delighted.'

'Then you must go on – I'll expect to see a lot more of your work. Now, shall we go and eat?'

'Oh yes, I hadn't realised I was so hungry.' I put the

article away carefully in my bag, and then Noel pulled me to my feet and I stood closely held in the shelter of his arms. He laughed teasingly down into my face, then taking hold of my hand started to pull me up the dune towards the path.

With Mark there had been youthful hope that our future lay together, and there had been hope with Desmond, too – blind hope that centered on a remote future, a sort of belief that what we had together was unique and precious. I had no such hope with Noel: I knew that one day, any day, it would end – but for the time being there was a glorious free enchantment.

Noel showed me the Hong Kong he knew well – Shanghai Street with its kites and paper symbols given to the dead, where fortunetellers traced our fortunes in grains of sand spread out on the pavements before them, and the Night Market where everything made under the sun was for sale and where one night we sat entranced to watch Chinese Opera.

At the jade market he bought me a bangle, a beautiful object fashioned in many different colours of green and which I knew had been very expensive, but when I remonstrated with him he merely laughed and extravagantly picked out a tiny Chinese Buddha on a carved rosewood stand which he said would bring me eternal good luck.

We drank scented tea in old tea-houses and walked through the bird market where the afternoon was filled with song and where parakeets performed enchantingly on tiny roller skates and scooters.

At night we drove out to the old walled village of Tsang Tai Uk where life went on as it had done centuries ago, and through the Sai Kung Country Park. In the village of Tai Po, Noel was again extravagant when be bought a beautiful rug for me at the carpet factory, but he insisted, 'I'm not paying the prices your place charges – this is cheap by comparison.'

Our days together lengthened into months. One evening he asked me, 'Do they ever give holidays at that gallery of yours?'

'I think so, I've never asked. Just being in Hong Kong seems like a holiday to me.'

'I have to go into the New Territories soon and you could come with me. Then there's Thailand and Macau – you may never see the Far East again after you've left it, so why not make the most of it now?'

'I would need to ask, but I'm very tempted, Noel. I want to see so much.'

When I made enquiries I was told that for every year I spent in Hong Kong I could ask for a month's leave. Delightedly Noel urged, 'Spend the first two weeks in the New Territories with me, then if my job and Providence permit, we can go on from there.'

It was the start of a glorious adventure. Moving out from Kowloon on the fast train for Canton I sat with my eyes glued to the window, memorising the long dun-coloured paddy fields and the people working in the deeply cut furrows: women with pointed hats like lampshades, carrying babies on their backs and men raising their eyes to the speeding train, gazing after it with dark inscrutable eyes.

We left the train at Canton and Noel hired a pack of mules so that we could travel slowly through the villages towards the mountains and the valley of the Yangtze. He also hired two smiling youths who looked after us and our animals with simple courtesy and I discovered a rare and primitive charm in our meanderings and a humility when I listened to Noel talking about China.

I had loved Desmond but always there had been that sense of guilt which no amount of modern sophistication could eradicate. There was no guilt in loving Noel – we were both free – but there was always the feeling that our love was transitory. This time it would not be another women that divided us, but his way of life – a life filled with danger which he had never felt he should ask a woman to share. Of course, there had been other women

215

in Noel's life, but I asked no questions. All I had was the here and now. I knew it would be death that kept Noel away from me, and I became doubly convinced of this when two of his cameramen were killed in a skirmish in Manila several days after he had left on a new mission.

Then suddenly one glorious sunlit afternoon he was back, handsome and smiling, showing me a bandaged shoulder grazed by a flying bullet with little boy pride. In the spring we went to Thailand and I wandered with Noel entranced through the palace of the King where they had filmed the story of Anna and the King of Siam. We explored the floating markets and laughed uproariously at the antics of the vegetable sellers and as we passed a tiny boat piled high with flowers the friendly girl at the prow placed a huge bunch of mimosa in my arms.

On our last afternoon we drove out to where elephants were working in a forest clearing and I marvelled at how these great patient beasts toiled with enormous tree trunks, obeying implicitly the instructions of the little men sitting easily on their huge shoulders. Noel told me that the working life of an elephant was usually from the age of fourteen to the age of sixty-five and in that time they normally stayed with the same handler so that they both more or less had the same working life.

I fell in love that afternoon with the most enchanting baby elephant who stayed close to his working mother, then after the day's toil was finished we followed them down to the river where they played and splashed in the water and where the baby mischievously sprayed me with water before we fed them huge bunches of bananas.

In the evening we sat cross-legged on the floor eating meat and rice with chopsticks, tools with which I was now expert, while before us, girls performed the graceful patterned dances of Thailand. Their long graceful fingers were like flowers, and their jewelled head-dresses were ornamented with tiny silver bells which tinkled prettily with every movement of their bodies.

As we walked back to our hotel through the scented dark I thought I had just spent the most enchanted day of my life. From our balcony we could hear the sound of temple bells and the insistent chirping of the cicadas. The night was perfumed with the scent of a thousand blossoms and inside our room the mimosa was powerfully sweet.

My whole being ached with love for Noel. I felt a blinding desire to tell him, to place fetters around him that would bind us together forever but I kept silent, allowing my body to show him the power of love while my lips remained silent. Tomorrow we were going back to Hong Kong, to its clamour and its colonial insularity.

When Noel drew up outside my apartment block, he leapt out, opened the boot and placed my suitcase on the pavement. Then he reached inside the car and took a brightly wrapped oblong parcel out of the glove compartment and placed it in my hands. It felt heavy, but when I started to thank him, he waved my thanks aside saying gently, 'Tell me some other time if you like it. Sleep well, Nancy.'

He went round to open my door and I stared at him uncertainly. On other nights our farewells had been warm and passionate with desire, but tonight his friendly smile made me lift my head proudly. If this was to be the end of it then I wouldn't let him see how much I cared. Bidding him a small goodnight I lifted my suitcase and went off up the steps leading to the flats. Before I entered the door I heard his car roar away into the night.

Normally we would have made arrangements to meet again, but now that old feeling of rejection swept over me and I sank down onto the nearest chair trembling with hurt. I stared at the parcel in my hands. It was obviously a farewell gift, and with some annoyance I threw it across the room and left it lying on the carpet near the window.

I had been in bed several hours, unable to sleep, when I remembered the parcel and left my bed to retrieve it. Curiously I cut the string and removed the paper then I was staring down at the faded covers of a book entitled *Love is a Many Splendoured Thing*. A note fluttered down onto the carpet.

It was very brief. '*I hate saying goodbye so please bear with me. I'm off in the morning to the Middle East where once more there is mayhem. Those fortunetellers were wrong when they promised us Christmas together, it would seem we shall be far apart for many months. Read the book, my darling, it will help you to understand.*' It was signed quite simply *Noel*.

Every spare minute I had during the following days I sat with my nose buried in the book. I wept hot salty tears for the Eurasian girl in love with an American war correspondent, for their love story that blossomed on the shores of Deep Water Bay – a love story that ended tragically with his death in Vietnam. When I found I could cry no more, I found comfort in the story: it was Noel's way of telling me that this was a fate that could happen to us, to any woman in love with a man who lived dangerously.

21

My life in Hong Kong resumed its familiar pattern. Occasionally I went out in a foursome with Sally and Guy, but I remained true to Noel, who wrote to me whenever he could. I followed his stories of the troubles in the Middle East avidly, listening attentively to the comments of those who knew him, and in my quieter moments I asked God to keep him safe.

Whenever I met Mrs Etherington-Grant I was aware of the look that said 'I told you so', but I greeted her respectfully and hoped she was a little disappointed that I gave her no further cause to think I was in the need of advice.

Aunt Susan wrote to me twice a year, on my birthday and at Christmas, and her letters were invariably strictures on warm clothing and foreign food. Maisie wrote now and then, occasionally including the odd bit of gossip about Amelia.

Mrs Etherington-Grant informed me one day that Desmond had received a Knighthood on his return from Russia. She added unnecessarily, 'I don't suppose it will make any difference to Celia, she was Lady Celia anyway, but I do wish they'd live together in London, it's so much more circumspect. How long are you in Hong Kong for, Nancy dear? Surely you must soon be due to return to London?'

'I'm not quite sure yet.' I smiled at her politely, determined not to let her upset me.

Shortly after that encounter, Sally informed me that she was getting married quietly in Hong Kong before returning to England when Guy had his next leave. Once home, they hoped to have a big party for her very large family and his widowed mother. I was delighted to be her only bridesmaid at the end of August and then I was waving them off on their flight to London.

I was cheered by a letter from Mr McKay informing me that my long series of articles on life in Hong Kong had been a very great success. He reaffirmed his offer of a job should I ever decide to return to the north. He knew how to flatter me, saying I was wasted selling expensive art objects to people with too much money, and that I had a natural flair for journalism. My father would have been delighted to read my articles, and even more delighted to think I was working on a paper again.

I considered his offer, but honestly didn't feel I could take up a life in Greymont with any ease. I was now nearly twenty-eight and I couldn't in all honesty envisage living with, or even near, my dominating Aunt Susan. I had no intention of being ruled by her, as my mother had been. Consequently, I thanked Mr McKay for renewing his kind offer, and promised to contact him if I wanted to take it up.

All thoughts of Greymont were swept out of my mind, however, when I received a letter from Mr Papadraos to say my term in Hong Kong was nearing its end. I was being replaced by a young Chinese gentleman who had been born in London but was of Hong Kong origin. He was also a nephew of Mr Ho Ying.

He arrived three days before I was due to leave, a slim charming young man with a grave gentle face, his eyes a dark limpid brown behind his thick horn-rimmed spectacles, his hair shining like black jet. He listened carefully to everything I could tell him but I quickly realised that he was every bit as knowledgeable as myself, in some respects even more so, so I gave myself two days' leave which I spent haunting the sites I had visited with Noel.

I would miss Hong Kong, its life and its colour, its incomparable brashness and its brilliance but I was not sorry to be going home, in spite of the fact that home meant London. Then an old and half-forgotten disquiet came to haunt me . . . For the first time in months I thought about Desmond, wondering idly what sort of girl was in his life now, or if he and Celia had resolved the differences in their marriage after their stay in Russia.

I turned the key in the lock before looking up for the last time to the first-floor windows of the flat I had shared for the past four years. My taxi waited at the kerb, a new white Mercedes. The company were doing me proud.

The airport was a hive of activity but it was incredibly efficient, from the smartly-dressed, helpful police to the smiling men who handled our luggage and the pretty girls in attendance at the desks. For a few minutes I stood at one of the large windows looking out to where the ferries plied across the harbour and even as I watched, a huge plane descended out of the clouds and seemed to skim the water as it dropped onto the runway. Then a monotonous voice announced in a faintly singsong tone that our plane to London had just arrived from Sydney and I turned to make my way to the passenger lounge.

That was the moment when I found myself looking into the cool appraising eyes of Mrs Etherington-Grant, who appeared remarkably pink and white and British in her favourite pastel colours. There was no opportunity for me to avoid her. She came forward with a bright smile, her hand outstretched saying, 'Why of course, Miss Graham, you're leaving us. I'd quite forgotten – so many people have been coming and going recently.'

I took her hand in its pale grey suede glove but she applied no pressure and I was glad to release it.

'We're here to meet my husband's new assistant and his wife. One has to make a gesture, I'm sure they'll be feeling a little strange. You must reassure them, my dear, that in no time at all they'll become one of us. After all, you were very quick to find your feet. Are you sorry to be leaving?'

'It will be nice to see England again.'

'Well of course, and what could be nicer than England

in the springtime? We miss it terribly and unfortunately we have no plans to go back there this year. Will you be returning to the gallery?'

'For the time being.'

'You are thinking you might move on then?'

'There is always the possibility that I might.'

'Actually, my dear, I think it would be a very good idea if you moved right away. Your memories will be none too happy and I don't suppose you wish to rekindle anything that can have no future. Do you hear from Noel at all?'

'Sometimes. I don't believe he has time to write many personal letters.' I didn't tell her that Noel seemed to have stopped writing to me and that I feared his love for me had died through our long absence from each other. That was my private sorrow, and one I would admit to nobody.

'Noel is a dear boy, we've known him for years. I doubt if he's the marrying kind, but then you probably know that without my telling you. He's very attractive and a great charmer: I tried to warn you in the early days of your friendship but you didn't take too kindly to my advice. I simply felt that you'd had one bitter disappointment, I didn't want you to have another.'

I felt a ridiculous desire to strike that pink and white smiling face with its gently smiling mouth and eyes like pieces of blue flint. I knew she was a silly poisonous woman who would have rejoiced when Noel left Hong Kong but not for the reasons she wanted me to believe.

I was relieved to see her husband walking across the hall accompanied by another man and a woman. He smiled toothily and politely held out his hand saying he hoped I had a pleasant journey home, and would not forget Hong Kong and the friends I had made there. It was a pompous little speech to which the other three listened admiringly, then he added, 'Look after yourself my dear, a pretty girl like you can't afford to be too careful these days.'

222

I felt angry and unsettled by the encounter but there was little time to think about it because almost immediately the passengers for the London plane were being called. After a brief goodbye I walked briskly across the hall, willing myself not to turn around, but with the feel of at least one pair of eyes boring into my back.

I was lucky enough to have been allocated a window seat, and as the plane rapidly filled I saw that my seating companions were Asian so I doubted if there would be much conversation on the long haul home. As the plane banked I looked my last on the crowded harbour of Hong Kong below me, the bustling ferries and the Chinese junks, the towering skyscrapers reflecting the morning sun in their maze of windows, and I sat back with my eyes closed.

All around me I could hear the vociferous chatter of numerous tongues, but in my imagination I could still smell the pungent aroma of incense and joss-sticks that is Hong Kong, and all around me people were straining their heads for a final glimpse of one of the most crowded and fascinating islands in the world. The plane soared like a giant bird into the brilliant blue of the sky and now there was nothing to see but white billowing clouds below us and I closed my eyes again to shut out the light. The hum of voices and the throb of the engines sent me to sleep but it was a light, easily-roused sleep, and by the time we were landing in Bangkok I was wide awake and staring down on the strange Eastern city sweltering under the midday sun.

A handful of people joined the plane including two nuns, strangely sombre in their black garb and seeming even more so beside a group of Thai monks in their saffron robes. Earnest young men with pale faces and shaven heads, I couldn't help thinking they would strike an incongruous note on the streets of London. My companions chattered together in Cantonese, handing me coffee and an English newspaper with bright smiles.

The newspaper was yesterday's and the news it contained uneventful. It was then I remembered the airmail letter in my handbag and I took it out and scanned the writing with a puzzled frown. The postmark was smudged so badly I couldn't read it, and when I opened the envelope I could see that it contained two sheets of pale blue writing paper. My heart missed several beats when I read the address printed in dark blue on the first page. *Garveston Hall, Ampledean, Lancashire.* Quickly I turned the pages over to look for the signature which read simply *Amelia.*

Memories were poignant at that moment and I turned my head towards the window impatient with the treacherous tears that filled my eyes. It was several moments before I felt sufficiently composed to read Amelia's letter and all the time I was reading it I was picturing her sitting calm and elegant in the drawing room at Garveston Hall, a slight frown between her eyes. It was probably a difficult letter to write – I can't believe it was an easy thing to span the years when she had ignored my existence for so long – but there would be a vague gentle smile on her lips, her soft dark hair falling over her face, occasionally pushed back by long slender fingers, then satisfied, the final flourish as she signed her name. How had Amelia managed to find me?

'*Dear Nancy,*' she wrote. '*I've had such trouble finding you! I tried your Aunt Susan who had unfortunately mislaid your last letter and then I asked Maisie Standing, but she said she hadn't heard from you for ages. I finally wrote to the gallery who were kind enough to give me your address in Hong Kong; how wonderful to be so well-travelled.*

'*I hope you haven't forgotten that in five months' time it will be ten years since we left Lorivals and I remember standing on the steps waiting to be picked up and saying we must all meet again in a decade, no matter what we were doing or where we were living. That is why I'm giving you so much notice.*

'*I see Maisie in the village occasionally but I have of course written to her with this invitation. I have also written to Barbara in Cheltenham. I propose that our reunion should take place here at Garveston Hall, from Friday afternoon on the twentieth of July until Monday the twenty-third after breakfast. That will give us Saturday and all day Sunday to revive old memories.*

'It's all so terribly sad that there can't be the five of us but I know Lois would want us to meet, I remember she welcomed the suggestion.

'Please write soon, dear Nancy. Yours ever, Amelia.'

I sat back stunned, allowing the letter to flutter on to the floor and the girl sitting beside me retrieved it and handed it back to me with a bright toothy smile.

I was remembering the scene vividly: five girls standing at the top of the stone steps above the drive, kissing and embracing, the air vibrant with their laughter. And yet Amelia had never tried to keep in touch . . . it was a mystery that after all these years she should suddenly remember that promise.

I would make some excuse of course, for how could I possibly spend a weekend listening to the gossip of wives immersed in their domestic wonderland? I would write to her nearer the time to say I was too busy with my job in London. I folded the letter carefully and replaced it in the envelope, then I pushed it away at the bottom of my handbag just in time to accept the tray containing my lunch from my travelling companion. She smiled again saying, 'You live in London?'

I nodded, returning her smile and thinking it was not going to be such a silent journey after all.

'You like England?' she continued.

'Yes, of course – it's my home. Is this your first visit?'

'Yes. I go to work for English family, to look after two children. I work for them in Hong Kong, now they have sent for me.'

'Are you happy to be leaving Hong Kong.'

'Yes, very happy. I want to travel, see the world. This is my one big chance.'

225

'I hope you'll be very happy in England. Will you be living in London?'

'No, in Colchester, Essex. You like?'

'I'm sorry but I don't know Colchester at all. It is one of our oldest cities though.'

At that moment the man sitting on the other side of her said something and she twisted around. It was several minutes before she turned back to me to say, 'He too is going to England for the first time. He's going to work in a hotel, a grand hotel like the Mandarin.'

I smiled. I had spoken to many young men in Hong Kong and always they were coming to work in some quite opulent hotel; they believed that every hotel in London was as sumptuous as the Mandarin. I was not going to be the one to shatter their illusions, but I couldn't help remembering the Mandarin on Hong Kong Island, with its gracious rooms, fabulous shops .and obsequious, soft-footed servants: not even the Savoy could compete with this Eastern magnificence.

The trays were taken away and conversation ceased while the in-flight movie was being shown on the massive screen set in front of us. My neighbour sat up keenly with every anticipation of enjoying the next couple of hours. For my part I was completely indifferent about the film. It was a comedy thriller, high in violence and risqué dialogue, and I was glad to close my eyes and listen to gentle taped music through my earphones, shutting out every other sound.

The rest of the journey was uneventful and I thought I had never felt so unutterably weary when fourteen hours later I stepped down onto the tarmac in a cold grey English dawn.

22

For a generous tip the taxi driver carried all of my luggage to the front doorstep of the house in Hammer-smith, and after paying him I looked at the familiar outside and garden with the utmost astonishment.

The old house had undergone a transformation. The entire paintwork looked brand new, in sparkling black and white. The path up to the front door had been newly paved and our poor dilapidated house which no amount of amateur renovation seemed to improve was suddenly a most desirable residence.

Even as I stared around me, a man approached pushing a wheelbarrow from the back of the house. I stood watching him for several minutes before he saw me, but he only raised his battered hat politely before going on with his work. There was a new shining brass knocker on the front door and in some anxiety I raised it and brought it down heavily, then stood waiting for the door to be opened.

The man left his flowerbed and came over to me. 'I should try the bell, miss. If the wife's in the kitchen she'll never hear the knocker,' he advised before returning to his work.

I heard the bell echoing shrilly inside the house and waited again. In just a few minutes however I heard footsteps crossing the hall, then the door was opened wide and a small plump woman was looking at me enquiringly.

She smiled and in some confusion I said, 'Good morning, I'm Nancy Graham. I wrote to say I'd be arriving this morning.'

Her face cleared. 'Of course, miss. I was told you'd be coming back but they didn't seem to know just when.

I'll get Joe to bring in your luggage; you and me will never manage it on our own.'

She called the gardener over and tucking one case under his arm and carrying the other two by their handles he followed us inside the house. I looked round at the familiar hall curiously. It had a tiled floor that had been mopped and polished so that it shone, and there was a new Turkey red carpet on the stairs. On a dark oak table set against the wall stood a tall vase filled with spring flowers and seeing me glance at them the woman said, 'They arrived yesterday and Miss Marcia arranged them when she came in last night. My, but they must have cost somethin' shockin'. It's a bit early for them and they're that expensive.'

Joe stood at the foot of the stairs looking at me for instructions.

'My room's at the front of the house, the second on the right at the top of the stairs.'

Nodding briefly, he picked up my suitcases and started to climb the stairs while the woman said, 'I expect you're ready for a cup o' tea, miss, so I'll go and put the kettle on. My name's Mrs Tunstall but mostly I gets called Emmie. Joe's my husband.'

'I'd love a cup of tea, Mrs Tunstall. Would you like me to come into the kitchen?'

'No miss, I'll bring it up to your room. And please call me Emmie – it's more friendly-like.'

'How long have you been here, Emmie?'

'Around six months. We're very comfortable – we have our own quarters and the young women are not much trouble, really. I reckon they could be a bit tidier but I cope pretty well. Will you be here for good now, Miss Graham?'

'I'm not quite sure what my future plans will be, Emmie, although I expect I shall be back at work quite soon.'

'Of course and you've just got to get used to living in England again. I'll get yer tea.'

She bustled into the kitchen and I started to climb the stairs. I met Joe leaving my room and he smiled, stepping back so that I could pass him. I've put the cases just inside miss, so watch you don't fall over them,' he said.

'Thank you, Joe.'

My room had an unlived-in look. It was too tidy, too impersonal but there was a new fitted carpet on the floor and new drapes at the windows. Somebody had been very generous and my heart sank a little when I thought how much I would be expected to contribute to this transformation. Still, it was good to be back in my old room, kept vacant for so long.

There was only one picture on the wall, a school photograph taken during our last year at Lorivals. I took it over to the window and stared down at it. I sat between Maisie and Amelia on the front row; I saw myself as I was then – a girl with pale blonde hair and a smiling pretty face, sitting with my friends, all of us looking so impersonal in our school uniform, alike and yet not alike.

Amelia was so very beautiful with her dark pansy brown eyes and soft cloudy hair framing a face as delicate and exquisite as a cameo, and so very different from Maisie with her tousled red curls and plump well-scrubbed look of robust health.

I found Barbara on the second row, tall and slender, her dark hair swept back from a faintly bored face; even in those days there had been a sophistication about Barbara beyond her years. Lois stood at the end of the row, her small gamine face expressive, wearing the large glasses that hid the beauty of her grey eyes, and the long enamelled earrings that Miss Clarkson had angrily commanded her to remove, but too late to keep them out of the photograph.

I looked up into the mirror on my dressing table and back again at the photograph. There were lines of weariness round my eyes now and the smiling happy girl in the photograph had become a tall slender woman whose fine fair hair framed a wistful face.

There was a soft knock on the door and Emmie came in carrying a tea tray on which rested a plate of biscuits and the welcome cup of tea. 'Dinner's at seven tonight, miss, but I never know who's coming in for it. I asks them over and over again to tell me what time they'll be in but they never do. It's difficult for Joyce but Marcia and the new lodger here, Phillipa, work in London, after all. They just forget most of the time.'

'Who is Phillipa?'

'She works at the same place as Marcia. She has the room at the end of the passage, the spare room.'

'I didn't know.'

'Well, there it was standing idle and Marcia said Phillipa was looking for somewhere decent to live. She was glad to come here. Now, do you need any help unpacking?'

'No thank you, Emmie. I'll remember that dinner is at seven; I'm looking forward to it.'

So Marcia had let Lois' room; she had never been squeamish or sentimental about things. Perhaps Phillipa had something to do with the transformation of the house.

I sat on the window seat to drink my tea watching Joe busily turning over the garden soil, then suddenly curiosity overcame me. I left the room and walked down the corridor. I hesitated at the door of Phillipa's room, still a little too nervous to enter, then I knocked lightly on the door and receiving no answer opened it cautiously.

It was totally different from the room I remembered. The furniture had been changed, the colours were different and on the bed lay an outsize teddy bear with a blue ribbon round his neck. Beside the bed lay a pile of magazines and on the chair near the window was a pile of flimsy underwear.

I had thought that memories of Lois would confront me as soon as I opened the door, but everything was so changed the memory escaped me. It was only when I left the room and stood momentarily with my back to

230

the door that I was able to conjure up the memory of Lois sitting cross-legged on her bed, her grey eyes filled with pain, her anguished voice reciting the actions she had been able to discover about the man she was so in love with.

Joe stood talking to a delivery man at the gate, and while I still watched from my room, a girl sprang lightly off the bus and entered the garden. She waved gaily to Joe and hurried up the path. I had never seen her before so assumed at once that this must be Phillipa. I started to unpack my cases, listening all the time for her footsteps to pass my door.

I could hear her singing as she ran up the stairs, then there was a light tap on my door and without waiting for an answer the door opened and a girl's blonde head appeared round the door. She had a remarkably pretty face, alive and smiling. 'Hello,' she said brightly. 'I'm Phillipa Darwen, Emmie told me you'd arrived. We didn't quite know when to expect you.'

I smiled in return, then observed, 'You're home early. I understood Emmie to say you worked in Westminster.'

'Yes, I work at the FO with Marcia, but it's a half-day for me today. I'd better hurry and get changed, I have a date. I'll see you tomorrow, Nancy, then we can really get acquainted. Marcia'll be in around six-thirty.'

Phillipa seemed a likeable sort of girl, but I couldn't reconcile the tasteful alterations to the house and gardens with the rather ordinary picture she presented. I also felt reassured. Phillipa did not appear to be a sensitive soul, unlikely to discover a lingering sadness in the room she occupied.

After a while I heard her singing in the bathroom, then soon after that came the sound of her busy footsteps going past my room again. I went to the window, and there she was hurrying down the path wearing a pale cream coat, her blonde hair piled on top of her head. For several minutes she hung about the gate, then a low bright red sports car containing two boys and a girl

231

pulled up and she climbed into the back seat. They drove off in a flurry of chatter and exhaust fumes leaving Joe staring after them shaking his head.

I finished my unpacking, then carrying my washing and the tray Emmie had brought up I went down to the kitchen. I could smell meat or poultry cooking and there was a sound of clattering pans and crockery. Emmie was busy at the stove and once again I turned to stare at the transformation. Gone was the old rusting washing machine and cooker, and in their place stood a new sink contained in a light oak unit and a brand new shining washing machine and dryer.

Emmie stood with her back to me, stirring something in a pan on top of the cooker. She heard me putting the tray down on the top of one of the units and turned with a smile saying, 'Are you all unpacked then?'

'Not entirely. I've left one suitcase – I'll do it later.'

'Leave your washing there love, I'll put it in the machine.'

'I don't expect you to do my washing.'

'That's what I'm paid to do: the cleaning, the cooking and the washing. Joe does the garden, decorating and odd jobs. We're both very happy here and more than satisfied with the money we get.'

'Who employed you, Emmie?'

'Well, Marcia did. She interviewed us and offered us the job.'

'I see.' I didn't really see. Marcia had always been short of money, always the one to borrow until the end of the month, and now she could suddenly afford all this. Either she'd come into money, won the pools, or she'd found someone willing to finance her.

'Was the house like this when you arrived here, Emmie?' I had to ask. I was completely baffled.

'Oh yes, lovely it was, and I've worked in some pretty awful places I can tell you. Of course the garden wasn't much. Joe's responsible for the way it looks today. The advertisement said a couple was wanted to look after a

232

large house and garden occupied by four businesswomen. We've always worked in old folks' homes before, and this seemed like a nice change. It's a lot less trouble, I can tell you.'

'Marcia will be in for dinner, I believe.'

'Yes miss, there'll be just the two of you. The young lady who works for the airlines is not back until Friday. I'll be serving dinner in the dining room around seven; me and Joe eats here in the kitchen. Young Phillipa's gone out, I hear. She's having a rare old good time at the moment but then, she's not the sort to settle down in a hurry. She's too fond of a laugh, she is.'

I smiled and let myself out of the kitchen door. Marcia would tell me all I wanted to know about Phillipa. However, there was no time to talk to Marcia before our evening meal. I heard her running up the stairs then the slamming of her bedroom door, and looking at my watch I saw that there was only a quarter of an hour before Emmie would be dishing up.

After a short nap, I had bathed and changed into a fresh skirt and blouse and so I decided to wait for Marcia in the dining room. Here again I was due for a surprise. Our old scratched dining table which we had bought for a song from a secondhand dealer in Pimlico had gone, and in its place stood a large oval dining table in rich mahogany while round it were placed six matching chairs, their seats covered in wine-coloured velvet.

Wine-coloured velvet drapes hung at the windows and a plain grey fitted carpet covered the floor. I took my place at the table and waited for Marcia who arrived minutes later flustered and still struggling to fasten her skirt just as Emmie appeared pushing her trolley. She rushed round the table and kissed and hugged me before taking her place directly opposite, then we sat in silence while Emmie set down the vegetable dishes on the table and a platter containing slices of beautifully cooked chicken.

I suddenly realised I was very hungry. I had only eaten

biscuits and drunk several cups of tea since leaving the plane that morning; now I helped myself from the dishes on the table with every expectation of enjoying my meal.

'What a rush!' Marcia complained. 'The traffic was worse than usual this evening. Oh Nancy – you look marvellous. So tanned and pretty and fit. I suppose Phillipa's gone out – did you get to meet her?'

'Yes. I believe she works with you?'

'That's right. Poor kid, she was in the most awful bedsit with a crowd of other girls; there was absolutely no privacy and I got fed up with hearing her complain every morning, particularly when there was a room vacant here.'

'She doesn't mind it being Lois' old room?'

'Well of course not, why should she? After all, one can't go on forever walking past it on tiptoe, talking in whispers whenever we pass the door. It was all terribly sad but life has to go on you know, and to be honest, we were glad of the additional rent.'

I went on with my meal. There were a great many things I needed to ask Marcia, but they could wait until the coffee stage when we were less likely to be disturbed.

Marcia prattled on. Office gossip mingled with questions about my life in Hong Kong and I sensed that she too was waiting for Emmie to make her final disappearance before we embarked on more serious conversation. At long last we sat with our coffee and I said feelingly, 'The meal was lovely, we obviously have a treasure in Emmie and Joe. There's just one thing I'd like to know. How can we possibly afford them?'

For a moment she stared at me in a puzzled fashion, then asked, 'You haven't said what you think about the house. It's cost a bomb to refurnish and do all that was necessary after the old lady died.'

'Did you get a bank loan or something? I have the distinct feeling I owe you a great deal of money. And like I said, Emmie's a treasure but do we really need her? We never had a housekeeper before.'

'You really don't know, do you. He didn't write to tell you.'

'I don't know what you're talking about.'

'I'm talking about Desmond, for heaven's sake. He paid for it all. He also engaged the Tunstalls, oh, not personally, but through a reliable employment agency. They think I'm the one who asked for them.'

It was my turn to stare now and I could feel myself trembling with the old emotional mixture of anger and resentment – and a strange kind of helplessness. 'I didn't know, he didn't write to tell me. Oh, why did he do all this?' It's been four years! My life has nothing to do with him now. How dare he act as if he owns me!'

'Conscience, Nancy. It probably began to bite when you weren't waiting for him to return from Russia. I'd love to have seen his face when he heard you were in Hong Kong for a few years.'

'If I'd been here I would never have allowed him to do this. What on earth are people going to say when they know? They'll think I'm a kept woman and I'm not!'

'Calm down, Nancy. Nobody knows except Desmond and me and I'm the soul of discretion. If anybody's going to be talked about it's me. I spend long hours in his office talking about the house, and I get the strangest looks from Marion Wilton. Nobody knows about this place, and I'm not really concerned what they say. Anyway I'm leaving the Foreign Office at the end of this month.'

'Leaving the Foreign Office! But why?'

'I'm getting married, my love. If I don't grab hold of this chance I might never get another.'

'Oh Marcia, I'm so glad for you! Who is he – is he nice?'

'I've known John for years, since I was about five, I think. He runs a fruit farm and a huge market garden in the Vale of Evesham. There's nothing I haven't learned about spring onions and radishes, when to plant

235

and when to reap, they even have a section selling caged birds and funny little things like mice and the like. It'll be a far cry from the corridors of power to cleaning out the cage of a golden hamster.'

'You haven't said what he's like or if you love him.'

'He's nice. He's tall and lanky and I've never seen him in a suit; he's usually in corduroys and wellies and he's got the brightest blue eyes and a face that smiles an awful lot. I'll be living in an old oak-timbered house that needs the earth spending on it – this place is a palace by comparison – but yes, I do love John, and the fact that I love him never ceases to surprise me. Now enough of me, what about you and Desmond? He'll be wanting to see you, Nancy, and you can't afford to look a gift horse like this in the mouth.'

'For the last time, Marcia, I don't want anything from Desmond. It's over,' I said stubbornly.

'Well, at least wait and see what he's offering.'

'I know what he'll be offering: the mixture as before – the secrecy, the loneliness. It was easier when I loved him, but I don't love him any more. There are no pieces to pick up, no loose ends. I even hate this house – it puts me under an obligation to him, and I don't want to feel I owe him anything. He's a fool.'

'How are you going to avoid him if he's so determined? He knows where you work and where you live.'

'Oh God,' I sighed, feeling utterly depressed and beleaguered. 'Marcia, I don't want to spend my life as somebody's mistress. It might suit some girls but not me – those few years before I went to Hong Kong showed me that. You more than anybody should understand.'

'I do. All these years I've been running around in circles and right there on my mother's doorstep was somebody nice and decent who's been in love with me for ages. His father was our local vicar – we even went to school together.'

'I'm happy for you but wish you weren't going. What's

going to happen to your room here when you move out?'

'Darling, there's a queue a mile long waiting to take my place. I nearly forgot – there are some letters for you in the hall. I'll get them.'

She jumped up and went out, returning almost immediately with a small pile of letters which I leafed through quickly. There was an envelope in Aunt Susan's writing and another bearing a Canadian stamp, both possibly welcoming me back to London, and then my heart skipped a beat when I recognised Desmond's flowing hand. Looking up in confusion I met Marcia's gaze.

'From him?' she asked.

'Yes.'

'Well, you go ahead and read it, while I take the coffee cups into the kitchen. Then I'm going upstairs to write a few letters. You may feel differently about everything when you've read what he has to say.' As she left the room she pointed idly to a large bowl of carnations on a small table near the window. 'From him,' she said briefly, 'simply to welcome you home.'

I could smell their perfume, and in that brief moment I could also feel Desmond's presence in the room, smell his aftershave, see his thin clever face with its world-weary countenance which could quickly turn into that little boy lost expression – the look that had first captured my foolish young heart.

'*Dear Nancy*', the letter began formally enough. '*I've thought about you so often over the last few years, often in the hope that you were missing me as much as I was missing you.*

'*I owe you so much, Nancy. You brought youth and joy and laughter back into my life, things that had been missing for a very long time, and I know now that I should have been completely honest with you where I had only been half-honest before.*

'*Marcia told me about your pregnancy and termination, and I realise there is so very much I need to make up to you*

237

and I am starting with that dreadful old house. I hope before you arrive home that it will have been completely transformed into a more fitting background for your grace and beauty.

'I know from Mr Papadraos that you will be back in England at the weekend but unfortunately I shall be in Brussels for the next ten days. I shall, however, look forward to our meeting as soon as I return. You will have so much to tell me, whereas life for me has been very much the same. Goodnight my dearest Nancy. Yours as always, Desmond.'

I put the letter down and sat staring at it for several minutes. Once again, I felt that surge of unreasonable, savage anger towards him, and a cynicism alien to me. Mine as always! When had Desmond Atherton ever been mine? Desmond had never belonged to anybody, not to me nor to his wife – he had belonged only to himself, the sublime egotistical product of his background and his environment, surrounded by admiring colleagues or sycophants who were merely stepping-stones in his way to the top.

I slept badly and when morning came I felt at a loose end. Mr Papadraos was not expecting me back until the following Monday but I decided I must get back there and do something, for anything was better than hanging around the house with my heart plagued with uncertainties.

They greeted me warmly at the gallery. Mr Ho Ying beamed through his thick glasses and the young girl in the office plied me with coffee and shortbread. They were eager to hear all my news and Mr Ho Ying queried softly, 'You met my nephew? He's a very nice boy.'

'Yes indeed, Mr Ho Ying.'

'You like Hong Kong?'

'I had a wonderful and interesting time.'

'You go to plenty parties, to the racecourse, Ocean Park perhaps.'

'Yes, all of those things.'

'And into China? There it is most beautiful.'

'Yes I loved it all.'

238

He nodded, happy with my reply, then Mr Papadraos was there shaking my hand and saying, 'Come into my office, Nancy. We have a great deal to discuss.'

For what seemed like an eternity he sat behind his large cluttered desk without speaking until I began to feel nervous. My anxiety ceased however when he smiled, looking at me kindly out of shrewd eyes. 'Are you happy to be home?'

'I'm not sure, it's too early.'

He nodded. 'Everyone says the East does that to you, but never with me. I am always glad to leave Singapore, Hong Kong or Bangkok – all of them. I am happier in London than in Athens, my home.' I smiled dutifully. 'And are you happy to come back to us at the gallery, to take up life as it was before you went away?'

He was looking at me so closely I could feel the warm blood colouring my cheeks and I knew that he was aware of my thoughts and understood them. I had to be as honest with him as with myself. 'Mr Papadraos, I *don't* want to take up my life as it was before. I've loved working for Treasures of the Orient, I've adored handling beautiful precious things which I know I shall never be able to afford, and I shall be eternally grateful to your kindness to me . . .'

'But?' he ventured.

'I want to leave London. I didn't know when I came in here this morning that that was what I wanted, but I think it's the only answer. I don't want to drift back into something I might bitterly regret. I want to make another whole new beginning, but at the moment I don't quite know how. Last time, you sent me to Hong Kong!'

'It is Mr Atherton, is it not? Poor man, he is sad and lonely and he was completely shaken to know you had gone away to work for us in Hong Kong, but will he want you to go back to him on the same terms? That is the decision is it not, Nancy? It is not your work, not a new life, simply an ending to the old.'

'Yes. I'm no longer in love with Desmond. I don't

239

want to take anything from him, and if I stay here he'll try to persuade me to go back to him. If I can't go back out of love, I don't want to go back out of pity.'

'Ah no, a man does not want pity from the woman he loves. What will you do then, go back to the north, go back into journalism?' He was staring at me keenly, and at that moment my heart gave a sudden excited lurch and seeing my eyes light up he said smiling, 'Ah, I see that I have given you the idea. The articles you sent to the *Gazette* were very interesting, very good. We have them all, since Mr McKay was good enough to send them on.'

'You didn't mind?'

'Mind? Of course not – it made our name known to those in the north who are looking for something special. There is life north of Watford, Nancy?'

I laughed. 'I shall go and live with my Aunt Susan until something else crops up. Must I serve a month's notice?'

'How long is Mr Atherton away?'

'He comes home next weekend.'

'And you wish to be gone before then?'

'I would like that, but if it isn't possible then I shall abide by your rules.'

'It is possible. I too think you should be gone before he returns. He will ask for you and I will tell him that you had this yearning to get back into journalism. That it is a local paper you are going to might puzzle him a little, but he will not argue with me.' For a few minutes he looked at me with a gentle smile playing on his face, then he rose and extended his hand across his desk. 'I wish you good luck, Nancy Graham. You are a very unusual girl.'

The Tunstalls showed no surprise when I told them I had decided to return to the north of England. I expect by this time they were growing accustomed to the comings and goings of their household. Marcia on the other hand was amazed at the speed with which I had made up my mind.

'What are you expecting to do, surely not live with your dreadful Aunt Susan?' she asked incredulously.

'I shall have to for a time, until I find somewhere of my own. At least she'll be pleased to see me, although I expect to be nagged half to death.'

'And what about a job?'

'I'm going to ask if they'll take me back on the paper.'

'I hope you'll still come to my wedding, Nancy.'

'I'll be very hurt if you don't ask me.'

She accompanied me to Euston Station that same night. I had booked a sleeper on the midnight express and as we embraced on the platform she said, 'You realise Desmond is going to ask me an awful lot of questions, Nancy?'

'Yes, I'm sorry about that, but I'm doing the right thing. We can never go back. I don't know about Desmond but I'm a very different girl from the one he knew four years ago. I fell in love with somebody else, somebody I don't want to talk about. It wasn't in the least like Desmond and me, the only similarity was that there was no future in it for entirely different reasons. In time I'll get over it but it's got to be at my own pace.'

She asked no more questions and I realised how much I liked this woman. She was a good friend, and there were tears in my eyes when I embraced her before stepping into the train. I was glad that Marcia was in love and I reminded her again to write and invite me to her wedding.

23

How strange to come home to one's roots after such a long time away. To see the rolling dark hills and the white floating clouds casting shadows on the lonely fells. A pale early sun gilded the imposing dome of the Town Hall and warmed the Pennine stone of the Parish Church. The market traders were setting up their stalls in the square before the library and I realised that I had completely forgotten it was market day in Greymont.

The town was coming to life. Newsboys were busy on their paper rounds, early shoppers were on the street looking for fresh fruit and vegetables before the bustle that would come later, and looking across the square I could see the sun glinting in the windows of the *Greymont Gazette*. I was pleased to see that the woodwork had had a recent coat of paint. How I had loved going to that office as a child, pounding with two fingers on one of the aged typewriters while my father wrote his column . . .

There was a taxi rank outside the library but no sign of a taxi so I could only assume I was too early. While I waited a postman came to empty the postbox and seeing me waiting he grinned cheerfully. 'You'll 'ave a long wait, luv,' he said amiably. 'They don't usually bother to get down till ten and the streets are aired. Far to go?'

'Yes, to Ellwood.'

'Well, the buses only come every hour and you're pretty loaded down. Ring up Dan Lowther – he runs a taxi service. Like as not he'll come down for ye.' He fished in his pocket and brought out a small pad and pencil, then tore out a page and wrote Dan Lowther's telephone number on it.

I thanked him warmly for his trouble then with a friendly wave of his hand he was away in his van and I was humping my luggage round to the post office where I knew I would find a telephone booth.

Fortunately Dan Lowther was in, and in less than ten minutes I was sitting in his taxi with my luggage stacked round my feet. He was a chatterbox and immediately started to ask questions. Had I come up on the London train, how well did I know Greymont, how well did I know Miss Susan Lester?

I answered his questions easily by telling him I had grown up in Greymont and that Miss Lester was my mother's older sister. At that piece of information he chuckled before saying, 'She's a mighty formidable lady, miss. I should know – my son's teaching her to drive.'

'Drive – Aunt Susan!'

'Bought herself a little runabout, she has. She tells me she's paying no more taxi fares since they went up and our George has been commissioned to help her pass her driving test.'

'Will she, do you think?'

'He's not hopeful, luv, but I wouldn't like to be the examiner that fails her. Is she expecting you, then?'

'No, I wanted to surprise her.'

'And how long are ye thinkin' of stayin' wi' us, like?'

'I'm not sure. It may be for some while.'

'Ye say yer were brought up around here. Where would that be, then?'

'On the corner of Park Road.'

'Ye mean them big terraced houses with the nice rockeries and the long back gardens?'

'Yes. My father was a reporter on the local newspaper. Arthur Graham – did you know him?'

'Well, no, I can't say I did. I'm a Shropshire man miself, married a local woman and came to live in her mother's house we did. I had a good taxi business in Shropshire but mi wife allus hankered to come back to Lancashire. Her mother left the house to us so we came to live here permanently.'

He started to hum a popular tune when we were at

243

last on the country road driving out to Ellwood and I was left to look out across the fields to where the spire of St Mark's Church seemed to tower over the tiny hamlet. There was a straggling high street of small stone cottages ending with The Barley Arms with its cobbled forefront and the flagged bridge over the stream that ran the entire length of the street and into the pond in front of the stone-walled churchyard. The church stood high on a hill so that there were steps from the gates up to the doors and across from the Inn several old men sat on the seat which surrounded the giant yew which was the pride of Ellwood.

The gardens surrounding Aunt Susan's house were immaculate. The grass was short and green, the beds and borders were tidy and there was an ordered pattern of azaleas and other shrubs that lined the drive up to the solid stone house with its diamond-paned windows and tall chimneys.

'How much do I owe you?' I asked Dan after he had carried my luggage to the front door.

'It'll be six pounds, luv.'

I smiled, handing over the six pounds plus a generous tip, and I thanked him warmly before he drove slowly down the drive and out of the gates.

I rang the doorbell and waited. At last I could hear shuffling footsteps crossing the hall, and then the sounds of the bolts being drawn back and Sarah's muttered grumbling. She stared at me in utmost surprise and then cried, 'Come in, come in, love! Why on earth didn't you write and let your aunt know you'd be coming? She's still in bed. Doesn't get up till around ten these days.'

I followed her across the hall and into the kitchen after leaving my luggage just inside the door. My first thoughts were that nothing had changed. A large oak dresser occupied the entire length of one wall and willow pattern china still took pride of place on the shelves. In the centre of the room was a large oak table on which stood a teapot and the remains of Sarah's breakfast.

244

'Come on love,' she said cosily. 'Take your coat off and sit at the table. Now, have you had any breakfast?'

'No, but I'm not very hungry. Still, some tea and toast would be nice.'

'We've good bacon and sausages. You can chat to me while I'm cooking them.'

'How are you, Sarah? You never seem to change in all the years I've known you.'

'Oh, I'm getting older, just like your aunt. This big house is too much for me to handle on my own – it was a mistake to buy it, in my opinion. When your grandfather died we should have looked for a smaller place, not one like this. Still, it's not for me to complain. I'm only the housekeeper.'

'Do you see much of Maisie, Sarah?'

'I've seen her in the town shopping once or twice and sometimes she helps Tom on the milk-round. Right bonnie the children are and she always has them nicely turned out. They're a credit to her. Her brother Bob and his wife don't have a family yet – maybe they don't want one, like that other friend of yours, Barbara Walton.'

Sarah kept up a steady flow of conversation while she cooked the bacon and when she set the meal in front of me she took her place opposite with the idea of disclosing as much village gossip as possible before Aunt Susan appeared. When she ran out of steam she enquired, 'Breakfast to your liking, then?'

'It's lovely, Sarah. Ooh, I'd forgotten what country bacon tasted like, or new-laid eggs.'

From the realms above we heard Aunt Susan's voice calling, 'Who have you in the kitchen, Sarah? If it's that gardener he should be out in the garden doing what he's paid for.'

I raised my eyes heavenwards saying, 'Nothing's changed, I see. Her tongue's as caustic as ever.'

Sarah yelled upstairs from the kitchen door, 'We have

a visitor, Miss Lester, arrived an hour ago and waiting to see you.'

'Who is it?'

Sarah quietly closed the kitchen door, chuckling quietly to herself, and in a few minutes we heard Aunt Susan's footsteps descending the stairs. She grinned. I knew that would bring her down.

To say that Aunt Susan was surprised to see me would be an understatement. She looked dumbfounded for a few seconds, then after I had kissed her she said sharply, 'Why didn't you write, Nancy, and why all this haste to get here! Have you lost your job?'

'I have an awful lot to tell you, Aunt Susan. I hope I'm coming to work here again, at the *Gazette*. Mr McKay has always said that any time I wanted to come back, there would be a reporter's job waiting for me.'

'But you had a job at the *Gazette* once and you couldn't wait to get away!'

'That's quite true – but now I can't wait to get back to it.'

'There's more to this than meets the eye but I haven't much time to talk now. I suppose you'll be wanting to live here?'

'Only if it's convenient, Aunt Susan.'

'You know you're always very welcome here,' she said, 'but I suppose if anything else takes your fancy you'll be off like the drop of a hat. You can have the room at the side of the house – you always liked the view from the window and it's warm being over the kitchen.'

'Thanks, Aunt Susan. I will look around for something of my own later, perhaps a little flat in the town. I don't want to impose on you.'

'And have all the neighbours say that I wasn't prepared to give you a home? If you're working in Greymont you're to live here.'

I gave in meekly, too tired to argue. 'Thanks Aunt Susan, I won't be any trouble.'

246

The team at the *Gazette* greeted me warmly, and Mr McKay seemed pleased that I had decided to return there.

'We trebled our sales with your articles, my dear. They were something a bit different from the usual run of material, and people looked forward to reading them. I'll show you some of the letters we received about your column – the articles sparked off quite a correspondence. You must remember that local folk had a great regard for your father and your grandfather. Are you quite sure you won't be bored with life here after London and Hong Kong?'

'It'll take a bit of getting used to, and to be honest I probably will find the pace a bit slow for a while, but it's what I want. I'll soon get back into the swing of it.'

In the course of my duties, I came across Dan Lowther again, who encouraged me to take driving lessons with his son, as well. What is more, he found me a car! He took me himself to the garage where he had found it: it was a white Mini, not in its first youth by any means, but it had been pampered by the boy who owned it and the mileage for its age was not excessive.

Nine weeks later I passed my test and Aunt Susan failed her second attempt. When I arrived home that evening Sarah met me in the hall saying, 'I wouldn't advise you to cross her tonight – she's failed her test again and she's got a look on her face that'd turn the milk sour.'

I had it all through our evening meal: how the examiner hadn't been clear in his instructions, other road-users had confused her by driving too fast and it was time she changed her driving instructor. I made the appropriate expressions of sympathy but the meal was a silent one in the main and afterwards I settled down to write letters while Aunt Susan sat glumly staring into the fire.

I felt her eyes upon me, and looking up recognised at once that she was in one of the vindictive moods I had dreaded as a child.

'I've been patiently waiting for the last two months for you to tell me why you suddenly decided to leave London, Nancy. You owe me a proper explanation, my girl! I suppose it was some man you met in Hong Kong.'

'No Aunt Susan, it wasn't a man I met in Hong Kong.'

'Well, I think I'm entitled to know why you came back here, particularly when you were so keen to get away before. Did you make such a mess of the job that you had to leave Hong Kong? Is that it?'

'No, they didn't ask me to leave – in fact they were sorry to see me go.'

'Well, then?'

'I wanted to get back into journalism.'

'To the *Gazette*! I can't believe you intend to make working on the *Gazette* an ambition for life. No, there's something else behind all this and if it wasn't your job at the gallery then it must have been some man or other. I suppose he was married.'

'Perhaps your work on the Bench has made you look for things that aren't there, Aunt Susan.'

'Don't play games with me, young lady. It's made me a student of human nature, and I'm old enough and wise enough to know that a girl like you doesn't suddenly decide to throw up a good job she's fond of to come running back to the country in search of her roots. Besides, you're living under my roof, I have a right to know what's going on.'

'Yes, of course you do, and I am grateful for everything you've done, but there's nothing going on. There *was* someone before I went to Hong Kong, but now it's over – it happens to a lot of people.'

'He was married, wasn't he?'

'Yes.'

'And living with his wife?'

'When it suited him.'

'I see.'

'No, Aunt Susan you don't see, and I'd rather not talk about it if you don't mind. Like I said it's all over and done with. I'm happy here in Greymont, I wouldn't have been happy in London.'

I could tell she wanted to pursue the questioning but there must have been something in my expression which made her change her mind, for instead she picked up her knitting and the irritable clicking of her needles told me quite plainly that she was far from satisfied.

Silence reigned for some time, then she asked, 'Did Lady Garveston write to you, by the way? She asked me for your address but I'd misplaced your last letter and I couldn't remember it offhand. She said she'd ask Maisie Standing.'

'Yes, I heard from her just before I left Hong Kong.'

'What did she want after all this long time?'

'She'd remembered that it was almost ten years since we left Lorivals. We'd all said we'd meet in ten years wherever we were and whatever we were doing. She wrote to remind me.'

'And are you going to meet?'

'She's suggested a weekend at Garveston Hall.'

'When?'

'The end of July.'

'You're going, of course?'

'I'm not sure, Aunt Susan. We've lost touch. Only Maisie and I have anything in common these days – it's years since I saw Amelia or Barbara.'

'Well, you've been in Hong Kong for the last four. If Lady Amelia's made the first move then you should accept. You can't treat her in the same sort of cavalier fashion as you'd treat Maisie. Barbara Walton will have had the courtesy to accept long before this, I'm sure.'

'Did you hear about it from Barbara's mother?'

I watched her face and was rewarded by seeing the rush of colour into her cheeks, then tartly she said, 'She mentioned it several weeks ago, said Barbara and Martin were going and wondered if you'd been asked. I told her I was sure you would be. I can't understand you at all,

Nancy. What possible difficulties can there be attached to accepting Lady Amelia's invitation.'

'I'm not very sure that I want to spend a weekend at Garveston Hall. Amelia has largely ignored our existence so far. Why has she suddenly decided to remember that old promise from five girls hankering after the old and afraid of the new? And Aunt Susan, I would never treat Maisie or any of my friends in such a cavalier fashion.'

'I suppose you don't want to meet Mark Garveston again now that he's married to Amelia. Really, I'd have thought you'd have put all that behind you!' she expostulated.

'My going or not going will have nothing whatever to do with Mark,' I insisted steadily.

'I don't suppose she'll have invited that Maisie and her husband.'

'She has, as a matter of fact. Maisie was one of us at Lorivals and besides, Amelia was always nice to Maisie. Come to think of it, she was nice to everybody.'

'Then why are you so stubborn about her?'

'I'm not. I just don't understand her, that's all.'

'Well, she didn't have your upbringing, did she? Heaven knows your father could argue the hind legs off a donkey, and Joe Smythe's a local councillor it's true but that's hardly comparable to being a Peer of the Realm. Lord Urquart's daughter would have stuck out like a sore thumb in the Jayson household.'

'What a snob you are, Aunt Susan.'

'I'm not in the least snobbish but I do know what's what. I meet Lady Garveston at the Magistrates' Court because we're both on the Bench but I don't grovel like some of them do. She respects me for that, consequently we get along very well.'

'I'm glad to hear it.'

She looked at me sharply in case sarcasm was intended, but I returned her gaze with bland innocence and somewhat irritably she muttered, 'If Barbara and Martin Walton are there they'll be full of themselves. Nellie

250

Smythe's a positive bore on the subject of their fine house, their influential friends and their big parties. Just don't you let them get away with it. Talk about your years in the Far East and your work in London, at least it'll be better than listening to the Waltons and Maisie going on about her children.'

The trouble with the evenings Aunt Susan and I spent together was her assertiveness and my reticence. We were three women living in the same house. She and Sarah had always argued, now here was I controversial and at times difficult. I would never discuss Desmond with her and Noel had been a dream, a charming diversion that had somehow disappeared, and I had been wise to accept what I couldn't change.

Spring turned into summer and my aunt became increasingly involved with local flower shows and fêtes. I too was kept busy reporting on these activities as well as writing up other regional events. This meant that we were not thrown together quite so much and were happier that way.

One bright sunny morning at the end of June I had been attending a Council meeting at the Town Hall when I saw Amelia arriving at Merton's, Greymont's most expensive department store which was situated directly across the square. I was standing on the steps chatting to Councillor Smythe when he interrupted his flow of conversation to say, 'There's Lady Garveston's car, Nancy. Looks as though she's going into Merton's.'

She was driving the car herself. It was a new BMW and a commissionaire hurried forward to open the door for her. Councillor Smythe chuckled, saying, 'They must have known she was coming, lass. There's just enough room for her to park her car.'

She opened the back door of the car and two girls stepped down on to the pavement. They were dressed exactly alike in pale blue coats and berets, and as they waited for their mother to join them she leaned back inside the car to speak to someone waiting inside it.

'She's had her older sister's daughter staying with her quite a lot recently,' Barbara's father informed me. 'I expect she's left her sitting in the car. Poor creature she is, crippled after meningitis, so I heard.'

He left me then and I couldn't stop myself from crossing the square and approaching the BMW. A nurse sat primly upright in the back seat and beside her was a teenaged girl, her head lolling against the cushions, her eyes vacant and expressionless. She had such a look of Desmond! Her mouth was open and a rush of pity and love filled me: I yearned to open the car door and take her in my arms.

At that moment the commissionaire came down the steps carrying a wheelchair and I stood back while he gathered the girl into his arms and placed her in the chair, while the nurse went to help him. Dorinda, sat in ungainly fashion, her head rolling sideways; passers-by looked on with sympathy while the two adults pushed the chair across the pavement and manhandled it up the shallow steps.

One lady standing beside me said compassionately, 'No amount of money can do much for that one. I've got two harum-scarum grandchildren who can't keep still for five minutes but I'd rather see 'em like that than in that state.'

At that moment the girl in the chair started to whimper; it was the ugly lowing of a cow in pain, and she began to struggle so that the chair was in danger of collapsing. The nurse and commissionaire wrestled to keep it upright. I rushed forward to help and it was then I felt the girl's hands clinging to me, holding my wrist in a grip of iron. I gasped with pain. I could never have imagined that this puny figure could have such power in her twisted fingers and when at last we were inside the shop the commissionaire said anxiously, 'She's strong, miss. You'll have some bruises on your arms after this.'

The nurse turned to thank me, assuring us that she

252

could now manage without our help and we watched her pushing the screaming girl through the store.

'Poor lass,' the commissionaire said softly. 'She can't hear and she can't see, she only senses things and she seems to know when Lady Garveston leaves her. All those folk milling around outside didn't help, either. Here, let me take a look at your arm.'

My arm was discoloured with red and black bruises, and bleeding where Dorinda's fingernails had cut into the flesh.

'I knew it,' he said gently. 'Get some salve on them bruises as soon as you can. I don't envy her ladyship. She's had that child a whole lot over the last few months, and it's too much with children of her own to see to.' He turned to a young shop assistant who was just passing. 'Will you get this young lady a cup of tea and see if you can find something in the office for her bruises.'

'You're very kind, but really I'm on my way home now. I'm perfectly all right.' Nevertheless, I felt shaken with a mixture of emotions, and my arm throbbed painfully.

'I'll see you to your car, then. Is it parked handy?'

'Across the way in the Town Hall car park. There's really no need for you to come with me.'

He insisted and I rather thought he was enjoying acting as my protector. As we walked to my Mini he confided, 'The girl is Lady Garveston's niece, you know. The sister leaves her here when she goes abroad.'

'She's abroad at the moment, then?'

'Canada, staying with relatives. I did hear she was run down, had some sort of breakdown. Mind, I'm not surprised after coping with that one.'

I thought about Dorinda all the way home, and about Desmond, lonely in London, his wife in distant Canada, and his disabled child screaming her head off in the store in the centre of Greymont. Despite her physical resemblance to her father, I couldn't reconcile that child with Desmond, not with her loose wet mouth and vacant

253

rolling eyes. I thought of his fastidious elegance, the near orderliness of his impersonal flat, and from Desmond my thoughts turned to Amelia . . .

Amelia had always been kind, a beautiful gentle girl who had floated like a celestial being through my young girlhood, but I was having difficulty in reconciling that kindness with the years of indifference that had followed. Apparently the kindness was still there or she could never have suffered her sister's child, and once more I asked myself if somewhere between the kindness and the indifference there was another Amelia, a person I had never known.

That night I wrote to her to say I was back in Greymont working on the *Gazette* and very much looking forward to our reunion in July. I did not tell her how long I had been back in Greymont and each day I waited for a reply, a small note saying we must meet, that now that I was so close wasn't there time for coffee or a cup of tea.

Inevitably I realised that there would be no letter from Amelia. We would meet as planned at the end of July and the four of us would discuss how the last ten years had treated us, then after that, there would again be silence. At least, that's what I believed.

24

Marcia was married at the beginning of June and I was invited to stay with her fiancé's sister in the Vale of Evesham in a huge rambling vicarage. In no time at all I was surrounded by dogs and children and all the warmth and companionship of a large happy family.

I liked Marcia's fiancé on sight. John was exactly as she had described him, tall and lanky, with a nice lop-sided smile and a lock of dark hair that fell boyishly over his forehead. He took my hand in a firm grip saying how glad he was I had come, and instinctively I knew he meant every word of it.

Joyce was in Tokyo, unable to attend and Phillipa was coming up on the day with her current boyfriend.

Marcia sat on the edge of my bed and chatted. I could tell that she was happy, for the bored look she often wore had been replaced by a happy acceptance of life, a belief in the future that I felt all new brides should have.

'We shan't be having much of a honeymoon,' she informed me. 'There's the new intake of finches to see to and the bedding-out plants. And, of course, the fruit harvest to plan. The nieces and nephews have promised to help while we're away but John won't rely on them for long, he'll be itching to get back. We're driving into Wales for a few days. Can you imagine – my thoughts on a honeymoon used to lean to the Bahamas to say the least! Now it seems there's no really convenient time to take a honeymoon, and nothing longer than a few days.'

'I've never seen you looking so happy.'

'I am happy, but what goes with you? Have you really settled down to working on that country paper again?'

'Yes, I really have. I can't say I'm all that happy living

with Aunt Susan, though. I have a lot of my father in me and they never got along.'

'You haven't asked about Desmond, Nancy.'

'No. Was he very angry when he knew I'd left the house and the Gallery?'

'Desmond Atherton's a diplomat and diplomats don't betray their feelings.'

'No of course not. I saw his daughter Dorinda in Greymont, she was staying with his wife's sister. I felt so sorry for her, Marcia, for all of them.'

'What was she doing at Garveston Hall? I thought she wasn't happy without her mother.'

'Celia is in Canada, apparently.'

'There's been some talk lately. Desmond has never been the sort of man to discuss his private life with anybody, consequently stories are invented and rumours run riot. It surprised me that you got so close to him. I suppose it was your youth and freshness – heaven knows, there were enough worldly and sophisticated women only too anxious to get their hands on him.'

'What is happening about the house?'

'When I told him you'd left London and didn't intend coming back he closed up like a clam and I knew he would not discuss you or anything about you with me again. I left two weeks later and haven't seen him since. He had to go to Amsterdam, I believe.'

The wedding went off without a hitch and Marcia made a beautiful bride in a pale blue wild silk dress and a large blue hat. John's two nieces were her bridesmaids, alike as two peas in their blue floral dresses. Later when I complimented Marcia on her choice of dress, she said with a smile, 'I was never the sort of girl who wanted ethereal white. I expect my wedding dress will come out of the wardrobe whenever John can spare the time to take me somewhere special. I hope it doesn't date though, because I'm thinking in terms of the next ten years or so!' She giggled merrily.

I left for home with a car packed with soft fruit and

new potatoes, two plump chickens ready for the oven and a large bunch of asparagus which I knew Aunt Susan adored. Several days later I stood at the edge of the hockey field watching a special, summer-term match between the girls of Lorivals and a team from the local Grammar School. Next to me was one of the *Gazette*'s photographers. He was young and cheerful, and kept up a spate of conversation as he snapped cheerfully away.

'I expect these'll end up in the family albums, Nancy. I'll just go down to the other end of the field – the view's better from there. I'd stay here if I were you, it's a bit muddy on that side of the field.'

I watched him walk on round. A handful of parents stood observing the match as well as several teachers from the two schools so I did not immediately pay attention to the solitary figure of a man walking with his head bent against the sharp wind which swept across the pitch from the fell, despite the June day. Once or twice he paused to watch the girls who ran too close to him, then he came on, and it was only when he paused several yards from where I was standing that we stared into each other's eyes and I felt the warm blood rising into my face and a sudden rush of panic.

He didn't smile, but there was no reproach in his gaze, only a strange sort of sadness, a resignation if you will, and this time I could not run: in all that vast open space there was nowhere to hide.

'I rang the *Gazette* and they told me you were here covering the match,' Desmond said calmly. 'Didn't you feel that we had to talk, Nancy?'

Tongue-tied and stupid I could only shake my head, and then he was standing beside me and I was looking up into a face I had never wanted to see again. It was a face that charmed me still, a thin, clever face with straight brows and blue eyes, a gentle smile playing around firm chiselled lips. I had loved that face, the memory of it had haunted my young impressionable life, but now it was just a face, and in that first joyous moment

257

I knew it would never have the power to haunt me again. I smiled, the sort of smile I could afford any man I had once known and liked.

'Why didn't you answer my letter?' he asked quietly.

'There was nothing to say. I had simply decided to come home to work on the paper.'

'I see. Did you like the house?'

The question was banal, but I answered him honestly. 'It was lovely Desmond, and very kind of you.'

'No, Nancy, it wasn't kind at all. It wasn't nearly enough, but I had to do something. How you must hate me.'

I stared at him in surprise. 'I don't hate you, Desmond. I thought I did when I went out to Hong Kong, but I got over it. You were always very honest with me – I knew about your wife, I knew about Dorinda, the only thing you were not honest about was the fact that Celia was going with you to Russia. Yes, I hated you for that, but after a while I didn't think I should. You had a good reason for doing what you did and your career is very important to you.'

'Did you stop hating me when you found someone else?'

'Perhaps. That wasn't important, either. He too has a career and I was dispensable.'

'I'm sorry. Was he anyone I know?'

'Nobody I want to talk about. I saw Dorinda in the town, Desmond. She was crying after Amelia.'

I did not miss the sudden sharp pain which crossed his face, and he said bitterly, 'If you saw Dorinda you must surely understand one of the tragedies in my life.'

'Believe me I do. I wanted to put my arms around her and hold her close. I wanted to weep over her, instead I wept for you. Desmond, I hope you haven't come here just to find me.'

He shook his head and I was glad that he could still be honest with me. 'I came here to take our daughter and her nanny back to Cornwall. It's a long journey and she will need to be sedated otherwise it would be impossible. I have a few days' leave before I need to get back to the Foreign Office.'

'You'll spend it in Cornwall, then. It can be beautiful at this time of the year.'

'I have told Celia that we need to talk about the future – Dorinda should not be allowed to ruin our lives, there *must* be some other way, but in the end I fear we shall be no nearer resolving things than we have been over the last seven years. It would appear the match is over.'

I looked round me in surprise. Girls were hurrying across the field and friends and parents were making their way towards the gates. The photographer marched across the pitch, his shoes caked with mud, his macintosh flapping in the wind. 'Thank God that's over,' he said smiling. 'The car's in the lane, Nancy. Are you coming back with me?'

'You go ahead. I'll walk it. Tell them I'm on my way.'

It seemed odd to be walking with Desmond along the country road on the outskirts of Greymont. Whenever I had thought about him I pictured him in softly-lit restaurants, in the gentle darkness of his car, or the austere comfort of his flat. I had always been careful to be suitably dressed, not as I was now with the wind blowing through my hair, and my old mac belted tightly against the damp wind.

Almost as though he could read my thoughts he said tensely, 'Heaven's but it's cold. You shouldn't be standing about muddy fields – is it often so wet at this time of year up here?'

'Yes, I'm afraid it is.'

'Don't tell me you enjoy it. Really, Nancy, you're capable of so much more than this! Why ever did you leave the gallery? I thought you were happy with the people at Treasures of the Orient.'

'I was, terribly.'

'Then why?'

'I didn't want to drift into something I would bitterly

259

regret. I didn't want us to start up where we had left off.'

He turned to face me, staring down at me with hurt, anxious eyes. 'You hate me as much as that?'

'I've told you – I don't hate you at all, Desmond. In fact, I'm very grateful to you for so many things. You taught me how to appreciate music, food, paintings, beautiful scenery . . . I was so immature, so ignorant. Now I know my perception is much finer, more intense. Nothing we had together was wasted, it was simply a good time to end it.'

'But a small-time newspaper, Nancy. I don't suppose this job of yours is even well paid. You surely don't intend to spend the rest of your life in this sort of work?'

'My father did, and he wasn't too unhappy.'

'Surely he must have hankered after something better, a national newspaper at least.'

I didn't answer him. I was not prepared to tell Desmond about my father's frustrations or yearnings for other things, and the next moment he was urging me, 'Come back to London, Nancy. I know a great many people who would be willing to give you a chance. I'm not asking you to come back to me, only to make a better life for yourself.'

'It's very kind of you, Desmond, but I've got to stand on my own two feet. If I make something of my life then it must be because I'm worth more, not because you've pulled a few strings here and there. Besides, I don't want to go back to London, not yet at any rate.'

I had seen that look on his face before, cold and withdrawn. In no time at all Desmond would convince himself that I was a fool, too stubborn and stupid to be bothered with. He would wonder why he had been foolish enough to squander his intellect on one such as I.

We walked on in silence, but it was not a comfortable silence. He surprised me suddenly by asking, 'Who was the man you met in Hong Kong? Was it someone in government circles?'

'No.'

'You mean you're not prepared to tell me.'

'That's right, I'm not prepared to tell you – but he definitely wasn't in government circles.'

'And you were in love with him?'

'Please, Desmond, I don't want to talk about it. I could have been, but right from the beginning it wasn't possible.'

'You mean he was married?'

'No, he wasn't married.' His stare became more intense. 'There were other reasons. Please don't ask me any more.'

He stared down the empty road, his face suddenly bleak and across the way I saw his long expensive car waiting to take him back to the Hall. 'Can I give you a lift into town?' he said evenly.

'I think I'd rather walk if you don't mind. Are you leaving in the morning?'

'Yes. It will be a long harrowing journey. Dorinda will be asleep I hope. I'm accustomed to travelling in silence.' He continued to stare down at me for several seconds, then briefly, without holding out his hand he said, 'Goodbye, Nancy. Who knows, we might meet again one day.'

'Goodbye, Desmond.'

I waited on the pavement while he got into his car and drove away without a backward glance. I felt the sudden sharp sting of rain on my face, and then I realised it was my tears.

25

When I suggested looking at a new block of unfurnished flats to rent that were being built near the park in Greymont, Aunt Susan refused to accompany me.

'Haven't I done my best to make you comfortable here in Ellwood?' she demanded irritably. 'You'll find a big difference when you have to pay the rent they're asking and keep yourself at the same time.'

'You've been wonderful Aunt Susan, but it's time I started fending for myself. I should have a place of my own nearer to town. I'll come and see you often and I hope you'll come to see me.'

'Those flats look downright poky to me. If you have a ground-floor one you'll have people tramping over your head, and if you have one higher up, it'll be like living upstairs.'

'How do you know what they're like if you won't look at them,' I protested. 'I really do need some advice about carpets and curtains, and you have such good taste. Oh, please come!'

Slightly placated, she agreed. After viewing the flats, though, she said it would be like living in a rabbit hutch – the rooms were too small, the kitchen was a disaster, and the plumbing was inadequate . . . but later, when we started to look at curtain material and carpets she became more enthusiastic.

I decided on a first-floor flat overlooking the other side of the park from where I had been born. Aunt Susan said I would get a lot of noise from the children's playground, and because it faced west I wouldn't get the sun until the evening.

'Well, that's all right, since I shan't be in until evening,' I replied brightly.

In spite of my aunt's many misgivings I went ahead with the flat, and on the day I moved into it with my new carpets and curtains and the few pieces of furniture I had managed to afford she said, 'Wasn't that house in London furnished? Why aren't you bringing some of that up here?'

'It went with the house, Aunt Susan.'

'You mean none of it was yours?'

'Some, but it had been bought from sale-rooms. It wasn't worth much.' I hadn't told her that the house in London had been transformed and I had no intention of asking Desmond if I could transfer any of its contents to the north.

Aunt Susan generously supplied me with dusters and teacloths, towels, sheets and pillowslips from huge chests in her attic and when I thanked her gratefully she snapped, 'I'll expect you every Sunday for lunch as usual; it'll probably be the only day you get anything decent to eat. And make sure you write and tell your mother what's going on.'

I was blissfully happy in my little flat. Maisie came with her children and pronounced it 'very nice but small'. She arrived with a huge castor oil plant which looked ready to take over half the lounge and ruefully said, 'This'll not do, Nancy. It needs a plant or two in here but I reckon I'll take this back and bring something small. What do you think?'

'Well, yes, if you don't mind – perhaps an African violet or something!'

'I'm used to the big rooms at the farm. A place as small as this would suffocate me.'

All in all I might have felt disenchanted with my tiny flat but I didn't. The windows overlooked the park with the great trees in full leaf, and the cheerful sounds of children's voices reached me from the area set aside for them with slides and swings.

I gave a housewarming evening for my friends at the *Gazette*, to which Maisie and Tom were invited, and they

263

sat on the chairs, the arms and the floor enthusiastically drinking wine and eating the repast I had provided.

It was a period in my life of no regrets and no thoughts of the future, a time of the present, when I lived every day for itself until that afternoon when I arrived in the office late to find the place agog with a rare excitement. Mr McKay said with a bright smile, 'You have a visitor, young lady. He's waiting for you in your office.'

'A visitor for me? Who is it?'

'Why not see for yourself.'

I opened my office door cautiously, and then I was looking into the laughing eyes of Noel Templeton. He was sitting at my desk with a sheaf of my notes in his hands. He jumped quickly to his feet and came to take me naturally into his arms, his keen blue eyes smiling deeply into mine. 'I'm in the north to see Dad,' he explained briefly. 'I tried to ring you in London but they told me you were up here working in your old job. I'm free until my train leaves at seven, can we walk somewhere?'

'I could make a meal at my flat.'

'Can't we walk on the fell instead? It's years since I was up there.'

'Yes, if that's what you want.'

All eyes were on us as we walked through the office, and Noel smiled warmly and said goodbyes all round.

It was warm on the fell; the sun shone out of a bright blue sky and overhead two lonely curlews circled lazily, calling their sad cries. Noel looked up, shading his eyes from the sun with his hands, then putting his arm in mine he confided, 'I used to come up here with Dad when I was just a kid. There were always a pair of curlews then – I don't suppose these can possibly be the same pair. Why did you suddenly decide to come back here to work?'

'I was ready for a change.'

'They didn't mind?'

'Mr Papadraos said they would be sorry to lose me, but he understood my reasons for leaving.'

'Because you couldn't wait to get back to reviewing local weddings and small-town events, or for some other more pressing reason?'

'You're too astute, Noel. You know the other reason without my having to tell you.'

'Are you sorry, though? That's what counts.'

'No, I'm glad. I'm not sure that I want to spend the rest of my working life at the *Gazette* – I have too much of my father's ambition to want that – but I suppose it's a start. And one day there might be an opportunity to move on. You say you're going back this evening, back to London?'

'For the odd night or two then I'm off to the Middle East once more where the action is.'

'And after that?'

'More action. There's always plenty of that, somewhere in the world. Life's never boring, Nancy. I could do with it being a bit less exciting some of the time.'

'I should feel very honoured that you can spare this time to look me up.'

I felt annoyed with myself. I hoped he didn't read the sarcasm in my voice and in the next moment I felt duly chastened when he said soberly, 'I always make an effort to come north to see Dad. He's not getting any younger and he worries about me.'

'Yes, of course,' I muttered miserably.

With a little laugh he held me close to him. 'Of course it's doubly fortunate that I can spend a little time with a gorgeous girl on a summer fell. It's not that sun-kissed hill in Hong Kong Nancy, but it's a good second-best.'

'And we're not two star-crossed lovers that death is about to separate,' I murmured gently.

'No, we're not that. There'll be no eternal devastation at my early demise. That's why I prefer to keep my friendships light-hearted – it's better for all concerned.'

I thought it was time to change the subject, so pointing

down to where we could see the tall chimneys of Garveston Hall I said, 'I'm going to spend a long weekend there very soon. I was at school with the present Lady Garveston.'

'Isn't she Lord Urquart's daughter?'

'Yes, I was very fond of her at school.'

'That's nice, do you see much of her?'

'No. This is something we arranged when we left school. A reunion in ten years' time.'

'Celia Atherton's her sister, isn't she?'

'Yes.'

'And you don't find that in the least dangerous, Nancy?'

'There's no reason why I should. Neither Celia nor her husband will be there and Amelia doesn't know Desmond and I were friends – at least, I don't think so.'

'I see.'

'There'll be a few of us invited – two more girls we knew at school and their husbands.'

'Hasn't she asked you to take someone?'

'No, as a matter of fact she hasn't.' For the first time I began to think that rather strange. Had Amelia assumed that I was on my own, or had she learned all that from Aunt Susan? I resolved to ask her at the first opportunity.

Noel consulted his watch saying reluctantly, 'We should be getting back. Much as I love these fells the train won't wait.' We turned and he took hold of my hand and hurried me down the hillside towards the lane. When we reached it we were breathless and he laughed a little. 'Heaven only knows when I'll be climbing the fells again, but I only know I shall,' he said confidently.

'It's strange we never met on the fells as you love them so.'

'I didn't spend much time around here. I was born in the North Riding of Yorkshire, not far from Wetherby. My mother died when I was four and Dad got a job on the *Gazette* here so we moved. I think Yorkshire held too many memories for him, he wanted a fresh start.

'Then his oldest sister came to live with us. She was a bit of a martinet, I can tell you. She and Dad didn't agree together for long, but she was a great one for what she called family duty – a little bit like your Aunt Susan, I should think. I went away to school when I was nine then Dad got a job with another paper and bought a house in Applethwaite. Do you know the village at all?'

'Oh yes, I love it there. I used to go fishing with my father. We sat on the banks of the Lune for hours and I was forbidden to speak otherwise it would frighten the fish away. I love the cobbled streets and the narrow alleyways – I always wished we lived there, it was so quaint.'

'It hasn't changed much in the heart of the village but of course suburbia has spread everywhere. There's an awful lot of new property on the outskirts of the village. If ever you get up to Applethwaite why not call in to see Dad? Tell him about your father and the *Gazette* – he'll be delighted to talk over old times with somebody.'

'Wouldn't he think it very presumptuous of me, and what would your aunt think?'

'Ah, that's another thing. Aunt Alicia went on a holiday to Bournemouth when I was sixteen and there she met a certain Mr Robert Shaw, a retired grocer and a bachelor. Four months later she married him much to Dad's delight, and they now live in Weymouth so we don't see them all that much.'

'So your father lives alone with nobody to look after him?'

'He's very spry. He loves his garden and argues with the vicar who lives next door at the vicarage. He still does a bit of freelance work and bores everybody to death by telling them about me. You can't miss the house Nancy, there's only the two of them at the end of the High Street, the Vicarage and Rosedale.'

'I take it he's a rose grower.'

'He is, but the house is named after a moor near

267

Whitby, a moor of which he and my mother were particularly fond.'

By this time we were walking briskly along the main street leading into the town and I had to hurry to keep up with his long strides. When we reached the front door of the *Gazette* office he paused and smiling down at me with what must surely be the most fascinating smile in the world he said, 'This is goodbye once again, Nancy. Will you be reading my reports?'

'Of course.'

'Who knows, one day you might be doing something similar in some Godforsaken place with the world crashing around your ears.'

He bent down and lightly brushed his lips against my hair, then he was gone, striding away from me along the street and I stared after him until he crossed the square. Not once did he look back.

My head told me I must not go to Applethwaite; my heart led me there the following Saturday. The village had small cobbled footpaths and larger cobbled streets, narrow alleyways between whitewashed shops and cottages, and a long straggling main street with the square-towered Norman church at one end and The Speckled Fleece at the other. Walkers and shoppers sat at the wooden benches outside the public house while they drank their refreshment, and on the seats surrounding the church yard were old men with their dogs, nodding sleepily or exchanging views.

The vicarage stood next to the church and next to that was Rosedale, a house that charmed me instantly. Built from warm Pennine stone, its lawns swept down to the stone walls surrounding it; the garden was alive with shrubs of many varieties, their colours mingling exquisitely, while several varieties of clematis climbed up the trelliswork beside the house. It was an idyllic spot with the birds singing in the branches and the scent of roses filling the air and I paused shyly to absorb the beauty of the setting, and wishing my courage would not fail me.

A fat tabby cat sat on the wall near the gate washing its face. When I spoke to it green eyes looked back at me composed and tranquil and the cat got to its feet and arched its back, purring gently, inviting me to stroke it. Its soft fur was thick and silky, and the more I stroked it the louder it purred and a voice said softly, 'Matilda'll stand that all day – she's been waiting for somebody to talk to her.'

I looked up at the man who had spoken and I knew immediately that this was Noel's father. Mr Templeton was tall and lean, and his deep blue eyes stared out at me from a tanned face, older, but so very much like his son's. I smiled, feeling the cat's body grow suddenly taut as two finches sped chattering across the lawn, and he tapped her sharply saying, 'Oh no you don't, you naughty girl. Haven't I told you the birds have as much right in this garden as you?'

'You have a beautiful garden,' I told him.

'Yes, I spend most of my time in it but the results have been very rewarding this year. Do you live around here?'

'No, I live just outside Greymont. I used to come here often when I was a little girl; my father was fond of fishing. I don't remember that he ever caught very much, though.'

He smiled. 'There's fish in the Lune all right, but I never caught much either, as I'm no great shakes as a fisherman. Would I know your father? I used to work on the *Gazette* in Greymont, years ago, of course.'

'My father worked on the *Gazette* too. His name was Arthur Graham, he was a reporter.'

His face lit up. 'Of course! Noel has spoken about him in the past. I knew Arthur Graham well, we worked together as young men. Don't tell me he never moved away. He had such ambitions then.'

'No, he lived and worked in Greymont all his life. Did you know my mother?'

'No he wasn't married when I left the *Gazette*. Marriage does make a difference to a man's career sometimes. I married young and my wife died when our son was only four, so I moved around a bit, particularly after Noel went away to school. You may have heard of him – he's Noel Templeton, and he's a war correspondent now.'

He could not keep the pride out of his voice nor the shine of fondness from his eyes and quickly I said, 'I think most people have heard of Noel Templeton. I met him in Hong Kong and I saw him for a few minutes last week.'

'Are you the gorgeous girl he was hoping to see in Greymont?'

I laughed. 'Did he say that?'

'Well, he said he knew a girl in Greymont, a gorgeous girl he thought he'd call on. Come along in my dear, we'll have a cup of tea together, or would you prefer something else?'

'No, tea would be very nice, thank you.'

He opened the gate and we walked together towards the house. Matilda left her perch on the garden wall and scampered in front of us and Mr Templeton said, 'She was my sister's cat, but when Alicia decided to get married she stayed on with me. Cats don't like upheavals, they like plenty of peace and quiet and a world of familiar things. I'm glad to have her, she's nice company. She's getting on now though.'

'You must get very lonely without your son, Mr Templeton.'

'I've not seen much of Noel since he was a boy, what with boarding schools and University, holidays when he went off climbing or sailing somewhere or other, then this career of his which keeps him out of the country most of the time. I'm very proud of him, he's made his

270

mark, but I must confess there are times when I wish he'd chosen a safer, more ordinary profession.'

'A nine to five job, you mean. I can't quite see Noel living like that.'

He smiled. 'Nor can I, but sometimes I hanker after a son who brings his wife and children to tea every Sunday. Do you have brothers and sisters?'

'No, there was just me. My name's Nancy, by the way.'

'Nancy Graham. Yes, Noel did tell me your name. Now sit here on this chair on the terrace and I'll put the kettle on.'

'Can I help?'

'No, Matilda'll keep you company. I shan't be long.'

Matilda settled down at my feet, the end of her tail twitching gently as she watched two sparrows squabbling over a titbit they had found on the lawn.

Noel's father reappeared after a few minutes with tea and biscuits and settled himself down in the chair opposite while I poured out the tea. I felt completely relaxed in his company. He talked easily on several topics, from the local countryside to his memories of the years he had spent in Greymont, and in turn I told him about my father, the ambitions that had been doomed to failure and a little of my time in Hong Kong.

'What momentous event made you give up everything to work on a small-town newspaper?' he asked curiously. 'I would have thought once you'd made the break London or abroad would have been offering far more than you'll ever get at the *Gazette*.'

'Perhaps I'm a country girl at heart,' I said lightly.

'No doubt you are, but there's more to it than that. Are you satisfied that you did the right thing?'

'I think so.'

'Only time will tell, though.'

'Perhaps.'

'How well did you know my son in Hong Kong, or is that a question I shouldn't be asking?'

271

'We met at a function we both found very boring so we left together and went to some little restaurant Noel knew. When he was in Hong Kong we spent a lot of time together, but he was always going off somewhere or other.'

'Naturally, and no girl would be willing to put up with that sort of thing.'

'I wasn't Noel's girl, Mr Templeton. I was just a girl.' His eyes searched my face and I smiled back confidently. I had come a long way since a man's eyes could make me betray my innermost thoughts or allow him to see into my heart.

It was late afternoon when I left Mr Templeton. He invited me to stay and eat dinner with him but I told him I had an engagement in Greymont. It was true, since I had promised Aunt Susan to accompany her to a play given by one of the local amateur groups, but he said firmly, 'You must come again, my dear. I've enjoyed chatting to you and I see very few young people. The vicar comes in three times a week to play chess and I have a daily woman who keeps me up to date with all the local gossip, a mine of information that woman is.'

'She probably appeals to the journalist in you.'

He laughed. 'Perhaps she does – once a journalist always a journalist with a nose for news.'

26

As the day grew nearer to our reunion I was wishing more and more that I hadn't said I'd go. However, on 20 July I was up early, packing a weekend case with the things I would need. At first I had reservations about the jade green dress, but when I took it out of its wrapper it seemed entirely suitable, despite its age. It had a time-less expensive simplicity and I breathed a silent thank you to Lois, who had donated it.

I had no doubts about the black gown which Desmond had loved, and which Noel had complimented me on one evening in Hong Kong. This was the dress that had raised Mrs Etherington-Grant's eyebrows enviously and brought admiring glances from every man in the room.

When I left, it was a golden afternoon with a light mist shimmering on the distant hills; shoppers walked along the pavements in bright cotton dresses and children crowded the play area in the park. The leafy lanes were an enchantment as I drove the few miles to Garveston Hall and the tall iron gates were open in anticipation of the arrival of guests. A little girl in a gingham dress waved to me from a swing in the garden of the Lodge House and before me swept the long drive and the ter-races and towers of the Hall.

I could see several cars parked on the lower terrace so I drove towards it, bringing my Mini to rest beside a long new Jaguar that looked as if it could have eaten my car alive. I took my case out of the boot and turned to look up at the house. Geraniums bloomed in giant stone urns along the terraces, and all in all the old house had a total air of well-being, with its fresh paintwork and the beauty of the gardens in which several gardeners were at work.

Before I had reached the end of the terrace I was hailed by a man running down the steps. Then Mark was there, holding me close to him, his face alive with warmth and I was staring at him in stunned surprise.

'Here you are, Nancy! I've been looking out for you all afternoon.'

'I'm sorry Mark, I had work to do this morning and a report to write up. I do hope I haven't inconvenienced Amelia. Her letter said Friday afternoon around four. I'm afraid it's half-past now.'

'We're having afternoon tea on the south terrace. The Waltons arrived over an hour ago, and I've been wanting some light relief from him.'

I laughed. 'Bad as that, is it?'

'You know him of course?'

'Not very well. I knew him as a boy, but I haven't seen him since their wedding years ago.'

'Which I made a good excuse not to attend.'

'Not a particularly good excuse, Mark, at least I didn't think so at the time.'

He laughed, unabashed, tucking his arm in mine and carrying my suitcase in the other one. 'You're looking marvellous, Nancy. I hear you're back in Greymont.'

'Yes, working on the paper.'

'I'm looking forward to hearing about your adventures during the next few days, but isn't this all a bit of a change from London?'

'Yes, it is.'

'You're living with your aunt then?'

'No. I have a small flat near the park.'

'I'll know where to come then when I'm in need of tea and sympathy.'

'There's a tenancy agreement which forbids me to entertain married men in my flat.'

'Whoever invented that?'

'I did.'

He threw back his head and laughed. 'Still the same old Nancy. We must have a long talk about all the things

274

you've been doing since we last met. What do you think about the Hall? My father let it go to seed, but Amelia's worked wonders – Amelia *and* her father's money.'

I detected a cynical note in his voice but by this time we were entering the Hall where a manservant relieved Mark of my case and we joined the others on the terrace. We walked through a large room where french windows stood open onto the patio. It was a room warm with sunlight, with a deep Chinese carpet on the floor and crystal chandeliers overhead. From beyond I could hear voices.

Mark drew me out onto the terrace and then Amelia was there, kissing my cheek and I could smell her perfume, gentle and lingering, and when I looked into her brown eyes the years dropped away and it could have been that morning in our dormitory at Lorivals when I first met her and instantly adored her.

Martin had risen to his feet and took my outstretched hand, then Barbara was greeting me effusively and for the first time in many years I really looked at her. I had imagined her like this, sophisticated and stylish, her dark hair swept up in a fashionable style, wearing a Chanel suit that breathed money, beautifully made up and smelling of Arpège. From the top of her gleaming dark hair to her expensive narrow shoes she was a product of money. She advertised the fact that she was the wife of a successful man and yet her face had developed a hardness that had not been evident in the old Barbara.

I sat beside her on the swingseat and immediately she started to bombard me with questions until Amelia remarked, 'We started without you Nancy, so I'll ring for some more tea. In the meantime, do please help yourself.' Mark helpfully brought plates of sandwiches and small dainty cakes from the table to my side.

Martin did most of the talking. We heard about his directorship in several companies – he had moved on since his early days as a young solicitor – and we heard about his powerboat in the harbour at Falmouth and their holidays in the Caribbean and Bermuda.

'We're off to the States in September,' he informed us. 'I have business interests there and of course, we have friends in Boston and New York. Have any of you been to America?' he asked with a superior smile. 'It's a rare experience, I can tell you.'

We all denied having had that privilege but Mark added wryly, 'I'm for old countries myself and Amelia doesn't care for foreign travel. She leaves that to other members of the family.'

'Oh, where are they?' Barbara asked.

'Mother and Father were in Egypt all during the winter,' Amelia said, 'and my sister's just come back from Canada. My brother always maintains there's enough beauty in this country, that one should never go abroad, but then he's in the Royal Navy so he has many opportunities for foreign travel.'

'Oh well, of course he's right,' Martin agreed pompously. 'In my case we have to travel for reasons of business, but we do enjoy it, don't we Barbara? She'd lie on a beach forever, she tans so beautifully.'

Barbara's tan was deep and golden while mine had quickly faded in the months since I left the Far East. 'I'm getting rather tired of Europe and the West Indies,' she remarked. 'I'd like to visit the Middle East – Jordan, I think. I'd especially like to see Petra. I read all about it quite recently.'

' "The rose-red city, half as old as time",' Mark quoted, but immediately Martin said testily, 'We're certainly not going to the Middle East! You want to read Noel Templeton's article in the *Times* this morning – there's no chance of *us* being caught up in any of that.'

Barbara's expression was bored and faintly cynical and Amelia said quickly, 'You've not said very much, Nancy. Perhaps you'd like to tell us what Hong Kong was like.'

Before I could answer Martin said, 'That's an idea, Barbara. Long before Hong Kong reverts to China, how about going there this year? I could see some business colleagues and others in Singapore – kill two birds with one stone so to speak.'

Ignoring him Barbara said coolly, 'Your aunt told my mother you were in Hong Kong, Nancy. I'd have thought you'd have met some divine man out there that you wanted to marry. What was the social life like?'

'In the main I enjoyed it, it's a different world.'

'How about you and me taking a turn around the park?' Mark said to Martin, rising to his feet.

Martin said self-importantly, 'Good idea, we'll walk this excellent tea off. I must say it's all looking very prosperous these days. We used to come camping in the field on the other side of the river when I was a boy, and the Hall looked decidedly seedy then.'

I did not miss the flicker of annoyance that crossed Mark's face at this rudeness nor the dry sarcasm in his voice. 'My father never had much interest in the place, he preferred to spend his money on other things. We owe all this to Amelia and her father, isn't that right, my dear?'

Without another word he walked down the steps from the terrace and Martin followed. We watched them walking at a brisk pace across the grass towards the river and after a few minutes Amelia said gently, 'This is how I imagined it would be when I thought about our reunion – just girls talking about old times and laughing about all the things we did at Lorivals. We should all be swapping stories about our babies and our husbands – I never intended the men to be here. Time alters many things.'

'Well, my life's been much as I hoped it would be,' Barbara announced. 'I always wanted Martin Walton: I knew he'd get on, I knew the sort of life we'd be living and neither of us were keen on children. I don't regret any of it, and I'd certainly have been bored out of my skin listening to three girls prattling on about babies.'

'But we were to have been five girls,' Amelia reminded her. 'You and Maisie were the predictable ones, and I suppose I was too, although it was to be Phillip, not Mark I would be chatting about. That was the first thing that changed and Lois was the next. How could any of us have visualised the terrible thing that happened to her.'

'Why on earth should she have done that?' Barbara asked us. 'I always thought she was paranoid about her father's activities but she had a good job, never seemed short of money and presumably had plenty of friends. I suppose it was some man, probably some married man. Surely you know, Nancy. You were living in the same house.'

'We didn't see a lot of one another. We had different friends, different jobs. I was as shocked as the next person.'

'But there was a man,' Barbara persisted, ignoring my signals of distress.

'Lois was secretive about her friends.'

'It was quite terrible for her father,' Amelia said. 'David Brampton was devastated by it, apparently.'

'You've spoken to him about it?' Barbara asked.

'No, but one hears these things.'

At that moment the servants came to clear the table and we sat in silence. Before us stretched a scene of incredible beauty, far removed from turmoil and sudden death. The wide sweep of the river was calm and placid but I knew that long before it reached the gardens below Lorivals it would fall swiftly over the weir where ahead lay the rocks and dangerous undercurrents in keeping with life itself.

Amelia's thoughts too must have been following a similar pattern because she said softly, 'It's such a beautiful afternoon. It's hard to imagine it on a wild windy day in March with the river in spate.'

'Oh well, it looks as if we're in for a spell of gorgeous weather,' Barbara said complacently. 'I always understood that mist on the lakeland hills was a good sign: if they were clear we were in for rain.'

278

Amelia's face lit up with a sudden smile, and rising to her feet she went to stand at the edge of the terrace looking out to where two children were riding their ponies towards her. She waved, and turning to us announced, 'Here are my two little girls come to say hello. I told them we'd be here this afternoon.' She introduced them with pride – Pippa and Berenice. Pippa resembled Mark, while the other was more like Amelia, but both of them possessed their mother's sweet gentle smile. They left their ponies tied to the terrace pillars, champing the short sweet grass, and then came to sit with us in the chairs vacated by the two men. Amelia encouraged them to talk to us about their interests, their ponies and their lessons at the small prep school they attended.

'Aren't they going to Lorivals one day?' Barbara asked curiously.

'Yes, of course, when they're old enough. You're both looking forward to that, aren't you darlings?' Amelia asked, and the two girls smiled in agreement.

'Why don't we show Barbara and Nancy around the house,' Amelia said brightly. 'I'm sure they'd like to see your rooms.' So we trooped into the house and listened to Amelia proudly telling us what changes she had made since coming to Garveston as a bride.

'Mark is often resentful that I was able to make these changes,' she confided, 'but inwardly he knows they were necessary. I couldn't have lived in this house the way it was. Can you believe it, many of the carpets were threadbare and most of the pictures needed restoring. It took a great deal of money to put it all right. Now Mark thinks we should open the Hall up to the public, or, if not the Hall, then certainly the grounds.'

'Don't you agree with him, then?' Barbara asked.

'I'm considering opening the park on certain days next summer, but not the house. I'm a very private person, and I don't want people I don't know tramping round indoors. We'll go to the girls' rooms first.'

279

Pippa's room overlooked the Forest of Bowland at the back of the house. Large, and beautifully decorated, it was lined with shelves on which children's books were stacked as well as dolls and other toys. A large dolls' house stood in the middle of the room, and there was a light oak desk in front of the window. One child's high chair stood in a corner and seeing us look at it Amelia said quickly, 'That chair used to belong to my niece, Dorinda. She was here for several months recently while Celia was in Canada. Dorinda isn't well, she's been more or less an invalid since she was three and like me she was more or less an afterthought in her parents' lives. We love having her, though. My children adore her, don't you darlings?'

I found myself remembering Dorinda, that sad travesty of a person who could never be anything but herself, who had no conception of good or bad. How could these two normal charming little girls see anything but tragedy in a life so different from their own? They smiled politely at their mother's words, but I did not miss the look of perplexity that passed between them.

Amelia and Barbara had moved on and Pippa said softly to me, 'Mummy always tells people that we adore Dorinda. That's so that Aunt Celia feels she can leave her with us when she has to go away.'

'I hope she doesn't come next year if Aunt Celia goes away,' Berenice muttered sharply, and Pippa said, 'Sshh, don't let Mummy hear you. She says we have to love Dorinda; she can't help it that she's not like us.'

'Come darlings,' called Amelia from the doorway, and the two little girls hurried to her while I walked after them thoughtfully. In the small morning room Amelia said, 'This is my favourite room – I call it my sitting room. Mark said it was his mother's favourite as well, – and it was the only room in the house that they'd managed to preserve reasonably well.'

It was charming, with its pastel carpet and delicate chintz covers. On the walls were several attractive water colours, and large windows overlooked the sweeping fell and distant lakeland hills.

'I do all my correspondence in here,' Amelia explained, 'and it's here I like to sew and read to the children. Mark says it's insipid, but I tell him it reflects my personality. Perhaps that too is insipid, I don't know.'

'I doubt if you'd think much of our house,' Barbara said. 'It's a large modern place with a big garden, extremely functional and with absolutely no character. Martin chose it.'

'Surely he consulted you about what you would like, the furnishings and other things?'

'Yes of course, but it's not a house that lends itself to water colours and the like. It was designed by a friend of Martin's, a young up and coming architect who's very much a creature of this generation. His first thought was a swimming pool in the garden and a kitchen the size of your largest drawing room – not a bad thing, since we entertain quite a lot. Martin considers we've got quite a showplace, but it's definitely not *this* sort of showplace.'

'Oh well,' Amelia said with a gentle smile, 'it wouldn't do for us all to like the same sort of thing. We couldn't turn this into a modern dwelling if we tried. I do hope none of you are going to be bored during the weekend, as we don't usually do much except chat. I thought we'd dine at eight then if you like we could play bridge. Mark may have suggestions to make.'

'I'm no great shakes as a bridge player,' Barbara said quickly, 'but naturally I'll fall in with what everybody else wants to do. Will there just be the seven of us for dinner?'

'The children will eat much earlier. There'll be just the five of us. Maisie and her husband are not joining us until Sunday evening.'

'Then we'll have the farm and the children, I suppose. I can't think Maisie's changed much.'

'Her children are very nice – I see them occasionally at some summer fête or other, and Maisie is a very good farmer's wife.'

'Oh, I'm sure of it.' As we walked down the staircase together Barbara whispered, 'I do hope Tom doesn't arrive in the sort of awful thing he wore at the dance. Remember him, Nancy – those great clumsy brogues and that thick sweater.'

When I didn't speak she gave a little laugh saying, 'I know, you still think I'm a first-class bitch and you're probably right. Don't catch my eye though if he does arrive looking as if he's just come in from milking. I won't be able to stop myself laughing.'

'You're likely to have a very pleasant surprise.'

'Really? Do tell me in what way.'

'Wait and see. I like Tom, I always have.'

'Oh I know, you always liked Maisie even when we used to fight like mad. Why don't we take a walk across the park and see what the men are up to. We can't spend all afternoon talking about them and the babies we haven't got. What do you say, Amelia?'

'Of course. Collect your ponies, girls, you can come with us,' Amelia replied, while the two girls ran across the hall and out through the french windows.

We walked towards the river, surrounded by the humming of bees and trilling birdsong. After a while Barbara said curiously, 'What do you do all day surrounded by all this tranquillity? Don't you ever get bored?'

'Well no, I have many interests,' Amelia replied. 'I'm a magistrate and the chairwoman of this and that, then there are the children. I like to think I help with their education.'

'Don't you do anything with Mark? I know he likes race meetings and racing cars, but I take it you have no interest in such things,' Barbara persisted, posing questions I could never have asked.

'Occasionally we have house-parties when our guests go to race meetings and sometimes I accompany them. I love horses, I ride with the children, but my guests understand that I'm not keen on actual racing. Mark doesn't mind, he knows it bores me. I always think the river is so beautiful here – must be the willows that make it so perfect. We have one guest who comes down here again and again just to paint this spot. I have one of his pictures in my sitting room.'

Amelia had changed the subject adroitly and I was glad that Barbara did not pick it up again. For a while we strolled along the river banks while the children trotted beside us on their ponies, then Mark and Martin were approaching us while the two girls rode off to meet them.

That night while I dressed for dinner I asked myself if I would have anything to contribute to the weekend. In the old days at Lorivals I had been immune to it, but now I felt it forcefully, the barriers of class of which I had so often been aware with Desmond and occasionally with Mark. Cushioned by her money, Barbara would never feel it, but Maisie in her honesty had always recognised it.

Amelia the schoolgirl had tried to be one of us and had in some measure succeeded. Amelia the mistress of Garveston was different. I felt her remoteness, a certain wariness behind the serenity but I doubted if Barbara had noticed. Barbara's veneer of sophistication was more than paper-thin, it was an enamel crust deep and impenetrable.

Before I went downstairs I stared at myself in the full-length mirror. The jade silk gown fell in graceful folds to my feet, and it brought back poignant memories of Lois and that fateful weekend in Gloucestershire. The gown was the same, the woman inside it different. The woman I stared at now had lost forever that bright puppy shyness. Lois's father had stared at me on that evening in the Cotswolds and told me I was beautiful: it had been the beauty of a young girl emerging from her chrysalis, untried and unversed. The face in the mirror did not have the brittle sophistication of Barbara, but it had a strangely sad and haunted look. Perhaps the memory of Lois had put it there, or thoughts of happier days before the classrooms of Lorivals had become lost amid the sterner classrooms of life.

I heard Barbara's voice outside my room, so I picked up my evening bag and after switching off the light let myself out into the corridor. The guests had gathered in the drawing room for drinks before dinner, the men attired in dinner jackets and the two women in long gowns which made me feel relieved that I had chosen correctly.

Amelia as always looked cool and entirely elegant in beige silk, while Barbara wore a dress of deep blue. Thin straps left her shoulders slim and bare, and the bright blue against her tanned skin made her look alien and exotic. She eyed my jade dress with some interest and I smiled to myself, thinking that she would already have assessed its age and worth. Sure enough, with a conspiratorial tone she said, 'I can't think your years in London or Hong Kong were spent over a sewing machine, darling – that dress was made to see Life.'

'Do you like it?'

'Well, of course – it's charming! Who was he, Nancy?'

'He was Lois' father David. He took me to a house-party in the Cotswolds when Lois was ill in hospital with pneumonia. I had to have something decent to wear.'

'Of course. Is that all you're prepared to tell me?'

I smiled. 'There isn't anything else. The others were all years older than me. I'd taken the place of his daughter, that's all. There's really nothing else to tell.'

'This is Barbara you're talking to Nancy, not Maisie Standing, nor Amelia either for that matter.'

I turned away to accept the glass of sherry Mark was handing to me. It was easy to allow my mind to wander over dinner. The conversation had reverted to holidays again and Barbara's penchant for the Middle East. Martin's face was sulky and Amelia in a conciliatory tone said, 'Why not try Egypt? My mother said it was beautiful and tranquil on the Nile – haven't either of you been there?'

Neither of them had, but Martin was quick to say that he didn't think a holiday spent looking at pyramids and tombs was exactly his forte, and Barbara retorted, 'Marian Jefferson says they have divine sporting clubs for people just like you.'

'What is that supposed to mean?'

'People who are not interested in classical Egypt but are merely looking for England abroad.'

Martin decided it was time to change the subject so the conversation reverted to the many pictures ranged around the room. 'I suppose all these are very old,' he began. 'Do you ever pick up something contemporary?'

'Now and again Amelia buys something, some water colour that takes her eye. I go in for sporting prints myself.'

'I managed to get hold of a couple of Lowrys last year. They cost a lot but I had to have them. They'll grow in value, of course, and they're both signed by the artist.'

Across the table my eyes met Mark's and he smiled. I knew he was remembering that disastrous day when he had argued with my father. Intent on keeping the conversation alive he said, 'You're keen on Lowry, are you?'

'Actually I'm not. I don't flaunt them, they're out of sight in the upstairs corridor but I do happen to know their worth.'

'I couldn't live with a picture I didn't like simply because it was worth a lot of money,' Amelia said evenly. 'There are pictures here that I don't really like but they belonged to the Garveston family and went with the house. I've done a bit of changing around since we married.'

'I hung the Lowrys in the lounge when I bought them,' Martin said, 'but I'm so fed up with my friends asking is Lancashire really like that, and having to explain that it isn't.'

Barbara picked up the story lightly by saying, 'We now have hunting scenes on the drawing room walls in

285

spite of the fact that Martin's never ridden a hunter in his life. My father would have gloried in one of his Lowry pictures but he won't part with one of them, even if they are tucked away out of sight.'

'I didn't buy them for your father, Barbara,' Martin said sharply. 'Heaven knows, he gets my sweaters, my ties and my golf clubs. I draw the line at the Lowrys.'

'We're only paying them back a little for all they did for us when we first married, for my expensive education and in the early days your Golf Club subs.'

Across the table my eyes met Amelia's and I knew what was passing through her mind. Mark and Martin should never have been sitting at the table with us on this occasion. Left to ourselves there would have been other things to talk about and I sensed her embarrassment.

Barbara declined to play bridge, and for a while we sat chatting until Mark said, 'We have videos of my recent trip to Kenya and there are family occasions you might be interested in. What do you say we go into the drawing room to look at them.'

We trooped after him and waited while he arranged chairs and furniture before sitting us down. Then Mark produced the screen and the videos he intended to show. Once during the film of Kenya I looked up to find Amelia sitting back in her chair staring in front of her, uninterested and detached until he began to show the ones of family. We saw the christening party for the girls and their emergence from babyhood into childhood, then there were other pictures, of Amelia's parents sitting in the gardens or walking across the lawns with an array of dogs. We were shown Amelia and the children riding their ponies along the country lanes, and Amelia presiding graciously at some function where she appeared to be handing out prizes.

Then there came another video devoted to Dorinda, the most unkind one of all. Mark should never have shown it. We saw Dorinda appealing and beautiful in a pale pink dress sitting on a motoring rug in the middle of the lawn on a sunny afternoon, her brother waving a toy fluffy rabbit to catch her attention, her parents proud and smiling beside them. I looked at Desmond's face, more serene than I remembered it, more carefree, and Celia laughing up at him with obvious delight. Then followed the harrowing pictures of Dorinda after her illness, showing the grotesque caricature of the child she had once been, the empty eyes and gaping mouth, the flopping limbs that obeyed no signals from a brain that was destroyed. Now Desmond was absent from those pictures and only Celia smiled as if nothing was wrong with her child.

After the long silence that followed the showing of this home-movie, it was Barbara who said in a small horrified voice, 'How terrible for that to have happened. Can't anything be done?'

'I don't know what made me choose that film. I'm sorry. Look – they've had the best doctors in the country,' Mark said quickly, 'but there's nothing any of them can do.'

'She's a very sweet child,' Amelia put in quickly, 'and she's not a lot of trouble. She knows her mother and me, and her nurse of course. Both my children adore her, we all do.'

'But what will happen to her when she hasn't got her mother?' Barbara went on relentlessly. 'I do think children like that should be put into a home where they're with other children like themselves. It's so unfair on the rest of the family who are expected to cope with them.'

Amelia's face was icy and controlled. Turning to her husband she said, 'Do you have that video of Mummy and Daddy's trip to the Holy Land, Mark? They're not actually on it, but they bought the video because they'd had such a marvellous time there.'

The film was produced and we sat back to watch it. I was still aware of a constrained atmosphere, however, and once Barbara and Martin exchanged glances which showed plainly that they were uncomfortable. I think we were all glad when the tape ended and Amelia suggested we returned to the drawing room for coffee.

Conversation became normal again and Mark said pleasantly, 'I usually play a round of golf on Saturday morning, Martin. Perhaps you'd like to join me? Did you bring clubs?'

'I put some in the car as an afterthought,' Martin said in a pleased voice. 'I'd like very much to play.'

'Then I'll walk round with you,' Barbara said quickly. 'I didn't bring clubs but I'd enjoy watching.'

'How about you, Nancy?' Mark said, smiling in my direction.

'I'll amuse myself. Perhaps I can keep you company, Amelia,' I suggested.

'Well, actually, I always ride with the girls on Saturday morning, they expect it, but there's plenty to occupy you in the house. You can take a look at the library and the portrait gallery, then there's the conservatory. I'm sure you won't be bored.'

After a few minutes Mark put a record on the hi-fi, saying, 'What do you say we dance? I know there's an odd one but that's no problem, since Amelia goes to bed early.'

'I'm for bed too,' Martin said, rising to his feet. 'We had a long drive up here and I was in London all day yesterday at several business meetings. I promised myself an early night if it was possible. How about you, darling?'

'I'm ready to dance the night away,' Barbara responded. 'I'm willing to take part in everything Mark proposes.'

I was near enough to hear him whisper, 'Everything!' and hear her arch reply of, '*Everything*, darling.'

Martin made his excuses and retired to bed, and turning to me Amelia said, 'Are you also ready to dance the night away, Nancy?'

'No, I shall go to bed. Perhaps I'll read a little.'

Together we walked up the shallow curving staircase and I wondered if she might come into my room to chat, but at the door she merely turned to smile saying, 'Goodnight Nancy, sleep well.'

How I wished at that moment that Monday would come quickly.

27

I couldn't sleep. I was surrounded by a deep impenetrable silence. Outside, the park was bathed in soft mellow moonlight but the birdsong was stilled, and not even a gentle breeze came to sway the branches of the giant beech trees or rustle their leaves. I strained my ears for the sound of a dog barking in the distance or the swift fluttering wings of a night owl, but I was greeted with silence, and if Mark and Barbara danced to music in the room downstairs I could not hear it; the doors were stout, shutting out the normal sounds in a sleeping house. This was a house built to last indefinitely against all the winds of change.

The book I had brought with me was banal and predictable and I wasn't enjoying the prospect of lying sleepless for hours. Unable to stand it any longer I decided to go down to the library to see if there was anything else, maybe some newspaper or magazine carrying Noel's articles on the Middle East troubles.

Outside in the corridor it was murky dark, but as I descended the stairs I found I didn't need to switch on any of the lights. Bright delicate moonlight came in through the long windows in the hall, lighting up the staircase, and I paused to listen for any sounds from the downstairs rooms. I was startled to hear the sound of clocks chiming somewhere but the chime was not on the hour and I had left my watch on the table near my bed. I knew it must be long after midnight so it was possible Mark and Barbara had retired, all the same I crept across the hall, opening the library door carefully so as not to make a sound.

Here again moonlight illuminated the room so I was able to walk easily to the table where magazines and newspapers were stacked. Most of the magazines were devoted to dogs and horses, hunting and motoring, but I did find a *National Geographical* with a write-up on 'Hong Kong Today' and a *London Illustrated* showing page after page of devastation in the Lebanon. People, many of them children, were lying dead or injured in the streets amid the burned-out cars and tanks and on one page, Noel's face was staring grimly at the sight of a nursery school blazing fiercely across the road.

Picking up the magazine I crept back to the door. Opening it gingerly I stood rooted to the spot. The drawing room door was open and Amelia stood on the threshold staring into the room with a strange expression on her face. I did not know how long she had been there, but suddenly she turned away and across the expanse of the hall our eyes met. She showed no emotion, no acknowledgement of my presence, and like a sleepwalker turned gracefully and walked unhurriedly up the stairs, a pale ethereal figure in a flimsy white robe, trailing her hand along the balustrade. After a few moments she disappeared into her room and I was left gazing after her, puzzled and uneasy.

I paused outside the drawing room and because Amelia had left it open I was able to look inside. The room was in darkness except for the moonlight filtering through the long windows. I thought at first that it was deserted and then I heard low voices and laughter and realised that Mark and Barbara were still in there. I could not see them but I knew they were lying on the couch in front of the fireplace, and with my heart thumping wildly I ran noiselessly across the hall and up the stairs. I had only just reached the last step when I heard Mark's voice muttering testily, then the door was shut firmly and I escaped into my room wishing fervently that I had never left it.

I no longer had any interest in the magazine. It was a warm summer's night but I was shivering, and for what seemed hours I tossed and turned sleeplessly in my bed.

I suppose in the end I slept fitfully, but the first pale lights of dawn found me wakeful. I dawdled over my toilet, taking a long leisurely bath. I was still in my dressing gown, hunting in the wardrobe for what I would wear for the day when there was a sharp tap on the door and a young maid entered carrying a tray on which rested a silver tea set and a cup and saucer.

She smiled, setting the tray down on the table next to the bed. 'Good morning, Miss Graham,' she said. 'I hope you slept well.'

'Yes, thank you. Is everybody up?'

'Oh no, miss. The master and Mr Walton are in the breakfast room but Mrs Walton's still upstairs and her ladyship's ready to go riding.'

She let herself out of the door and I went to the window in time to see Amelia and the two girls walking along the path towards the stables. Mist lingered on the slopes and on the river and as yet, the pale tentative fingers of the sun still struggled to light up the parkland. It was a mist that heralded a warm and sunny day and I was wishing Amelia had asked me to go riding with them. I wasn't an expert horsewoman but I was adequate, and I didn't think Amelia would be too adventurous in the company of her young daughters.

I dressed in my good tweed skirt and silk blouse, and left my room to see Barbara closing her door behind her. She greeted me with a smile saying, 'I wish I hadn't promised to walk round the links, I'm too sleepy. You look very nice, Nancy.' She was wearing beige slacks and a pale blue cotton sweater, and although there was nothing unusual about her attire there was a cool elegance about her, an elegance she had always had even as a child.

As we reached the hall we could hear voices coming from the breakfast room and with a little grimace Barbara said, 'That's Martin talking shop, as usual. We must rescue Mark before he dies of boredom.'

'Does he always talk business over breakfast?'

'And lunch and dinner. I've developed a second skin. I say yes and no in all the right places so that he thinks I'm hanging on to every word.'

'You make your life together sound very boring.'

Ignoring my remark she said, 'What are you going to do all morning? I must say Amelia isn't putting herself out to entertain us. I mean, she's not changing her routine, is she?'

By this time we had reached the breakfast room and there was no need for me to reply. The two men were at the toast and marmalade stage and Barbara said, 'I only ever have fruit juice and coffee. I watch my figure very carefully.'

'I wouldn't have thought you needed to,' Mark said, his eyes on her breasts.

'You'd be wrong. I put on almost a stone during our last trip to America. They eat the most enormous meals there – I got to the stage when I couldn't face food after I came home.'

My eyes didn't miss the look that passed between the lovers but Martin was oblivious, enlarging on a recent business adventure, and I went to the side table to help myself to cereal and juice.

Mark passed the morning papers around and Martin said, 'I see Templeton got caught up in some particularly nasty fighting in Tel Aviv yesterday – there's another cameraman killed. One of these days these journalists will be taken hostage like some other chaps.'

I felt my heart lurch sickeningly and Barbara responded, 'All that risk in the cause of news! I'd hate to be married to a man like that.'

'I've never heard that he's married,' Mark said. 'I shouldn't think he is.'

'He isn't,' I couldn't resist saying.

For the first time since I arrived I had their undivided attention. 'You mean you've actually met him?' Mark asked.

'Yes, in the Far East.'

'What a dark horse you are,' Barbara said admiringly. 'Do tell, did you have a wild romantic affair?'

'I said I met him. It was at a party soon after I arrived.'

'Is he as goodlooking as his photographs?'

'I think so.'

'Is that all?' she said, disappointed. 'I was hoping there'd be more.'

'I saw Amelia leaving the house with the children,' I said quickly. 'Do they always ride so early?'

'You're changing the subject,' Barbara accused.

'There isn't any more to tell.'

'I must say you don't seem to have made the most of your opportunities in the Far East. You tell us you've met a divine man like Noel Templeton at a party and that was the end of it. Really, Nancy.'

'And she's blushing,' Mark said, laughing.

'Barbara could always make me blush,' I replied. 'She could always say the most outrageous things – ask Maisie when you see her.'

'Oh, of course they're coming, I'd almost forgotten. Tonight or tomorrow?' Barbara asked.

'Tomorrow.'

'Do you see much of her?'

'Quite a lot actually.'

At that moment Martin consulted his watch saying, 'What time are we starting out, Mark? I usually try to get on the course around nine-thirty.'

'I'm ready when you are, we're just waiting for Barbara.'

'I'm ready. Are you going to come with us, Nancy?'

'No, I'm having a lazy day. I think I'll do what Amelia suggested, take a look in the library and at the house.'

'Try the portrait gallery,' Mark suggested, 'you'll find all my worthy ancestors there, some of them quite disreputable, and there's a stack of family photographs all over the house. Or if you want to walk, there's a very nice path through the beechwood to the village.'

The house felt strangely empty after they had all left

294

but I was glad to be alone with the morning papers and Noel's latest report on the fighting around Tel Aviv. His smiling face stared impudently back at me from the front page and a quite unreasonable anger set my hands trembling so that I had to put the paper down sharply on the table top. He had made me love him. How dared men like that make any woman love them, when all they cared about was excitement and danger.

Amelia had created a treasure trove out of the old, somewhat decrepit Garveston Hall. I spent an enchanting time wandering through the vast rooms and thickly carpeted corridors. Over the marble mantelpiece in the library hung a huge oil-painting by Turner and I could understand Mark's antipathy towards my father's treasured Lowry print. Mark had been polite, my father audacious – how could I ever have thought that either of them would understand each other?

I was intrigued by the portraits in the gallery of long-dead Garvestons in their ruffles of lace or old armour; high-born patrician faces, dissolute lechers, ethereal beauties and dominant matriarchs, they were all there. Mark's parents were painted standing in a group with him and his older brother Phillip; his mother was pale and delicate, his father rotund and with a red smiling face.

At the head of the stairs on the first landing stood a large portrait of Amelia and Mark; she was elegant and graceful from the top of her brown cloudy hair to the hem of her pale cream gown. Her eyes looked serenely out of the picture and the artist had caught her expression of gentle enquiry so perfectly I spared Mark only a perfunctory glance.

I found the photographs in the drawing room and morning room more personal. Here were family snapshots of the children playing with their dogs, or riding their horses, people standing about the lawns on a warm summer's day, Mark with his hair tousled by the wind at the wheel of his new sports car and Amelia distributing silver trophies at the end of the judging at the Agricultural Show.

There were photographs too of Amelia's parents; her mother was as I remembered her, a little old-fashioned in brogues and a shapeless jacket over a tweed skirt and sweater, her father tall and distinguished despite the battered trilby, ancient sportscoat and plus-fours.

In Amelia's sitting room, photographs of her family took pride of place. There was one of a handsome man in Naval Officer's uniform and I guessed this to be her younger brother Cedric. Celia was there in a white ball gown, looking incredibly like Amelia, her expression was one of cool assurance; then I saw Celia as a bride, smiling up at Desmond, a strangely young and carefree Desmond. There was a family group similar to the one I had seen in Desmond's flat and yet another of Desmond standing alone wearing formal morning dress on the steps of St Peter's in Rome. A more mature Desmond, more like the Desmond I had known.

I held it in my hands staring at it and my heart felt shaken by an old and remembered pain. Desmond had been my joy, he had filled my young impressionable heart with tender and delirious love. I had not believed in those early heady days that they would be followed by a hurt so intense I would feel destroyed by it.

I had not heard the door open, I did not know that I was no longer alone. I did not see Amelia's hand reach out to take the photograph from my hands, I only looked up to see her watching me intently while my eyes filled with treacherous tears. I wanted to escape, but there was nowhere to run to. Amelia remained silent waiting for me to regain my self-control.

It seemed to take an age before I felt confident enough to face her. She was standing at the window staring out towards the fells and in those first few moments I wondered how much she knew. I was not left long in doubt. I went to stand beside her and when she turned to face me I saw that her expression was sad. In a voice little above a whisper she said, 'I thought I would hate the girl Desmond was in love with, but I'm not very sure if I can hate you Nancy.'

'How much do you know?'

'A woman my sister knew in the Far East told her Desmond was seeing some girl in London. Celia didn't believe her, as this person has a reputation as a gossip and is not a particularly nice woman, but just before they went to Russia she asked Desmond if there was any truth in it. He told her that there was a girl, a girl he had met at some function or other and they had been going around together. He blamed it on the separateness of their lives, on the barrier Dorinda's illness had put between them but when Celia asked him if he wanted a divorce he denied it was so serious. I don't know how much my sister believed him but she was very aware of his ambitions.

'It was another time to patch up their marriage. She went to Russia with him and Dorinda came with us. Things moved pretty quickly when they got back. Desmond received a Knighthood, Celia came for Dorinda and I knew she was still unhappy. Desmond had rejected divorce as an answer to his problems, but however much he might deny caring for the girl in London the fact was that he had changed. He was staying with Celia for the sake of his career, nothing more. Were you very much in love with him, Nancy?'

'Yes, but not any more. I got over Desmond, I had to. He never lied to me Amelia, he never promised marriage or even that we had a permanent future together. I knew about Dorinda, I knew about his ambition and if I was foolish enough to hope that one day it might be different I was fooling myself.'

'Did you know that he was married to my sister?'

'Not at first. I saw a photograph in his flat once; you were in it and I recognised Drummond in the background. Desmond told me that his wife was your sister, and he was frank about Dorinda and her illness.'

297

'Was this your way of paying me back for taking Mark away from you?' When I stared at her blankly she said quickly, 'I knew about you and Mark and I felt responsible for it. I was the one who had introduced him to you at that wretched school dance. I hadn't bargained on you falling in love with him but I knew he'd never marry you. If he hadn't married me he'd have married Jane Leadbetter. When Phillip was killed it all changed. I was a coward about you, Nancy. I knew you'd never be able to understand the way things were, the way people like us think. So, was this your way of getting back at us?'

I stared at her aghast. 'How can you even think such a thing? I wasn't in love with Mark when he married you – I'd got over him a long time before that. I was very sorry when Phillip Garveston was killed. I wanted to see you, Amelia, to tell you how sorry I was but you were always so aloof, so unapproachable after we left Lorivals. I couldn't reconcile the Amelia I had known there with the Amelia who treated me to a cool nod and a frozen smile whenever we saw each other. Surely all that wasn't because of Mark.'

Her smile was bleak. 'I'm not a very good student of human nature, am I, Nancy? I felt guilty about your loving Mark, I thought you must hate me, then just now I almost accused you of getting back at me through Desmond. I have to ask you though, for Celia's sake: is it finally over between you?'

'Would I be here working on the local rag if it wasn't? I think I know the name of the woman that told your sister about us. She is a poisonous gossip and she told your sister a mischievous story but I can't deny the truth of it. I loved him, Amelia, even when I knew he would never leave his wife and children, he made that very plain. I went to Hong Kong loving him, and hating him because he promised me nothing. Now I'm out of his life and I no longer love him. I hope for all your sakes

298

that your sister and Desmond can finally sort out their destinies.'

I had not told Amelia the full story, as so much of it was locked in my heart forever, but I did feel a certain relief that perhaps one day we could recover our old comradeship.

Saturday evening passed quietly enough. Amelia said she had letters to write so the four of us played bridge. Barbara refused to partner her husband because she said they always quarrelled, so I played with Martin until eleven o'clock when Mark suggested we put on a few ballroom records and dance.

'What did you find to do all alone in the house this morning?' he asked, as we waltzed round the room.

'I enjoyed myself, Mark. I looked at your pictures and photographs, but I was rather disappointed not to find a single Lowry in sight.'

He grinned. 'I was a bloody-minded clot to have that argument with your father. I can't recognise a Constable from a Gainsborough, I've never been into art, but I can recognise a Lowry with all those matchstick figures. I was too sensitive, too quick to take offence and he knew it.'

'I can't think why. I told him it was his fault, that he had been too insensitive.'

'He made me feel an aimless clod and I was. I hadn't a job, I was living on anything my father cared to dole out. Come to think of it, things haven't changed an awful lot.'

'What do you mean?'

'Well, I still haven't got a job. I run the estate with the help of a good Estate Manager and we farm a bit. Your friend Maisie's husband would regard our style of farming as pathetic but my wife's money keeps us very buoyant. Does that shock you, Nancy?'

'Are you trying to shock me?'

'Not particularly. I'd much rather shock Walton, he's

299

so puffed up with importance I'm not surprised his wife's looking elsewhere for a bit of excitement.'

'She's not seriously looking elsewhere, surely.'

'No, perhaps not seriously, but she's a very bored lady and bored women get into mischief.'

'Have you anything planned for tomorrow?'

'Well, Amelia'll be going to church very early, and after that we'll get our heads together and plan the day.'

When Amelia joined us later she reaffirmed that she would be going to the village church early next morning and I asked if I could accompany her. She seemed pleased that I had asked, and just then Martin invited her to dance.

Barbara said quickly, 'I'm not a heathen Nancy, but honestly seven-thirty on a Sunday morning is a bit much.'

'The service is at eight actually.'

'You'll be walking through the park, that'll take at least half an hour. I expect Amelia'll soon be stating her intention to go to bed, but I for one would like to go on dancing.' When I didn't speak she gave a little laugh saying, 'I've spent some very boring days in the country, I hope tomorrow isn't going to be one of them.'

'I'm sure Mark has something planned. He said we'd talk about it together.'

'I do hope so. I don't want another day walking round the links and we've got the exhilarating prospect of Maisie and her husband in the evening.'

28

It felt like the old days walking through the park with Amelia on our way to church, and something of the same must have communicated itself to her, for when she said, 'Do you remember those old church parades, Nancy? How organised and decorous we were. I see the girls from Lorivals often in the church near the school, as for my sins I'm on the Board of Governors, and they look exactly like we did. Uniform is a great leveller, I think.'

'I wonder if some of them will agree to meet in ten years' time.'

'I'm sure they will. I think you've changed the most, Nancy.'

'I!'

'Well, yes. Barbara has hardly changed at all except that she's an adult woman. She was always abrasive, always very sure how her life was going to be. She got exactly what she wanted, Martin and money. Maisie hasn't changed at all, but you are the one who is hiding behind normality, nursing too many hurts, too many disappointments.'

'You're very perceptive, Amelia.'

'It wasn't just Desmond, was it Nancy? If there was just Desmond you'd never have been able to run away, you'd have gone on hoping for something permanent to come out of it. Something or someone else gave you the courage to run away.'

'Yes, somebody else I met in Hong Kong.'

'Another married man?'

'No. There was no wife involved, only a job that took him into danger. Perhaps he didn't care enough, maybe he cared too much, I'll probably never know.'

'Have you had friends you could talk to? I've been such a bad friend, Nancy.'

I was saved from replying when at that moment we were hailed by the vicar running along the road, his gown flapping round his ankles, a smile of greeting on his face. He was in the mood to deliver a long sermon and the service went on rather longer than expected so that Amelia said when we emerged from the church, 'We'll return to the house by the road. Mark will be so cross if we're late, he's sure to have all sorts of suggestions for the rest of the day.'

The others were sitting in the morning room reading the papers when we arrived back and Mark said somewhat petulantly, 'How late you are. It would have been nice to get off early instead of killing time in here.'

Amelia blushed, saying in a gentle voice, 'I'm sorry dear, it was a very long sermon. Are you wanting breakfast, Nancy? I rarely eat breakfast on Sunday, just fruit juice and coffee.'

'That's what I would like.'

'Well, do hurry,' Mark said briskly. 'If we leave it much later the roads will be crowded and most of the car parks full. We've decided to head for the lakes, that's if you two agree of course.'

'That would be lovely Mark, we're using two cars of course?'

'We'll all pile into the Space Cruiser. One vehicle's easier to park than two.'

We hurried over our frugal breakfast and Amelia said with a smile, 'Mark's so impatient when he's decided to go off somewhere. I live my life on a far more even keel.'

The six of us piled into Mark's Space Cruiser assisted by one of the staff who handed up baskets of refreshments as well as chairs and rugs for us to sit on.

The sun was already warm and the lake shimmered enticingly. We found a pleasant picnic area under the trees where we could watch the wild ducks cavorting in the lake and eat our lunch. I sat a little apart from the others on a rug and after a while Mark came to sit beside me, making a show of refilling my coffee cup before lying back with his eyes closed, saying, 'Enjoyed your weekend Nancy?'

'Very much, it was kind of Amelia to invite us.'

'She's given you ten years to get over me, but how long did it actually take?'

'I don't think I should answer that one.'

'I told Amelia I was never destined to be the solitary passion of a lifetime, and there was no reason on earth why she couldn't invite you over much earlier, or keep in touch at any rate. Were you very surprised when I married Amelia?'

'No, I don't think I was. It was sad about your brother.'

'Yes, he understood Amelia more than I've ever done, and they had more in common. He loved the Hall, he'd have enjoyed working on it, making a success of the farming side of it, whereas I'm often straining at the leash. I like motor racing and the horses. Amelia and Phillip liked the same sort of people, too. She's never been keen on any of my friends, but then neither were you Nancy.'

I nodded quietly and after a while he said sombrely, 'Dad had no means of repaying all the money Lord Urquart had spent on Garveston when he thought his daughter was going to marry my brother, so I was the sacrificial lamb.'

'But you must love her, Mark? She's so very beautiful, and you have two lovely children. I always loved Amelia, she was somebody very special in my young life.'

His face was pensive and he remained silent for so long I believed he intended to ignore my words then he said softly, 'You're a loyal little thing, Nancy. I never deserved you, but Amelia and I deserve each other.'

'What exactly do you mean by that?'

'I have a lot to thank the Urquart family for but the reminders have been pretty constant over the years.'

Amelia and Barbara were standing near the lake and suddenly Amelia turned and walked back towards us. 'Mark,' I said urgently, 'please be careful with Barbara. Amelia saw you together on Friday night.'

He grinned. 'I know somebody opened the drawing room door. There's nothing of any consequence between Barbara and me – she's just bored and so am I. We're a lot alike, selfish and greedy, and we're also pretty reckless as you've probably gathered. Besides, she's bored out of her skin with that husband of hers. Wouldn't you be?'

'I would never have married Martin Walton.'

'Well, of course not! I can't see what a bright girl like Barbara ever saw in him. Hello, it looks as though Amelia's decided to pack up.'

I jumped to my feet and gathered our rubbish into a small heap, then I went to help Amelia to clear up the rest of our belongings. She smiled brightly saying, 'Martin's suggested we drive up to Ambleside and take a boat out on the lake. I hate rowing boats, so it's got to be something bigger than that. Mark has a small yacht he keeps there, so perhaps he'll agree to us taking that out.'

Mark was only too pleased and we spent a delightful afternoon cruising from one end of the lake to another. Martin was enthusiastic about the boat and Barbara said darkly, 'He won't rest until he's got one of these, now. He was like that until he got the power boat and yet we hardly ever use it these days.'

'Don't you have a say in it?' I asked innocently.

'Not when it's something like this – a boat, a car or a holiday. I get my way about the house then he starts to add to it.'

Amelia warned us we had to get back to the Hall in time to change before dinner when Maisie and Tom would be joining us.

'What's she like these days?' Barbara asked as we walked together to the car.

'Maisie doesn't change. She's totally happy with her life and her children are a credit to her. They're doing very well at school.'

'Do farmers have to be clever?'

'They'll probably never be farmers.'

'Does Amelia see much of her?'

'I really don't know. Probably at the agricultural shows and church fêtes. Amelia's on so many committees and Maisie attends all the functions.'

'Are you leaving directly after breakfast tomorrow morning?'

'Yes, I'm going into the office when I get back. Why, has Martin got the day off?'

'Martin takes time off whenever he feels like it, for golf, racing and weekends in the country. He's the big boss, he doesn't need to ask anybody.'

'How nice.'

She grinned at me. 'I'm not showing off, Nancy, I'm stating a fact. I knew he was going far – nothing Martin has achieved has surprised me.'

'Are you calling in to see your parents on the way back?'

'Heavens yes, Mother'll be waiting with baited breath to hear about the weekend. She'll dine out for months on the pictures, the furniture and the weekend generally.'

'She and Aunt Susan'll have a lot to talk about when they next meet.'

'I'm sure Mother bores everybody with Martin's achievements, our fine house and our committees. I never tell her that for most of the time I'm fed up with entertaining the same old people, and I'm often alone. Martin's away a good deal.'

'You always wanted him, Barbara.'

'I know, but it sometimes happens that the things we want at seventeen are the last things we want ten years later.' I stared at her curiously, then with a little laugh she added, 'We'd better go, Amelia's waiting. I can't say

305

I'm looking forward to a night of Maisie, the farm and the children.'

I had never seen Maisie looking prettier. The green dress she wore for dinner complemented her auburn hair and tanned face, and although she was inclined to be plump the folds of the dress made her seem taller, endowing her with a rare grace. Tom was wearing a dark lounge suit, and as always he looked robust, his face shining and ruddy over his white shirt.

Mark and Amelia were all charm, Martin somewhat sulky, but Barbara admired the gown and after a few minutes Maisie sat down between Amelia and me while Tom stood with Mark looking out across the parkland, discussing his farm, I felt sure.

The meal was excellent, the talk general, and Maisie was encouraged by Amelia to tell us about her children, after which we heard little else beyond Peter's excellent school report. Barbara raised her eyes heavenwards and at one stage I wanted to laugh when the talk got on to farming and Mark encouraged Tom to open up so that there followed a long discourse on crops and livestock, leaving Martin looking openly bored.

The evening passed pleasantly enough. After we had eaten Maisie followed me closely so that we could sit together in the drawing room. Martin talked about Mark's yacht, indicating that he would like to buy one and would Mark advise him when the time came, while Barbara spoke endlessly about the delights of shopping in Cheltenham. Maisie muttered in my ear, 'She's not changed, has she? Still showing off.'

I had little to contribute. There were times when I felt invisible, a single woman sitting with three others who were married, and Amelia, perhaps unconsciously, was making me doubly aware that I was different – whatever might have happened in my life was unimportant. My mind wandered; the hum of the conversation in the room meant nothing to me and I had grown tired of pretending an interest I didn't feel, particularly when the others showed so little interest in me.

Soon after ten Maisie and Tom said they must leave and Mark put in heartily, 'I expect you'll be up when the cock crows.'

'Earlier than that sometimes,' Tom said earnestly. 'Farming's a round the clock thing, there's no days of rest.'

'No, that's true. I've often thought we could make more use of our land, particularly that bit near the moor bottoms.'

'I've been sayin' that for years,' Tom agreed. 'Mi father always said it was good farmland goin' to waste.'

'If I decide to do anything about it would you be willing to lend a hand?'

'Just ask. I haven't a lot of time, but I'd be willin' to come over and tek a look.'

'And that's probably the last you will hear of it,' Amelia said with a gentle smile. 'Mark's always going on about that land, but he never does anything.'

'Perhaps we should mention it to your father the next time they're up here. He'll no doubt know what's needed and how much it'll cost.' His tone was sarcastic, and immediately the rich colour flooded Amelia's face and I saw her hands clench tight against her skirt.

For a little while after Maisie and Tom had left we remained in the drawing room listening to Mark and Martin discussing the attributes of different power boats and motor cars, then Barbara yawned and said, 'Well, I don't know about the rest of you but I'm for bed. I'll do a bit of packing, as we'll want to be away directly before lunch tomorrow.'

'I have a meeting in the village hall tomorrow,' Amelia said. 'I couldn't put it off but it won't last long. It's the agricultural show at the end of August and I'm the chairwoman. I'll be home before eleven, in time to see you off.'

The three of us walked up the stairs together leaving the men drinking their whisky, their voices following us upwards and Amelia said softly, 'They'll go on talking for hours if it's something they care about. Goodnight, both of you.'

I undressed, feeling relieved that there was to be no more repetition of Barbara and Mark's love-making, and for a while I lay in bed with a book open but I was not reading. The house was so still; occasionally I could hear the wind rustling through the trees in the park and there were no signs of human habitation, no voices, no chiming clocks or dogs barking. Once again I was struck by the same impersonal feeling the house inspired in me – it might have been unlived-in, a beautiful background, a golden cage for Amelia's beauty and her imagined perfect world.

I was up and out on the fell before the others were awake the next morning. I needed this little time to myself in the fresh morning air: I was glad the time was fast approaching when I could conveniently drive my Mini through the gates and back to Greymont. Even on the hottest days of summer there was a breeze on the fells. The tough moorland grass sprang strongly under my feet and although it was only late July, already the heather bloomed blue and purple all around me, and tiny fluffs of cotton fluttered bravely.

How I loved it, the big sky and the gently sloping fells, the high rugged crags and the lakeland hills covered with haze. It was on the fells where I had poured out my childhood dreams and longings, my adult miseries. I had walked towards the summit of this same fell after Grandfather died, with a sad heart plagued with memories and questions and it was here where my father had found me. We had sat together looking out across the moors while he tried to explain to me the mystery of death, something he hadn't understood himself.

I had walked here again after my father died, infinitely more tragic because Grandfather had been old and weary,

308

whereas Father was still relatively young and interested in the life that went on around him. I had sat with my back against the crags in a cold wind that had brought the tears to my eyes, thinking about Desmond and the sudden coldness in his face, loving him and hating him, wondering if he would be at the station waiting for me when I stepped off the train. I was so engrossed with my thoughts that I didn't hear a sound until Barbara stood beside me on the hillside.

'I thought I'd find you up here,' she said cheerfully. 'I saw you leaving the Hall and head towards the fell but Martin was going on and on about that damned boat until I thought I'd scream. He's gone off with Mark now. He knows somebody in Kendal who has a boatyard and could probably put him in touch with a supplier.'

'Will he keep it up here on one of the lakes?'

'Heaven knows where he'll keep it. We live in the Midlands, remember. A motor launch can be kept on the Severn or the Wye, but this will have to be bigger and better than anybody else's. Oh, the whole thing is so silly. Martin's always like this when he gets a bee in his bonnet. He's done remarkably well, I always knew he would, but he constantly has to prove it to himself, to me, to everybody. This means a bigger house, a more powerful car, more expensive holidays, and now it's the boat. This is why my father gets so angry about him.'

'I don't suppose it's anybody's business if he can afford these things.'

'It isn't, but my father'd have been much happier to see me like Maisie with a nice house, a family and a husband contented with his lot.'

For several minutes we sat in silence looking down on Lorivals below us. Men were working in the gardens and the playing-fields while a small black dog raced exuberantly across the short cropped grass. There was no sign of life from the school, no girls sauntering along the paths or active on the tennis courts, no sounds of music or laughter; the men were left to get on with their work unhampered by chattering schoolgirls and Barbara said softly, 'I wonder how many of them vowed to get in touch in later years and how many of them really meant it.' When I didn't answer she added, 'I suppose Clarkie gave them her usual pep talk on being the chosen ones so that they left in a haze of euphoria believing that the world was their oyster.'

'We've all had our chance. The school wasn't to blame if we messed things up.'

'It must be nice for Clarkie to refer to Amelia as a former pupil, and Mother never misses an opportunity of letting her know what sort of financial circumstances we're in. Then there's Maisie's very proper contribution as the wife of a yeoman farmer. Three out of five can't be bad. You're the dark horse Nancy, and enough said about Lois the better.'

She went on, 'I must say I was surprised when Amelia actually remembered to invite us. It was a rash idea, after all. Amelia lives in a dream world – the perfect wife, the perfect mother, in a dream house – talking about that poor daughter of her sister's as if she'd simply broken a leg or something. Did you know that she and Mark have separate rooms?'

'No, I didn't know.'

'I wouldn't have known myself but I had a pressing invitation to go into his bedroom last night. Before that it had just been a romp – I wasn't looking for anything else, but Mark evidently was.'

'Isn't it time we were getting back?'

'I suppose so.' She grinned, and suddenly I had a vision of the old Barbara, and felt warmer towards her.

We strolled back to the Hall to find that Amelia had returned and they were all standing on the terrace awaiting us.

'Martin's anxious to get away,' Barbara observed. 'He's brought the luggage out but I want to call in to see my parents. Oh, I do hope they're still not talking about that dratted boat. We really don't need another.'

310

Her wish was a forlorn one, for as soon as we reached the terrace Martin informed Barbara that he had put down a deposit on a yacht and intended to keep it up at Ambleside. Shrugging her shoulders indifferently she turned away to ask Amelia how her meeting had gone, and sensing the tension Amelia said lightly, 'You really wouldn't think people could argue for over an hour about which field the dog show should be held in, and in what order the dogs are shown.'

'Doesn't Maisie interest herself in things like that?' Barbara asked curiously.

'Well, of course. Tom owns the field so naturally he's on the committee. Maisie comes to the show with her children, and she's good at exhibiting her cakes and preserves.'

'Bully for Maisie.'

'Sometimes I think I sit on too many committees. It's difficult to decide which ones I should give up.'

'I do know what you mean,' Barbara said feelingly. 'To get on the committee at the Golf Club is to be little less than canonised.'

Mark grinned at me across their heads, and Martin made a move to pick up his luggage. 'Is this the lot,' he said, eyeing Barbara's pale cream monogrammed week-end case.

'The rest is in the boot. Didn't you put it in earlier on?'

I saw then that my own luggage stood ready on the terrace and Mark picked it up cheerfully. Amelia bade us goodbye graciously on the terrace steps, embracing Barbara and me warmly, saying, 'It has been wonderful, hasn't it? We must do it again in another ten years if not before, it's so necessary that we keep in touch.'

We smiled politely, and Mark said evenly, 'I'm always in Cheltenham for the racing, shall I see you both there?'

'Well, I'm not really a racing man, but it's possible. Perhaps Barbara might care for it.'

Mark looked at her enquiringly and with a smile she

said, 'Yes, we always have a large house-party during the race week. Most of them are Martin's business friends and we'd be delighted to have you join us.'

Barbara and I embraced swiftly and she whispered, 'Can you even begin to think about another weekend in ten years' time, Nancy? We'll all be pushing forty, and I for one won't be here.'

Mark and I watched while the Walton's big car left in a puff of smoke, then they were driving down the long-lined drive and out of the gates. 'Have lunch with me one day,' Mark suggested casually.

'I'm a working girl, Mark. I get an hour for lunch if I'm lucky, and people will talk.'

'We could drive out to some little inn in the country – will you think about it?'

I smiled but made no promises. We shook hands briefly, then I too was driving away from him, and through my driving mirror I saw that he watched until I reached the gates. At that moment I felt as though a great weight had been lifted from my shoulders. Nothing from the past would ever hurt me again – not Amelia with her cool indifference nor Mark who had been my first love. As I drove through the sunlit country lanes I felt suddenly light-hearted. There was something strangely comforting in being a small-town girl, independent and fancy free, able to think in a singularly detached sort of way about the love that had coloured those years in London. The memory of Desmond's charming clever face had lost its power to hurt me – it had gone forever that compelling domination he had exercised over me. It had been Noel who had finally convinced me that I had no place in Desmond's life: it was Noel who had made me strong . . .

29

The office was quiet. There were several messages for me but no particular assignment so I left to go home and unpack.

The memory of Garveston Hall made my small flat seem smaller but it had never seemed so homely or lived in. The books in the bookcase were shabby and used compared to those vast shelves in the library at Garveston, where great shining volumes stood side by side, looking as new and unread as on the day they had been placed there. Instead of giant porcelain vases filled with exotic blooms from the glasshouses I had a small vase filled with roses, their petals already beginning to fall on to the top of the coffee table. Here were no bronze busts or suits of armour, only old and well-loved china figures of no specific value, relics from the house on the corner of the road where I had spent my childhood.

I changed into a pair of slacks and started to unpack my case and put things away. I was thinking of telephoning Aunt Susan when there was a ring on my little front door and I wasn't unduly surprised to see her standing on the doormat.

'I was passing,' she explained, 'so I thought I'd call in to see if you'd enjoyed yourself at the Hall. I noticed your car was parked across the road.'

I smiled. I doubted if Aunt Susan could have contained herself until my dutiful visit for lunch next Sunday. I went into the kitchen to make coffee and she followed me, making it necessary to chat.

'Lady Amelia was at the agricultural meeting this morning – I was surprised to see her there,' she began. 'She cut the meeting short by saying she had guests and wanted to get back.'

'While she was away, Barbara and I walked across the fell and the two men drove to Kendal to see about a yacht Martin wanted to buy.'

'I thought he already had a boat. I could swear Barbara's mother said they had one down south somewhere. I see that Barbara's called in to visit her parents. The Waltons were just leaving when I passed the house.'

'She hasn't stayed very long, then.'

'That's what I thought.'

I poured the coffee and handing a cup to her indicated that we should go back to the sitting room.

'Well,' Aunt Susan began, 'I want to hear all about it.'

So I told her all about the gardens and the house, the food we had eaten and the dresses the women had worn, and when I had finished she said tartly, 'You've not told me anything at all about what you actually talked about all that time. I thought it was silly to have the men there.'

'Not really, Aunt Susan. Maisie wouldn't have gone without Tom and Martin was very anxious to see the Hall. Besides, Mark was at home.'

'That must make something of a change.'

'I don't know anything about that.'

'It's true nevertheless. Amelia covers up beautifully, but all those weeks when she was coping with her committees, her own children and that child of her sister's he was away, in Kenya I think.'

'They seem happy enough.'

'I expect she's expert at putting a good face on it by now. I don't suppose Maisie Standing had much to say for herself.'

'On the contrary, she talked a great deal – and she looked lovely. I've never seen her look so blooming.'

'She probably spent a lot of money on a dress she's not likely to wear again.'

'Oh, I don't know. The children are growing up now and she and Tom will be able to go to functions together.'

314

'I suppose Barbara Walton wore something quite extravagant.'

'Barbara always dressed well, I expected her to look nice.'

My aunt sniffed audibly, then suddenly recalled, 'I almost forgot, a gentleman telephoned yesterday. He'd got my number from your office, he wanted to contact you.'

'Did he say who he was?' I asked, my heart leaping strangely.

'I forgot to ask him. I told him you'd be home this morning but he didn't say whether he'd phone again. He was nicely spoken, quite charming. I wish I'd asked his name, but he was very brisk when I told him you were away. I gave him your number.'

I could only think of Desmond. Desmond could be charming, nobody more so, and I had had experience of his briskness – but why was Desmond telephoning me at Aunt Susan's? I had made it very plain that our association was over, and it wasn't like Desmond to grovel.

After a while Aunt Susan left. I jumped nervously when the telephone rang in the early evening but it was only Maisie wanting to know how the rest of the weekend had gone.

'We quite enjoyed it,' she said. 'Amelia's nice, isn't she? She could always make me feel comfortable and she was pleasant to Tom.'

'Why shouldn't she be, Maisie?'

'Well you know, he's only a local farmer, not in big business like Martin Walton. Did Barbara say anything about my dress?'

'Only that you looked very nice.'

'I felt a bit overdressed. I'm not used to wearin' something so classy – goodness knows when I'll wear it again.'

'But you will, Maisie. You and Tom'll be going out much more now that the children are growing up.'

'Well yes, perhaps we will. Did Amelia say anything about keeping in touch, about meeting again?'

'In another ten years perhaps.'

There was silence at the other end of the telephone and then Maisie said breathlessly, 'Oh Nancy, I shan't want to go, not after all that time. There'd be even less to talk about. Was she serious?'

'Perhaps not.'

'Would you go?'

'Ten years is a long time, we don't even need to think about it.'

'No, I suppose not. You'll call to see us, won't you?'

'Yes, of course.'

The telephone didn't ring again that night.

Mr McKay greeted me next morning with some relief. He sat behind his big desk in his shirtsleeves looking harassed, his desk littered with papers.

'I'm so glad you're back Nancy,' were his first words. 'Joe Gorman's fallen and broken his leg so he'll be off for a while and Alison's just handed in her notice. She's wanting to go to college to do some course or other that she's dreamed up. She wasn't much good around here anyway.'

'Is there something urgent?'

'There's Councillor Downing's funeral to cover, then there's that garden party at Mrs Smithson's in aid of the church roof. She'll expect some coverage on that. Can you do both?'

'Yes, of course.'

'Fred'll go with you to the funeral, and he'll take a few pictures of the civic party. You'll need to change into something pretty for that, mind.'

'I'm not a guest, Mr McKay.'

'Nevertheless you know what Mrs Smithson's like; it'll be all floppy hats and flowers. Bring back some of the goodies, by the way, they'll be very acceptable.' I grinned at him. He was a large man who admitted to a weakness for rich cakes and pastries.

It was late afternoon when I returned to the office carrying a cardboard box filled with cream cakes and pastries. Fred met me in the hall, his voice hushed. 'You can't go into the big boss' office now, Nancy. He's got a visitor.'

I shared the cakes around the office, being careful to keep Mr McKay's favourites intact, then I sat down at my desk to munch at some fruit cake and compose my report. I had not been there long when Mr McKay's door opened and he called, 'Can you come in, Nancy?' Surprised I looked across the room at Fred who shrugged his shoulders philosophically.

I stared at Noel Templeton who was sitting on the corner of Mr McKay's desk. He was smiling but offered no greeting and Mr McKay said, 'Mr Templeton's got something to ask you, my dear. I'll leave you two together as I don't want to influence you in any way.'

He closed the door behind him, then Noel went to sit in his chair, indicating that I should sit opposite him. I stared at him perplexedly: this was not exactly how I had pictured my next meeting with Noel Templeton – even supposing there *was* to be one – and seeing my bewilderment his smile broadened.

'I telephoned your aunt yesterday Nancy, but she said you were away for the weekend. Enjoy it?'

'Yes, thank you.'

'I'm up here again to see Dad so I thought I'd call in on you in person rather than telephone. Now, how do you feel about a job on my team?' I stared at him incredulously, and Noel's smile deepened. 'I know it's a bit of a shock but there's an opening for you, if you're interested. You haven't had much experience in my kind of journalism but I like your style, it's promising. And don't get any romantic notions that you'll be a high-flier to begin with: I can only promise you dirt and grime, danger and much suffering. There may be times when you don't have a decent place to lay your head, and you'll be a general dogsbody for the rest of us, but you'll

317

learn, and one day people will read what you write, and listen to you.'

'But why me?' I burst out, excited and appalled. 'I'm just a small-town reporter – I'm nothing special, Noel. There must be hundreds of girls better qualified than I am. Look – I don't feel capable of being one of Noel Templeton's team.'

'Will you let me be the judge of that?'

'Suppose I don't measure up, then what?'

'Mr McKay'll be glad to have you back. He's already said so.'

'I see.' My brain teemed with conflicting thoughts and emotions.

The smile left Noel's face and suddenly it became very kind. 'We're not talking about your failure, Nancy, we're talking about the great success you're going to be. I liked those articles you wrote about Hong Kong, they showed a great deal of originality, and I liked your guts in getting away from London even if it was only to a small paper in a country town. I know exactly why you did it, too, and that showed guts as well. A great many women would have taken the easy option. Now, you haven't asked any questions.'

'You haven't given me much time!'

'Ask away. You might not even be interested when you hear what's in store.'

'Is it in the Middle East?'

'No, South America this time.'

'And there's trouble?'

'Naturally. Isn't there always trouble where I'm sent?'

'Will there be just the two of us?'

He threw back his head and laughed. 'That sounds cosy, Nancy, but actually there'll be five of us – Alec Fielding and myself, you've heard of him of course, two photographers and you. For a while you might not even get to write a word that's published, and like I said you'll be the general dogsbody, but you'll learn if you've any sense and if you're not in too much of a hurry. I'll

318

supervise what you write: I'll either approve of it or tear it to pieces, but I can tell you now, young Nancy Graham, you won't ever be coming back to work here.'

'When do we need to leave?'

'At the end of next week. Can you be ready by then?'

'Yes.'

'Good girl. I'll be in touch with final instructions. I know it doesn't give you much time.' His smile was encouraging, but then he was gone leaving me to stare into space, dazed and bemused.

Mr McKay was sorry to lose me but he was unashamedly proud. 'Your father'd be so pleased with you, girl,' he said gently. 'It was always his dream to do the sort of thing Templeton does, and you couldn't have a better example. You must have made quite an impression on him, but can I give you a word of advice? It's the sort of advice I'd give my own daughter if I had one.' I smiled, knowing exactly what was coming. 'Will you keep both feet on the ground, love. You're a pretty girl and he's a charming presentable man with a silver tongue: will you be able to think of this as professional business and not go confusing it with anything else?'

'I promise I won't even think of anything else.'

'That makes me a lot more comfortable.'

Aunt Susan was horrified. To go off to some uncivilised place where they shoot people, put them in prison for no reason so that they're never heard of again – what had English people to do with such things? Why did British journalists even have to write about such happenings. Oh, and why wasn't my mother at home to reason with me! Why had it always to be her who was expected to sort things out.

'Aunt Susan, I'm twenty-eight years old. I'm not a child, I'm capable of making my own decisions and living my own life,' I prevaricated, but it made little difference, the nagging went on and on.

Later on, I received a telephone call from Barbara, whose father had sent her the cutting from the local paper which informed Greymont at large that Nancy Graham was to be one of Noel Templeton's team of journalists in South America.

'How thrilling for you,' she enthused. 'Martin's just about exhausted our weekend at Garveston Hall, so now he can conveniently dine out on you for the next few weeks.' I asked myself if she could still love him when she understood his foibles so well.

It was a time of meeting people on the street and having them express their enthusiastic or apprehensive feelings about my future. Maisie thought I was foolish. 'You have a nice flat and a good job, what do you want to go out there for, putting your life in danger? Tom says Noel Templeton's been injured several times quite recently – next time it could be you.'

I received a brief notelet from Amelia congratulating me on my new appointment and wishing me well. It was impersonal, as was the short letter I received from Desmond. I doubted if the news of my appointment had made the London papers so I could only guess how he knew about my future. A few months before his letter would have unnerved me, set my mind alive with questions and doubts, but now it was just a letter from an old friend. The exciting things that were happening to me in the present were making memories of Desmond illusive and transient.

'I should get rid of the flat,' Aunt Susan advised fussily. 'If you're away any length of time it will get damp or be burgled and you could probably do with the rent money. In any case, you can always come back here, you always have.'

'I'll hang on to it for the time being, Aunt Susan, and I'll keep the Mini.'

'If you ask me, that young man's never home long enough to do anything, and you'll probably be the same.'

Mr McKay said, 'You're never coming home Nancy, you're leaving us for good this time, so let me advertise your flat and rent it out for you. Surely your aunt'll let you garage the car until you need it.'

So it was settled. My flat went in the newspaper at the weekend and the Mini went into Aunt Susan's garage alongside her own. Most of my clothes were in the wardrobe in one of her bedrooms and packed in the grip I was taking with me were casual clothes – slacks and sweaters, tracksuits and the odd cotton dress. Supervising the packing Aunt Susan was scathing about it. 'You're taking the most unattractive clothes you can find! If they're all you're going to need for the life you're expecting to lead you must be out of your mind. I knew it would come to this one day, I told your father we'd have trouble with you, you were always too independent. Don't you want what other women want, a nice house, a nice husband and family? I suspect it was listening to your father that changed you.'

'I thought you said I was always like this.'

'Yes, but he made you worse. I shan't know what to say when I write to Mary.'

'I've already written to Mother, but tell her I'm very happy and looking forward to the future. Tell her I love her.'

She drove me to the station and Sarah came with us so that my last view was of them standing on the platform, Sarah tearful, Aunt Susan stiff-necked and disapproving. I stood at the window until I could see them no more.

Twelve hours later I was with Noel and three strangers in the lounge of Heathrow Airport waiting to be called to the plane. Alec Fielding grinned at me cheerfully but the two photographers seemed more concerned with their array of equipment than with the advent of a raw reporter who had yet to make her mark.

For a few minutes in that crowded bustling place Noel and I were alone. He looked down into my face with keen quizzical eyes asking, 'Well – how do you feel, Nancy? No regrets?'

321

'No, none.'

He smiled. 'Nothing I told you deterred you – nothing you ever read about our exploits discouraged you?'

'Nothing.'

He took hold of my hand and held on to it. 'That's my girl,' he said gently.

There was so much strength in the clasp of his hand, so much promise in his smile, then his eyes darkened and I surprised in them a sudden and unexpected tenderness. 'Always remember you're my chosen one Nancy,' he said lightly. 'Never let me down.'

My heart lifted, my spirits soared. For the first time in my adult life I believed in a future bright with promise, coloured with joy. I felt his hand under my elbow guiding me towards the departure gate and then we were joined by the others. Halfway along the corridor a man carrying a camera stepped forward to bar our way. We stood together in a smiling group while he took the photograph, then with a laugh and a whispered, 'Good luck!' he walked away.

Noel laughed, but I knew his words were for me. 'Tonight and tomorrow we'll make the national press. Very soon, the world will be waiting for our story.'

I thought about his words as we swept through the midnight sky. The lights in the plane were dimmed, and beside me Noel slept calm and unruffled by the prospect ahead of him. He looked so boyish asleep, the shock of dark hair falling across his forehead, long lashes sweeping his cheek, making me long to put my arms around him and hold him close.

I had been too excited to think about them before but now I could consider them calmly and logically: how would the people who had made up my life receive the story we had to tell?

Aunt Susan would be more proud than disapproving when she'd had time to get used to the idea, and Miss Clarkson would lose no opportunity to inform the pupils at Lorivals that one of their Old Girls was a member of

Noel Templeton's team. What would Amelia think? I pictured her and Mark sitting in polite isolation at the breakfast table. Mark would no doubt comment that I must have lost my senses before he turned to the sporting pages, but for Amelia there could only be relief that I was no longer a threat to her sister's marriage. Then I thought about Desmond, his clever goodlooking face pensive, perhaps a little disdainful. He would follow our story I had no doubt, but I would never know his real thoughts.

I felt Noel stir beside me and when I turned to look at him he was peering at his watch, muttering, 'Heavens, is that all it is, there's hours yet. Have you been asleep?'

'Not yet, I'm far too excited.'

He smiled, then taking hold of my hand settled back in his seat. 'I'd try to get some sleep if I were you, Nancy. Make the most of this bit of peace and quiet.'

It was good advice. I must forget the past with its doubts, all the broken dreams and pledges that had coloured it, for in a few hours I would be stepping out into a new day, a new life.